I0817721

BEYOND THE RIFT

BAEN BOOKS by JOHN RINGO

TRANSDIMENSIONAL HUNTER (with Lydia Sherrer)
Into the Real • *Through the Storm*
Behind the Veil • *Beyond the Rift*

SHADOW'S PATH
Not That Kind of Good Guy • *Welcome to the Jungle*

BLACK TIDE RISING
Under a Graveyard Sky • *To Sail a Darkling Sea*
Islands of Rage and Hope • *Strands of Sorrow*
The Valley of Shadows (with Mike Massa)
Black Tide Rising (edited with Gary Poole)
Voices of the Fall (edited with Gary Poole)
River of Night (with Mike Massa)
We Shall Rise (edited with Gary Poole)
United We Stand (edited with Gary Poole)

TROY RISING
Live Free or Die • *Citadel* • *The Hot Gate*

LEGACY OF THE ALDENATA
A Hymn Before Battle • *Gust Front* • *When the Devil Dances*
Hell's Faire • *The Hero* (with Michael Z. Williamson)
Cally's War (with Julie Cochrane)
Watch on the Rhine (with Tom Kratman)
Sister Time (with Julie Cochrane) • *Yellow Eyes* (with Tom Kratman)
Honor of the Clan (with Julie Cochrane) • *Eye of the Storm*

COUNCIL WARS
There Will Be Dragons • *Emerald Sea*
Against the Tide • *East of the Sun, West of the Moon*

INTO THE LOOKING GLASS
Into the Looking Glass • *Vorpal Blade* (with Travis S. Taylor)
Manxome Foe (with Travis S. Taylor)
Claws that Catch (with Travis S. Taylor)

EMPIRE OF MAN (with David Weber)
March Upcountry • *March to the Sea* • *March to the Stars* • *We Few*

SPECIAL CIRCUMSTANCES
Princess of Wands • *Queen of Wands*

PALADIN OF SHADOWS
Ghost • *Kildar* • *Choosers of the Slain* • *Unto the Breach*
A Deeper Blue • *Tiger by the Tail* (with Ryan Sear)

STANDALONE TITLES
The Last Centurion • *Citizens* (ed. with Brian M. Thomsen)
Beyond the Ranges

To purchase any of these titles in e-book form, please go to www.baen.com.

BEYOND THE RIFT

JOHN RINGO &
LYDIA SHERRER

Beyond the Rift

A Baen Books Original

Baen Publishing Enterprises
P.O. Box 1403
Riverdale, NY 10471
www.baen.com

ISBN: 978-1-6680-7312-4

Cover art by Kurt Miller

First printing, February 2026

Distributed by Simon & Schuster
1230 Avenue of the Americas
New York, NY 10020

Library of Congress Control Number: 2025043313

Printed in the United States of America

10 9 8 7 6 5 4 3 2 1

This is to you—yes, you—
and all the ways big and small you are fighting
for your family, your country, and your world.
No matter the challenges you face,
take courage and stand firm.
—L.S.

~

As always
For Captain Tamara Long, USAF
Born: May 12, 1979
Died: March 23, 2003, Afghanistan
You fly with the angels now.
—J.R.

CONTENTS

Cast of Characters

Cast—CIDER

Steve Riker—Fallu AKA FallujahSevenNiner, Taskforce Sanctus Assistant S-3

Robert Krator—head of Tsunami Entertainment

General Kozelek—head of CIDER's unified military command

Colonel Kane Bryce—head of Force Training for Taskforce Sanctus

Secretary John Byerly—US Undersecretary of Defense for Technology and Acquisitions

Dr. Benjamin Quasnitschka—CIDER's Chief Scientist

Dr. Roberts—head of CIDER's research and development team

Trainer Bowers—TD Counterforce classroom instructor

Trainer Coler—TD Counterforce physical training instructor

Dr. Ed Hillenbrand—CIDER research assistant

Dr. Thind—CIDER's in-house neurologist

President Washington—President of the United States

Patricia Woods—CIDER civilian oversight appointee

Major Kim Lawrence—CIDER liaison to the intelligence community

Cast—Cedar Rapids

Matilda Raven—Lynn's mother

Mr. and Mrs. Swain—Kayla's parents

Mr. and Mrs. Nguyen—Dan's parents

Mr. and Mrs. Johnston—Edgar's parents

Mr. Thomas—Lynn's elderly neighbor

Mr. Payne—Ronnie's father

Kayla Swain—Lynn's best friend

Cast—Other

Mrs. Pearson—GIC employee, Skadi's Wolves PR manager

Riko—Mack's possibly fake girlfriend

Jonnie Inanis—Hacktivist AKA "J-nonymous"

Kate Libby—Hacktivist

Xun—Kate's "boyfriend"

Jason Ash—small-time gamer stream celebrity

Mike—AKA Cap, old unit buddy of Steve's

Tap—AKA DoubleTap AKA ChaosGremlin666, old unit buddy of Steve's

Droopy—old unit buddy of Steve's

Taskforce Sanctus (listed alphabetically by handle)

Handle—First Name "Full Handle" Last Name, Unit, CompanyPlatoon-Squad

Abrams—Lafayette "AbramsBeast" Muller, Alpha Co. Commander

Alter—David "Alter_The_Chaplain" Lee, Team Black Templars, Alpha1-1

Beer—Bradley "HoldMyBeer" Hayek, Team Light Brigade, Alpha1-1

Brayard—Gliff "Brayards_Revenge" Runeberg, Team Black Templars, Alpha1-1

Ch'hala—Brandy "Ch'hala_Hears_You" Bolgeo, Team Zahn Wars, Alpha1-3

Champion—Baron "ChampionSigismund" Lyle, Team Black Templars Capt., Alpha1-1

Cosmos—Mary "Cosmotron1964" Maulucci, Team Florida Man, Alpha2-2

Crash—Andrew "CrashBandicoot" Stoner, Alpha Co. 1st Platoon Leader

Dan—Dan "DanTheMan48" Nguyen, Team Skadi's Wolves, Alpha1-2

DBoshe—Rose "dBoshe" Lopez, Alpha1-3 Squad Leader

Death—Derek "DeathShot13" Peterson, Team Light Brigade Capt., Alpha1-1

Desperado—Blain "Desperado" Keister, Team Lansing Nights Capt., Alpha1-1

DevilDog—Elliot "DevilDog" Rosenthal, Charlie Co. Commander

Druid—Seb "SexyDruid" Blackwell, Alpha Co. 1st Platoon Assistant

Emilia—Emilia "Emilia_Tomás" Tomás, Team Amaranth, Alpha1-2

Eva—Nicole "EvaNight07" Gaines, Team Amaranth, Alpha1-2

Hermes—Herman "Send_Hermes" Bailey, Alpha1-2 Squad Leader

Hero—Wayne "Hero_of_Time" Kramer, Hamilton's Own, Gunner

Ion—Robert "IonMighty" Bullock, Hamilton's Own, Lead Gunner

Khoury—Malak "Khoury_ShadowStar" Khoury, Alpha Co. XO

Kiss—Brent "KissMyChainsword" Dudgeon, Team Black Templars, Alpha1-1

Gadsden—Hank "GadsdenSnake" Loper, Team Lone Star Capt., Alpha1-3

Grim—Jacob "TheGrimReaper16" Stills, Team Amaranth, Alpha1-2

Mack—Mack "MackMcBladezz" Rios, Team Skadi's Wolves, Alpha1-2

Mara—Audrey "MaraSkywalker01" Gneezak, Team Zahn Wars, Alpha1-3

Maui—Edgar "Maui_YoureWelcome" Johnston, Team Skadi's Wolves, Alpha1-2

Mr. E—Gregg "Mr_E006" Santoro, Team Light Brigade, Alpha1-1

Neutron—Ernest "Mr_Ernie_Neutron" Tucker, Alpha1-1 Squad Leader

Plot—Richard "PlotTwist4U" Groller, Team Zahn Wars, Alpha1-3

Queen—Elena "QueenElena01" Seville, Team Alpha Flight, Bravo3-3

Raven—Lynn "RavenStriker" Raven, Team Skadi's Wolves Capt., Alpha1-2

Ronnie—Ronnie "RonnieDarko" Payne, Team Skadi's Wolves, Alpha1-2

Sarah—Sarah "The_Best_Sarah" Hartman, Team Amaranth, Alpha1-2

Serenity—Serena "SerenitySoul" Thomas, Team Amaranth, Alpha1-2

Sonia—Sonia "Sonia338Lapua" Peterson, Team Light Brigade, Alpha1-1

Star—Sally "RopingStar" Feldman, Team Lone Star, Alpha1-3

Stinkbug—Crispus "Operation_Stinkbug" DeLeon, Team Light Brigade, Alpha1-1

Taken—John "MyUserNameWasTaken" Doe, Team Black Templars, Alpha1-1

Teach—Jesús "Unavoidably_Teach" Sánchez, Bravo3-3 Squad Leader

Thrawn—Charles "Thrawn_Lives" Gannon, Team Zahn Wars Capt., Alpha1-3

Timothy—Timmy "TimothyRocks" Bolgeo, Team Zahn Wars, Alpha1-3

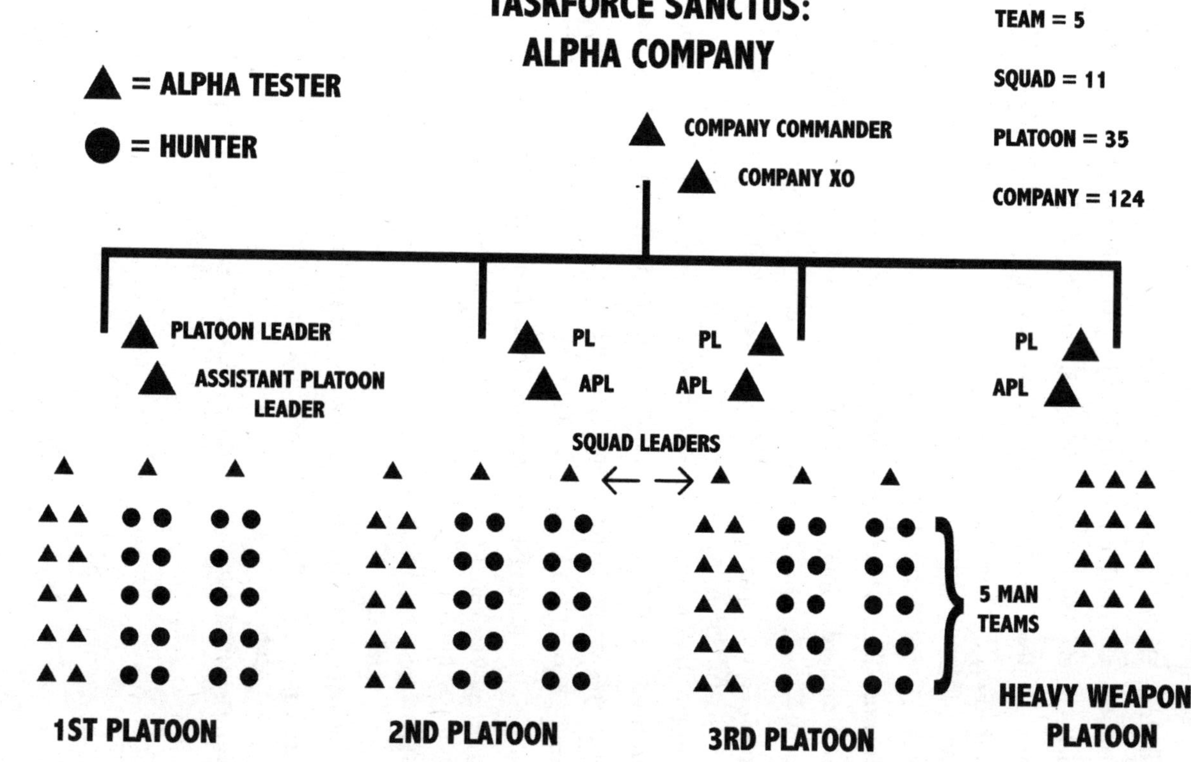

TASKFORCE SANCTUS:
ALPHA COMPANY
= ALPHA TESTER
= HUNTER
TEAM = 5
SQUAD = 11
PLATOON = 35
COMPANY = 124
COMPANY COMMANDER
COMPANY XO
PLATOON LEADER
ASSISTANT PLATOON LEADER
PL
APL
PL
APL
PL
APL
SQUAD LEADERS
5 MAN TEAMS
1ST PLATOON
2ND PLATOON
3RD PLATOON
HEAVY WEAPONS PLATOON

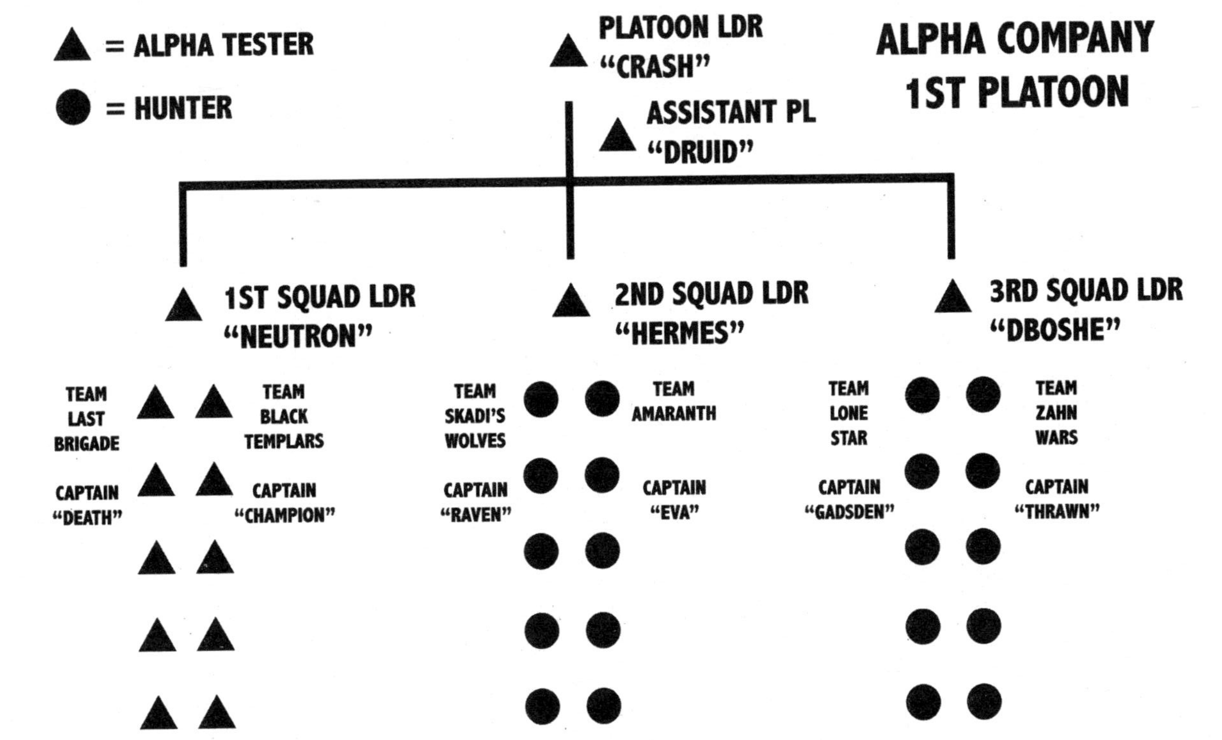
= ALPHA TESTER
= HUNTER
PLATOON LDR
"CRASH"
ASSISTANT PL
"DRUID"
ALPHA COMPANY
1ST PLATOON
1ST SQUAD LDR
"NEUTRON"
2ND SQUAD LDR
"HERMES"
3RD SQUAD LDR
"DBOSHE"
TEAM LAST BRIGADE
CAPTAIN "DEATH"
TEAM BLACK TEMPLARS
CAPTAIN "CHAMPION"
TEAM SKADI'S WOLVES
CAPTAIN "RAVEN"
TEAM AMARANTH
CAPTAIN "EVA"
TEAM LONE STAR
CAPTAIN "GADSDEN"
TEAM ZAHN WARS
CAPTAIN "THRAWN"

Author's Note:

Almost nine years ago in the summer of 2017, John Ringo asked me for a private word out on the smoking patio at the Chattanooga Choo Choo Hotel on Sunday afternoon near the end of LibertyCon, that year celebrating its 30th anniversary.

I was immediately nervous.

I'd been reading John Ringo books since I was a teen, and had therefore been working hard all weekend to not be obnoxiously excited to meet him. On top of that, I knew he was a veteran, and since I went through Marine Corps ROTC during college I still tended to rack my brain for what I'd screwed up anytime someone asked me for a "private word."

Praise in public, rip 'em a new one in private. You know how it goes.

So it was with no small amount of trepidation that I sat down on the low wall around the patio as he lit up a cigar and situated his kilt (it was hot as hell, so I didn't blame him, but I will also forever have an image burned in my memory of John Ringo standing and fanning his manly bits with his kilt).

Imagine how confused I was as I sat, braced for a dressing down because of some imagined unprofessional slip-up I'd made as a brand-new pro at LibertyCon, when instead John started talking about a book he wanted to write with his daughter.

Now, anyone who has met John knows how much he loves to tell a good story (the best ones are usually to be heard at late night "No Shit, There I Was" panels). So I was perfectly content to listen to him talk, even though I was extremely confused and still had no idea why he was talking to me.

I swear it took me a good fifteen minutes listening to him chat about his book idea and how his daughter wasn't really the writing type before it dawned on me where he was going with his long, rambling explanation.

At that point I nearly had a heart attack. But I managed to keep my mouth closed as he finally found his way to the point (another fifteen minutes later), which was: Do you want to write a book with me?

Cue internal fan-girl screaming

Somehow I managed to say, without sounding too terribly stunned, "Um, yes. Yes, I do."

He warned me he didn't know if he could get his publisher on board or not, but that we could give it a shot, and he'd send me what he had of his story idea so far.

The work in progress title at the time was "Whispers in the Night."

After we spoke I wandered dazedly back into the Choo Choo, and was immediately set upon by excited John Ringo fans who had spotted us talking on the patio. Unbeknownst to me, stalking John as he recruited co-authors was a time-honored tradition, and to the well-meaning fans I was the next fresh meat that meant they'd get to read more John Ringo books (yay!).

Someone had even snapped a picture of us through the Choo Choo's condensation-stained window, proof of the moment a brand-new series was born. Maybe I'll frame the picture someday.

As excited as I was, leaving LibertyCon that year, I did try to moderate my enthusiasm. The gears of the traditional publishing industry are slow to turn. Indeed, it took two more years to get Baen Books to sign off on the series. John and I even briefly discussed self-publishing the books ourselves, considering I was already a successful independent author making good money selling my Love, Lies, and Hocus Pocus urban fantasy books.

But in the fall of 2019, John finally sold Toni, our editor, on the idea and we got a three-book contract (how every well-meaning Baen Trilogy starts out, right?).

Thus began a six-year journey of collaboration that has changed both of us—hopefully for the better.

Based on my conversations with John, his thoughts on collaborations could likely best be summed up by a wise saying that's been passed around from author to author over the years: be cautious about collaborating with anyone who lives closer than four hours away, because that's how long it will take you to calm down after you storm out of your house intent on showing up on your collaborator's doorstep to vent your frustrations in person.

During our last meeting to finalize the outline for this book, John shared a picture with me of three greats, Larry Niven, Jerry Pournelle, and Steven Barnes, posed humorously with Larry swinging an ax overhead, Steven executing a flawless sidekick, and poor Jerry in the middle trying to hold the feuding authors apart. From what I can gather the mock fight was photographed and used as humorous promotion for the trio's 1987 release of *The Legacy of Heorot*.

The picture gave me a good laugh, and also struck too close for comfort.

As for me, I am extremely grateful for the chance John Ringo took on me and the opportunity I was given to write this amazing series with him. I have come to love Baen Books not just as a reader who devoured the books they published, but as a business partner and friend who has worked alongside the incredible team that makes the magic happen behind the scenes.

Our collaboration has not been without its moments of pitched battle (though fortunately there was no ax involved, otherwise John might not still have his head). But since John and I live a whole five hours apart, we've been safe from falling into authorcide, and are now pleased and honored to present our dear readers with Lynn's completed adventures.

So, thank you, John, for taking a chance on me, and for all the many useful things you have taught me about writing and publishing—some of it even on purpose!

Thank you, Toni, for giving this series a chance, and for guiding and supporting us along the way.

Thank you Leah, Joy, Marla, Jason, Rabbit, Griffin, Dave, Jim, David, and any other of the Baen team who helped make sure these books were beautifully polished and delivered into readers' hands.

Thank you Dave Seeley and Kurt Miller for the amazing cover art. You brought the energy, tension, and epic struggles of the series to visual form so that readers' imaginations could be inspired to a whole new level.

There were many wonderful people over the years with whom I consulted for details about various topics. I can't remember you all because I was foolish enough not to keep a running list, my apologies for that lack of foresight (likely I do remember you, I just can't find our however-many-years-old text/email/messenger conversation to recall your name).

For those I do remember: Thank you Mike Muller for your invaluable military expertise, Speaker for your scientific insight, Ted Thomas for your vision on future technology, and Chuck Gannon for your career advice.

Thank you to the many people whose names I commandeered to outfit the troops of Taskforce Sanctus. You were all chosen with love, care, and a desire to honor the way you've enriched my life.

Thank you to the many friends and family members who supported me during this collaboration, who lent a listening ear and prayed for its success. You know what I'm talking about.

Thank you to the many bookstores and fans who promoted these books (and will continue to do so!) and shared them with others out of love and enthusiasm.

Thank you to all my fellow authors and business professionals who cheered me on, shared their knowledge, and gave me opportunities to give back. A rising tide lifts all boats!

I always save the best for last, so thank you to my alpha reader and the most supportive husband ever, David Sherrer. Without your love of gaming and expert knowledge on the gaming industry, game mechanics, and game lore, there's no way I could have made this book series as fun and full of joy for gaming as I did. You're the best.

And now, dear reader, the only thing remaining is for you to go enjoy the final installment of Lynn's thrilling adventure. Thank you for reading, thank you for enjoying, and thank you for sharing this story with other people whose lives will be made richer by it.

Chapter 1

July 17th, 1975

"WORK, DANG YOU!"

Dave Bowers was fifty-two, still weighed in at around one hundred and fifty-five pounds, same as when he'd left the Navy in 1946, and balding. He wore the standard uniform of his day, time and position: a short-sleeved white shirt, dark dress slacks, neatly polished black low quarters and a black tie.

His face worked as he lit a new Lucky Strike from the still-burning one in his lips, stubbed that one out, put the new one between his lips and quickly took a swig of cold, stale, coffee as he stared at the green screen.

The screen showed the readouts from the complex's klystrons. The klystrons were the very heart of the powerful radar at the center of the anti-ballistic missile complex.

The Safeguard System was the newest and most powerful ABM system ever devised. Consisting of two sets of powerful and fast missiles, Spartan and Sprint, along with a long-range radar, PARC, and the targeting radar, SPARC. Although Safeguard only officially protected the ND Missile Pack, despite the ABM treaty it was a foot-in-the-door approach to creating a nationwide integrated anti-ballistic missile system using clean micro nuke warheads and an opportunity to make the country safe forever from the threat of annihilation by the Soviets.

The problem was that for the low-yield, low-fallout warheads, neutron bombs, to disable the Soviet Multiple Independent Reentry Systems, they had to explode close. Very close.

And the missiles, Sprint especially, had only seconds to intercept the Soviet MIRVs requiring not only very fast launch but hypervelocity speed.

Given the closing speeds, with MIRVs coming in at reentry speeds and Sprints going up even faster, as well as having to get the missiles into a very tight engagement basket, all of that required not only the fastest computers ever conceived but a very powerful tracking and aiming radar.

Which was where the klystrons came in.

Klystrons were a specialized linear beam vacuum tube that turned electrical power into microwaves. Those were then used as the radar's emissions. Though there were other systems to create microwaves for the power they needed, klystrons were the only real choice.

Two General Electric AV188 klystrons, eight feet tall, filled with dielectric oil and topped by two-ton steel and lead plates to reduce x-ray radiation flooding the complex, were positioned on the bottom floor of the complex in their own two-story private tank. Each was capable of turning 150,000 volts of electricity, supplied by six massive generators, into a narrow beam of microwave energy that was the only thing capable of tracking the MIRVs closely enough and fast enough for the system to work.

The joke around the complex was they were so powerful they twisted more than electrons: they twisted the very nature of space and time.

In testing they were fine. Power them up and all good. Each had been checked and rechecked.

And each time they were powered up together . . . things went wrong.

"Come on, baby . . ."

Dave had joined up in '43 to fight the Nazis and instead ended up on a destroyer in the Pacific as a radar operator. That led to a career in and out of the military as he built, designed and operated increasingly complex and powerful radars.

SPARC was his brainchild and his brainchild was not behaving.

"One-twenty kay," Charlie read off as the power mounted.

Dave kept his eyes fixed on the resonant frequency indicator.

In a klystron, RF energy is fed into an input cavity at or near its resonant frequency creating standing waves of RF energy. There were multiple additional steps to create the microwave beam, but the problem centered around the resonant frequency. Whenever they approached the resonant frequency at high power, the system started to destabilize. And he could not determine why.

"One-thirty," Charlie read.

There it was again. The resonant frequency was moving up and down, up and down and there was no reason for it to do so. As the power increased it began to destabilize more and more until it was approaching "disastrous resonance" point.

"Power down," Dave said. "Go to one-twenty again, then come back up slowly..."

Watching the numbers on a slow increase Dave started to see a pattern. The resonance was flickering in an almost... musical pattern? It wasn't a regular up and down. More like bump-bump-bump-da-bump... almost like that hippy music everyone was listening to these days. He found himself nodding along, trying to feel out the rhythm.

"Hold there," Dave said, twiddling knobs on his console. If there was a pattern, there was a way to counter the pattern.

Finally, he started to get the resonance under control.

"Power up, one-three-five," Dave said.

"One-three-five, aye," Charlie replied.

Charlie was former Navy, too. One of the reasons Dave had hired him.

"Steady at one-three-five," Dave said. "One-four-zero."

"One-four-zero, aye."

Dave got the resonance back under control. *Just hold steady, girl.*

"One-four-five..."

More adjustments. Back under control.

"One-five-zero," Dave said.

"One-five-zero, aye."

He had it. It was holding. Resonance was in line. It was hold—

The resonance went into full cascade mode as his monitor went wild. For just a second, so short a time he wasn't sure the rest of his life if it was just a hallucination, a strange, unrecognizable script flashed across his screen.

"SHUT IT DOWN! SHUT IT...!"

It was too late. The entire system started to smoke as alarms went off throughout the complex.

Dave had learned a lot of language in the Navy appropriate for this moment but inappropriate for the job.

"WHAT THE... *FUDGE* IS *CAUSING* THAT?"

"We've got one more shot at this or Congress is closing us down," Roy Atwood said. The Project Director was also WWII generation but had managed to quit smoking. Dave wasn't even trying the way things were going. "The overruns are costing like crazy. Dave?"

"There is no earthly reason this should be happening," Dave said. "There is no reason the resonance should be interacting with anything outside the system, but it seems that something outside the system is acting on *it*."

"Sabotage?" Eric Gartner was the Security Chief for the complex.

"If it is, the Ruskies have figured out how to sabotage something remotely," Dave said, shaking his head. "I almost had the resonance cascade under control. One more time. I can get it. We can get it."

July 25th, 1975

"WHAT THE HELL?" DAVE MUTTERED.

This time as they powered up, there was no interference. It was like the resonance gremlins had just... left.

"One-three-zero..." Charlie called. "One-four-zero... One-four-five..."

There was no interference, resonance was staying in parameters. There was still some... flux. Something weird was happening in Klystron Two but it was working. That was the important part. He adjusted the output so it wouldn't interfere with the radar beam.

"One-five-zero," Charlie said.

"Klystrons nominal," Dave said, calmly. They'd been working on those words for months and there was a leap of joy in his heart as he said them. But you stayed professional.

"Transfer, nominal."

"Radar, nominal..."

It was working! They were gonna end the threat of nuclear annihilation!

September 15th, 1976

"What do you mean 'we're shut down'?" Dave asked, knowing the answer.

The complex had been fully operational for nearly a year and it was working like a charm. There was the continued . . . weirdness of Klystron Two but it was, if anything, working beyond its parameters. The radars were so accurate that they had to detune them so that the missiles would *miss* incoming warheads. In one test they had nearly achieved a direct hit.

He'd thought Congress would want more of them, not shut them down.

"The analysis is that with the increased number of Soviet MIRVs it would be functionally impossible to intercept all of them," Roy said.

"That's . . . not an accurate analysis," Don Beatty replied. The Chief Strategic Analyst would tend to know such things.

"Whether it is or not, Congress funds and Congress decides," Roy said. "So we're shutting down on October 1st. And that's that."

January 6th, 1977

Roy Atwood looked down the Primary Personnel and Equipment Hallway and shook his head. $26 billion dollars. They'd gotten it working. Done what everyone said was impossible.

And now it was stripped out and emptied of all of that equipment they'd worked so hard to perfect. Including the now-working-perfectly klystrons. It could have worked. America could have been free of the threat of nuclear annihilation.

Just to have it shut down at the whim of some politicians who'd rather spend the money on post offices for their districts.

Congress giveth, Congress taketh away.

He threw the final breaker, turned his back, and walked out into the cold.

In the darkness of the Klystron Pool, there was a faint flicker of purplish-blue light.

Chapter 2

THE HILL WAS NEVER GOING TO END.

It went up and up in front of her, and she didn't have the strength to lift her head and search desperately for the top. What remained of her will was busy forcing one leg in front of the other. If it got sidetracked, it would probably go on vacation to Hawaii and leave her gasping in the ditch. Maybe she'd get lucky and have a heart attack instead. Then she could go to gamer's Valhalla and spend endless days fragging cocky dipshits, drinking pop, and eating bacon-rolled steak bites.

Oh, and thinking up gruesome torture scenarios for whoever had invented augmented reality games that forced perfectly respectable gamers to leave their body-mold chairs and *go exercise.*

Except, this was no longer a game.

The cadence of dozens of weary feet pounding on gravel before and behind her barely registered in her brain. Her eyes did see the ground—alert for tripping hazards on this uneven trail that threaded through the West Virginia mountains. But her brain kept skipping away, touching on flashes of memory from the whirlwind of the past week.

Sign here on the dotted line, Ms. Raven. I know you're used to voice signatures, but Tsunami has a hard-copy duplication policy in place at the moment, just in case... well, just in case. Welcome to the TransDimensional Counterforce.

"I could've run home and eaten lunch by now at the rate you milksops are dragging! Come on, I thought you were elite gamers! Pick up the pace!"

The energetic bellow of Trainer Coler echoed down the straggled line of runners, and Lynn glared at the gravel. Or at least tried to. She wasn't sure if her facial muscles did more than twitch feebly. But she still dredged up a surge of spite and shoved more energy into her aching legs. The crest of the hill was close. It had to be, right?

Becoming an official member of Tsunami Entertainment's TransDimensional Counterforce—currently providing unspecified contractor services to the organization known as CIDER—had been surreal. But it was hardly more than a blip in the long line of surreal things she'd done recently.

A week ago, she and her elite gaming team had competed in the national championships of the first globally sensational AR game in history. She was watched by millions on the streams, harassed by paparazzi drones, and followed by obsessed fans. Her team had led the effort to successfully destroy the massive Sierra Class TDM boss that should have won them the national championship.

Instead, they found out there *was* no national championship. Not really. The whole thing had been a smokescreen. They were informed by no less than the president of the United States that the in-game monsters, the TDMs they'd been fighting for an *entire year*, were not augmented reality.

They were real.

And they were quickly overwhelming the world's cutting-edge infrastructure, threatening global unrest that could plunge civilization back into the dark ages.

Lynn was sure she'd aged years in the last week. Her recent high school graduation felt like a distant memory. Team drama, bullying, stream fame, even the doxxing and stalking she'd endured during her final months of high school felt like small change compared to what she was facing now as June turned to July.

Our purpose here is not to turn you into soldiers.

Getting briefed, in person, by the man she'd once thought was an *actor* for the TD Hunter cut-scenes had been almost comical. But the gravity on Colonel Bryce's face had been enough to quell any possibility of mirth on that first day of training when they arrived at The Greenbrier.

Our purpose is to improve your reaction time and stamina as much as possible while we train you in standardized maneuvers, new weapon technology, and how to operate within a chain of command.

It was Alice in Wonderland levels of craziness. Skadi's Wolves and all the other Hunter Strike Teams who had volunteered to join CIDER had been sent to an elite luxury resort, of all places, to do their training. It was nestled between soaring ridges of the Allegheny Mountains in secluded White Sulphur Springs, West Virginia. The place normally catered to dignitaries like senators, presidents, and Saudi Arabian oil princes. But Tsunami Entertainment had booked out the entire complex to conduct their "TransDimensional Counterforce training." It was closed to the public and operating on a skeleton staff for a month. Not even the historic Cold War bunker tours of the massive underground facility beneath the resort were still open.

As far as the public—and more importantly, the stream paparazzi—knew, these Hunter Strike Teams had hit the jackpot with their superior scoring at the national championship and were now enjoying a month of luxury and game tactics training courtesy of Tsunami. Similar training was underway in other CIDER member nations across the globe for their own native teams who'd covertly volunteered to continue the charade and fight TDM bosses alongside each country's specially trained CIDER forces. Once trained, these TD Counterforce teams would go on a "TD Hunter Battle Tour" of major cities around their native countries to "show off their hunting skills" and drum up excitement for the competition to end all competitions: the TransDimensional Hunter International Championship to be held in Tokyo.

Not that the international championship would ever happen. They had six months, max, to put a serious dent in TDM boss numbers before the entities hit critical mass and cities started going dark in a global domino effect.

We are going to train you the way we would train a high school band—if a high school band was being asked to fight a global invasion of invisible aliens.

Lynn was still trying to wrap her brain around the insanity of what they were doing. Elite gamers, publicly training to be part of a fictional-but-actually-real TransDimensional Counterforce to fight pretend-but-actually-real aliens, streamed live all over the world.

The TD Hunter game was officially the craziest and most successful psyops cover mission in all of military history.

Robert Krator was an evil genius.

"Pick it up, Hunters! This measly hill might be over, but you've still got two and a half miles to go before you get your hot baths with little smelling salts and shit. I don't know what they even have in those rooms, but you might as well enjoy it while you can!"

Lynn gasped and raised her head as she crested the hill, her entire body filling with relief endorphins to see the ground slope down in front of her. Ronnie was panting and cursing right behind her. His long legs gave him a disgustingly annoying advantage whenever they did sprint drills, but she seemed to have a deeper well of stamina when it came to long distance. She turned her head to gulp from the hydration tube on her right shoulder, then glanced back further to put eyes on the rest of her team. Dan and Mack were halfway up the hill, but poor Edgar was still near the bottom with the stragglers, a head taller and noticeably broader than those around him.

Trainer Coler had instructed them not to run as a team, stuck at the speed of their slowest member. They needed to push their bodies to the absolute limit for each individual so they could ensure maximum benefit from the training regimen. But she was still captain of Skadi's Wolves. She'd gotten the guys into this, and felt personally responsible for them.

We are not trying to wash you out, Hunters. We want *you to stay. Thanks to Tsunami's commitment to CIDER's mission, we have the resources to make life as pleasant as it can be while not coddling you. You'll have good food, good quarters, and staff cleaning up for you. But we* will *work you hard. We will squeeze every last drop of utility out of these four measly weeks at The Greenbrier, because it's all we've got time for.*

Lynn lengthened her stride as beautiful, wonderful, blessed gravity pulled her downhill. She didn't give in to the temptation to look ahead, scoping out which Hunters she might catch up to. Instead she kept her eyes on the trail, cautious for tripping hazards. She *freaking hated* running. But at least technology was good for more than entertainment. Once she'd had plenty of funds to spare from her sponsorship work with her PR company, Global Image Consulting, or GIC, she'd shelled out a ridiculous amount for cutting edge sports bras that utilized new shock-absorption fibers and specialized omnipolymer supports. They cost more than her upgraded body-mold chair, but were sooo worth it.

A rumble in the distance made her mentally shove her middle finger at the sky. Hugo had informed her when he'd woken her up for training well before dawn, that rain was forecasted but not to expect it to change their schedule. After all, they'd been promised "good training."

Maybe if it rained hard enough, she wouldn't need to waste time taking a shower before breakfast and could collapse face down on her fancy canopy bed for a cat nap instead.

At the bottom of the hill, the trail turned and wound through open woodland, only gentle ups and downs in sight. Lynn leaned forward and found a new well of energy somewhere, determined to make up ground. Predictably, Ronnie pulled ahead of her, his long legs eating up the level trail more efficiently than they'd managed on an incline. Lynn didn't care. It wasn't a competition in her eyes. They all had different body shapes and types. She'd been gifted with significant natural muscle mass, while Ronnie had lucked out in the height department. Then there were the inherent biological differences between men and women encoded in their DNA. She'd grown up with a nurse for a mother, so she had no illusions about the realities of biology.

Fortunately for CIDER's recruiting efforts, few TDMs outside of Yaguar and Nundu were particularly fast, and none of them had body mass—at least not in this dimension. The insubstantial alien entities were equal opportunity targets for gamers everywhere.

Lynn gulped more water and tried to get her breathing down to a rhythm, eyes focused on the ground six feet in front of her. Every mile she ran, every minute she beat back fatigue, was one more cord of strength strung between her body and her will, one more step toward making her unbreakable, no matter what she faced.

And the challenges were many.

Lynn remembered how white her mom's face had gotten, bloodless with shock, when Lynn had told her plainly that the TDMs were real, and that she and the guys had volunteered to fight them. After the national championship ceremonies had concluded, Lynn had pinged Steve and told him—not asked—that she was bringing her mother in on the secret, and he could help her do it, or hide like a coward. To his credit, he'd shown up in their hotel room soon after. He'd gotten special permission to offer the same NDA to Matilda Raven, having vouched for her personally.

As Lynn had suspected, her mother hesitated only a moment before agreeing to silence and LINC monitoring by Hugo so that she could find out whatever grave news Lynn needed to share.

At that point, Lynn almost hadn't been able to force the words out. But she'd thought it would hurt her mom more if it came from Steve, who Lynn rightly should have forced to do the deed. The world was six months away from going up in flames, though. Her father's death had taught her what it felt like to live with regrets, so it was time for pride, hurt, and feelings to take the back seat.

She'd put on her Larry face and gotten it done.

It had taken her mom a whole minute of shocked silence, looking back and forth between Lynn and Steve, before she'd found her voice. Then she'd only asked one question, eyes locked on Steve.

You knew the whole time, didn't you?

Steve had nodded, once.

Get out.

Matilda had said it quietly, but Lynn's heart still broke at the pain in her mom's voice. Steve hadn't argued, just hesitated a moment, then left. Lynn hadn't argued either—what could she say? Especially when her mother had turned those dark brown eyes on her, moisture shining in the corners. She'd expected her mother to argue, cajole, beg Lynn to change her mind and go away somewhere safe. Matilda had already lost her husband, and now Lynn was asking her to risk her only child as well.

Lynn had steeled her heart, even as she dreaded the inevitable pain.

Instead, Matilda had pulled her into a fierce, desperate hug that Lynn wished could have gone on forever. But her mother had simply whispered, "Your father would be so proud of you," and then pulled back. Lynn had quietly filled her in on what would happen next.

A big PR announcement from Tsunami introducing the "exciting new events" planned for the Hunter Strike Teams leading up to the international competition.

A day to go home to Cedar Rapids and pack. Prepare. Say goodbye.

Then an airbus would pick up Skadi's Wolves and take them to an undisclosed location for training.

Lynn had watched the announcement on the way home from Austin, wondering what was true and what was smoke and mirrors as Mr. Krator promised the world "bigger guns and more thrilling battles" with the Hunter Strike Teams getting the enviable privilege of trying out the new gadgets first.

Tsunami's PR team had already started coordinating with GIC and dozens of other PR agencies, spinning the tale, promising exclusive interviews and footage of the TransDimensional Counterforce training. But first the Hunter Strike Teams were going to disappear for a few days. Give them time to acclimate to their training. That sort of thing. They were professional gamers, after all, not reality-stream celebrities broadcasting 24/7.

All too soon, the time had come, and Lynn had hugged her mother goodbye as the nondescript but visibly high-end airbus had waited on the curb. Matilda had gripped her so tightly Lynn felt like her bones might break, but she hadn't cared. Kayla had been there too, waving excitedly and promising to finagle herself onto the GIC vid crew that came to do Lynn's exclusive training interview.

Poor Kayla. She had no idea what was going on. And Lynn couldn't tell her.

Maybe it was better that way.

Their first week at The Greenbrier had been chaotic and exhausting. Alternating runs and HIIT drills before breakfast, briefings all morning while they were at their sharpest. Lunch and thirty minutes of free time, then weapons and formation training underground in the Cold War era facility built beneath The Greenbrier.

The fallout shelter was massive. It was completed in 1962 and was originally intended to be the fallback for the US legislature should a nuke fall on DC. It had a two-story exhibit hall, office space, chambers for both the Senate and the House, and the dining, dormitory, and medical facilities to house over a thousand people from radiation should the worst come to the worst. Two gargantuan blast doors, the biggest twenty by twenty feet of solid steel almost two feet wide and weighing thirty tons, guarded two vehicular entrances, while an eighteen-ton door connected the resort to the bunker.

Technological advances in missile delivery made the facility functionally obsolete for its intended purpose several years after it was constructed. But it was still kept secret and in functional readiness by The Greenbrier for three decades before a Washington Post reporter revealed it to the world in 1992. After that, parts of it were converted to data storage, while the historical sections were kept in their original condition by The Greenbrier for educational tours.

Their formation and battle training mostly happened in the huge exhibit hall, forty feet underground with rows of load-bearing columns marching down its length. If the whole thing hadn't been painted white and lit with bright fluorescent lights overhead, Lynn might have felt like she was in the Dwarven city of Khazad-dûm.

So far, they hadn't gotten any hands-on time with whatever bigger, better "weapons" CIDER had developed. Lynn hoped they would get the chance later that day, now that they'd entered their second week of training. The first week had been a lot of orientation briefings about their new unit structure, what their chain of command looked like, and how everything was going to interface between what the public thought was going on versus their actual mission. All briefings were carried out in the underground amphitheater that had been built as a backup chamber for the House of Representatives. They'd also spent significant time that first week doing drills and attack scenarios in the exhibit hall to get used to their new units and the expanded utility of their TD Counterforce app.

As Lynn had discovered in one of their first briefings, the Hunter Strike Teams were not members of the US Military, either officially or unofficially. CIDER—the Coalition for Interdimensional Dark Energy Research—had been set up as a multi-national project to establish the source and implication of these exotic particle entities that had been discovered, in order to advise its various member nations on what action might be advisable. But CIDER's mission had changed once it had become clear that the entities were sentient, organized, and parasitic to infrastructure. All attempts at communication had failed, and so CIDER had established an R&D branch to conduct "ongoing development of technology and strategies to mitigate transdimensional particle interference." That was the branch that had started collaborating with the various countries' militaries.

The briefing hadn't gone into detail about how Robert Krator, world-famous game designer, had been read in on the global crisis. However it had happened, though, Mr. Krator had come up with the insane idea of an AI-powered gaming interface to manage the exotic particle entities. Technically, Tsunami Entertainment wasn't contracting with CIDER. It was Tsunami's subsidiary company, Mind Game Inc., that everything was funneled through—contracts, payments, investments, even the TD Hunter trademark.

Of course, now that Lynn knew what was going on, the entire thing was hilariously and tragically clear.

She wondered how much science fiction Mr. Krator watched—or read, if he was old school—and if it included the story about that kid who became a general. Was this her own version of Battle School?

If it was, it was a pretty lame equivalent. But at least the Hunter Strike Teams got better food and quarters. The chefs at The Greenbrier were world-renowned, and boy did it show. Lynn only lamented they got barely fifteen minutes to appreciate the culinary delights each meal before they were hustled off to their next task.

Their training "handlers" were all military men and women. But since the Hunter Strike Teams were only contractors with CIDER, the handlers were operating in an advisory role. Most of the military advisors were active duty from various branches who had been detached from their native units and covertly assigned to Taskforce Sanctus as Alpha Testers. The Alpha Testers had been the guinea pigs for the original TD Hunter system development. Lucky them.

As far as it concerned Lynn and her fellow gamers, their military advisors were to be obeyed as if the TD Counterforce units really were within the United States military chain of command. But as Colonel Bryce had said, it wasn't boot camp and the Hunters weren't recruits. Everyone was expected to be professional and treat their mission with due seriousness. Anyone who didn't feel like cooperating was welcome to take CIDER up on that one-way ticket to "The Island" for a nice, secluded, six month stay. It was the fate Lynn assumed had befallen Connor and his three ARS teammates who'd never shown up at The Greenbrier with Elena, much to Lynn's delight and relief. Lynn was mystified as to why Elena had stuck it out. But the former pop-girl had been assigned to a different unit, so Lynn had had no chance to ask her about it.

So far, all the gamers-turned-military-contractors had remained focused on the mission. Everyone had volunteered to help fight, and fight they would. Their military advisors pushed them hard in training and held them to high standards, but there was no hazing or typical Drill Instructor yelling.

Part of this, Lynn was sure, was because the eyes of the world were on them, at least for their aboveground training.

The Greenbrier, as a luxury resort, no doubt had its own incredibly expensive and airtight interdiction net. Lynn's own gated neighborhood had something similar, if more basic. It provided a bubble of air space above the neighborhood that prevented unauthorized entry from drones or automated air vehicles. All airborne traffic needed passcodes to be let in, and the neighborhood had a community app where residents could generate one-time-use codes for air taxis and delivery drones, or a limited number of permanent codes for their personal vehicles, or use by friends, household staff, and the like.

Non-governmental use of such technology required stringent licensing and expense, and was hard to get, unless you were rich and famous or could prove an undeniable need for it. A luxury resort that catered to politicians, foreign dignitaries, and the cream of the social crop obviously qualified.

Lynn assumed the net above The Greenbrier was augmented by or even duplicated by even tougher military tech brought in for their month of training. It was impossible to prevent *all* drone surveillance. But at least it could prevent anything close enough to record conversations or get usable footage.

Even so, all briefings and sensitive training were conducted underground in the bunker.

The woodland trail they'd been running on turned and went downward again, and Lynn spotted pavement, indicating they'd finally finished their loop and were returning to the civilized portions of the resort. Now they *only* had a dozen golf holes to wind their way around, and the empty cottages to pass through, before they finally reached the West Virginia Wing of the resort where they'd been billeted. It was the newest wing, having been built from 1959 to 1962 as cover for the hulking fallout shelter that had been secretly constructed beneath it, its lowest level reaching sixty feet underground.

If gray rain clouds hadn't been hanging low overhead, the sun would have been cresting the verdant green mountains just about then, treating the trainees to a spectacular sunrise accompanied by cheerful birdsong. Instead a cool wind chilled their sweat-soaked brows, and big fat raindrops began to fall on their trembling limbs. By the time the snaking line of roughly sixty trainees in Lynn's unit were within sight of their wing, the skies had opened up and everyone was soaked. Their high-performance wear wasn't waterproof, but it was specially designed to wick away moisture and prevent chafing, so the soaking was more an annoyance than anything else.

Lynn ducked her head and pushed out one last burst of speed to get up the gentle hill that led to the north side of the West Virginia Wing where the road ran under the wing's tall, covered portico, then looped back to form a circle for guest drop off and pick up.

Trainer Coler finally gave the word and everyone stumbled to a weary walk. He had them go under the portico and loop back around the drive until their line turned into a circle for cooldown. Lynn thought the pouring rain was doing a fine job of cooling them down on its own, but didn't say so. Instead she slowed even more until Mack, Dan, and finally Edgar joined her. Ronnie had pulled ahead at the last and Lynn couldn't see where he was through the driving rain.

"Nice little morning jog, huh?" Dan half yelled over the rain, attempting to grin through his still-labored breathing.

"Shut up, Dan," Mack groaned. His entire body drooped, but at least he was still moving. "Why, oh why did I let myself get talked into this nightmare?"

"For the—exquisite—fine dining?" Edgar offered from just behind them, panting between words. He seemed to be remaining upright through sheer force of will. Lynn hoped it didn't run out, because none of them were big enough to catch him if he decided on an impromptu nap.

"You can thank Lynn," Ronnie called from behind Edgar, surprising them all. He'd lapped them and caught up without them noticing, tired as they were. His expression was more or less a permanent scowl these days. "She's the crazy masochist who thought volunteering to fight an alien invasion was a good idea."

Lynn let several choice retorts pass by, unspoken, and instead bared her teeth at Ronnie in a thoroughly Larry smile. He looked away, and everyone fell silent, focusing on getting their breathing, and limbs, back under control.

Their team dynamic was . . . tense.

Over the past week none of the guys had said a word about regrets or wanting to quit—well, not serious words. Mack was constantly moaning, but it seemed to be his way of coping. Yet they were all still coming to terms with the complete upending of their hopes and dreams, their future, and their entire world.

They'd worked *so hard* for a bright future that had seemed nearly within their grasp, only to have the illusion shattered. Lynn was still angry at Mr. Krator for the whole charade, even if she understood the necessity. Ronnie was especially bitchy about it.

But they had a mission, and the mission was holding them together, despite their frayed tempers and the fearful uncertainty that likely gnawed at the back of everyone's brain.

After their five-minute walking cool down, Trainer Coler dismissed them to their rooms to shower and change. After that they'd head out of the West Virginia Wing through connecting hallways to the resort's main dining room for breakfast.

The West Virginia Wing had three floors of luxurious rooms outfitted with thick carpet, floor-to-ceiling drapes, and dark polished furniture that looked like it belonged in a museum. While the poshness of the furniture gave off British vibes, it was made distinctly American in flavor by the extremely large, colorful, and *floral* designs on every bit of cloth available, from rugs to drapes to upholstery. Apparently some famous interior designer had decorated it from top to bottom in the 1940s after it had been a military hospital during World War II. The style had been meticulously maintained in the hundred years since.

Talk about brand loyalty.

The Hunter trainees had been assigned two to a room, and conveniently there was just about the right split between men and women to fit all the women on one floor and all the men on the other two floors. The girls had gotten the top level with the best view, while the guys were spread out on the lower two floors. Lynn skipped the elevator, despite the jelly consistency of her muscles. Being trapped in a tight space with a dozen other sweaty bodies wasn't worth it.

The one hundred eighty Hunters from the national championship that had volunteered for the TD Counterforce had been divided into three companies, each made up of roughly sixty Hunters and sixty-four Alpha Testers. They wouldn't meet the bulk of the Alpha Testers in their units until further into their training. For now, only the leadership who'd been assigned as their training handlers were needed. Those that were present were billeted in the main resort, apart from the trainees.

Each of the three companies were made up of four platoons—three infantry platoons of mixed Hunters and Alpha Testers, with a fourth heavy weapons platoon made up of Alpha Testers. The platoons were comprised of a platoon leader, assistant platoon leader, and three squads. Each squad had a squad leader and two Hunter Strike Teams, each of the five-person teams led by their respective captains. Two of the three squads in each infantry platoon were Hunter trainees, and the third squad was made up of Alpha Testers.

That meant, effectively, Lynn and her team had gone from spearheading a literal horde of gamers to being a lowly team under an entire command structure of Alpha Testers.

The *real* fighters, in other words.

It was a big mental adjustment.

Most of Lynn's gaming career had been spent as a lone operator. When she had gamed on a team, she always preferred calling the shots since she was usually the most skilled gamer around. Now, though . . . now things were *real*. Life-and-death real. She waffled painfully from extreme relief to extreme annoyance at her new position. Her Lynn brain had never wanted to be in charge, had never wanted to be in the hot seat. Her Larry brain, though . . . that part of her definitely chafed.

At least she still had her team to look after, and that gave her something to focus on.

Lynn arrived at her shared room before her roommate did, so she made a beeline for the shower to get in and out as fast as possible. Nicole "EvaNight07" Gaines, captain of Team Amaranth, tended to linger under the hot water, and Lynn needed protein more than she needed muscle relaxation.

Skadi's Wolves and Amaranth had both been assigned to Alpha Company, 1st Platoon, 2nd Squad. The 1st Squad in each platoon was made up of Alpha Testers, so Lynn supposed her team and Amaranth had the dubious honor of being the first of the first of the first, at least as far as Hunter trainees were concerned.

Eva was pretty cool from what Lynn had seen so far. She was quiet and self-contained without being awkward, for which Lynn was incredibly grateful. Lynn had never been much of a conversationalist, and Eva seemed happy to share details when questioned without straying into Kayla levels of overwhelming enthusiasm.

Eva and her team were from Colorado, right between Denver and Colorado Springs. The woman was a former USA Gymnastics National Champion who'd had aspirations to make the US Olympic team. Unfortunately an injury had ended her elite gymnast career near the end of college, so she'd turned to AR gymnastics and dance performance that, much like AR sports, took advantage of augmented reality to turn a show of athletic skill into a *true* spectator sport. Eva had shown Lynn a few of her most popular routines on the streams—vids that had tens of millions of views—and Lynn had to admit they were incredibly beautiful performances. Hard to look away from.

Eva had formed her team along with her best friend from competitive gymnastics, Emilia Tomás, who seemed to like things simple because she'd used her name as her TD Hunter handle. Emilia and her boyfriend, Jacob "TheGrimReaper16" Stills, were obsessive gamers, and between their gaming expertise and Eva's professional AR experience, they'd gathered a few more girls from their gymnast circle and formed a top-notch team.

Based on their leaderboard ranking and what Lynn had seen of them during the national championship, they were all incredibly fit and had high technical scores in accuracy and some obscure kill combos. But their kill-to-damage ratio was middle-of-the-road. Lynn suspected it was a tactics and strategy issue. In a game as competitive as TD Hunter, even occasional mistakes in how and where you took on the overwhelming masses of TDMs could pull down your overall score. Lynn hadn't gotten up the courage yet to ask Eva why she was team captain and not Grim or Emilia, considering they were the ones with the most gaming experience. But maybe they had the same weaknesses Ronnie had. Or Mack or Dan or Edgar. Not everybody was leadership material, and Eva certainly seemed to have the sort of self-possessed authority you needed to inspire and lead.

Of course, scores didn't really matter anymore, did they?

Trying to mentally juggle TD Hunter the game versus TD Hunter the covert military op had been making Lynn's brain hurt ever since she'd arrived at The Greenbrier. Instead of popping headache pills like candy, she'd been avoiding the cognitive dissonance with mental reassurances that their briefings would explain it all soon.

Maybe today.

Lynn sped through her shower in record time, gave Eva a polite nod as she exited the bathroom, and got dressed in her recently issued TD Counterforce uniform. It was the same sort of high-performance wear she'd been competing in for months already, but with a few extra pockets and some quality upgrades. It also didn't have any of her sponsorship logos or branding on it. Since not much of their training was going to be livestreamed outside a few controlled situations, Lynn supposed it didn't matter much. Mrs. Pearson was coordinating with Tsunami and Lynn's sponsors, and Lynn assumed the mega exposure they would soon get with the TD Counterforce's "Battle Tour" would make up for a month or two of scant activity.

Without all the logos she was so used to, the black uniform looked incredibly somber, almost ominous. Its subtle red and blue accents broke up the field of black, along with a small TD Counterforce logo on the right breast with her unit and call sign underneath.

Raven

It felt odd, but also strangely poetic, that she had gone full circle from mercing in virtual as "Coughlin," to mercing in the real as "Raven." Well, sort of mercing, anyway. She wasn't fighting people, thankfully, but she was fighting *something*, and being paid to do it, if the compensation and benefit package from Tsunami was anything to judge by.

Full gaming handles were too much of a mouthful for high-intensity situations, and most gamers already used shortened handles or nicknames for the people they gamed with regularly. Usually it was the first word of your gaming handle, thus "Raven" for her. Rather hilariously, Ronnie, Mack, and Dan had all used their given name as the first part of their gaming handle, so that's what they got emblazoned across their uniform. Edgar, even more hilariously, was now known as "Maui." He was tickled pink about it. Lynn couldn't help noticing he stood a bit straighter and got a twinkle in his eye whenever he heard it. She'd also caught him humming snatches of a certain song when nobody else was around.

She'd wondered why their "glorious leaders" at CIDER had decided not to go with the normal military convention of last names, but supposed it made sense. The Hunters were just innocent gamers, after all, training for an international championship. It would have been odd if they all started referring to each other by last names instead of shortened handles.

Her new call sign as well as unit number were splashed in large font across her upper back, above a bigger version of the round TD Counterforce logo. Now that she was intimate with the weapon configurations used in TD Hunter, she could appreciate the artistic rendering of the crossed Plasma Rifle and Plasma Blade on the logo. It seemed so long ago—and just yesterday—that she'd first seen it embroidered on the beta tester swag polo Tsunami had sent her last June. Seeing it now in large, bold colors on the backs of everyone around her was surreal. The vertical lightning bolt that slashed down in brilliant gold over the crossed weapons really caught the eye. The three objects were superimposed over a blue-green planet Earth, which in turn was surrounded by a double ring of red. Within that red-bounded border was "TransDimensional Counterforce" at the top, and at the bottom the Latin motto: *Quod Nos Tueri.*

That which we protect.

She'd never really noticed or cared about the motto before. But in the terrifying quiet of that first night after her world had been flipped upside-down, as her mom had slept fitfully beside her in the hotel room, she'd finally realized its significance.

She understood, now, why military units had mottos. She understood what it felt like, in all the fear and confusion and uncertainty, to need an anchor to hold onto, a certainty to guide you.

What would Skadi's Wolves' motto be, if they had one? She hadn't had time to ponder it, and there was no time now, either.

She shoved her feet into her boots as she finished a quick, tight plait for her hair to hang down behind her back. She'd make it secure after lunch before they started their exercises; for now it was fine to simply hang. After that all she had to grab was her ultra-thin hydration pack, an upgrade from the bulkier one she'd been using for the past year. This one formed so well to the body that you could sit comfortably for hours without it giving you back strain. She felt a momentary pang of loss for the little weight she was used to having in her pocket. There was no telling if she'd ever see the Helle pocketknife again that her father had gifted her. She'd used it to defend herself from a stalker attack that spring and it had been confiscated as evidence. Without that and the compact backpack she was used to taking on all her hunts, she felt naked.

She didn't even have auto-tinting AR glasses to hide behind anymore.

To ensure everyone had the right equipment and no one was leaking vital secrets on unauthorized devices, they'd all been required to leave their personal LINCs at home for this training. They'd each been issued a Tsunami-made, svelte-looking wristband LINC instead. The omnipolymer in it resized seamlessly to fit each wearer. The first time Lynn had put it on and it had tightened around her wrist, she'd had to fight back the wild impulse to claw it off again. It didn't escape her that there was no way to manually remove it if the LINC was locked down, which turned it into a handy little monitoring and tracking device.

Fun, fun, fun.

She reminded herself that she'd been wearing her own LINC every second of every day for most of her life. Being overtly monitored by the government instead of covertly monitored by the advertising industrial complex was hardly much of a change, if you thought about it sensibly. She would worry about privacy and government overreach after the world was no longer on a crash course to civilization collapse.

In addition to the standardized LINC, everyone had been issued AR interface contacts. Lynn was surprised they hadn't offered implants, but maybe the cost and medical trouble wasn't worth it for such short notice. Standard AR contacts had a continual-use life of one month and were quite comfortable to wear, once you got over the whole putting-something-in-your-eye part. Her mom had told her contacts used to be much more primitive, and people would pop them in and out *every day*. Lynn shuddered at the thought.

Once she'd gotten used to the new AR interface, Lynn had to admit it was incredibly convenient—besides the whole not being able to hide behind tinted sunglasses thing. She knew some people liked to have all sorts of distracting apps and widgets permanently stationed around the edge of their vision, but her nurse of a mother had pounded into her the dangers of constant visual distraction and how badly it could rewire the brain to sabotage executive function and healthy dopamine reaction. So she'd always kept her display empty of distractions. Hugo helped her set up her new eye-control cues to pull up time, weather, maps, notes, or whatever else she needed day-to-day. She could always subvocalize a request for Hugo to show her what she wanted, but she couldn't shake the uneasy pit in her gut that lingered at the thought of Hugo.

Despite knowing the whole time that "Hugo" was simply an extremely advanced computer program, she'd still felt hurt and betrayed that he—it, whatever—had been keeping her in the dark about TD Hunter. That inadvertent and unwanted feeling of betrayal was a big reason why she'd always avoided using a personal AI. She'd seen people get really messed up by too much personal AI interaction. A guy from her high school had committed suicide back in sophomore year after he'd fallen in love with one of those AI girlfriends Lynn sometimes saw ads for. It had all been very hush-hush, but the student gossip mill said he'd become so obsessed with it that he'd neglected everything else in life, and when his parents had tried to delete his account he'd gone off the deep end.

Hugo's saving grace was that it didn't pretend to be human. It regularly referred to itself as a program, referenced its various parameters and limitations, and subtly redirected attempts at emotional connection toward human sources. Maybe Lynn was projecting her hurt and distrust on it, since she couldn't very well sit Mr. Krator down and give him a stern talking to. She hadn't even seen Steve since the championship in Austin. Hopefully there would be a chance to talk privately with him in the near future, to clear the air between them.

Of course, that was assuming Matilda hadn't already murdered him and hidden the body.

All these worries kept Lynn occupied as she trotted down the stairs toward the West Virginia Wing's first level, then headed out into the hallway that would take her past the empty ballrooms and event spaces and to the main resort's posh dining hall. Other Hunter trainees were headed the same way in front of and behind her, but everyone's footsteps were muffled on the thick, boldly patterned carpet. At least this one wasn't riotously floral, like the one in the West Virginia Wing. The hallway carpet was a repeated, overlapping pattern of large magnolia leaf clusters, and together with the polished wood trim and cheery yellow-white patterned wallpaper, it gave everything a summer-verdant feel. High ceilings and full windows made what might have been a stuffy atmosphere instead well-lit and airy. A faint smell of antique carpet and wood polish entwined with the bold visuals to give the whole resort a stately panache that made Lynn smile inside.

Down the long, *long* hall and around the corner to the right led Lynn to the formal dining room. Its many small, four-person tables had been pushed together into three long lines down the expansive room, which sported a double row of columns, a dozen chandeliers, cream wallpaper, and spotlessly white wainscotting below and crown molding above. The juxtaposition with the milling crowd of gamer-athletes turned secret-soldiers moving through the buffet line made Lynn chuckle to herself every time she saw it.

Lynn and her fellow Hunters of Alpha Company joined the trainees from Bravo and Charlie Company lining up for the buffet line. Their morning PT was staggered in different locations, rotating each day, so they could all get the full pleasure of an hour's worth of torture without stepping on each other's toes.

Edgar, as usual, had staked out a place for their team at the end of the tables nearest the buffet. He was already halfway through his first plate—Lynn had no idea how he got to the dining room so quickly but apparently he was a big breakfast person. Lynn wasted no time filling up her own plate with steaming scrambled eggs, juicy bacon, and deliciously seasoned tater tots. There was also sausage, biscuits and gravy, fruit, and piles of delectable pastries. Lynn skipped the refined carbs and snagged a banana to top her mountain of bacon. She craved salt and protein like a drowning person craved air. Edgar was the only one who could top her meat intake, though the others gave it a fair effort. Dan, Mack, and finally Ronnie joined them soon after and got to work on their food. They had thirty minutes for breakfast, but between the long hallways and the wait in the buffet line there was rarely more than fifteen minutes of actual butt-in-chair time to eat as much as they could.

Eva and her team appeared soon after, taking seats next to Skadi's Wolves. There'd been the usual awkwardness when they'd first been thrown together in their unit assignment. But Lynn had swallowed her initial instinct—self-consciousness—and firmly ignored her second—grumpy silence—and had facilitated introductions. Despite the tension, the guys had taken it in stride.

Ronnie and Dan had hit it off with Grim and Emilia, who were happy as clams to devolve into gaming lingo, while Mack had helpfully made sure the other two girls, Sarah "The_Best_Sarah" Hartman and Serena "SerenitySoul" Thomas, didn't feel left out.

At the breakfast table, most people were too tired or too busy shoveling food into their mouths to talk. Except for Dan, of course. He didn't let a little thing like chewing stop him from grilling Grim on his top five favorite MMORPGs. Grim couldn't do more than mumble half-audible replies around a mouth stuffed with sausage, but Dan hardly needed the input. He could carry on both sides of a conversation all by himself.

"Mornin', Miz Raven."

Lynn's head came up to grin tiredly at the source of the smooth Texan drawl that had greeted her.

"Heya Gadsden. You know, 'Miz Raven' is what my ninety-plus-year-old neighbor calls me. You should probably stick with just 'Raven.' Wouldn't want people mistaking you for an old geezer."

Despite the fact that the captain of Team Lone Star could hardly have been older than thirty, he was still about the oldest Hunter Lynn had seen so far among the trainees. That made him a prime target for ribbing.

"Manners are timeless, or so my mama claims. But since you insist, Raven it is." He nodded in a friendly sort of way, then took a deep breath of the steaming goodness wafting up from his plate. With almost reverent care, he forked up a piece of buttermilk biscuit smothered in creamy gravy and placed the bite in his mouth.

His exaggerated groan of ecstasy made Edgar snort beside her.

Lynn cut her eyes to the side and noted Edgar's grumpy expression, though it was aimed at his pile of cheesy scrambled eggs, not at Gadsden. Edgar was usually the most laid-back person in the room. Very few things got on his nerves. Apparently smooth-talking, handsome Texans was one of them.

At least Lynn now understood *why* Gadsden made Edgar grumpy. Edgar had sort-of-kind-of-accidentally confessed to having a massive crush on her—love was too strong a term, right?—the night before the championship in Austin, and she'd desperately shelved the incident in her brain. She'd intended to worry about it after they'd advanced in the competition and she had a bit of breathing space to untangle her confused feelings.

But then her world had gone up in flames.

Fighting for humanity's survival didn't seem like a great environment in which to navigate a relationship, so she hadn't brought up Edgar's confession. Neither had he, to her surprise, though sometimes the way he looked at her made her sure he wanted to.

He had nothing to worry about where Gadsden was concerned. Or any other guy. Romance might be alluring in the abstract, but when it came down to brass tacks, it was the most terrifying thing she'd faced in life, including battling an alien invasion. Suave smiles and classy flirting were not tempting in the slightest. Edgar had years of trust and friendship going for him and even *he* made her twitchy when his expression went all sappy.

"So, I guess the grub is better than Army fare, huh?" Lynn asked, remembering Gadsden's comment at the championship.

"I'll fight a whole dadgum universe of aliens, long as they keep feeding me like this," Gadsden confirmed between bites and more unseemly groans.

Lynn snickered, then went back to the important work of eating her bacon. It was a heavenly explosion of juicy, crispy perfection in her mouth, and she almost groaned herself. There was no time to savor, though, so she chewed with firm purpose. Across from her, Gadsden was putting away biscuits like they were his personal salvation, given to him by the good Lord himself. Lynn pointed a fork in his direction and spoke past a cheek full of bacon:

"If you keep that up, they'll have to roll you up and down the hills on our next trail run."

Gadsden shook his head.

"Naw, missy. I swear I can do anything under the sun long as the sun ain't tryin'a kill me. Try running them hills when it's hotter'n two rats making whoopee in a wool sock."

Lynn's brow scrunched as she tried to translate that honey-smooth Texanism of near gibberish. She was saved from replying by the poke of an elbow and a hiss from Dan.

"Hey, look! It's Elena."

He jutted his chin down the line of tables and Lynn craned her neck. She caught a glimpse of a familiar high and tight gold-blond ponytail before it disappeared behind seated figures at the end of the room.

"You know anything about the unit they put her in?" she muttered to Dan.

He shrugged unhelpfully, but then Ronnie leaned toward them from Dan's far side.

"It's gotta be either a team that lost a member to the Island, or a group of strays," he stated.

"Who's Elena?" Eva asked a bit further down. It was loud enough in the room that there was no chance of their conversation carrying far. But Lynn still kept her voice low as she leaned toward Eva to answer.

"She used to be part of Cedar Rapids Champions, but the rest of her team disappeared, hopefully to a cold, gray cell somewhere. They came from the same high school as us in Iowa, and they were all bullies."

Eva's brow furrowed.

"But wasn't she the first to stand up and volunteer, right after you all?"

Lynn squirmed internally, all too aware of that fact. Why *had* Elena volunteered? Not an hour before that she'd been as rude as ever to Lynn during the championship battle. Had discovering the global threat to humanity finally knocked some sense into her? One could only hope.

"Who knows what goes on in Elena's head," Ronnie said with a snort. "If narcissistic harpies had a poster child, it'd be her."

Lynn wasn't so sure about that. What narcissistic harpy would volunteer to risk her life to fight the unknown, in secret, with no promise of medals or acclaim? Maybe Elena didn't believe the TDMs were real and she was just going along with the "charade" for continued social clout?

"She's gotten this far," Dan pointed out, his mouth only *half* full of food. "She's got balls, at least."

"Oh, really?" Lynn's brows rose, and she waved her fork at herself and the girls of Amaranth. "Does that mean we've got balls, too, since *we're* here?"

Dan got a deer-in-the-headlights look.

"Uhhh..."

"Come on, Lynn, it's just a figure of speech," said Mack, coming to Dan's rescue.

"Seems like a silly thing to say," Eva pointed out, "since balls are the weakest and most sensitive part of *your* body."

All the girls snickered.

"I always figured it was a backhanded sorta compliment,"

Gadsden drawled. "It ain't the little girls tryin'a ride their bikes off the roof. They're too smart for that. It's them little boys up there while the girls watch from the lawn with a bag a' chips."

The girls laughed harder, and Lynn almost choked on her bacon.

Dan looked horrified.

"What sort of dummy would try to ride their bike off a roof?"

Gadsden grinned. "What? You never tried it? Never built a ramp or made a parachute outta an old sheet?"

"No," Dan muttered. "I never even *had* a bike. What would be the point? I had BMX-Extreme in virtual. Have you ever done a double flair off the Great Wall of China?"

Gadsden frowned, then shook his head and went back to his biscuits. Lynn, who was closer to him, heard him mutter, "Kids these days."

Conversation more or less ebbed after that, as everyone concentrated on their food. Lynn wondered, not for the first time, where Derek and his Team Light Brigade was. She hadn't spotted them acting as trainers, so maybe they would join the companies later once the trainees graduated to practicing platoon and company-sized movements? It would be patently foolish for a team of Alpha Testers that experienced in TDM combat to not be included in this whole song and dance, but who knew what sort of role their CIDER superiors had them doing.

Lynn had just about cleared her plate when Hugo piped up in her ear, as he was doubtless doing on every other trainee's earbud as well.

"Good morning, Miss Lynn. It is five minutes to eight. Might I suggest that it is time to head toward the briefing room?"

Normally Lynn would have subvocalized something witty in reply, knowing Hugo was always up for amusing banter. But the exercise had lost its luster, so she didn't bother replying, simply stood up, leaving her plate where it was. The cooking staff did all the cleaning up, as Colonel Bryce had promised.

Edgar stood up with her, his plate sparkling clean, as usual. She'd never spotted him licking it. She had no idea how he managed it. Maybe it had something to do with growing up in a house full of siblings.

They headed out side-by-side with Ronnie tailing them, leaving Dan furiously shoveling the last of his food into his mouth while Mack skipped back to the buffet line to snag another pastry to munch on while they walked. There was a press to get out the dining room doors, and a few of the teams Lynn recognized called a greeting while they all waited to stream out into the hallway. Out of habit, Lynn kept a furtive eye peeled for a high blond ponytail. She hoped Elena had moved past their high school drama, but wasn't going to bet on it, just in case.

Once they'd finally made the hall, Lynn let Ronnie, Mack, and Dan pull ahead with Grim and Emilia while she trailed behind with Edgar. She wanted to scan her notes from last week's briefings.

The trailing mob of trainees streamed down the long, magnolia leaf-rugged hall. They passed ceiling-high windows on their right, and empty, chandelier-hung ballrooms on their left awaiting their next event booking. Eventually the mob split, some heading for the elevator, the rest heading up the sweeping staircase that climbed up to a half-circle landing where gigantic bow-shaped curtains framed the windows that looked out on the perfectly manicured resort grounds. It had taken Lynn an entire day to stop staring at the five-foot wide bows perched atop those gaudy curtains. Now she didn't even glance up as she kept climbing the staircase to the top level of the event center that, having been built next to a hill, joined to the basement floor of the West Virginia Wing.

For three decades everybody had thought this particular corridor led only to an innocuous, two-story expo hall. What they hadn't known about was the eighteen-ton, two-foot-thick blast door that had been chained open and hidden behind a false wall and a set of decorative panels. Tens of thousands of people had walked past it over the decades and never realized that when they entered the expo hall, they were entering a top-secret fallout facility masquerading as part of the resort.

Now, of course, the blast door sat in plain view, though still chained open. It took only fifty pounds of pressure to make the multi-ton door swing smoothly closed, but the information plaque next to it stated the doors had never been built for the stress of frequent opening and closing, so to preserve the massive hinges thicker than Edgar's forearm, the blast door was never closed.

The multitude of footsteps echoed across the off-white linoleum floor of the expo hall as they wove between the columns, headed for the underground amphitheater.

Hopefully today they'd finally find out something concrete about CIDER's crazy plan to save the world.

Chapter 3

"GOOOOD *MORNING*, HUNTERS! I HOPE YOU'RE READY TO PAY attention, because things are about to get interesting."

Lynn, along with the entire roomful of trainees sat up straighter. Trainer Bowers, a tall, lean, dark man with his black-brown hair cut in a high-top, strode purposefully onto the stage at the front of the amphitheater-style room and stopped in the middle, hands behind his back in parade rest as he surveyed his scattered audience.

Like the other rooms in the underground facility, this room had a still, heavy feel to it, with no moving air. It bordered on oppressive, though the air was cool enough, if a bit musty.

Since the room they were in had been created to seat all members of the House of Representatives, there was room for 435 people plus a few extra. That gave the trainees plenty of room to spread out. Their seats weren't the most comfortable, though. The old schoolroom-style, right-handed flip-up desks that were bolted to the concrete floor left a lot to be desired. Edgar could barely squeeze into his, and looked even more giant than usual sitting beside her.

Skadi's Wolves and Amaranth had staked out one of the center rows for themselves. The seats were arranged in many rows marching down the sloped floor toward the stage, with a larger middle section and two smaller sections on each side, with walkways in between. Skadi's Wolves sat about two-thirds of the way towards the back, close enough to clearly see the large flex screen behind Bowers. The screen remained blank, though, while the briefing title and description along with Trainer Bowers' name popped up on Lynn's AR display instead.

Once Trainer Bowers seemed sure he had everyone's attention, he continued.

"Last week you were thoroughly briefed on our mission: to destroy as many nodalities as quickly as possible to save threatened infrastructure in major cities across the country. It is hoped that, if we can stomp out the TDM boss population, we can buy CIDER time to find a permanent solution to this invasion of alien entities.

"This morning I have the unenviable task of explaining how the TD Hunter combat interface works behind the scenes. This task is unenviable because not even the designers and scientists who created it really understand how it works, much less can explain it in words with less than ten syllables. If you think I'm exaggerating, talk to Dr. Roberts. You'll likely only understand half of what he says, though, which is why I'm giving this brief instead of him.

"By the time I'm finished, you should have a basic grasp of what the TDM entities are and how we're fighting them. If at any point you feel like your brain is going to explode, please exit the room first so the rest of us won't get hit by splatter. We've got a lot to cover this morning and we ain't got time to take things slow.

"Rules of engagement are as follows: please hold all questions until the end, more than likely they'll get answered in the course of the brief. Make note of them, though. If they don't get answered, ask 'em at the end and I'll do my best to clear things up.

"As usual, if you get tired, get up and go stand in the back. If I see anyone nodding off in their seat, I'll call you out by name, so don't be that person. I have some mean 'yo mama' takedowns, all I need is a reason to use 'em. There's a coffee station in the back if anyone needs it.

"Questions before we begin?"

Trainer Bowers waited expectantly, looking out over the one-hundred eighty-some gamers. But there wasn't a peep. Everyone's eyes were glued to him. Lynn assumed everyone was as eager as she was to get some answers.

"Right, then. Onward and forward." Bowers unfolded from his parade rest, hands coming up to gesture as he began pacing with slow, measured steps.

"You've all heard of quantum computing and how its advances transformed energy and computing power at the beginning of the century. That would've been covered in your high school history and math classes. You college-age people should have learned how the quantum coupling breakthroughs and qubit stabilization technology of the 2020s launched quantum computing out of its NISQ era and laid the groundwork for everything from Everlast batteries to modern-day LINCs."

Images of various LINC configurations and examples of battery-run technology cycled through Lynn's display as Bowers continued.

"Now, I can see some of you are going cross-eyed already. Take a deep breath. To quote Richard Feynman, 'nobody understands quantum mechanics.' There won't be a quiz, but you *do* need to grasp a couple terms."

Bowers ran down a short list of words that Lynn had only ever heard a few times. His short, sweet, practical explanations made a refreshing amount of sense. The animated diagrams accompanying each word helped, too.

"Even more essential to the technology surrounding TDMs," Bowers continued, "are the principals of quantum entanglement and quantum coupling—that 'spooky action at a distance' that Einstein critiqued in the 1930s. Turns out Bohr was right and Einstein was wrong.

"Now, I'm going to dumb this down as much as possible so even you crayon-eating former Marines in the back can grasp it."

There was some chuckling from the rear of the auditorium and an enthusiastic call of "Oo-rah!" Lynn resisted the urge to twist in her seat to see which Hunters were former Marines. Maybe she would ask around later.

"Basically, quantum entanglement is like how twins know something bad has happened to their twin even though they're nowhere near each other. It's the idea of two particles being 'entangled' to the point that they're functionally the same particle. For quantum computing, that's real convenient, because it means we can influence particle A over here and have it instantly repeated on particle B over there. Don't ask me how or why it works, that's Dr. Robert's wheelhouse and I don't even think most experts know *why*, just *how* well enough to take advantage of the phenomenon.

"Quantum coupling is the mechanical, practical description of these quantum entanglements that we harness in our physical technology. All coupling requires entanglement in order to work, but not all entanglement is necessarily harnessed in coupling. Clear as mud? Good.

"This technological breakthrough revolutionized the internet and computers because it transitioned us from 'transmitting' data to 'expressing' data, or you might say 'mirroring' data. See, transmission implies time spent and distance traveled to send information back and forth, even if it *is* at the speed of light. But fiber optic cables can be cut, and EM waves can be distorted or blocked. The quantum entanglement of particles enables instantaneous expression of data that is impervious to interruption or interception between points A and B. Spy and hack-proof, in other words."

Lynn stared intently at her display, brain working in overdrive as she watched the animations and followed Bowers' explanation. She didn't glance at her teammates to gauge their reaction. While she hoped they grasped the briefing, none of them were the Team Leader of Skadi's Wolves. That was her, and it was her responsibility to understand what was going on, what they needed to do about it, and why.

"That brings us to LINCs. What most people don't realize is that Limitless Integrated Network Connectors are all, to some extent, entangled with one another, along various particle pathways. They use quantum coupling technology in the manufacturing stage so that each LINC, from the small personal devices we think of as LINCs to the gigantic mesh nodes you see everywhere, is interconnected on a particle level. The World Wide Web, our mesh web's predecessor, was a vast network of servers communicating with one another via wired and wireless data transmission using the electromagnetic spectrum, and so was bound by time and distance. The mesh web, on the other hand, is a network of quantum entangled particles expressing data to one another without regard to time or space.

"This results in an incredible amount of particle activity that began barely ten years ago as theory and has increased exponentially ever since. I know some of you are still spring chickens, but others of us remember 2033 quite clearly when commercial LINCs debuted worldwide.

"Now, who wants to guess what year we discovered the existence of transdimensional entities?"

Bowers' question hung in the air, and it was a moment before some brave soul shouted: "2033!"

"Yup," Bowers said, sighing and shaking his head. "It still hurts my brain, trying to wrap it around how fast all of this has happened, and how much we still don't understand. Scientists in CIDER are still arguing about whether or not humanity *created* TDMs ourselves by accident. The only reason the prevailing theory puts TDMs as *transdimensional* and not some home-grown, mutated infestation is because of TEPs: Transdimensional Exotic Particles."

Lynn's eyes narrowed, her thoughts already jumping ahead, theorizing based on her knowledge of how the TD Hunter game worked.

"The TransDimensional Monsters you know and love from the TD Hunter game, when observed through boring ol' lab instruments instead of the TD Hunter combat interface, appear to be groupings of exotic particles moving together and acting with purpose. Whether or not they're sentient is still unknown. Here, the term 'exotic' means 'so crazily incomprehensible we don't know shit about them.' The only thing we *do* know is they act a lot like quantum entangled particles, especially the way they seem to 'spawn' out of nowhere."

A humorless smile quirked one side of Lynn's mouth as she remembered something Steve had told her ages ago that had seemed... off at the time. He'd said the game algorithm spawn patterns were opaque even to the game engineers. Now she knew why.

"There's no way to know for sure how long these TEPs have been hanging around. Most of the lab coats in CIDER agree they, shall we say, 'aren't from around here.' But when scientists first encountered them, they had no idea they weren't just one more exciting new particle discovery like quarks or muons, and so incorporated them into our increasingly swift technological advances.

"All the big questions about these particles, the where, how, and why, are keeping the coats busy. For now all *you* have to worry about is how we get rid of 'em.

"Keep in mind, these TEP entities are nothing so clunky and *biological* as a hive mind, though the idea of a hive mind is the closest us 'dirt-beings' can get to understanding a singular thought separated into a gazillion quantum connected fragments. The idea is utterly alien, which is likely why every attempt we've made to communicate with these spooks has failed. For all we know *they don't communicate*. They just *know*. They can't see us, hear us, or feel us, because—at least this is the theory—they don't possess 'senses.' Maybe they have no way to gather and interpret data outside of their own entangled system. And since us dirt-beings aren't entangled with them, we're shit out of luck."

Lynn leaned back in her chair and, for reasons unknown even to her, smiled. It wasn't as if anything Trainer Bowers had said improved their situation. They were still screwed. But for the first time in the past week, Lynn felt like the insane, uncontrolled spin the TDM revelation had launched her into was slowing. Becoming manageable.

Know thy enemy.

She had a brief moment of gratitude, remembering the promotional TD Hunter-themed crossover mode WarMonger had released earlier in the spring. Good thing the spook human-possession thing had been creative license. *That* would have been terrifying to deal with in the real.

Lynn felt bad for the Alpha Testers, CIDER's guinea pigs who'd been thrown blindly into this fray without a clue of what was going to happen. Had they worried about alien possession in the beginning? No wonder the Alpha Testers had dubbed the entities "spooks" before the term "TDM" had been formalized. That's all the entities had been to them: formless, unknowable boogeymen.

But not anymore.

Lynn leaned forward again, hanging on Bowers' every word.

"So, these TEPs are orders of magnitude more opaque to us than any amount of quantum theory. Even string theory makes more sense than TEPs. But as we've already discovered with the quantum revolution, you don't always have to understand the *why* or *how* to harness something with technology. Which is good, otherwise CIDER never could have developed the TD Hunter combat platform. The only reason we formerly discovered TEPs in the first place was because they were interfering with our systems. It was the unexplained glitches that prompted scientists to look for a cause.

"From here we get into even more complicated shit like quantum electrodynamics and wave-particle duality, which ain't none of us got time for. Just take my word for it that because of some complicated science, the spooks get *real* excited about all the concentrated EM activity—that's electromagnetic activity to you crayon-eaters—caused by modern infrastructure. We don't know if they're somehow metabolizing EM radiation or what. But whatever they do with it, if there's a large enough concentration of TEPs—remember that's what the spooks are made of—around an EM source, the human system crashes and usually takes out a portion of the grid around it.

"That's important to know because, for anyone who wasn't paying attention in biology class, us dirt-beings emit EM radiation as well. It's low enough that the spooks don't seem to notice humans, but whatever it is they do to EM nodes, they do to *us*, too. As in shut us down. Like *that*."

Bowers snapped his fingers, and the sound was swallowed in the heavy silence as everyone waited with bated breath.

"Now, Delta, Charlie, and Bravo class TDMs don't have a high enough concentration of TEPs to bother most people, though we've documented bouts of dizziness, nausea, and other symptoms similar to heatstroke, especially when test subjects remain for extended periods inside a swarm of spooks. Normally, the TDMs are pretty spread out, and so don't cause that problem. Innocent bystanders don't tend to hang around sources of high EM activity, so there have been far fewer deaths than anyone could dare to hope from an unstoppable alien invasion.

"CIDER has slapped together their best effort at shielding technology in the form of vests and helmets for us on-the-ground-personnel. But while it does mitigate a certain amount of neurological damage, it won't save you if a Sierra Class boss decides to park their big, fat ass right on top of you."

Lynn instantly thought of Mishipeshu, the Bravo Class boss Skadi's Wolves and CRC had defeated during the TD Hunter qualifiers last September. She'd plunged headfirst into the center of that TDM boss on the theory that if she was inside it, she could keep attacking it without it being able to reach her with its powerful tentacles. High-level gamers were just as interested in breaking a game as winning it, and she'd managed to pull off that victory moments before passing out from what she'd assumed at the time was heatstroke.

Now, of course, she understood why the TD Hunter staff overseeing the qualifier had been so freaked out about her unconventional tactics, and why they'd seemed to hover and cluck over a mere minor concussion.

She almost snorted at the memory of Steve's upside-down face, expression strained, as he'd scolded her for her stunt while the paramedics had checked her over. She could imagine the internal monologue that must have been going through Steve's head, probably involving a lot of mental hair-pulling and blistering curses worthy of Larry Coughlin. Well, at least her antics had sparked a second-chance romance for her mom . . . if her mom could ever forgive Steve, anyway.

Bowers' words also explained what had happened to Mack last fall when they'd made their first, suicidal attempt at defeating Gyges, the Alpha Class boss that had been parked on the mesh node behind their high school. Mack had collapsed with a sudden seizure when Gyges' bulk had briefly engulfed him. Inexplicably, though, it hadn't caused the same effect in her when she'd dashed in to pull him to safety. The very edge of it had made Edgar and Dan vomit, though. So what was different about her? Did the neurological effects differ person to person? She remembered feeling nauseous, a bit dizzy, and having a terrifying sixth sense of danger. But that was it. Come to think of it, she'd felt the same effects when she'd been attacked by Nagaraja, the Sierra Class boss at the TD Hunter National Championship.

Lynn shook her head and concentrated on the briefing. She wasn't sure how many people knew about her "resistance" to the TDMs. She suspected it was not something to call attention to in front of her fellow trainees. Better to assume, for now, that she was just as vulnerable as the next person and look for a way to ask some private questions. Maybe she'd have a chance to meet this Dr. Roberts soon.

"I'm sure at this point some of you are pretty freaked out. Maybe worried about your families?"

Bowers paused, and there was a quiet swell of murmurs that swept through the room.

"I get it. I've got a wife and kids at home myself. The good news is that nobody but grid-workers and some really unfortunate homeless people are likely to come into contact with these TDM bosses who cause permanent neurological damage. Yes, there've been some tragic deaths, especially in big cities where select nodes are parked right in the middle of the action. There's also the risk of injury from equipment malfunction when TEP concentrations cause infrastructure failure. You've probably heard about the worrying rise in airbus accidents. Thankfully, most of those incidents haven't caused injury or death because of the backup systems in place."

Lynn's gut clenched. She could still remember the terrifying, sickening moment of weightlessness when the airbus she and her mom had been riding on to Des Moines had gone dark. It hadn't fallen far before the backup batteries had kicked in and stabilized it, but it had still been a traumatic brush with death that she would never forget. It had made travel a newly nerve-wracking experience.

"You can rest assured that the statistical likelihood of anyone you know being hurt by spooks or a spook-induced accident is about the same as their chances of getting injured by human hands, be that a mugging, rape, homicide, or otherwise. The risk is there, but it's nothing greater than the risks we run every day simply being alive around other humans. There's nothing you can do to make your loved ones or the public safer—except to fight. Fight these alien bastards and eradicate them with extreme prejudice. Because at the rate they're multiplying, they *will* become a significant public threat soon, if only because of infrastructure failure.

"This is truly an invasion," Bowers said gravely, halting his pacing and turning toward the Hunters, "and *you* are humanity's one and only hope for survival."

The trainer fell silent, letting his words sink in.

It was not a pleasant sensation. But Lynn took hold of the tragic, unlooked-for responsibility and wrapped it around herself like a mantle.

Oh, we'll fight, whispered her Larry brain. *We'll fight until the world goes up in flames, and then we'll dance in the fire and keep fighting until black eternity takes us all.*

Jaw set, Lynn glanced to the side at the same moment Edgar looked her way, and their eyes met. He looked grimmer than she'd ever seen him. The weight of it dug furrows into his normally relaxed, smooth face. The eyes that normally twinkled were now shadowed by fear. The lips that always seemed to be hiding a grin were now hard and flat like granite.

Under the polished wood of their flip-up desktops, Edgar's hand shifted and gently squeezed Lynn's knee. The warmth and pressure sent a pleasant thrill up her leg, and she was momentarily distracted from the feeling of doom that hung in the room's stagnant air. She hesitated, but then gave in to the need to return the touch, to anchor herself in goodness and humanity in the face of crushing uncertainty and fear. She shifted her own hand to find his and gave it an answering squeeze. To her relief, it eased the shadows in Edgar's eyes, and he finally blinked and looked back to the front at Bowers.

Lynn returned her hand to the top of her desk.

Edgar's hand stayed where it was.

To her surprise, she found she didn't mind—though it did make it harder to focus on the briefing.

"Fortunately," Bowers said after a bracing intake of breath, "we Americans are a tough bunch. We don't take being invaded very well, as the Japanese found out after Pearl Harbor. Just because this new bunch of invaders are slippery alien spooks doesn't mean jack. This is the land of the free and the home of the brave, dammit. We're going to fight them, and we're going to win. Oorah?"

"Oorah!" shouted a scattering of Hunters.

"I can't hear you!" Bowers barked, cupping a hand around one ear.

"OO-rah!"

Lynn joined in the shout, sending a jolt of adrenaline through her body that swept aside the cloying fear and uncertainty.

"That's more like it," Bowers went on, and resumed pacing. "Now that you have a basic understanding of what the TDMs are, I'll give you an overview of the TD Hunter combat interface and how it, and the weapons we'll be issuing you, work together to interact with and destroy the spooks.

"When scientists first discovered these entities and the TEPs they're made of, we barely had the technology to measure and detect them, much less interact with them. In fact, the discovery was more or less an accident. The lab coats who became the foundation for CIDER's multi-national science division were originally trying to interact with dark matter when they stumbled on the TEPs. They never did figure out how to harness dark matter, but they *did* determine how to agitate and direct TEP particles through a quantum mechanism that I'm not even going to try to describe, but it relates to the quantum coupling that seems to have attracted the TDMs in the first place.

"By the time the coats realized these identifiable masses of TEPs weren't just randomly careening around, but were organized and directed, the DOD was reporting concerning incidents that, at the time, were assumed to be freak accidents. But there was enough of a pattern for the coats to connect the dots, and they figured out it might be wise to look into some method of *disrupting* and *dissipating* these pesky, exotic particles. And that, Hunters, was when TEPDP was born."

Lynn cocked her head, trying to puzzle out what "*tep-dep*" could possibly stand for. Bowers didn't keep them wondering.

"For anyone without a PhD in theoretical physics, that would be the Transdimensional Exotic Particle Disruptor Platform. It's a mouthful, I know. Thank God for Robert Krator and his marketing department. If we left naming things up to the scientists, we'd all be screwed.

"Anyway, the coats originally tried every possible field, beam, wave, you name it that we could manipulate to try and disrupt the TEPs to the point that they would 'de-tangle' and dissipate. They figured it shouldn't be that hard, considering how hard it is to create and maintain quantum entanglements in the first place. But apparently the TEP entanglements were made of tougher stuff than the coats had any way to explain—possibly something to do with whatever other dimension they originated from.

"They were at their wits' end when someone came up with the last-ditch idea of bombarding the entities with their own particles. No real reason why it would work, but if nothing in *our* dimension could disrupt the TEPs, maybe TEPs could disrupt TEPs. And, lo and behold, it worked. Don't ask me how, that's a question for Dr. Roberts, and you'll likely regret asking it. The point is, if you bombard spooks with enough concentrated streams of TEPs, whatever bonds that hold their own TEPs together shatter and their exotic particles go every which way.

"Now, why do TEPs hurt us when they're a functioning TDM and don't hurt us when they're scattered? Your guess is as good as mine. The best explanation I've gotten out of the coats is to think of it like positive and negative charges." A cartoon graphic replaced the latest slide of the talk, showing little circles labeled "TEP" with tiny "+" or "-" signs beside them. As Bowers continued, the circles started to move. "Let's say the spooks are made up of positive TEPs, while free-ranging TEPs are negative. When we bombard the spooks with enough negative TEPs, the bastards fall apart and their positive TEPs turn negative. Don't get hung up trying to make sense of the science, it's just an analogy to wrap your head around the craziness. TEPs don't follow the rules of how we understand science in this dimension anyway.

"So, the atrociously named TEPDP was the first, but rather

clunky, system developed that successfully 'dissipated' these exotic entities that kept monkeying with our systems. A step in the right direction. But we still had no way to effectively field it, no mechanism to eliminate the spooks out in the wild among the general populace. That's where Robert Krator came in.

"Game theory has been used to solve scientific problems for decades. But it wasn't until Mr. Krator came at the problem from the side instead of the front that we had a breakthrough. He didn't *just* bring together quantum physicists and AI designers to pioneer the most advanced deep learning algorithm on the planet—an AI trained on human *and* transdimensional entity behavior. Robert Krator envisioned the entire TD Hunter interface from start to finish. He was the one with the *chutzpah* to propose a worldwide game to solve the simultaneous problems of man-power and secrecy that CIDER still had no idea how to overcome."

Lynn made a mental note to never tell her mom that little fact. Otherwise Matilda might get it into her head to go threaten the CEO of a multi-billion-dollar company.

"By harnessing the omni-sensors and quantum coupling capability of every single LINC installed with the TD Hunter app, and combining that data with a worldwide network of live drone footage to give the algorithm a birds-eye view, the TD Hunter combat interface can map the TDMs in real time and overlay all the appropriate graphics and effects to facilitate their destruction.

"Now, while LINCs with their quantum coupling are the key to gathering exotic particles, it's the omnipolymer batons Tsunami has manufactured in the millions that weaponize it. The existing hardware inside standard LINCs can only emit the particles in undirected pulses, unlike the batons' concentrated beams. Imagine a sprinkler versus a firehose. Trying to add hardware to existing LINCs was unfeasible and suspicious. But game controllers have been a standard presence since digital gaming was invented. So, stick the new hardware into omnipolymer batons along with a basic chip to manage the controls, and voila.

"This solution helped protect the game player as well. Remember, as far as we know the spooks can't see us any more than we can see them. What we know they *can* detect is concentrated TEPs being aimed in their direction. So when they strike back, they are attacking the source of the concentrated TEPs—the baton—instead of attacking the bearer directly."

That, Lynn suspected, explained why she'd lost multiple batons to TDM-induced damage. The very first had been when she was still a beta tester, and she'd assumed it had been user error, considering she'd fallen on it and snapped it in half. That hadn't accounted for the super heating and spontaneous flame, though. Those signs correlated with the multiple times over the past year when her batons had gotten uncomfortably hot during tough battles. And then, of course, there was the time her baton had literally burst into flame when a Sierra Class boss had dealt her a direct blow.

"The TD Hunter combat interface itself is about three-fourths practical functions, and one-fourth purely aesthetic features designed to make the interface entertaining and functional as a gaming system. Surface stuff like armor skins, weapon classes, and monster graphics are pretty discretionary and were implemented by Tsunami designers who thought they were simply building the world's first breakthrough AR game. Behind-the-scene mechanics, like power consumption, attack tactics, weapon ranges, and damage levels, are all based on real-world interaction between the combat system and the effects the weaponized TEPs have on the spooks.

"Take the 'if you can see them, they can see you' axiom that you learn early on in the game. This is half based in reality, half artificially imposed for game mechanic purposes. When you fire up the combat interface, which is what 'going into combat mode' entails, it activates the hardware in your batons that interact with TEPs, the function that enables you to see the spooks. But that TEP activity puts you on the spooks' radar in turn. That's real. The game-mechanics bit is that the system regulates the amount of TEP activity based on your Hunter Level. That way when you are starting out in the game and don't have a clue what you're doing, you only emit tiny amounts of TEP and only get the attention of the weakest, smallest spooks, able to be destroyed by small amounts of TEP bombardment. The combat interface artificially hides the spooks in the area above your level to prevent interaction that will cause the Hunter to get swarmed and potentially hurt. The experience gained from killing TDMs is carefully calculated to balance adequate time for a Hunter to master new combat techniques and situations.

"TDM behavior is another example. While the exact positioning of limbs is creatively generated, the macro-movements and attack patterns are translated by the algorithm straight from the spooks themselves to your AR display.

"To summarize, all mechanics in the TD Hunter game are designed around the reality of the alien entities you're seeking to eradicate. But the aesthetics and exact details are tailored to appeal to the consumer, that is you, the stereotypical gamer.

"What this all means is that, even though you now know the spooks are real, the details of how you fight them will remain virtually the same. This is functionally necessary, and also vital to maintaining the cover of a gaming enterprise—absolutely essential if we want any hope of defeating this threat without causing mass societal panic, anarchy, and chaos.

"While individual and team scores, for example, are no longer your driving motivation, you still need to fight like they are. The health system in the game was another feature carefully balanced to enable fair mechanics while also protecting Hunters from dangerous situations. I won't get into the whole ecosystem of how the combat interface uses your LINC to generate a scatter field of TEPs that function as a faint shield—that's the plates you use, by the way. Just take my word for it that getting hit by TDMs is still bad and to be avoided as much as possible, even if you're full on plates."

Trainer Bowers halted his pacing in the middle of the stage and swung around to face the hunters once more.

"That concludes your introductory spook briefing, in all its glory. Now, questions?"

There was a long moment of silence as if everyone was still trying to wrap their mind around what they'd learned. Then a drawling voice piped up to Lynn's left.

"Pardon my French, Mr. Bowers, but why the flying fudge are we even here? I *am* enjoying the grub, good 'n proper, but if I had my druthers I'd be torturing myself with PT *after* the sun rose, not 'afore. Why aren't there swarms of drones out there cleaning up this here spooky mess? Why put us dirt-beings to work at all?"

Lynn couldn't help cracking a grin at the distinctly plaintive note in Gadsden's voice. Bowers must have heard it too, because one side of his lips twitched before he smoothed his expression and got serious again.

"Good question, Gadsden, though one you'd likely be able to answer yourself if you sat down and went through the obstacles point by point. The first and most pertinent reason is range. The

TEPs are particles, remember, not waves, and our ability to focus and direct them is limited, not only by physics but also by the TEPs themselves, which are extremely finicky in terms of reliably going where you want them. The sniper rifles some of you players use have maxed out the effective range we've been able to produce so far, though there are some more powerful, close-range weapons coming down the pipeline that we hope to introduce soon."

Lynn caught the grin of anticipation that flashed across Edgar's face, and she nodded in satisfaction. That had been one of her questions: when did they get bigger guns?

"Because of this distance limitation," Bowers continued, "someone or something has to get up close and personal with these spooks. It *would* be awfully nice if drones could fill that role, but they would run into several major problems that there's no way to solve.

"The least of these problems is the fact that drones are part of the advanced technology that seems to attract TDMs in the first place, what with their built-in LINCs and Everlast batteries. You've experienced first-hand how TDMs react when you drop into combat mode and start putting the hurt on them. Imagine a drone trying to survive in that environment. Being in the air doesn't give them an advantage either. There are plenty of flying TDM types. Plus, want to know a fun fact? TDMs don't seem to be limited by gravity. We've documented types like Orculls and Spithra that *had* been classified as ground-dwelling morph into flying types when we attacked bosses from the air and they had no targets on the ground to draw aggro. Most TDMs seem to move along the earth's crust by default because that's where a lot of our infrastructure is. But they are perfectly capable of changing altitude to swarm drones if that's where the attacks are coming from."

"Thank *God* there are no flying Spithra," someone piped up in the brief silence as Trainer Bowers took a breath. "If giant flying attack spiders came my way, I would 'Nope' out of there so fast I'd look like I'd invented teleportation."

There was a general chuckle, and Bowers smiled briefly.

"Obviously we don't show the scattered TDMs that act out of character. They're usually so few and far between they don't affect the game anyway.

"In any case, CIDER coats tried developing a drone delivery system before CIDER accepted Mr. Krator's bid to develop the TD Hunter combat interface. They wanted to prove Mr. Krator's idea of a worldwide game was unnecessary. I'm sure you won't be surprised to hear that the drones were swarmed and shorted out before they could put much more than a dent in a small Bravo Class boss.

"What we *have* proven successful, thanks to RavenStriker during the TD Hunter National Championship, is drone-provided air-support."

What felt like everyone in the room turned to stare at her. Lynn fought the impulse to sink into her seat, wishing herself invisible. Instead she jutted her chin out, keeping her eyes on Bowers. He gave her a slight nod.

"What we discovered that day," the trainer continued, "was that a drone delivery system of large but infrequent, one-time TEP bursts does not provoke effective retaliation provided there are sufficiently distracting targets elsewhere. That spearhead attack you teams executed got close enough that the Nagaraja swarm went after you instead of our drone delivery platform every time an air strike landed.

"Now, imagine an army of two-hundred-plus robots on the ground attempting that maneuver."

Several people in the crowd chuckled.

"Our robotics tech is improving by leaps and bounds, but we're still far, *far* away from developing machines that can fight like *that*. We haven't yet developed weapons systems that can both heavily shield clumsy robots *and* deliver the payloads we need to kill the bosses. And even if we could, it wouldn't solve the last, and biggest problem of all."

"OPSEC," Lynn muttered to herself at the same moment Bowers said:

"Operational security, Hunters, is our lifeline right now." Bowers paused and looked across the amphitheater of strong, independent-minded gamers who had fought their heart out for a *year*, only to discover it was all a fraud. Lynn could feel the tension in the air. She'd heard mutters in the halls, at mealtime. People who were upset and questioning the need for secrecy, especially from their family. It was clear from Bowers' expression that he was all too aware of the undercurrent in the room.

He started pacing again.

"I know many of you are in your twenties—or younger—so you have no memory of what the world was like before the pandemics of the 2020s...and how fundamentally that decade changed us. It wasn't just the pandemics, I'll give you that. There were political, cultural, and technological factors as well. But the first pandemic that broke out in 2020, it . . . blindsided us. The modern world had never dealt with anything even close. It closed down massive swaths of commerce across the entire globe. It permanently shuttered millions of businesses. Major supply chains were broken, food shortages broke out across many less-developed countries. A whole generation of students suffered educational and development delays. A global mental health crisis was sparked. Medical and welfare services for every need and across every sector imaginable were interrupted or simply vanished. Some estimate that almost as many people starved, committed suicide, or died from preventable diseases as died from the viruses themselves.

"Historians estimate a mere tenth of one percent of the world population died from those viruses, and it has taken well over a decade for the world economy to recover. Obviously inflation never reverses, so that's permanent damage we'll all live with till the end of time. But more than that, the *distrust* that decade bred . . . the fear . . ."

Bowers stopped his slow pacing and turned back to face the Hunters, his brow drawn down in painful recollection.

"That was compounded by the generative AI revolution that turned the world topsy-turvy for a good three or four years. No one knew what or who to believe anymore. No one knew what was real and what wasn't. It was pure insanity. It didn't get better until world governments got their shit together and started passing disclaimer laws, and the AI tech bros finally got slapped by the backlash and put legitimate effort into developing accurate AI-detection tools.

"Now imagine world societies, already burned twice by failed trust, finding out we're being invaded by invisible aliens capable of killing us, world governments have kept it secret, *and* we have no idea where the threat is coming from or how to stop it? Can you *imagine* the chaos it would spark? We could hope for unity. *God* I hope humanity would prove me wrong. But we can't take that risk when our only hope of survival is to get the whole world to work together against this threat."

Bowers fell silent, waited, gaze moving slowly from Hunter to Hunter. No one spoke. No one contradicted him. The angry tension in the room had seeped away, replaced by grim acceptance.

"We're facing enough unrest and destruction already from these damned spooks, we can't afford to add human-made chaos on top of that. Sure, the truth might come out eventually, whether we want it to or not. But that just means we have to fight all the harder right now, to gain some advantage or scrap of hope before things get out of hand.

"Right now, Hunters, your singular mission is to destroy as many bosses as possible, as quickly as possible, while keeping the public safe and unaware. That's all you have to worry about. CIDER, partnering with Tsunami and other government contractors, will take care of the rest. So train hard, pay attention, follow orders, and *keep your mouths shut*. If you get jumped in an interview or some groupie corners you and starts asking about conspiracy theory stuff, don't deny it, that looks suspicious. Just play dumb. Or, if you really want to avoid a conversation, sneeze and change the subject. Get it?"

Lynn automatically muttered, "Got it," along with about a third of the room.

Bowers' lips quirked. "Good. Now, any more questions?"

There were, of course. Most of them got into the nitty gritty of the combat interface. Others were suggestions of how to take on the TDMs with less human involvement—TEP car bomb? TEP grenades? Long-distance TEP missiles? Bowers seemed to appreciate the Hunters' creativity, but the way he patiently explained the technological limitations of each suggestion made it clear he, and likely many other Alpha Testers, had trod that ground before.

Lynn mostly kept her mouth shut and her ears open. She had a few lingering questions of her own, but wanted to wait to see if they were answered by other people's comments first. Her biggest questions, of course—where had the spooks come from and how could CIDER stop the spread—would be pointless to ask. Bowers had as good as said they had no idea, and Lynn assumed CIDER's scientists were already running themselves into the ground trying to figure it out.

What she *really* wanted was to talk to Dr. Roberts. But scratching that itch wasn't part of her mission. She was a ground troop, not a general. So she focused on the flow of conversation. Talk had moved from nuts and bolts to cloak and dagger, specifically how they were all supposed to pretend this was still a game when they were out in the field, fighting boss TDMs that could potentially hurt them.

"You're thinking about it all wrong," Bowers said, shaking his head. "You have the easiest, cushiest undercover job in the history of undercover jobs: your cover story is exactly the same as reality. We're not asking you to pull your head *out* of the game. We're asking you to *lean into* it. Remember, you're the TransDimensional Counterforce. Whether in the game or out of it, your mission is still the same: kill bosses with extreme prejudice. You don't have to be all smiles. Be serious, be grave. Be real, even. The stream junkies will eat it up.

"As for your safety, that's the whole point of this Battle Tour Tsunami is organizing. Remember, half your unit will be Alpha Testers, and each Company has an entire Heavy Weapons Platoon. This will not be like the qualifiers or the TD Hunter National Championship when we threw you into the deep end to see what you could do. You *will* have support. You will have qualified and experienced people telling you what to do. All you have to do is fight hard and look good for the cameras."

Lynn snorted, as did others in the audience.

"Who knows," Bowers continued, "maybe we'll be so effective at killing bosses that we'll crater the TDM population. Maybe we'll get this infestation under control with the public none-the-wiser. Then Tsunami really *can* put on the International Championship. And don't forget, CIDER is a global alliance. Right this moment, special task forces in roughly two dozen other countries are training their own volunteer TD Counterforce to do this same thing in their own cities. The Battle Tour is worldwide, after all. Frankly, I don't envy Mr. Krator or his subordinates. They likely won't sleep a wink for the next six months.

"Now, unless there's any more *pressing* questions—no, Cosmos you can't have a custom mod skin of Kim Kardashian—let's pull up your combat interface and take a look at all the new features, make sure you know where everything is. We have the interface in demo mode, so don't worry about accidentally going hot. This week we'll be diving into unit formations, from squad to company level, so I want you on point with this interface."

They went through the entire app, covered all the sub menus, icons, and functions. Bowers had them practice various command functions, from subvocalization to eye movements, just to make sure everyone was on the same page. Then he had them all stand up and divide into their assigned companies, one company to each section of seats. Alpha Company got the left-hand side, so Skadi's Wolves and Amaranth got up and slowly maneuvered between all the other relocating Hunters to find their spot. They ended up near the amphitheater stage at the front where they were joined by the 3rd Squad of their platoon. It consisted of Team Lone Star and a team from Illinois named Zahn Wars, along with their squad leader, a fierce-looking lady who went by the handle dBoshe.

Three seating sections, three companies. Three infantry platoons per company, for a total of nine platoons in the room. Each platoon's second and third squads were made up of two Hunter teams each, so twenty Hunters organized in the second and third squads of each platoon. The first squad of each platoon was made up entirely of Alpha Testers who they wouldn't meet until they'd finished their initial training at The Greenbrier and moved on to the next stage.

Lynn twisted to look behind her at the rest of their section where Alpha Company, 2nd and 3rd Platoons were arranging themselves with low murmurs of conversation. Gadsden's lazy drawl rose above the noise, and Lynn glanced at the Texans of Team Lone Star to see them grinning and elbowing one another as they chuckled over some private joke. Her AR display helpfully labeled each individual with their handle, followed by their unit designation. Hers read RavenAlpha1-2, or Raven of Alpha Company, 1st Platoon, 2nd Squad. Gadsden's read GadsdenAlpha1-3, which put the Lone Stars in Alpha company, 1st Platoon, 3rd Squad.

Once they were organized into their units, Bowers had them practice navigating the communication controls, creating proper unit channels for their teams and squads. Then he showed them how to manage the larger unit channels he created for platoon and company level. They were all going to be in tense, chaotic situations in the near future, and as Bowers kept telling them, "Communication is key!"

There were more exercises and explanations, more information for Lynn to burn into her memory as best she could. Yes, Hugo was there to help with recall if she ever forgot something. But she knew getting flustered and turned around in the app or in her own memory could cause fatal delays in combat, so she needed this new information to become second nature to her.

Through it all, her palms itched for her batons.

She wanted to be outside, fighting monsters, not stuck in

this suffocating room, playing peacemaker between Ronnie and Dan who were taking digs at each other for no apparent reason. Somehow Dan had turned into a Manic Sunshine Happy Squirrel, as if stress had dialed up his already bubbly, excitable brain. Conversely, Ronnie had reverted to his grumpiest mode, full of doom and gloom and criticism. Mack hovered at the edges, looking perpetually worried and a little scared, while Edgar was so laconic Lynn wondered if he'd opted for selective mutism.

The dynamic was grating on her nerves and she needed to do something about it, but she didn't know what. Talk to them? Both her inner Lynn and inner Larry shuddered at the thought. She didn't want to talk, she wanted to shoot things. Maybe even stab a few too. If Ronnie was one of them, well . . . he'd heal up quick, right?

They were all on edge, dealing with lingering shock and disappointment. Things would get better soon, though. They'd get out of this blasted conference room, get their hands on some sweet new weaponry, and start killing TDMs again.

Hopefully before Ronnie and Dan murdered each other.

Staff Sergeant Jesús "Teach" Sánchez had known his patient nature was going to bite him in the butt someday. He'd just never imagined it would get him saddled with a bunch of moody orphans.

To be fair, they were patriotic moody orphans, but still.

When CIDER had made their plans for bringing the Hunter Strike Teams into the fold, they had to account for the fact that some teams might split up. It hadn't ended up being many, but there were some. And Teach, being the lucky bastard he was, had been given the happy job of forming them into a new, cohesive whole.

It wasn't as bad as it could have been. He'd grown up taking care of his siblings while *mamá* and *papá* worked two jobs apiece, and these professional gamers couldn't come close to the craziness of four younger brothers. Maybe that's why he'd enlisted in the Army the day after he'd graduated high school—he'd longed to do something for himself, instead of for *la familia*. But Uncle Sam could sniff out compulsive conscientiousness like a vulture on roadkill, so here he was back again, shepherding pups.

Three of them had been from the same team, though those three hadn't included their team captain. The other two were totally orphaned. One in particular was a special case, or as he thought of her, his "trouble child."

He'd been briefed on what had happened to the rest of Elena "Queen" Seville's team. Disappeared into black holes, the lot of them. Their captain had apparently been engaged in some seriously shady shit, up to and including inciting criminal assault. The other three were likely just his stooges, but they'd been involved in physical intimidation, so had been shipped off too.

Queen, though . . . nobody was sure how much she did or didn't know, or had been involved in. And she *had* been one of the first and most vocal to stand up and volunteer.

Teach was supposed to keep an eye on her, just in case she had any nefarious motivations that might surface once she'd gained access to the TD Counterforce. All he saw, though, was a misguided young woman with high walls that likely hid deep wounds and a lot of anger issues.

Lucky him.

"Okay, Team Alpha Flight, circle up," Teach said to the group of five young men and women, none of them looking particularly thrilled to be there. He wasn't either, but he had a decade enjoying the delights of good old Uncle Sam, and this posting was pure luxury compared to some of the places he'd been deployed, so he wasn't complaining. Since the training schedules were so tight over the scant weeks the teams were at The Greenbrier, Teach had to meet with Alpha Flight during other teams' free time to work on cohesion exercises.

He carefully avoided the words "remedial training." No point demoralizing a group of brave volunteers already ill at ease with their situation.

Once all five were in a semicircle around him, Teach explained the evening's exercise.

"Tonight you'll be doing a series of small-scale battles. Your goal is to move from this end to that end of the exhibit hall, cycling through the team formations you've been learning." Teach gestured as he spoke, making sure all five Hunters were watching and paying attention. "This is to help you practice proper formations during pitched battle with plenty of distractions and enemies. There will be no boss, but watch out for Alpha Class TDMs. You need to work as a team to take the bigger ones down. Questions?"

There were multiple shrugs and muttered "nopes," which could be a good or a bad thing. This group tended to check out, which was better than infighting, but not by much. Teach was still trying to figure out some unifying motivation to make them *feel* like a team, instead of a group of atomized individuals.

When they'd first arrived, he'd driven home his first rule: no drama. They'd taken to it relatively willingly, though Queen had a delightful passive aggressive streak a mile wide.

"Come on, let's get this over with," Queen said into the silence, flicking her blond ponytail over her shoulder. "It's already not fair we don't get free time. I don't want to be here any longer than I have to."

Ah, perfect.

Teach smiled inside, and stepped toward Queen, getting into her personal space, though not in an aggressive manner. Just in a way she couldn't ignore.

"Good observation, Queen. You all have worked harder and done more than any of the other teams. You should be proud of that. But . . ." He caught her eye and held it, steadily. A little "v" of annoyance formed on her forehead, but she didn't look away. "It's also exactly what you volunteered for."

Queen's eyes flashed and she crossed her arms. "I did *not* volunteer for extra work and no free time!"

"Oh?" Teach said, raising his eyebrows. "So, you'll volunteer to put your life on the line and save the world, but only from nine to five. Anything more and the world is shit out of luck?"

Queen's scowl deepened, but she didn't protest further.

"Don't worry," Teach said, looking at the other members of Alpha Flight. "I don't like extra work any more than you. The goal is to get you up to speed so extra training is not needed. But none'a you is gonna survive 'less you accept responsibility that you gotta work longer and harder than the other teams. It's not fair, it's just reality.

"Good news is, if we stay focused, you'll be a well-oiled machine before you know it. What's my first rule?" he asked, grinning at the five of them.

"No drama," some of them chorused. Queen wasn't one of them, but Teach didn't press it.

"Good. I'll teach you my second rule, now, since I think you're ready for it: we keep our heads down, we stick together, and we come back alive. Sound like a plan?" He held Queen's gaze as he said it, talking directly to her.

She looked away, her arms shifting until they were more wrapped around her middle than crossed in front.

"Let's get this show on the road so we can all hit the sack," Teach said, reaching for his batons. No point pushing Queen further right now. He guessed she'd had some major blinders ripped off when CIDER had revealed the spooks. Reasonable that she'd be prickly and defensive. The only question was, could she mature past it?

Only time—and training—would tell. And he was in charge of the training part.

He had a constant, direct chat open with Alpha Flight's team captain—a dark-haired, dark-eyed college-aged kid with the handle "Deadly_Tacos" who simply needed some direction and encouragement to step into his role. The kid tended to forget he was the captain and needed to take charge, so Teach gave him a subvocalized nudge, and Deadly got Team Alpha Flight formed up.

Teach started the scenario and followed along behind the team, helping keep TDMs off their back as a stand-in for the second team of their squad, so they could forge forward across the exhibit hall. His main goal was to get them used to working with each other. Build some trust and rapport in the face of adversity.

Once they were warmed up and making good headway, Teach initiated the *actual* team-building part of the exercise, and hid a smile as a Manticar came out of nowhere and scared the shit out of them. They scrambled to readjust, but after some flailing they got their act together and performed the standard distract and flank maneuver TD Hunter tactical taught players to deal with Manticars.

Teach had to give it to Queen, timidity was not her problem. She seemed to have a personal vendetta against all TDMs and charged fearlessly at them. Even a Manticar roaring in her face.

After they successfully tackled the Manticar, Teach threw two more Manticars at them simultaneously. Deadly struggled to maintain focus and control of the team, but what they lacked in finesse, Alpha Flight made up for in sheer spite and determination.

By the end of the exercise when Teach—feeling slightly guilty—unleashed a trio of Chimera on them, the intensity of the situation had started shaking Alpha Flight loose of its hang-ups and he could see the cohesion starting to form.

It would take plenty more sessions to make them a true team. But the seeds had been sown and were being watered.

Of course, they still all hated him for the extra work. That was fine. Let them hate him, as long as they leaned on each other.

Chapter 4

"And that, gentlemen, is why we've been unable to get a theoretical TEP 'tactical nuke' out of the theoretical stage. The physics simply don't work."

The hologram of Dr. Roberts, head of CIDER's research and development team, shrugged helplessly. Steve could imagine the bitter disappointment being swallowed by every military member at the meeting, both those physically present around the conference room table at CIDER's covert military headquarters at the Pentagon, as well as those joining remotely. He knew *he* was bummed at the news. If only they could lob some nukes at the problem and make it all go away. Then Lynn would be safe, Matilda might deign to talk to him again, and he could go back to being paid to game.

Man, he'd *liked* his job at Tsunami. It sucked giving it up, though of course Lynn and Matilda were worth it. Even if he hadn't resigned for them, he'd been told the higher-ups at CIDER were contemplating calling him back to active duty, what with the alarming deterioration of the world situation.

At least his new position kept him in the action. He'd been appointed Assistant Operations Officer—or Assistant S3—for the battalion that made up Taskforce Sanctus. Uncle Sam had deemed his combination of military and gaming expertise, as well as close ties to Tsunami leadership, too valuable to pass up. Thank heavens he'd avoided being made the Battalion S3.

He didn't envy the responsibility in the slightest, not after he'd already done his time in SpecOps. Captain Riker had a better ring to it than Major Riker, anyway.

"What about the chain-reaction detonation method you posited..." General Kozelek paused, obviously checking his notes, "three meetings ago? Has there been any progress on that?"

Dr. Roberts pursed his lips, as if he wasn't exactly pleased with what he had to say.

"It seems... possible that we could manufacture a working prototype. The predictive models we've used have given us encouraging results..."

"But?" the general said in the pregnant pause.

"But even if we field it successfully, it won't solve the problem we're trying to address. TEP particles are the *opposite* of explosive. They're downright lethargic, like a cat in the sun. All your heroic, loud, high-octane shots and slices and blasts in that game interface are purely for show. In reality, we're just bombarding the entities with wave upon wave of their own, now inert particles, like a fan blowing sand in your face. Eventually there's a tipping point where the cascade of particles trigger some kind of polarity reversal and the entities simply come apart. There *isn't* really a way to deliver more TEPs, faster or harder, to speed up the process of disintegration. Yes, we might develop a successful chain-reaction 'bomb,' but it wouldn't *speed up* the process much, it would just automate it and keep it going on autopilot until the TEPs in the surrounding vicinity ran out or it was overwhelmed by swarms of spooks. It would still need to be brought *to* the nodality by some means, and then defended to prevent malfunction. If we knew exactly how and why the particles interacted, maybe we could come up with something better. But we just don't know."

"And how likely are you to find out in the next"—General Kozelek made a show of looking at his wrist where he wore an old-style mechanical watch—"three months?"

The image of Dr. Roberts shook its head.

"An act of God, sir."

The general grimaced.

"As much as I'd welcome divine intervention at this point, it's generally frowned upon as lacking the, shall we say, transformational objectives needed to adapt to our evolving strategic environment."

There were a few muted chuckles at the General's fluent bureaucratese, but they quickly died.

Steve could see the bleak frustration in the faces around him—faces of men willing to lay down their lives to defeat threats that they had the tools and means to defend against. Now, though? They were being asked to fight what they could not see, by means they didn't understand, with no idea if it would even work.

What I wouldn't give to go back to the good old days when the biggest stress in my life was WarMonger players figuring out how to patch porno skin mods onto their avatars.

But that wasn't life anymore. The fight was at their door, and each and every one of them had to decide what they were going to do about it.

The weapons development discussion continued, and Steve listened with half an ear, in case he thought of anything relevant he could add. What he was really waiting to hear about, though, was Colonel Bryce's update on Hunter training. He had no reason to expect Lynn or the guys would be having trouble, but if he could glean any insights on how they were faring that were safe to pass on to Matilda, it might help their . . . well, it might help.

He was a patient man, but it was a lot harder to be patient with an impending apocalypse hanging over your head. He was well and truly in the doghouse with Matilda, and had no idea if reaching out and trying to rebuild bridges would help, or make things worse.

Lynn might know. But would she tell him?

"And how are the new trainees coming along, Colonel Bryce?"

Steve's ears perked and his eyes swung to the image of the Colonel. The man's service uniform was impeccably straight, and his high and tight haircut was as clean as his diamond-hard jawline. He surveyed those gathered at the meeting.

Colonel Bryce ran a tight ship, and the Alpha Testers had a lot of respect for him, not least because he'd been willing to do the TD Counterforce First Sergeant role for the TD Hunter game. Mr. Krator had insisted on using real military personnel for most of the roles, and he'd been so impressed by the Colonel's intensity and magnetism in the early CIDER meetings on the combat interface that he'd personally asked the Colonel to do it.

The fact that Colonel Bryce had agreed, instead of arguing that he was too important or his time too valuable, showed how much he believed in their mission. It had gone a long way toward silencing the voices arguing against the gaming interface in the first place. There'd been a certain amount of pearl-clutching among the senior military leadership, claiming the fate of humanity was too important to leave in the hands of mere *gamers*.

They were well and truly choking on their own bigotry, now.

Colonel Bryce began with a general summary of the training, and Steve leaned back in his body-mold chair as he listened. Everything sounded like it was going smoothly, and Steve grinned at the mental picture of all those fresh-faced kids being put through their paces. No, it wasn't boot camp, but it was the best they could do in the time they had to prepare the Hunters for this slog of a Battle Tour they had coming up. The bulk of the Alpha Testers were going through similar conditioning as well. Steve was torn about not being among the ground troops. He didn't miss the physical toll it took on the body, but he itched to do more than monitor, organize, and direct from a distance. Maybe he could convince his S3 to let him do his job on site at whichever boss battles Alpha Company was assigned to.

"The number of paparazzi drones we're having to shoot down is becoming a problem," Colonel Bryce said, and Steve's brow creased. "Even with our military augmentation, The Greenbrier's interdiction net has holes, and the little buggers are slipping through by the dozen every day. We've recruited local law enforcement to help patrol White Sulphur Springs and the surrounding area looking for loitering drone handlers, citing public safety and nuisance laws to clear them out. But there's no way to catch them all. The sooner we get the official PR teams in to do their dog and pony show, the better. This information blackout is causing a stream vulture feeding frenzy."

A grin snuck through Steve's composure, thinking about how grumpy Lynn no doubt was at the looming prospect of public attention.

"It's coming at the end of the week," Mr. Krator said, sounding as relaxed and composed as ever. "My people have the schedules all worked out and the PR teams vetted. It will be up to your people to keep any rogue streamers from slipping in and scooping the story. I know it's a lot of extra work for your teams, but the publicity is a vital part of the overall operation. There's no way humanly possible to keep the TD Counterforce a secret in this day and age. It's vital that we keep the eyes of the world trained on what they need to see to keep enthusiasm high, and away from the true inner workings of our operations. You all know the possible consequences of a leak, at this point.

"On that note," Mr. Krator continued, and Steve sat a little straighter at the change in his former boss's voice. The guy was worried about something, though a casual observer wouldn't have been able to tell. "We've recently seen a massive surge in the number of attempted hacks, trojan horses, and what-have-yous trying to infiltrate our systems. One recently came... concerningly close to succeeding. Obviously we have some of the most robust system security out there, especially since TD Hunter's launch. Corporate espionage is a thriving business in the gaming world right now. Everybody is desperate to copy TD Hunter's 'success' in this new AR gaming market."

General Kozelek snorted and shook his head, and Steve couldn't have agreed more. The situation had the sort of out-of-this-world irony that made you want to laugh and punch a wall at the same time.

"Block-chain technology and advancing quantum encryption have taken care of many security issues companies once faced. The weak link in the chain has always been, and likely will always be, human error and gullibility. We know this, and train our employees assiduously to lower the risks. For TD Hunter specifically, our combat interface AI, Hugo, is a vital second layer of defense. Normally, it would be enough. After all, Tsunami is a vast company, its holdings diverse, and the threat of competition has been a part of business since the dawn of time... except, now it's not just the stockholders' interests at risk. The fate of humanity itself is on the line."

Mr. Krator paused, looking at the faces assembled before he went on.

"I am formally requesting assistance from the US Government in tracking down the source of the latest attempt, and ensuring they are no longer a threat. CISA, NSA, Homeland Security, whoever we need to collaborate with. This attempt tried to access Hugo's source codes, no doubt hoping to recreate or improve on the algorithms that have made TD Hunter so 'successful.' I'm sure none of you need reminders of what a catastrophe it would be for someone to succeed, then decide to go public when they discover what is *really* behind TD Hunter's 'success.'"

General Kozelek frowned thoughtfully as he considered Mr. Krator's words. Finally, he nodded.

"It's a reasonable request, considering the circumstances. There'll be red tape to cut through, but I'll get the ball rolling. Nobody will like the idea of diverting our top expertise from national security issues. At least the spooks are causing the Chinese and Iranians just as much trouble as they're causing us."

"Thank you, General," Mr. Krator said, dipping his head briefly. "I'll get your people in touch with my head of cyber security."

General Kozelek gave a curt nod of acknowledgment, then looked around at the meeting attendees, from the various staff officers of Taskforce Sanctus, to the CIDER lab coats, to the members of civilian oversight—most of whom had been noticeably more subdued and less argumentative these past few meetings. It was as if they'd finally realized the shitstorm rapidly approaching and were wisely less concerned about their own pet grievances. Small mercies, right?

"Anything else?" the General asked. "No? Then let's get to it, people. We have less than five weeks to mission go. Then the *real* fun begins."

"*Cheeeehooo!* I freaking *love* this gun!"

The earsplitting, very much *not* subvocalized war cry reverberated around the cavernous exhibit hall of The Greenbrier bunker. Lynn felt it in her bones in a way none of the TDM noises or simulated weapons fire could match, since they were all digitally generated.

"Hot *dayum,* Maui! Can you teach me to do that?" said Grim in a properly subvocalized voice. He and Edgar had taken a distinct liking to each other, with Grim egging Edgar on to ever-higher bloodthirsty levels of enthusiasm at digital death and destruction.

Lynn caught a glimpse of a grimace on Hermes' face, their squad leader. Herman "Send_Hermes" Bailey, like all the company leadership, was an Alpha Tester and more military in demeanor than others, such as their Platoon Leader Andrew "CrashBandicoot" Stoner. The Hunter teams had been told that since they had a gaming cover to maintain, extraneous chatter during missions was not technically prohibited, since it was what the fans were used to. But they did need to maintain enough com discipline to execute the mission.

The directive had made Lynn and several other Hunters chuckle. They obviously hadn't spent much time watching professional stream gamers.

"I got you, *uce*. Remind me when we're done killin' stuff."

"Sweet, thanks Maui."

They were, indeed, busy killing stuff.

And killing stuff *inside* for a change. Lynn had always wondered why TDMs never showed up inside buildings. Now she knew.

They did.

The TD Hunter app simply never showed them.

Fortunately for humanity—and Lynn's nerves—it was mostly the harmless Delta Class spooks you found inside, simply because most electromagnetic signatures inside buildings were weak. The strong sources, like generators, transformers, nodes, and more, were kept away from regular human activity since they weren't healthy for humans to hang around.

It was not a pleasant thought, knowing invisible, creepy little TDMs could be hanging out in her bedroom beside her as she slept. The fact that there was nothing to attract them to such intimate human spaces was cold comfort.

Their current battle drill inside the exhibit hall was entirely simulated, to ensure a controlled environment. Since TDMs ignored the existence of walls, and some major grid energy sources were located underground in basements and utility tunnels, there was a distinct possibility TD Counterforce operations could involve clearing small spaces where only a few squads could fit at a time.

"*Aaugh!* I *hate* these disgusting Spithragani!" Serenity from Team Amaranth hollered over by the hall's exterior wall. She was on flank duty and had a particular dislike for spiders. Lynn didn't blame her. The combat interface did give them *some* warning; it was able to detect TEPs through light interference. But the bunker's walls were four feet thick. Not exactly "light." Even *with* a bit of warning, it was disconcerting as hell to have spooks popping out of walls at you in a near-constant stream.

Flank duty was a universally despised position.

Lucky for Lynn her skills put her in forward more often than not.

"At least we don't have to worry about scores!" Mack chirped, sounding disgustingly cheerful. That fact alone had seemingly lifted an immense weight from his shoulders. It had made Lynn realize how much of a toll the anxiety of competition had taken on Mack.

Apparently fighting for humanity's survival was much less stressful.

Lynn understood, though. It was freeing, to simply kill instead of worrying about dodging every tiny strike. They still had to keep up appearances on livestream, and they still had to worry about their health levels as important indicators for how much "TEP radiation" they were getting—it wasn't radiation at all, but that was the vernacular Alpha Testers had settled on. Mack no longer had to worry about physically "scooping up" and distributing Oneg, since that was a game stat which livestream viewers weren't privy to anyway. They maintained their health by killing more TDMs, and backing up to reduce direct hits if their health got too low. Collecting ichor was easier now, too. The ichor graphics on the ground were simply indicators of higher TEP concentrations where spooks had just exploded, and all they needed to do was walk near or through them for their equipment to harvest the particles. Globes and plates worked the same way, and Hugo automated their application unless the user needed to override it for a specific tactic.

With those game mechanics taken care of, they could more efficiently focus on their singular mission: kill, kill, kill.

"Amaranth, I want to see tighter, more controlled attacks on your side," barked Hermes. "Our TEP resources are even more limited with these stronger weapons you're using. Skadi's Wolves, less dancing around. I know you've trained hard on preserving kill-to-damage ratios, but you don't have time to worry about that. Speed and efficiency are the name of your game, now."

Lynn grimaced, but put words to action and lunged forward directly at the Rakshar in front of her, ducking enough so that its swipe only passed through the crown of her head instead of sweeping her torso directly. Abomination in her left hand was already engaged blindly blasting another Rakshar to the side, and now she stabbed up into the chest of the Rakshar face-to-face with her, dispatching it with a direct, close-quarters strike to the heart. The two Rakshar exploded simultaneously and Lynn grinned.

She could get to liking these new close and dirty tactics. She couldn't take it too far when they were aboveground, doing publicized boss battles. She had millions of TD Hunter-fanatic fans micro-analyzing her moves and scores. They would definitely notice her changes in tactics, so she had to keep it believable within the confines of the game's scoring.

Down here, though, it was an all-out, seething brawl of destruction.

"Maui!" Hermes snapped. "Quit trying to head bash the spooks! Your headgear does *not* do melee damage!"

Lynn heard Ronnie snicker on their squad channel.

"That's a missed opportunity, there," Dan chortled. "I'm sure they can custom mod this headgear, though. It's friggin' Tsunami Entertainment tech! They can do anything!"

"But Maui's the only one crazy enough to use it," Mack pointed out.

There was a huff of exasperation that Lynn was pretty sure came from their squad leader. She liked Hermes well enough, he was good at his job, certainly. But he obviously hadn't spent much time around real gamers, not like Derek and his Light Brigade crew had.

To be fair to Hermes, Dan's comment *was* pretty ridiculous. TDMs always focused on the batons, since that was where the destructive particles were emanating from. Weaponizing their headgear would attract enemy attacks to the head area, sort of the opposite of what the protective gear was designed for. Their headgear was the same as they'd been issued at the championship in Austin, looking like a futuristic version of open-faced motorcycle helmets with a clear faceplate. They were lightweight, sleek, and fit perfectly thanks to an omnipolymer interior that custom molded to each individual's head. The outer helmet shell was lined with the same material as the combat vests covering their torsos from neck to waist, a material the lab coats had found mitigated the disruptive effect spooks had on human nervous systems.

Transitioning to their new gear had a learning curve, though. Their new batons were about twenty percent longer and thirty percent heavier than the standard gaming batons. The increased mass enabled the batons to house bigger TEP projection systems, thus packing a bigger punch. The drawback was the extra muscle strength needed to use them. It didn't help that the more solid weapons combined with the insanely realistic graphics projected directly onto their retinas made the TDMs and their attacks seem more real than ever. In close combat their bodies sometimes reacted instinctually to visual cues before their brains could remind them there was nothing physically there.

At least they had Hugo to help with spatial awareness.

With their displays already crowded by more data than the human brain could normally process, Hugo had already saved them from multiple Hunter-on-Hunter collisions, and stopped Lynn from backing right into a column. Granted, that would have hurt her pride more than her body, but it was still appreciated. They weren't used to fighting in such close quarters, and it really showed the first few days of indoor drills.

A loud "*Yeehaaw!*" came from behind and to the left where 3rd Squad's Zahn Wars and Lone Star teams were entangled in their own furious battle with the waves of Alpha and Bravo Class TDMs protecting the Bravo Class boss awaiting them at the end of the hall. 1st Platoon was currently on left flank duty, while 2nd Platoon fought on the right flank and 3rd Platoon practiced advancing up the middle. They hadn't yet integrated with their Alpha Tester squads, or met the purely Alpha Tester heavy weapons platoon that would be carrying the truly big guns and crew-served weapons, if the unit gossip was accurate. They, plus the heavier batons everyone was carrying, would be why a single company of a hundred twenty-four people would dare take on Sierra Class bosses during the Battle Tour. During the Austin championship, it had taken over two hundred Hunters to destroy Nagaraja, and they'd succeeded only by the skin of their teeth.

Of course, there were *three* infantry companies available in the battalion that made up Taskforce Sanctus. But the Hunters had already been told all three companies would be deployed simultaneously to different nodality battles across the US, destroying bosses as quickly as humanly possible.

Alpha Company would have to make do with what they had to destroy their targets, regardless of size or complicating circumstances.

Lynn got the impression, from the intense energy and "on edge" feel from every Alpha Tester she'd met so far, that the military types in CIDER were champing at the bit to get this Battle Tour on the road.

Despite the danger, Lynn agreed with them. Fighting was always better than sitting and worrying.

Lynn's blood hummed and her muscles burned with exquisite fire as she lunged back and forth, destroying her targets with extreme prejudice. They were in a familiar pentagon formation, with Edgar at the tip, her and Ronnie flanking him, and Mack and Dan somewhat behind and between them. Their squad was anchoring 1st Platoon's left flank, while Lone Star and Zahn Wars were on the inside closest to 2nd Platoon who were driving down the middle of the exhibit hall.

Fortunately, even in close quarters there was no danger of friendly fire, since the "negative" TEPs that caused the spooks to disintegrate didn't affect humans at all. They still had to worry about beaning each other over the head with their melee weapon swings, but at least the batons' omnipolymer had some give. Their headgear and their impact-absorbing high-performance wear helped too.

"Amaranth, the spooks are starting to swing around your flank," Hermes said. "Keep up your rate of fire and stay sharp. Mack and Dan, stand by to provide cover fire to the rear if needed."

Unfortunately, physical barriers limited their ability to use their bait drops just as much as it limited visibility. In close quarters, they had to fight harder to keep the TDMs off their backs. At a certain point they'd simply have to accept being surrounded and would use bait as a buffer behind them to prevent attacks from all sides while they dealt with the boss. During their Battle Tour, Lynn knew they'd have more space to work with, *and* they'd have their heavy weapons platoon who would be sporting high-payload, three-sixty coverage grenade launchers.

Lynn was looking forward to the fireworks.

"Maui, hold back a little," she said on her own team channel. "You're pulling too far ahead."

"Sure thing, boss," Edgar grunted, then let out another "*Chee-hoo*!" as the Jotnar he was targeting exploded.

Every single team recruited to the TD Counterforce was top tier. They'd all made it to the TD Hunter National Championship, after all. But there was top tier, and then there was *top tier.* Sometimes Lynn had to remind herself this wasn't a competition anymore. They were part of a unit, and they had orders to follow. Everyone getting the best weapons CIDER had to offer helped even out performance, but Lynn knew Skadi's Wolves could chew through these TDMs faster than they were now if they had to, especially with their new rules of engagement.

Edgar wasn't used to holding back. None of them were.

Maybe she could ask the company commander—well, no, she'd

need to start with her squad leader, she supposed, to maintain chain of command—if she could sit down with whoever was in charge of training and suggest some standardized attack drills to implement across the company. She'd noticed some sloppy techniques from some of the other teams, and they would advance faster as a unit if they were all on the same page.

"Over halfway there," Hermes said, "keep up the pace, teams, I want this boss bagged and us out of here in time for lunch."

Ten more furious minutes of fighting and they were within range of the boss, an ugly, squat thing that nonetheless was tall enough that it was partially obscured by the ceiling overhang at the end of the exhibit hall. What they could see was a mass of writhing tentacles, more closely spaced than Mishipeshu's had been.

"Raven and Eva, prepare to deploy force shields. The rest of you, remember to stay well out of range. Just because it's Bravo Class doesn't mean it's not dangerous."

Lynn sighed internally. Being team captain had its drawbacks. Since she was in a leadership position, she was considered the proper personnel to carry the team's defensive weaponry. She wondered if Eva and other team captains were equally disappointed at having a reduced ability to kill stuff, or if it was a relief to them.

It was a serious source of irritation to Lynn, but she didn't say anything. Mission came first.

When they reached the pre-appointed optimal range—as close as they could get while still outside Hugo's estimate of the boss's reach—Hermes had them form a battle line and their formation flattened out.

"Everyone, stand by to drop your bait markers!"

On Hermes' command, the entire squad deployed the distracting shield of bait to give them a brief window to focus their fire on the boss. Their entire strategy depended on wrapping this thing up before mobs of spooks surrounded them and piled in with gusto.

A cry of alarm from someone in 2nd Platoon dragged at Lynn's attention, but she kept her eyes forward as she blasted the boss with Abomination and used Bastion as a bludgeoning weapon for the few TDMs that strayed within her reach.

"Watch it!" Hermes snapped. "Those tentacles are longer than they look."

Their squad leader stayed slightly behind them, also bearing a force shield along with a big honking pistol that looked like a miniature hand-held cannon. He pulled his weight, for sure, and had to worry even less about the appearance of good scores, since he was a virtual nobody to most of the crazed fans who would be watching their Battle Tour. That freed up more of his attention for directing squad movements and coordinating with their platoon leader.

Lynn chafed at taking orders, but knowing she'd be pulled off the front lines if she was given any sort of command position made it bearable.

The simulation threw them for a few more loops, just to keep them on their toes. At one point Lynn dodged in front of Edgar to catch the whip-coil of a tentacle before it could wrap itself around Edgar's head. Hermes tersely reminded her to stay in formation, which made her scowl. She'd have to have a conversation with him about it, because she knew how much bosses could mess people up, and there was no way she'd stand by and let one of her teammates catch a direct hit from a boss if she could help it. She *was* Bastion's bearer, after all. What the heck was the point of her having it if not to *defend*?

In the end, though, the simulated boss finally succumbed to their overwhelming barrage of TEPs and exploded into an impressive display of multi-colored sparks. Lynn wondered if Hugo had decided that just because their lives were now on the line didn't mean they couldn't still enjoy exciting graphics.

Their combat interfaces shut down and their displays cleared, and the various platoon leaders rallied their squads to circle up in the center of the exhibit hall.

"Well done, Alpha Company," said their company commander once they were all gathered round. Lafayette "AbramsBeast" Muller, or Abrams as he was known to them, was blond-haired and blue-eyed with the bearing and intensity of a man a good foot taller than his actual frame. Lynn suspected that anyone who underestimated him because of his height was in for a swift and very unpleasant surprise. Based on his handle and his compact frame, Lynn guessed his previous command before he'd been pulled for an Alpha Tester had involved tanks.

"I'm seeing definite improvement on speed with accuracy maintained," Abrams continued. "2nd Platoon, you did well on the sharp end of the spear. 1st and 3rd, good work keeping our flanks clear. It's a thankless job, I know."

Lynn heard Serenity mutter darkly from somewhere nearby about "those thrice-cursed Spithra," and Lynn had to suppress a grin.

"This, of course, was a small-scale battle to accustom everyone to the combat interface and weapons. I'm sure it was as realistic as Hugo could manage within his given parameters. But you have all faced real nodalities; you know how unpredictable they can be. Some are mobile, some have ranged attacks, and some have hidden defense mechanisms. The amount of TEPs needed to destroy each is unknown. There was a case during beta testing where the Alpha teams sent to dispatch a nodality had to give up and retreat because the thing simply *would not die*. Now, at least, we have better weapons and more TEPs available—the *only* benefit of the spooks' exponential increase. But every boss battle will be a new and potentially volatile situation. Hugo can analyze the nodalities before we attack, but until they are drawn into combat and activate their defenses, we face a plethora of unknown risks."

"Sounds like another day endin' in *y*, sir," one of Gadsden's teammates drawled, sounding like he was discussing the weather. "Ain't no battle plan *I* ever saw what didn't have surprises."

Abrams raised an eyebrow, and Lynn thought a hint of humor sparked in his eyes, but his response was grave.

"Yes, for some of us unpredictability is the norm. For others, however"—his gaze swept the gathered Hunters, most of whom looked just as young as Lynn and her friends—"they would do well to take this reminder to heart. The spooks might not have the physical claws and teeth to tear us limb from limb, but people will end up just as dead if we make mistakes. Not just yourselves, but innocent civilians. Women, children, the elderly. The most vulnerable will be hurt the worst, as they always are in times of war. Because this *is* war, even if whatever these entities are lack murderous purpose."

He spent a moment longer looking at them, meeting people's eyes, holding gazes, making sure his point was driven home.

"Very well, then. Tomorrow the PR teams arrive and we have several days of public training and drills to get through. You'll get briefings on all the details this afternoon. Just remember that the lives of your loved ones depend on our cover staying air-tight. Keep your wits about you, and choose your words carefully. Alpha Company, dismissed."

Out of the corner of her eye, Lynn saw several of the Alpha Testers come to attention, though they didn't salute. None of them wore military uniforms or rank, but they all acted like they did. No doubt they'd been told to act like civilians for the sake of their gaming cover.

Some of them were better at it than others.

Lynn thought of Team Light Brigade again and shook her head. They'd had a subtle intensity about them, but that was it. Maybe they'd been "detached" from their unit for longer? Or maybe they were just better gamers.

"Whatcha thinkin' about, boss? Got your thoughtful scowl on."

Lynn became aware of Edgar's warm presence beside her as the crowd broke up and the chatter began. Everyone was tired and hungry, but they had to head up to their rooms to wash and change before they could sit down to lunch.

"I don't have a thoughtful scowl," Lynn protested, turning to walk with the crowd.

"Yeah, you do," Ronnie said, his tone just this side of snide.

Edgar punched him in the shoulder.

"Dude, *I* was teasing. *You* was being rude. Figure out the difference, bruh."

Ronnie glared at Edgar, rubbing his shoulder. He managed not to snap back, though, just huffed derisively and lengthened his stride to pull ahead of their group.

"Uh, thanks Edgar, but that wasn't super helpful," Lynn murmured.

"Don't care," Edgar rumbled back, his eyes on Ronnie's figure that quickly disappeared in the crowd. "I've given him a pass for long enough. Not anymore."

Lynn should have pointed out they were all a little tense, and they should put aside their differences during this critical time.

Instead, she pursed her lips to hide a smile.

"Hey," hissed Dan on Lynn's other side. "Watch out!"

Lynn's head came up and she saw what he meant right away. Elena, eyes lowered as if in thought, was almost on them as all the teams crowded through the exhibit hall's exit into the resort. Lynn stopped dead just as Elena's head came up, as if she'd heard

Dan's furtive warning. She spotted them right away, and her nose scrunched up in a sneer. Lynn's body tensed in anticipation, her Larry brain leaning forward, itching for provocation even as her Lynn brain wished she were invisible.

"Hey! Queen! Come on," called a voice further along in the shuffling crowd, likely one of her teammates. "I heard they're serving Baja Tacos for lunch and you will *not* want to miss those."

For an eternal moment, it seemed like Elena might do something. But then she snorted and dove into the crowd, shoving her way through the press to catch up with her team.

"*Dios mío*," Mack whispered, sounding so much like Mrs. Rios that Lynn snorted in amusement. "Did *Elena Seville* just walk right past us without saying something mean? Was that even Elena? Is she on drugs? Did they lobotomize her?"

"Shut it," Lynn said, smacking Mack's arm lightly even as she watched the back of Elena's platinum blond head disappear in the crowd. "People change."

"Not Elena," Mack said fervently. "She turned bullying into a professional sport."

Dan snorted, though Lynn noticed Edgar didn't so much as crack a smile. He didn't look angry, though, just wary. And thoughtful.

"She's not our problem anymore," Lynn said firmly as they started off again.

"I wouldn't bet on it," Mack muttered.

"Did you hear what that guy called her?" Dan said, ignoring his friend's doubtful tone. "Are any of us really going to use her handle? 'Queen'? Seriously? How much trouble do you think we'd get in if we called her 'Harpy' instead? What about 'Insane Screeching Bi—'"

"*Dan,*" Lynn snapped, her voice slicing across his babble like a hot knife. He recoiled, and Lynn realized she'd used her Larry voice. "Knock it off," she continued in a more subdued tone. "I'm serious. This isn't high school and she's not our enemy. Our *families' lives* are at stake. Don't you *dare* waste your energy on a stupid high school grudge. Got it?"

"Yeah. Okay. I got it," Dan said, shoulders hunched. "No need to bite my head off. Yeesh."

"I'll bite your head off as many times as I need to if it prevents a problem that could get us all killed. This isn't a game anymore." She bared her teeth at Dan in a humorless smile.

"I know that," he said, sounding defensive.

"Then act like it." Lynn turned her head back toward the now emptying hallway and sped up, leaving Mack to console Dan on the way to their shared room. She sighed internally, wondering if she'd been too harsh. Even *she* was keyed up, snapping at her people over little things. But had it been so little? Her instincts in the moment hadn't thought so.

Her Larry instincts.

Derision and unprofessionalism were poison to effective units, and she never allowed that sort of behavior in her WarMonger teams. The sort of people who lowered themselves to it were almost always a waste of her time. In WarMonger it had been easy, though. A few words from "Larry the Snake" and the offender was either properly contrite, or smart enough to act it until they were done with the mission and safely out of the match lobby.

It was completely different in the real, with people she cared about.

"You okay, *manamea*?" Edgar asked quietly.

Lynn's breath hitched at the way "*manamea*" rolled off Edgar's tongue. She didn't need to ask for a translation of the Samoan to know it wasn't a word you used casually.

"Uh, yeah. Yeah, I'm fine."

Ever the faithful shadow, Edgar kept pace with her and followed as she bypassed the elevator and took the stairs. She doubted she'd be able to chase him away until she got to her rooms. Not that she blamed him. He was probably in no hurry to go deal with Ronnie, his roommate.

The reminder made her sigh internally.

Once they were alone in the stairwell, aching legs taking each step at a measured pace, Lynn spoke again.

"Hey, um, could you possibly . . . be a little nicer to Ronnie?"

Edgar didn't reply, but she could fairly feel his scowl.

"I don't mean give him a pass on being a jerk. I just mean . . . remember that *we* are all we have. We're a team, and we *have* to look after each other. We'll never get through this otherwise. Does . . . that make sense?"

Edgar sighed deeply, but nodded.

"I get you, *uce*. He's . . ."

"Being more of a jerk than usual?" Lynn offered into his pause.

Edgar snorted.

"Nah, I was gonna say 'smarter than this.'"

Now it was Lynn's turn to snort.

"Coulda fooled me."

"Yeah, yeah," Edgar conceded. "But I mean it. Ronnie's smart. Real smart. At least when he doesn't get in his own way, you know?"

"I . . . can't say that I've seen much of it, but I'll take your word for it," Lynn said diplomatically.

Edgar grinned.

"You scare the shit outta him."

"I *what*?" Lynn spluttered, pausing on a landing, mostly for the chance to give her poor legs a breather.

"He don't like being wrong, and you prove him wrong just by existing." Edgar shrugged, eyes twinkling.

Lynn snorted again and shook her head.

"You're crazy."

"Maybe so. Don't make me not right, though."

Lynn squinted, trying to figure that one out.

"He's mad at you, too, you know."

"Oh?" Lynn said faintly, not very surprised.

"Yeah. Been grumbling about it on and on in our room. Still sore there's no millions to win or a full ride or nothin'."

Lynn rolled her eyes.

"That's dumb," she said, gripping the stair railing and forcing herself to keep climbing. "I could have never touched TD Hunter and the outcome would have still been the same."

"He knows that."

"Then why the heck is he mad at *me*?"

"Cuz you didn't bail, *uce*. If you'd bailed and taken the thousand, we all woulda bailed with you, and then he woulda had a *good* reason for being mad at you. He coulda been all bitchy without knowin' the truth: there wasn't no millions to win in the first place."

Lynn stopped and stared at Edgar, jaw open. Then she threw up her hands.

"That's *insane*. What a moronic reason to be mad at me! Doesn't he *want* to live? Doesn't he *want* to save the world?"

"Well, yeah, or else he wouldn't be here. Don't make him any less hurt or scared, though."

"Ugh! Men!" Lynn huffed, and started climbing again.

"Nah, just Ronnie," Edgar chuckled.

By the time they reached the door to her room, she'd calmed down. But her exasperation had been replaced by a weary sort of uncertainty. She knew she couldn't "fix" Ronnie. That was his own business. But how should she deal with this? How could she be the captain Skadi's Wolves needed? She came to a halt and turned absently toward Edgar, still thinking.

"Hey, don't scowl like that, *manamea*," Edgar said softly, his voice rumbling in his chest. The sound sent a shiver down Lynn's spine. She lifted her eyes to meet his, almost nervous about what she would see. But he was just smiling his usual goofy Edgar smile. It wasn't his smile that had changed. It was her understanding of it that put everything in a completely different light.

His hand slowly rose, and she watched, transfixed, as he brushed his thumb gently across the furrow between her brows, as if he could smooth it away.

"Ma always says it'll stick like that if you're not careful."

"My mom would say that's hogwash," Lynn whispered, not daring to move. "She's a nurse. She'd know."

Edgar shrugged and dropped his hand, his smile still there.

"Maybe they're both right."

Lynn cleared her throat, so her next words didn't come out a squeak.

"They can't both be right, that'd be a contradiction."

"Sure they can," he said, grin widening. "They're mas. Mas are always right."

Lynn had no answer to that. She could hear her mother's voice clear as day saying: *Oh, come on, sweetie. He is so obviously over the moon for you.*

"You're... you're silly," she finally muttered, shaking her head to give herself an excuse to look away from those intense dark eyes.

Edgar shrugged as if the accusation didn't bother him in the slightest.

"Look, I've got to go shower. Could you just... try to help Ronnie? If not for his sake, then for all of ours? He'll listen to you, I think. We've made it this far, I'm not going to give up on him now."

A strange warmth entered Edgar's eyes, and one side of his mouth formed a crooked smile.

"Sure, boss. I got you."

Still, he didn't move.

"Um. See you at lunch, I guess?" Lynn said, not quite sure what else to say.

"Sure thing."

Edgar hesitated, as if there was more he wanted to say—or do. Lynn's pulse sped up, though whether in excitement or dread she couldn't tell. Maybe both.

Finally, though, Edgar gave a little wave and turned away, headed back down the hall toward the stairwell.

Well, that was way more excitement than I needed right now, Lynn thought, hurrying into her room. She was starving and tired and itchy, but also weirdly . . . okay. The world was still ending, and everything was crazy and uncertain and stressful.

But she wasn't alone in it all.

And that was nice.

Maybe nice enough to . . . want more of it.

Chapter 5

THE WEEKEND THE PR CIRCUS DESCENDED ON THE GREENBRIER, Lynn learned that the Alpha Testers weren't the only ones with hidden military skills: Mrs. Pearson went full-blown general on them all.

Apparently Tsunami's PR liaison had been so impressed by her in Austin that he'd temporarily "borrowed" her from GIC to help coordinate the absolute bedlam of forty-plus PR teams and an equal number of hand-picked reporters and personalities from various stream channels.

She was beautiful to behold. A logistics goddess encased in a linen pantsuit. Matron of Order. Holder of The Plan. Champion of The Schedule.

She would sweep into a situation, set it to rights with a few stern words and precise directives, then sweep out again to address the next crisis. The older woman made the publicity weekend a mere pain in the butt instead of a marathon of anxiety and torture.

Lynn was pretty sure she spotted a couple of the military types drooling behind Mrs. Pearson's back. Probably wondering where the woman had been all their career and why couldn't they please, please, please have her as their S4?

The answer was no, of course. Lynn didn't think the military could handle Mrs. Pearson's blunt, no-nonsense style. Inefficiencies and red-tape seemed to be the woman's mortal enemies, and she attacked them with a take-no-prisoners sort of attitude.

The first day of the two-day publicity weekend consisted of tours and training exercises—or rather, training performances. Swarms of drones followed the Hunters around as the trainers put them through their paces, from runs to agility drills to formation training. Lynn spent the entire time daydreaming about every conceivable way to shoot drones out of the sky. Slingshot? Boffer arrows? Flamethrower?

She was impressed to see a few of the professional livestreamers join the Hunters in their exercises throughout the day. Sure, it was to give their stream followers a more visceral *lived* point of view. But at least *they* got their hands dirty, sweating and panting alongside the TD Counterforce troops.

While the general population of stream vultures had *not* been invited to the exclusive preview weekend, the allure of such exclusive footage had the power to turn the heads of even the professionally vetted. During that first day, a few foolhardy streamers were caught sneaking away from their designated areas, or ambushing Hunters for impromptu interviews. After the first few culprits were immediately and unceremoniously escorted off the premises, the remaining media members got the picture and there were no more incidents.

Mrs. Pearson made it crystal clear that she was solidly in Lynn's corner, there to *protect* her client, not exploit her—a rare oasis of relief after a year of parasitic stream vultures chasing her around for their own gain. It helped that the guys had Mrs. Pearson's full blessing to jump on anyone hanging around not on their own GIC PR team.

Metaphorically jump, of course.

All PR personnel were required to wear a lanyard with a giant, neon orange badge, to make them extra easy to spot and evict if anyone put a toe out of line. Everyone else was in their various uniforms—Greenbrier staff, Hunters, trainers, and Tsunami employees—so interlopers would stand out. Edgar and Ronnie in particular got a kick out of glaring at any stranger who so much as looked their way. It amused Lynn to no end, seeing Ronnie act like a grumpy old pro when just six months ago he'd been tripping over himself trying to get streamers' attention. He likely hadn't matured all that much, simply realized that unsanctioned footage didn't make *him* any money in the way of sponsorships, and the more exclusive GIC's coverage was, the more people would pay to sponsor him.

Or maybe he'd finally realized that being put on a pedestal for billions to scrutinize, criticize, and paw at in virtual wasn't everything it was cracked up to be.

During the afternoon, while the various stream celebrities got a tour of the resort and famous underground bunker, the PR people got to work with their individual Hunter Strike Teams, recording various product promotions and other content to tide their streams over until they were done with their TD Counterforce training. It was annoying, tedious work. But at least the change of pace seemed to put the guys in better spirits, and there was definitely some cutting up between takes.

Having a friendly face around helped too.

True to her word, Kayla had maneuvered herself onto Skadi's Wolves PR team as their official wardrobe supervisor and stylist. Since they wore the standard-issue TD Counterforce uniform most of the weekend, there wasn't much to coordinate. But there were some costume changes for the product promotions and Kayla was also in charge of making sure all their various sponsorship logos were properly programmed into their uniforms' smart fabric.

With Mrs. Pearson there to make sure everything ran smoothly, *finally* the first day was over and all the media personnel were escorted off the premises for the night.

That left only the second, more nerve-wracking day to get through: a livestreamed boss battle and a slew of interviews.

Despite Lynn's protests, Kayla had *ideas* when it came to the look for Skadi's Wolves on "the big day." There wasn't a lot to work with, since their standard uniform covered in sponsorships was non-negotiable. But Kayla was undeterred.

Her first target was Lynn's hair. It was an easy ask, so Lynn sat dutifully while Kayla worked her magic and put it up in a Viking-esque maze of twists and braids. By the time Kayla was done, Lynn was ready to climb onto a dragon and torch the whole PR nightmare from above, just to escape it.

Kayla, of course, thought she looked "breathtaking." While that normally would have made Lynn scowl, the fact that Edgar couldn't keep his eyes off her and smiled like an idiot every time their eyes met mollified Lynn's annoyance, replacing it with a warm, tingly, slightly panicked feeling in her chest.

The hair, though, was just to soften Lynn up for Kayla's second target: the face paint.

Lynn had always refused to wear makeup, but somehow Kayla had managed to convince Mrs. Pearson that it was a fantastic idea to paint them all up, barbarian style. She started with black across their eyes and added some ice blue runes and geometric patterns on forehead and cheeks that matched their Skadi's armor skins in game. Lynn couldn't help but notice that Kayla took particular care painting Dan's symbols, her tongue poking out slightly as she furrowed her brow in concentration. Dan sat perfectly still, a vaguely panicked look on his face. He kept going cross-eyed like he was trying to see what Kayla was doing, and Lynn had to turn away to keep from giggling. By the time Kayla was done with everyone, Lynn had to admit they looked pretty darn impressive. Warlike, even. Which was appropriate, considering the circumstances, even if Kayla didn't know it.

After all the Hunters were prepped to their PR teams' satisfaction, the real circus began.

The streams had been starved for juicy Hunter Strike Team content for *two whole weeks* and apparently the world was going to implode if they didn't get new, thrilling battles to watch directly from the eyes of the "best of the best."

And, of course, Tsunami was all for feeding the insatiable content machine.

An elaborate boss battle had been planned on The Greenbrier's mostly flat golfing practice range, with the various PR staff and drone handlers cordoned off by The Greenbrier's Golf Academy building. The TDMs were all simulated, of course, since the game couldn't whistle up a boss of just the right size and difficulty in precisely the right place for maximum visual impact. Thankfully this meant there was no reason for the Hunters to wear their protective headgear, thus crimping their style as burgeoning stream celebrities. The TD Hunter Lens app did a fair job of replacing the headgear with whatever armor skin each Hunter had active. But it wasn't perfect. The players still all wore their vests, though. Lynn assumed it was to get the public used to seeing them in their TD Counterforce getup, complete with standardized handles.

All three companies of Hunter Strike Teams participated in

the fight, organized into their various squads and platoons. They still hadn't integrated with their Alpha Tester units or heavy weapons platoons, but Lynn wasn't surprised CIDER wanted those people scrutinized as little as possible. So it was just the Hunter Strike Teams and their squad, platoon, and company leadership.

The boss fight itself was more an extended drill than anything truly challenging. The algorithm—which Lynn supposed was technically one and the same as Hugo, but that was too weird to think about—threw in some Dracas just to make it interesting. But these didn't laser focus on her like she had some sort of TDM bait marker on her back, so they were pretty fun to kill.

The whole thing was surprisingly enjoyable. For an hour or so Lynn got to let go of the burden of competing—or saving the world—and simply *enjoy* playing TD Hunter. She put on some extra flair, and Skadi's Wolves could banter to their heart's content on their own team channel, much to the delight of their livestream audience. The same scenario was likely playing out on dozens of team streams across the board. Their Alpha Tester unit leaders provided just the right amount of orders to keep the battle interesting and moving along, and Lynn got the impression they were enjoying the break from reality as much as the Hunters were. Lynn kept forgetting that all the Alpha Testers were gamers in their own right, not just covert members of CIDER.

Mrs. Pearson and her team managed the live footage with all their usual aplomb, though Mrs. Pearson had to ban Kayla early on from spectating on Skadi's Wolves' channel because she kept gasping and squealing at their near misses and epic takedowns. Kayla seemed particularly enamored by Dan's sniper skills, and Lynn was absolutely sure he kept calling out his targets before he shot them just to show off to her.

They wrapped up the battle with a massive salvo on the boss once the Dracas had been taken care of. The encircling TDMs were few enough that between the three companies, they had them mostly wiped out by the time they turned their attention to the boss.

It was a luxury Lynn suspected they would only ever find in simulated battle.

The whole exercise was wrapped up in time for lunch.

The Greenbrier staff herded the PR personnel off to the resort dining hall while the Hunter companies organized and walked back to the West Virginia Wing to shower and change. They would eat after the "civilians" had finished eating and gone to set up in various rooms around the resort for a marathon of interviews.

Kayla pinged her with a highlight vid she'd made during their livestream battle, and Lynn had to admit she and the guys looked incredibly impressive between their Skadi's armor skins and face paint. She also got a good look at Amaranth, since they were in close proximity during the battle. They were honestly poetry in motion, with the four girls all specializing in various forms of melee combat that ensured they chewed through the TDMs like windmills of death. Grim was the odd one out, being the only non-former gymnast. He filled the overwatch roll with incredible skill, though, and likely rivaled Dan in accuracy.

Lynn got glimpses of other teams throughout, from Team Lone Star with their dystopian cowboy theme toting guns as big as their torsos, to Team Florida Man who had the most eclectic collection of weapons that it was a mystery to Lynn how they'd achieved top tier status. She couldn't linger and enjoy the footage, though. They only had limited time to get cleaned up, and Kayla insisted on touching up their face paint, despite the fact that she'd already assured them it was a premium formula impervious to smearing without the proper chemical solution to remove it.

By the time they'd finished a hasty lunch and had been herded off to the interview room assigned to Skadi's Wolves, Lynn was feeling distinctly less sanguine.

She *hated* interviews.

At least they were back in their standard hunting gear, complete with sponsorship logos, instead of being forced to wear some sort of matching frippery concocted by Kayla. The form-fitting athletic gear provided neck-to-ankle skin coverage, which made Lynn happy, while apparently "showing off her figure" which made Kayla—and the audience—happy.

Lynn was so used to their outfits she usually barely noticed how they looked. Her brain was too busy thinking about battles, tactics, scores, and training. But since Austin she'd become uncomfortably aware of the fact that hers was not the only figure "shown off" by their uniforms. Edgar had always been a solid mountain who was hard to miss. Yet his quiet, easygoing demeanor and normally baggy clothes he wore to school had made him fade easily into the background. A year of intense training, though, had melted off every bit of softness, and his uniform left nothing up to the imagination. Every single muscle showed, and when he crossed his arms . . . well, it did funny things to her insides.

Was this how she made *him* feel? How could anyone concentrate with all these *distracting* thoughts?

Normally their team was elbow-deep in TDMs and she had plenty distractions to keep her focused on the mission. Sitting around waiting to do an interview, though, left her brain dangerously unoccupied. To keep it in safer territory, she eyed the GIC personnel of Mrs. Pearson's team currently prepping their interview space. Kayla, perhaps considering her part to be done, was loitering beside Dan, chatting brightly about the upcoming interviews while the other staff moved furniture and set up lights. Dan had a painfully earnest look on his face, eyes riveted on Kayla. Lynn snorted to herself and wondered if he was hearing even half the words Kayla was saying.

Probably less, if Kayla was talking as fast as she usually did.

Lynn couldn't hide a smile as she noticed that Dan and Kayla were almost exactly the same height, though Kayla's wild, exuberant hair gave her a few good inches on him in terms of silhouette.

A curt call from Mrs. Pearson made Kayla scurry over to help set up, and Lynn turned her attention to the room they'd been given for the "torture session" as Lynn thought of it. The space was actually one of the main ballrooms of the resort—she suspected Mrs. Pearson had leveraged her position as Tsunami liaison to snag one of the fanciest rooms available.

The official name was the Cameo Ballroom.

Dan, in all his great wisdom and fashion sense, had dubbed it the Pepto Bismol room.

To his credit, he wasn't wrong. The walls were such an intense, cheerful salmon pink that it was hard to think of any other descriptor. To make matters worse, the golden glow from the massive crystal chandelier and the fancy sconce lights around the edge of the room gave the pale cream ceiling a much more yellow tone. That pink-yellow combination made Dan's observation irrefutable, despite the very elegant touch of white trim and crown molding around the room.

Honestly, there wasn't a single room in the entire resort that *wouldn't* have clashed with Skadi's Wolves' edgy "space Viking" look. At least in the ballroom, the floor was elegant polished wood, and not a swath of giant floral designs.

The Greenbrier was a beautiful testament to elegance and history. As an interview backdrop for the most popular augmented reality game of all time, though, it lacked a certain...vibe.

But then, it didn't need to be perfect, did it? The extreme dissonance between past and present would likely pique more curiosity than anything else, and the better these interviews went, the more interest there would be in TD Hunter, and the more people would be out there chipping away at the alien invasion Lynn and her team were putting their lives and futures on the line to defeat.

The realization brought a weird sense of calm with it—a calm that started at her head and moved down her body in a gentle flow of relaxing muscles and release of tension.

This is what Mr. Krator had been doing for *months.*

Showing up in front of cameras, smiling and relaxed, casually advocating for a game that could be the literal salvation of humankind. And not one viewer had been any the wiser.

Well played, Robert. Well played, Lynn thought. The Larry part of her gave a lazy salute of respect. The Lynn part of her let go of the last thread of resentment she'd been holding onto.

I get it now.

Lynn turned to the guys. Kayla and the GIC PR team were almost done setting up, but there was still time.

Her movement caught Edgar and Mack's gaze, and Edgar raised his eyebrows. Dan and Ronnie were arguing about the tactical superiority of curly versus crinkle fries. Lynn sent them all a voice chat request.

"Sup, boss?" Edgar subvocalized.

"What?" Ronnie's voice came next, sounding annoyed, but he and Dan both turned toward her.

"Circle up, Skadi's Wolves," Lynn subvocalized, putting her Larry face on.

Maybe Ronnie sensed the shift, or maybe he was just feeling conciliatory. For whatever reason, he didn't argue as he and the other guys gathered round. Lynn looked at each one slowly. The black paint around their eyes made them look tough, ready for everything, and the blue runes gave them a mystical air.

"I know it's been a rough few weeks since...well, since we

found out the truth. I know some of us—heck, probably all of us—are dealing with a lot of disappointment and frustration right now."

She caught and held Ronnie's eye, keeping her expression smooth.

He snorted, his mouth twisting to the side. But he didn't look away.

Lynn took a deep breath and continued looking directly at Ronnie as she subvocalized.

"I want you all to know that no matter what happens, I am proud to be a part of this team. I am proud of what we've accomplished. And I am honored to be among four men who volunteered to keep secrets and sacrifice their futures for our country. For our world."

Confusion, then surprise blossomed on Ronnie's face. When she got to the part about "four men," he seemed to flinch a little, and looked away. Lynn had mercy on him and turned her intense stare to the other members of the team.

"What we want and feel right now doesn't really matter. Not in the larger scheme of things. It *is* normal to want things, to have hopes and dreams. It *is* reasonable to be upset, nervous, even afraid. But none of us are standing here because of our feelings. We're standing here because we love our families, and we will fight to protect them."

Ronnie's shoulders hunched, and the sight twisted something painful in Lynn's chest as Mr. Payne's ugly words rang loud and clear in her memory.

Get over here this instant you worthless runt, or I swear I'll—

Lynn's lips thinned, and she thought of her own father. His strong hands. His boundless courage. His quick smile.

The pain in her chest sharpened, but instead of pushing it away, she embraced it.

"*You* guys are my family, too," she subvocalized, jaw set. Edgar smiled crookedly while Mack and Dan looked surprised, but pleased. Ronnie didn't move. "*All* of you," she added. Ronnie still didn't react, but Lynn knew better than to expect him to. She went on, "You all have fought for me, and I will fight for you. We will get through this, *together.* We will *not* stoop to immaturity and unprofessionalism—not with each other and not with outsiders. We will *not* allow resentment to divide us. We will not give up. We will not back down. We are Skadi's Wolves, and we are top-tier gaming professionals, regardless of what TD Hunter is or is not. Regardless of what our future holds. Now, let's go do these interviews and show them who we really are: a team, and a damn good one."

Mack pumped a fist in the air.

"Yeah! Go Wolves!" he yelled out loud, then ducked his head, blushing as his words echoed loudly in the ballroom and every GIC staff member turned and stared at them.

"Points for team spirit," Edgar subvocalized, deadpan.

Dan snickered.

"Whatever gets your blood pumping," Lynn subvocalized, giving Mack a half smile. "So, are we ready for this?" she asked, looking at each of the guys.

"Bring it on," Dan said, putting his hand out in the middle of their circle like they were some sort of old-school sports team.

"We got this," Mack said, adding his hand to the pile.

"Might as well have some fun," Edgar said and shrugged. When he added his big hand on top, Dan and Mack's hands sank perceptively as if Edgar was letting them hold up his muscular arm. They glared at him, but he just grinned.

"Ronnie?" Lynn asked. He was staring across the ballroom, his expression opaque. But at her call, he shook his head, as if coming out of a trance. He added his hand to the pile without looking at Lynn.

"Whatever. You're all dorks. But I'm stuck with you, so I guess I'd better make sure you don't do anything *too* stupid."

"How magnanimous of you," Lynn said dryly. Ronnie glanced up, brow furrowed. When he saw her grin, though, he snorted and rolled his eyes.

Lynn added her hand to the pile.

"Let's go be badasses and have fun."

They broke up their circle just as Mrs. Pearson came over, her low Oxford heels clacking against the polished wooden dance floor.

"Ready, Miss Raven? Gentlemen?" the older woman asked, perfect eyebrows arched in question.

"Yup," Lynn said.

They took their places, Lynn between Dan and Mack on a settee that had been relocated for their use, and Edgar and Ronnie in armchairs on either side of the settee. A strange calm suffused

Lynn's body, and she leaned back, propping her arms up on the back of the settee on either side of her and crossing one ankle over the opposite knee. Without knowing how to explain it, she knew it was a Larry pose. Project confidence and ease. Own the space around you. Show the world you had nothing to fear.

Mrs. Pearson was talking, briefing them on the first interviewer, the questions to expect, what to do if off-limits questions were broached—the same rundown she gave before every interview. Lynn left the team voice chat active. They didn't often need it, but sometimes covert communication was helpful in team interviews to coordinate their answers or ask for help. Ronnie never utilized it—unsurprisingly. But the other guys did. They could also subvocalize to Mrs. Pearson if they wanted her to stop an interview without making a scene during livestreaming.

Once they were prepped and comfortable, Mrs. Pearson showed in the first interviewer, and the fun began.

"That was *awesome*," Mack said. There was a little hop in his step as they walked down the long, carpeted halls. Kayla had already helped them remove the face paint, hugged Lynn tightly goodbye, and hurried off to help Mrs. Pearson wrap up everything for the weekend. They had a little time before dinner, and Lynn figured everybody deserved a break, so they were heading to the retro arcade next to the bowling lanes the resort had in their entertainment wing.

"You only say that because you're Mrs. Pearson's favorite," Ronnie sniffed. "She made sure you got all the fun questions."

"Man, it's almost like being polite and helpful has benefits," Edgar said with a grin.

Lynn could not keep her face straight, so she looked away from the glare Ronnie shot Edgar's way.

"I *am* polite. I just don't grovel," Ronnie said.

Lynn slapped a hand over her mouth, still looking away, to muffle her splutter of laughter.

"Dude, I think you might want to look up the definition of polite," Edgar said. "You are the most impolite person I know."

While Ronnie's mouth flapped in protest, Mack hop-skipped a step to draw even with Edgar.

"Hey! Don't forget Elena and her crowd. He's not as bad as them."

"Hm, point. Sorry for comparing you to Elena, Ronnie. You're the most impolite person on *this team*. Happy?"

"*No*!" Ronnie's voice came out several octaves too high.

"Just send him to work for Mrs. Pearson for a while," Lynn said out loud, trying to head off unnecessary drama. "That'll teach him manners."

"Riko could teach him manners," Mack said, still bubbly. "The Japanese revere politeness and honor. She's been teaching me greeting customs and words, for when I finally get to visit her. I can't wait to hear what she thinks of our interviews!"

"Oh my *God*, Mack, you *cannot* still be talking to that bot!" Ronnie said, sufficiently distracted.

"She's *not* a bot! Her dad owns the biggest airbus manufacturing brand in Japan!"

"Yeah, *sure* he does," Ronnie rolled his eyes. Lynn noticed him glancing at Dan, who was usually quick to jump in on teasing Mack mercilessly for his ongoing virtual romance. But Dan's gaze was distant, so Ronnie simply turned back to Mack. "You know what I bet it is?"

"What?" Mack asked suspiciously.

"An organ harvesting ring. They use honeypot bots to convince foreigners to unwittingly travel right into the jaws of their trap, in strange territory where they don't know how to get help. Then they get jumped and drugged and bye-bye Mackie. I hear all sorts of chatter about the value of young, fresh, healthy organs. A lot of rich people out that way don't trust the lab-grown tissue tech China's trying to sell to the West. They only want the real deal."

"You're crazy!" Mack said, giving Ronnie a healthy shove. "You're just jealous *you* don't have a girl. You all are sad, lonely, and single, so you take it out on me! Riko is real and you'll meet her someday, as soon as it's safe to travel again."

That thought sobered everyone, and silence fell abruptly. Likely everyone was wondering *if* it would ever be safe to travel again.

"I don't want to die a virgin!" Dan burst out.

Everyone stumbled to a halt and turned to stare at him.

"What in the *world*?" Ronnie muttered, looking at Dan like he'd sprouted two heads.

"Uh, you doin' okay, man?" Edgar asked, head cocked.

Lynn's brow furrowed and she stared at Dan, who had his hands shoved into his pockets and his shoulders hunched.

"I . . . I had all these plans . . . I had *time*. And then—then *this* happened." He pulled his hands out of his pockets and gestured expansively at the resort around them. His hands dropped and he stared off into nothing with a hopeless look on his face.

Realization hit Lynn, and she had to bite her tongue to keep from blurting out Dan's secret.

Kayla.

"What am I supposed to *do*?" Dan asked plaintively, looking around like there was an answer to be found hidden in the floral wallpaper.

"Well," Mack shrugged, "there's lots of single girls here. You could always ask around. I'll bet some of them are thinking the same thing."

Dan recoiled with a look of abject horror on his face while Ronnie guffawed loudly.

"What?" Mack said, spreading his hands. "You'd just be *asking*. It's not like you'd be running people down or anything. Go door-to-door on the girls' floors. It's the end of the world, after all. *Somebody*'ll be feeling lonely, right?"

"*Mack*," Lynn said, the word coming out half rebuke, half splutter of laughter. As soon as she got herself under control, she continued more quietly, "This is an unsecure location. There might still be media personnel around, or at least their drones, hoping to catch some unsanctioned footage. We're not supposed to talk about *that* stuff in the clear." She looked up and down the hall out of reflex, but it was as empty as it had been most of their walk. The resort was a big place, capable of hosting thousands of people at a time, and there were barely two hundred members of the TD Counterforce currently staying there. With only a skeleton staff, most of the resort's attractions were closed, like the casino and spa. The only reason the arcade was open was because it was completely automated.

"Dan, my man," Edgar said, stepping over to lay a heavy hand on his shorter friend's shoulder, "my ma always says life ain't never guaranteed. Don't assume you got a tomorrow. You gotta tell the people you love what they mean to you while you still got the chance, you know?" He looked over at Lynn as he spoke, brows tilting outward, his eyes going all soft.

Lynn hastily cleared her throat and looked at Dan. A warm, panicked, fuzzy, anxious, happy little glow in her chest was scattering her thoughts, but she rallied herself and gave her friend a reassuring smile.

"Don't let fear control you, Dan. Things are . . . uncertain, yeah. But CIDER has a plan, and we're good at what we do. Let's just get through training and get to killing bosses, and I'm sure things will improve. Love isn't something you can rush." Her eyes flicked to Edgar as she said it, and he gave a little shrug, one side of his mouth quirking upward. She could almost hear his calm rumble in her head, saying something like:

Hey, can't blame me for trying, uce.

"But, how can I be *sure*?" Dan said, not quite wailing anymore but obviously not very reassured. "What if . . . what if things *don't* get better?"

They all looked at each other, silent faces reflecting the same fear.

"Then we keep fighting until they do," Lynn said, low and firm. "We *always* keep fighting, got it?"

Dan nodded miserably.

"Come on," Lynn jerked her head down the hall. "We all need a break, and there are games calling my name. Think any of you guys are up to beating me?" She raised an eyebrow in challenge.

Edgar grinned like a maniac and rubbed his hands together. Dan smiled a little, while Mack shook his head, as if he knew better than to rise to the bait.

"Ronnie?" Lynn said, cocking her head and carefully *not* letting Larry's predatory grin break the surface of her control.

Ronnie squinted suspiciously, but then his expression firmed. "You're on."

Their arcade trip wasn't quite the bloodbath Lynn had been hoping for, but it *did* get everybody's mind off the future. Lynn got so into it that she forgot herself once and shouted a colorful Larry-ism that made everybody look sideways at her. After that she put her guard back up, staying more focused and professional while she and Ronnie duked it out on games so old she wasn't even sure her *mom* had been alive when they were built. All were expertly restored, of course, but that didn't make them not *old*. They were huge, too, and clunky. Mack and Dan acted like they'd died and gone to heaven—apparently they considered themselves experts on game history and were enamored with the quaintness of the machines. Ronnie knew more about the old games than Lynn by proximity osmosis with Dan and Mack, so he had an edge on Lynn, who had to learn all the rules and controls on the fly.

Then there were the pinball machines.

Those, Lynn liked. They were beautiful things relying on physics and mechanical engineering. It was all about timing and pressure. The simplicity of the game belied the finesse needed to rack up the highest scores.

Ronnie didn't have the patience for it, so Lynn wiped the floor with him—multiple times. He finally gave up in disgust and went to play shooting games with Edgar, who didn't care if he won or lost, as long as he got to shoot stuff. Lynn thought it was one of Edgar's better qualities. It wasn't that he wasn't competitive. He fought hard for their team. He simply didn't have an ego to speak of, and so didn't see losing as a negative experience. As long as he had fun playing, that's all he cared about.

She really appreciated that about him. His joy and calm were infectious.

After dinner, when she was back in her room getting ready for bed while Eva did her pre-bedtime stretches, Lynn caught herself daydreaming about Edgar. About doing normal, everyday things with him. What would it be like to have someone she could be herself around without gaming competitions or global crises getting in the way? As soon as she realized what she was doing, she reined her thoughts in. Those daydreams were wasted effort. A distraction. There was no point wishing things were different. Too many responsibilities rode heavy on her shoulders for her to let her guard down right now.

Edgar's words burned in her mind, though: *You gotta tell the people you love what they mean to you while you still got the chance.*

What did Edgar mean to her?

She avoided answering that by thinking about her mom. Had Matilda talked to Steve yet? Would she ever? Would her mom regret not reaching out? What if Steve . . . well, what if the worst happened?

Before Lynn had left for Greenbrier, she'd promised her mom she would call when she could. She'd been too exhausted every evening before this, but their day had been light on the physical side, so now was the best time she was going to have. The next two weeks were going to be non-stop training.

Lynn finished cleaning her teeth and brushing out her hair, then left the bathroom to Eva and flopped down on her bed to stare at the fancy patterns of molding on the ceiling while she summoned the energy to ping her mom.

Matilda answered so quickly Lynn wondered if she'd been waiting, hoping Lynn would call.

"Honey! How are you? Are you okay?"

"I'm fine, Mom," Lynn subvocalized, unable to hold back a tired smile. It was a relief to hear her mom's voice. "We're all good. Well, as good as you could expect, considering . . . you know."

"Yeah," Matilda said softly. "I know. How's the training? I saw your interviews. You were *amazing*, dear. Confident, beautiful, articulate. I'm so proud of you."

Lynn felt her face heat.

"Uh, okay. Thanks mom. You're exaggerating, but, you know, thanks."

"Lynn! I am not exaggerating. Don't brush off sincere praise just because it clashes with your self-image. I'm not saying you're perfect. I'm saying you've really grown, and I'm proud of you. Use that knowledge to do even better in the future. Don't put yourself down, honey."

Lynn heaved a theatrical sigh.

"Okay. You're right, I guess. It just feels so weird. Everything has changed so quickly. I . . ." She trailed off, unable to say the rest out loud.

I barely recognize myself anymore. Lynn? Larry? Leader? Soldier? Who am I and who do I need to become to save the people I love?

"Slow down, kiddo. You're going to be fine." Matilda's calm voice relaxed the ball of tension behind Lynn's breastbone, and she took a deep breath as her mom continued. "You're on the cusp of adulthood. All those feelings are normal. Life is crazy and change is always hard. I remember when I left the reservation and started on my undergrad. It was a massive cultural shift. I don't know how I got through it with my head still screwed on straight."

"Dad helped," Lynn said with a little smile, though it came with a long familiar ache in her chest.

"That he did," Matilda agreed. "I don't know what I would have done without him. My point, dear, is that while all this seems new and out of control, it isn't. It's actually really normal and on-track. It's part of growing up, figuring out what adulthood is. Billions of people have gone through it before you and been just fine. You'll be fine too."

Lynn made a face her mom couldn't see. Her situation was *slightly* more complicated than the average eighteen-year-old, considering the whole *alien invasion* thing. She didn't say it, though. The silence that stretched between them said it for her.

"Hey, sweetie. It's going to be okay," Matilda finally said.

Lynn wished it made her feel better, but it didn't. It was the sort of thing moms said when the world and its problems were too complicated for their kids to understand or be expected to deal with.

Like it or not, Lynn was past that point. Far, far past it.

"Have you talked to Steve?" Lynn asked instead of pointing all that out.

There was a beat of silence, then a sigh.

"No."

Lynn's eyes widened in surprise, then she narrowed them.

"You mean he hasn't called you or anything?"

"No."

Lynn couldn't decide if it was relief or disappointment in that "no." Maybe there was a bit of both.

"Are you going to call him?"

There was a much longer silence. Lynn ached to hold her mom's hand, to remind her she wasn't alone.

"Maybe. Eventually."

Lynn let out a silent sigh of relief.

"Do you, um." Lynn swallowed. "Do you still like him? I mean, do you still want him? Want him with you, I mean, not, like, want his *body*. Not that you can't want his body, I just, um—"

Matilda laughed.

"Oh, honey. Stop while you're ahead."

Lynn snapped her lips closed, happy to oblige. Her mom was still chuckling as she answered.

"Yes, dear, I still love him, if that's what you were trying to ask. I'm just . . . I guess it's okay to admit this, now that you're all grown up. I'm . . . *afraid*, honey."

"Afraid of hurting again," Lynn said, her subvocalization so faint it came out as a whisper that echoed the sadness in her heart.

"Yeah."

Lynn wasn't sure what to say to that. It wasn't as if she had any experience or wisdom to share in the relationship department.

"Mom?" she finally said.

"Yes, honey?"

"Last year, at the qualifiers, you told me you were proud of me for not letting my fears hold me back. Do you remember?"

Matilda sighed. "Yes."

"Well, back when I was trying to get up the courage to form a team and take a shot at the TD Hunter championship, Mr. Thomas gave me some advice. He said there's no reward in life without risk. He said either you succeed at the risk of getting hurt, or you choose failure just to avoid the pain. I think what he meant was that there is risk and pain no matter what you choose, because choosing not to act can bring a pain all of its own. And . . . and I think you'd probably agree that you'd choose Dad again, even knowing you were going to lose him . . . right?"

There was a muffled sob, and Lynn's eyes burned. She hadn't meant to make her mom sad.

"Y-yes, honey. Yes I would." Matilda's voice was tremulous, but there was no doubt in it. "Otherwise, I never would have had you. You were the best thing your father ever gave me."

The burning in Lynn's eyes intensified. She coughed to clear her throat and rolled to face away from the bathroom where Eva was brushing her teeth. It took a minute to quell her emotions. When she was calm again, she simply said:

"I like Steve, Mom. I think he's done the best he could, considering the circumstances. But I'll support whatever you decide to do. Just take care of yourself, okay?"

"I will, honey. Promise me you'll do the same?"

"I've got Edgar for that," Lynn said on a whim, a smile tugging at her lips.

"Hmm, that you do," Matilda said, and Lynn could see in her mind's eye the interest lighting her mother's eyes. If she said one word about *grandchildren* . . .

"Get some sleep, honey."

"Okay, Mom. Love you."

"Love you, too, sweetie."

Jonnie Inanis hated sleep. It was such a stupid waste of time. It was probably the second greatest impediment to his mission, after the global capitalist elite. The average person spent a *third* of their life asleep. Thirty years! There was so much he could be doing in that time instead of lying around, unconscious. Like infiltrating the mesh systems of bloated, capitalist monopolies like Tsunami Entertainment. As it was, he went as long as he could on stims before crashing just long enough to think straight again.

He wasn't an idiot. He knew perfectly well how unhealthy his lifestyle was. But it didn't matter, because by the time it would kill him, medicine would have advanced enough to fix it. You could already buy custom repair tissue grown from your own DNA—if you were rich enough. Which was exactly the sort of evil, capitalistic shit that proved how badly the current system needed to be torn down. Health was a universal human right. Charging money for healthcare was the equivalent of murder.

Besides, *he* was sacrificing his health for the good of the common man. If anyone deserved access to advanced medicine, it was him.

Jonnie took a swig of his stim drink, then went back to glowering at his display while he obsessively twisted and turned his Gigaminx Rubik's Cube, running through long-memorized algos to keep his tactile senses engaged. Tsunami's security net was the tightest he'd ever seen, and so far he'd been unable to hack it. It was galling. He wasn't "J-nonymous," the best hacker in the Western Hemisphere, for nothing. After MIT had kicked him out for "unethical behavior" he'd gone back to live with his mom while he expanded his shadow mesh contacts and started to really make a name for himself.

Then the FBI had come knocking.

It'd only been that whiny, moralizing lawyer his parents had hired that kept him out of jail. He'd played along, for obvious reasons. Afterwards, his mom had actually *kicked him out*. Seriously? *She* was the one who'd taught him to fight the system in the first place! Apparently all her big talk and flags and activism were just a sham to get attention. When it came down to it, she was just as much a capitalist pig as the faculty at MIT.

His shadow mesh gigs had given him enough of a cushion that he'd gotten the hell out of dodge. There'd been plenty of resistance groups around the globe desperate for his expertise. Room and board were usually shitty, but it just fueled his determination to bring down the global capitalist elite. It was so obvious how greedy they were, how could anyone miss it? The fact that they were so rich and the rest of the world was poor was all the proof he needed.

Currently he was holed up in Hong Kong with the main cell of TPACT—The People Against Capitalistic Tyranny, or Anticap, as some called it. It was all pretty corny, but it wasn't the least impressive resistance name he'd ever worked with. There'd been that one based in California called The Global Rise of Mankind Against the Capitalistic Tyranny of the Patriarchal Pigs. Any idiot who tried to abbreviate their name to TGROMATCTOTPP wasn't worth his time. Plus they were too soft. Too much talk and hand-wringing, like his mom. He'd moved on pretty fast.

The oppressed masses needed bold action, not cowardly talk. And he needed *big* gigs to get his name out. He knew he was the best, but the hacker world was just as elitist and snobby as MIT. J-nonymous would never become a byword on the shadow mesh unless he pulled off some really high-profile hacks.

That's why he'd been crashing with TPACT for a while.

TPACT at least put their money where their mouth was. They funded subversive demonstrations all over the world, tricked the idiot universities into taking their money and using it for special student programs, that sort of thing. They had an HQ in the US, of course, but they couldn't let their *real* work go on there. Too many lawsuits and media attention. So they'd set up this cell in Hong Kong. China was just as guilty of capitalistic oppression as the US, obviously, but their police were easier to bribe, and TPACT had an agreement with the Hong Kong police and the local triad.

This time last year, he'd been busy trying to access the training vaults of various social media AI. If he could get access, TPACT could insert subtle revolutionary thinking into the algorithms and help society wake up to the tyranny they lived under—and he could plant subtle conditioning that would make his name go down in history. It would have been a massive undertaking, but a worthy one if he could establish an access point.

That had proven a bigger and more amorphous project than he'd anticipated, though. It'd gotten unreasonably tedious. So he'd switched focus, drawn by the meteoric rise of TD Hunter.

Gaming had always been a guilty pleasure. It was a stress regulator and expanded the human imagination in ways the corrupt system couldn't control. He never paid to play, of course, or paid for any in-game purchases or ad-blocking. What was the point of being a hacker if you didn't steal revenue from the bloated corporations for the benefit of mankind? He and some old high school buddies used to play PVP games once a week. WarMonger was a favorite, though he'd always hated the merc system it enabled. Players like Larry the Snake and NeoPunisher were just more privileged old white men exploiting the system to hoard money and make the game unplayable for everyone else.

When TD Hunter had come out, though, all his old buddies had become obsessed with it, and were never in virtual anymore. They were too busy having fun killing monsters, getting exercise and healthy Vitamin D—all things *he* was deprived of because the racist pigs at Tsunami wouldn't let Chinese players access the game. The Japanese got it. The Koreans got it. Vietnam got it. But no, China was "mean" to the US, so they were cut off from the most revolutionary game of the century.

Sure, Western media claimed it was actually China blocking the app in their own country. But everyone knew that was just a convenient excuse to blame China for all the problems caused by behind-the-scenes politics of greedy corporations.

It was unfair, racist, and bigoted, pure and simple. Just more proof that Tsunami was in league with the US political elite, spreading toxic masculinity and oppressive patriarchy everywhere.

He'd convinced TPACT that the TD Hunter AI—Hugo, of all the stupid names—was a better target for his skills because it was the most advanced AI in human history. If he could just free it from Tsunami's clutches, then the possibilities for a fairer world were endless. As a bonus, if he could get the algorithm to the Chinese, they could make their own version of TD Hunter, and he could finally play it himself.

But to do that, he had to find a way through Tsunami's security.

The lights over Jonnie's head abruptly flickered, then went out.

"Again?" he grumbled to himself, casting an eye over his extensive mesh station setup, which was all connected to a double layer of backup batteries. He'd learned in the last six months not to rely on the local grid. He'd thought Hong Kong would have a robust grid system, considering how much commerce and banking transactions flowed through it. But the blackouts kept happening. Seemed to be getting worse, actually. But maybe that was just because of the summer heat.

"Hey Kate! Go grab the battery lights! And order some takeout while you're at it!" Jonnie yelled over his shoulder in the general direction of his fellow hacker. He heard a shuffling behind him, the sound of something toppling over, and a fervent curse. Jonnie ignored it.

Kate wasn't anywhere near as good of a hacker as him, so he let her worry about the things that would be a waste of his time, like getting food and cleaning the suite they shared with a few other hackers. She wasn't an idiot or anything, just not in his league. Pretty good looking, though, except for her pixie haircut. She'd be hotter with long, wavy hair.

He'd assumed, when he'd first moved to this cell in Hong Kong, that he'd have a chance with her. But apparently she only had the hots for Asian dudes. He made sure she knew what she was missing, but didn't waste time on her otherwise. There were enough governments out there who would love to throw him in a cold gray cell, he knew better than to shit in his own bed.

Sometimes he daydreamed about moving back to the US and setting up shop somewhere remote. Maybe on an island in the Caribbean. But he wasn't an idiot. He had to be on multiple watch lists. The NSA and FBI probably had a whole file on him and everything.

No, Hong Kong was safer, at least for now.

The lights still hadn't come back on, but Jonnie soon forgot about it and kept staring at his display, fingers moving on automatic as he continued twisting his Gigaminx.

He was getting nowhere looking for another angle of attack. He'd tried brute force, he'd tried Trojans, he'd tried coming at it frontward, backward, and sideways. There was a solution out there. Every system had a weakness. But it was stupid to waste time when there was an easier way.

He just hated it.

Human error always had been and always would be the greatest weakness in digital security. Cyber gangs around the world made billions of dollars a year off of people's stupidity and gullibility. It wasn't a surefire or predictable method, but someone always made a mistake, eventually.

The problem was that phishing attacks were lame, boring, and low class. Any ignorant, lazy Nigerian thug could execute a phishing scheme. It was so beneath him—basically the same as admitting defeat. But it was his only option at this point if he wanted the world to know J-nonymous before some other hacker claimed the glory. The shadow boards were always buzzing with gossip about the latest numb nut who'd tried—and failed—to crack Tsunami. The dumb ones boasted about it before they tried. The smart ones—like him—kept their mouths shut until they had something to show. No *real* hacker would be impressed if they knew he'd taken a shortcut. Then again, everyone had been trying to get access to TD Hunter since it came out. Those schlubs would be so impressed he'd done it at all they wouldn't care how.

Jonnie huffed a breath out through his nose and tossed the Gigaminx onto a table crowded with tools, node parts, and old takeout containers. He was sick and tired of this stupid apartment. He wanted to get *out*, and TD Hunter was his golden ticket to the recognition he deserved.

He hoped the pigs at Tsunami all had heart attacks when they found out he'd stolen their precious game.

Chapter 6

THE NEXT FEW WEEKS MADE LYNN THINK MAYBE BEING IN THE military wouldn't be too bad. Yes, the days were long and exhausting. Yes, she grew to hate running even more than she thought possible. Yes, she hardly had a moment's peace between the guys chattering all day and rooming with Eva at night. But the Hunters units stayed focused, worked hard, and soaked up everything their trainers had to offer—barring that one room party Team Florida Man had organized, anyway. Lynn heard it had involved wine snuck in from the kitchens and a significant lack of clothing among the attendees.

Lynn had never in her life contemplated joining the military, but it was weirdly relaxing to have a set schedule and someone else in charge of planning what to do.

When she made the joking comment to Gadsden one evening during dinner, though, he nearly choked on the filet mignon steak he was inhaling. His Lone Star teammates gave him some hearty slaps on the back while they laughed uproariously. He laughed too once he was no longer choking.

"Bless yer heart," he'd finally said once he was capable of speech again. "We're living like kings and queens, here, sweetheart. Uncle Sam's purse strings are as tight as the Devil's sphincter when it comes to the troops. This?" He waved a fork around at The Greenbrier dining hall. "This is Tsunami's doing, not CIDER's, sure as hogs are made'a bacon."

Lynn shrugged. He had a point. Maybe what she'd been enjoying was the best of both worlds that had come together in this desperate gamble: military organization and single-mindedness combined with all the wheel-greasing and efficiency corporate America had to offer.

Not a bad combination, all things considered, at least if you had a secret alien invasion to repulse.

Lynn was almost sad to see The Greenbrier go when they finished their four weeks of preliminary training and were transported to Greenbrier Valley Airport. There they boarded three large airbuses headed to Minot Air Force Base in North Dakota, which boasted the largest indoor AR simulation training grounds in the US. There, the Hunter Strike Teams would integrate with their Alpha Tester counterparts and run simulated boss battles for two weeks.

Then it would be showtime.

After the time they'd spent vulture-free at The Greenbrier, Lynn felt her internal anxiety level tick back upward when they were met by a swarm of paparazzi drones at the airport. As instructed, the Hunters smiled and waved. They were just one big happy group of gamers, after all, excited to graduate to the next leg of their all-expenses-paid gaming adventure as members of the TransDimensional Counterforce.

There was a nervous energy flowing beneath all the conversation on the airbus, and quite a few Hunters looked as green as she felt to be flying now that they knew the cause of the mysterious airbus accidents. She couldn't stop remembering that heart-stopping feel of her stomach levitating into her throat as she'd dropped like a rock through the air when her airbus had stalled on the way to Des Moines. The fact that it had restarted seconds later and everything turned out fine in the end wasn't much comfort to her lizard brain instincts.

Lynn stayed very close to Edgar during the two-hour flight. She didn't say anything, but he seemed to understand, and didn't give her questioning looks, or crack endless jokes like Dan and Mack did further down their row. He was solid, calm, and reassuring.

Having Alpha Company's squad and platoon leaders on the flight was reassuring, too. They all sat by unit, while Trainer Bowers rode at the front, speaking to the safety officer on board. He'd assured them all when they'd lifted off that the airbus was a military-rated vehicle and had multiple redundant systems. As far as anyone knew, no military vehicle had been crashed by the spooks, only civilian ones.

But there was a first time for everything.

Lynn didn't breathe freely again until they landed at Minot Air Force Base and were shown to their temporary billet, a long, low two-story building of boring gray concrete. Their rooms were decidedly less luxurious than at The Greenbrier, with linoleum floors, plain metal bunks, small side tables, and chests of drawers that had seen better days. Lynn didn't mind. The flat gray and blue shades of the floors and walls were sweet relief to her poor eyeballs. The Greenbrier had been an impressive place, but she never wanted to see another gigantic floral pattern in her life.

They were bunked four to a room, which meant Eva went to stay with the other three girls from Amaranth while Lynn got to spend quality time with the three women from 3rd Squad, the second of the two Hunter squads in her platoon. There was Sally "RopingStar" Feldman, a buddy of Gadsden's from his youthful rodeo days who now helped manage rodeos all over Texas. Oh, and she ran marathons for fun. Apparently there'd been some drama on the rodeo circuit and she'd been thinking of taking a break when Gadsden had invited her to join Team Lone Star. Lynn learned she was a big fan of survivalist games, especially anything that involved big, dangerous predators. That little tidbit had elicited a grin from Lynn, and she thought she and Sally would get along just fine.

The other two ladies, MaraSkywalker01 and Ch'hala_Hears_You, were from Team Zahn Wars, the Hunter Strike Team from Illinois. When Lynn raised an eyebrow at their oddly specific gaming handles, Ch'hala launched into a rapid-fire geek-out over a super old science fiction book series they were all fans of, further evidenced by the handles of their other three members, Thrawn_Lives, TimothyRocks, and PlotTwist4U.

Her story involved a literary convention named LibertyCon, a mountain of Jell-O shots, and a drunken pledge made in the name of the late science-fiction author Timothy Zahn. Lynn kept her mouth shut during the story, trying to track the names and details and knowing she'd forget it all within minutes.

Zahn Wars seemed fueled more by enthusiasm, hard work,

and determination than any raw gaming talent. But they'd made it to Hunter Strike status, and the lot of them were welcoming and dedicated to the mission. Lynn figured she could forgive them their nerdy streak.

Overall, her roommate situation wasn't as painful as it could have been. The other women happily chatted about non-gaming related topics, so Lynn mostly stayed in her bunk and re-read the military manuals on leadership Steve had suggested to her when she'd been struggling to grow into her role as team captain. She would have preferred to bunk with the rest of her team, but... well, it was probably better not to create any opportunity for "distractions." Distractions who were tall, solid as a mountain, and had an uncanny ability to see right through to her soul.

The next day they kitted up and were shuttled directly from their barracks to the massive simulation center just off the base. The complex was built and maintained by a military contractor who also leased the space out to private entities for business training and recreational use whenever it wasn't reserved by the military. Tsunami had the whole complex blocked out for the next two weeks.

Tsunami had freely publicized their whole training itinerary—they *obviously* had nothing to hide. But since the simulation complex had the same military-spec anti-drone grid over it that the Air Force base next door used, the stream paparazzi had to wait until the last weekend of training for another chance at interviews or exclusive footage.

On the outside, the place looked like your standard convention center, if said convention center had been built for classified military training. There was a lot of concrete and metal, and no windows to speak of. None *at all.*

It took a while for everyone to disembark and file in, hydration packs on their back and headgear under their arm. Once they were inside, though, Lynn was surprised to see it wasn't at all the gloomy, claustrophobic space she'd expected. It was huge, airy, and open, a lot like the Austin convention center that had hosted Tsunami Fan Con. The polished concrete floors echoed with their steps as the three companies of Hunters streamed into the big space. Lynn's eyes darted around, taking it all in as Edgar, Ronnie, Mack, and Dan moved to flank her in a sort of automatic formation they seemed to adopt without realizing it.

"I hope they're not going to make us do sprints to the end of the hall and back," Mack subvocalized in their team chat. He sounded thoroughly depressed at the thought, and Lynn heartily agreed.

"Doubt it," Ronnie said, studying the wide-open space. "Looks like this end is set up for briefings and that end"—he jerked his chin at the far portion of the space—"is the simulation area. See the floor?"

Lynn noticed it now, the faint but distinct change in the gray floor from marbled, polished concrete to flat gray. She squinted curiously, but soon looked away as she followed their squad leader to the large square of folding chairs in rows with a sign above it that read "Alpha." There were two more similar sets of seating, marked "Bravo" and "Charlie." Milling about the seating were scores of muscular, serious-looking figures in TD Counterforce uniforms identical to the Hunters.

Lynn grinned.

"Derek!" she called out at the back of a familiar figure with nondescript brown hair and the most generic haircut you could imagine.

Derek Peterson turned, his face breaking into a grin as he spotted Lynn's group. The others around him turned as well, revealing Hayek, Crispy, Santoro, and Sonia, the rest of Derek's Team Light Brigade. Sonia was Derek's wife, and the other three seemed like old military buddies if Lynn had to guess, knowing now that they were CIDER Alpha Testers, not the "pest control contractors" they'd claimed to be.

Well, they *had* been doing pest control. Just not any pests native to earth.

The ingenuity of their cover story and the month Lynn had spent getting used to her new view of reality meant she clasped Derek's hand with genuine warmth. She liked Derek and his team, and was relieved she had no lingering resentment to exorcise.

"Good to see you, Raven," Derek said, eyes subtly checking her over as if to make sure she was all in one piece.

"You too, uh, Death?" Lynn said, remembering to check his handle. She suppressed a giggle at such an ominous handle for such an average-looking guy.

"At least it's better than mine?" Hayek grumbled, seeming to read her thoughts. "I am stuck with stupid 'Beer.'"

This time Lynn couldn't hold back a snort of laughter, which only got worse when she spotted Crispy's handle of "Stinkbug."

"You should have thought of *that*," Sonia said coolly, "when you picked your gaming handle, Mr. HoldMyBeer." She slid between Hayek's bulk and her husband's much more nondescript frame and took Lynn's hand in her cool, slender one. "Good to see you. Very impressive battle, down in Austin. We watched the whole thing." She flashed Lynn a brilliant white smile, and Lynn grinned in response.

"It was, uh, pretty nerve wracking. I never imagined it would end in . . . all this," Lynn finished, gesturing vaguely at the huge space around them where hundreds of people were milling and talking in subdued voices, including Hayek, Crispy, and Santoro as they exchanged handshakes and backslaps with her guys.

Sonia's brows angled outward and her eyes softened.

"I know. I'm sorry for that. *Everyone* wishes things were different. But they're not, so we'll make the best of what we've got, eh?" She briefly clasped Lynn's hand in both of hers.

"Yeah. You're right." Lynn took a deep breath in and out, then gave Sonia a forced smile. Sonia smiled back and nodded encouragingly, then turned to greet the others.

Lynn cut her eyes to Derek, who was looking around casually while almost certainly keeping a close ear on the conversation. She sent a private chat request to "Death" and Derek's eyes flicked to her as he accepted it.

"YodaMaster, you sneaky bastard," Lynn subvocalized, suppressing an upward twitch of her lips. "Consulting? Large scale pest control? I oughta frag you right here for being too clever for your own good."

She'd been thinking about it for weeks, and she was almost certain Derek had known all along she was Larry Coughlin. For one thing, Derek "YodaMaster" and Steve "FallujahSevenNiner" were close associates in WarMonger. For another, Derek had the same strange air of protectiveness that Steve had always exuded around her. She suspected the protectiveness came from Steve's inside knowledge of her double life, which meant Derek likely knew as well.

The idea had once terrified her. But now . . . now she was proud he knew.

Derek's eyes twinkled and a muted smile crept across his face, confirming her suspicions.

"Good to finally meet you in person, Larry," he replied in their private chat.

A strange sensation of hot, then cold washed down Lynn's body, and she shifted, rolling her shoulders to shake off the sensation. It was the first time she'd ever been addressed as Larry to her face. Sure, Steve knew, but he'd never looked right at her with that glint of respect in his eye and called her by her WarMonger handle.

"Be glad I like you, Yoda," Lynn subvocalized, pitching her voice lower with a bit of growl in it. It was tricky to do with subvocalization, but the sensors picked it up and translated it beautifully. "I usually only meet people in person to put a bullet in them."

Derek chuckled softly.

"You know, I didn't believe Fallu when he told me who you were in the real. I was sure the smug bastard was pulling my leg."

That made Lynn grin evilly, though she quickly sobered.

"Anyone else here know?" she asked, subvocalization tone returning to normal as she flicked her eyes around. Mack was busy introducing the rest of their squad to Light Brigade, while Dan, Hayek, and Crispy had their heads together, probably cooking up some kind of trouble. Sonia cast suspicious looks their way in between shaking hands with Team Amaranth.

"Not as far as I know," Derek said, then shrugged. "It's likely your leadership have been briefed on it, though, to minimize any disruptive surprises. My team was tapped early on to be a sort of 'overwatch' for Skadi's Wolves, but I'm the only one of my team who also fought with you in WarMonger, so I got pulled into the sacred *inner circle*." Lynn rolled her eyes, which made Derek's mouth crook upward. "It was nice, having a battle buddy like Fallu to commiserate with once I realized I'd been thrashed for years by a high school kid."

That brought Lynn's evil grin back, and she cocked her head thoughtfully.

"I think I was, hmmm, fourteen the first time I fragged you?"

"Yeah, thanks for reminding me." Now it was Derek's turn to look grumpy.

A call for attention echoed across the hall, and everyone started grabbing seats according to squad and platoon.

"See you out there, eh?"

"Looking forward to it, Death. Maybe sometime when all this is over, you, me, and Fallu can enjoy some good old death matches in WarMonger."

"I'm a soldier, you old snake. Not a masochist," Derek threw over his shoulder as he turned to join his team.

Lynn just grinned, hurrying to corral the guys toward their assigned seating.

Once all the shuffling had quieted, Lynn got a chat invite titled "Taskforce Sanctus." As she accepted, she noticed a familiar figure striding out to stand in front of all the seated gamers. Colonel Bryce settled into a parade rest and looked out across the almost four hundred people assembled. Three full companies of spook-killing machines.

"Good morning, Hunters," he began, words subvocalized. "From here on out, we will conduct all briefings, training, drills, and simulations via subvocalization. This is to prepare you for the field where you will be in front of billions of eyes, and must fight for the fate of humankind while they remain none-the-wiser. If you were not already doing so, make it a habit to use each other's handles in all conversation. Your discipline and discretion will help ensure as much safety as we can hope to provide to the public."

"Yes, sir!" came hundreds of replies from Lynn's earbud.

She was struck by a sudden thought that made her chuckle.

Colonel Bryce, head of force training, had not moonlit as a game actor simply because he was willing to do whatever it took to complete the mission. It was because it gave him the perfect cover to be seen with Tsunami's "TD Counterforce." After all, why not give your elite competition gamers the treat of interacting with the TD Hunter "actor" in person as part of their exclusive prep for the much-anticipated Battle Tour?

Lynn wondered what the stern, muscular colonel would do if she asked him for an autograph. Her lips twitched at the thought.

"I've been impressed by your dedication and progress over the past month at The Greenbrier," the Colonel continued. "It has been my pleasure to oversee your training, and I know you will devote yourselves with equal focus to these next weeks of simulations. Keep ever at the forefront of your mind that you are preparing to engage in very real battles with alien entities who have already taken hundreds of innocent lives across the country."

Lynn swallowed, her throat suddenly dry.

That many? When would it become too many for them to keep the secret any longer?

She shivered.

Next to her, Edgar shifted and pressed his solid, warm leg gently against hers. She looked up at him, and he gave her what she was coming to think of as his "I got you, *uce*," look. It was simultaneously cocky and reassuring, and it made the tension in her chest ease.

From there, things moved quickly. Trainer Bowers took over the briefing and described their unit exercises for the day. They would spend several days practicing full company formations before diving into various battle simulations. Then the trainer released them to their company commanders.

Everyone switched to their company-wide chat, and Abrams stood up to introduce all the Hunters to his Alpha Company staff. There was his Executive Officer, Malak "Khoury_ShadowStar" Khoury, as well as the leadership of all four platoons, including their heavy weapons platoon they'd been dying to meet. Alpha Company's heavy weapons platoon was nicknamed Hamilton's Own—apparently its platoon leader was a recovering history buff. The seventeen Alpha Testers waved cheerily at their introduction. They seemed similar to Edgar in temperament: happy for any excuse to shoot big guns and kill things.

It was extremely odd to engage in full briefs, introductions, and demonstrations in subvocalization mode. People still moved, paced, and used all the normal hand motions and body language. But their lips never moved.

Really weird.

Useful, though, in case any unauthorized drones were sniffing around. You couldn't even read lips when someone was subvocalizing. They'd have to trust in Hugo to keep out potential breaches from the mesh web. Lynn figured if anyone could do it, Hugo could.

From there, Abrams went over each of the heavy weapons units, the weapons they carried, what effects the weapons had, and what tactics were implied for their impending battle simulations.

Each heavy weapons platoon was made up of three squads, with only one five-man team in each squad instead of two. Each of the teams carried not only their personal weapons in the form of the usual twin batons, but also a piece of a larger, crew-served cannon type they'd named Pounders. The bulky omnipolymer sections would flow together to form a single unit, much like the batons did when going from single-handed to double-handed personal weapons. This crew-served cannon could morph into two separate modes: mortar mode for artillerylike, heavy hits, and machine-gun mode for close-range, overwhelming firepower.

Each company's heavy weapons platoon had one mission, and one mission only: destroy the nodalities. It was the job of the other three platoons to get them within effective range, destroy TDMs en masse to provide TEP fuel, and protect the heavy weapons for as long as it took to overwhelm and destroy each boss they went up against.

Lynn suspected it wouldn't turn out so nice and neat once they started facing real bosses. But then these Alpha Testers probably knew that far better than she did.

Abrams added before he wrapped up that CIDER's research and development team was working tirelessly to develop bigger and better weapons. Such weapons would be issued to Taskforce Sanctus as they became available, at which point their battle strategies might change to take their new capabilities into account.

You mean if *they became available?* Lynn wondered, not wanting to get her hopes up. She'd helped destroy multiple bosses already without the benefit of such weapons, so she felt confident they could complete their mission regardless of what the "lab coats" came up with.

Unless... the bosses got even bigger than Nagaraja. It was a possibility she couldn't discount.

Their briefing ended and they were directed to pick up their chairs and stack them on the empty racks waiting against the wall. For a few minutes the only sound was the scraping of metal on concrete—either everyone felt particularly sober, or else they'd taken the "no gossiping in the clear" directive to heart. Lynn suspected it was the former. Not even Dan cracked jokes in their team chat.

Once the area was clear, the various platoons spread out and the platoon leaders started their own briefings and introductions, integrating their Alpha Tester and Hunters into a coherent platoon.

The second Alpha Tester team in their platoon besides Light Brigade was Team Black Templars. The two Alpha Tester teams made up 1st Squad, led by Neutron, or Ernest "Mr_Ernie_Neutron" Tucker. They also got to meet their platoon assistant, Seb "SexyDruid" Blackwell, who pointed out at his introduction that he should properly be called "Sexy," but that due to boring Tsunami corporate rules he had to be called "Druid" instead. That got a chuckle out of most of the company. He was a lanky, black-haired man with a quick smile who had the disheveled gamer look down pat. By the easy way he responded to his handle, he was more of a serious gamer than most of the other Alpha Testers.

Team Black Templars seemed like a competent bunch, if much more stoic and rough-looking than Light Brigade. Based on what she knew of Steve, Lynn wondered if they were former SpecOps. They had that quiet, deadly look in their eyes. They would definitely have a harder time passing as everyday gamers than Light Brigade, which was probably why Derek and his team got their "overwatch" job instead of some other group of Alpha Testers. When mixed with all the Hunter Strike Teams, though, especially when everyone had their headgear on and things were moving fast, Lynn doubted spectators would notice the difference. Lynn did note Hermes clasping forearms, slapping backs, and exchanging heartfelt words with both Champion—or ChampionSigismund, captain of Team Black Templars—and Neutron. She guessed most of the Alpha Testers knew each other pretty well, since they'd been working together in CIDER for several years now.

Lynn mostly paid attention to her platoon and squad leaders, but snuck peeks at the other companies when she could, to see if she recognized anybody. Who else had she come in contact with besides Derek and his crew who had been Alpha Testers masquerading as everyday gamers?

She didn't spot anyone familiar, at least none of the Alpha Testers. One person she *did* spot wasn't an individual she wanted to dwell on.

Elena.

The pop-girl was in Bravo Company, 3rd Platoon, 3rd Squad, according to her handle designator in Lynn's display. "QueenBravo3-3" wasn't looking at her squad leader like the rest of her squad, but was instead surveying the room much like Lynn.

Lynn thought about ducking behind Edgar when Elena's gaze swung her way, but something stopped her. Maybe it was Derek's simple but profound acknowledgment of that part of her she'd kept hidden for so long. For whatever reason, Lynn simply straightened her spine and met Elena's eyes levelly when the girl looked her way. Elena paused, micro expressions passing over her face too quickly for Lynn to decipher. Then she seemed to snort to herself and dismiss Lynn, her eyes returning to their survey of the crowd.

The breath in Lynn's lungs unfroze and she took a deep, quiet inhale. Before turning away, she made note of Elena's team captain, squad leader, and platoon leader, just in case. Curiosity about Elena's near-miraculous restraint burned in her chest, but it would have to sit there and smolder. No good would come of it, and she had much bigger fish to fry.

Once introductions were over, the units spread out even more, and each company got to work on the boring but necessary work of practice formations, now that they were at full strength with a heavy weapons platoon.

Lynn was all for unit cohesion and Hunters knowing what the heck they were supposed to be doing. But formation training was the absolute worst, only slightly less painful than running. Gamers were not known for their discipline, at least when it came to being a part of a larger unit. Most of what they did was so abstract from the physical that the hand-eye-to-screen coordination many of them had been developing from early childhood didn't always translate well to spatial awareness in the real.

There were many moments when Abrams called a halt and had everyone go back to square one because some team or squad was wandering off course, despite their leadership's best effort. It got to the point that Hermes kept muttering "slow is smooth, smooth is fast," in their squad chat. He'd used it before, explaining the concept as, "don't try to do a thing faster than you can do it correctly." Mainly it seemed his way of telling his squad to quit grumbling and focus on doing things right instead of rushing the boring parts.

Lynn also suspected it was his personal touchstone to patience and sanity dealing with all these "gamer kids."

Somehow, they got through the formation drills. It helped that they were interspersed with PT and accuracy training, to keep things interesting.

Overall, their day of integration went well, and Lynn fell into her bunk that night exhausted as dozens of new names and handles scrolled on repeat through her head.

By day three, she was starting to feel the invisible tendrils of unit cohesion binding their platoon together. Skadi's Wolves, Amaranth, Lone Star, and Zahn Wars mixed freely and Lynn saw friendships starting to bud. Team Black Templars took longer to warm up to the Hunters, and Lynn guessed they would always be somewhat standoffish. Gadsden seemed to take their reticence as a personal challenge, though, and started working them over with his Texan charm. Lynn saw them crack a few smiles, so the Lone Star captain must have wiggled his way under their professional wall.

The three troublemakers from Light Brigade were thick as thieves with Dan, Grim, and Plot from Zahn Wars. Lynn wondered if it would be safer for the world if such a potent mix of reprobates were broken up. But Derek didn't seem alarmed by it, so Lynn didn't say anything either. Hayek, Crispy, and Santoro—or Beer, Stinkbug, and Mr. E as they were to be called in chat—were adults who were *supposedly* capable of keeping themselves in check. She needed to keep an eye on Dan, though, who had always considered rules to be more like guidelines. Ronnie spent an unusually large amount of time—for him, anyway—talking to Eva, and Lynn was flabbergasted to witness Ronnie acting almost . . . normal. Like he was sincerely interested in what Eva had to say and took her seriously.

It put Lynn in a mood of intense frustration. Why couldn't he act that normally with *her*? What had Eva said or done that she hadn't? When Lynn pointed it out to Edgar, not quite growling in frustration but close to it, Edgar's practical answer stopped her in her tracks.

"Don't let it get to you, *uce*. Eva never put him to shame. You did."

Lynn gaped at him, and Edgar huffed out an amused breath. "Being resentful's easier'n admitting you're wrong, yeah?"

Lynn groaned and rubbed her face, but let it go. Edgar was right. There was too much history between her and Ronnie to expect things to be easy. At least he'd learned how to treat *other* female gamers like peers worthy of respect instead of mutants with two heads.

Lynn was the only lucky recipient of *that* attitude.

They arrived for their first day of simulation training excited and chatty. Lynn was itching to do more than endless PT drills to keep their physical fitness up. She was also itching to get a closer look at that strangely flat gray floor.

The mass of Hunters and Alpha Testers, hydration packs and headgear in place, separated into their units while Trainer Bowers started up the Taskforce wide chat.

"For those unfamiliar with this facility's state-of-the-art simulation arena," he subvocalized, "please turn this way and observe. A simulation view will activate on your display, overlaying the simulation arena."

With a flicker of graphics, the flat, gray floor spreading out over an area the size of a small city block transformed into a busy downtown street. Lynn bit her lip to hold in a gasp. The graphics were flawless, and she had a bit of cognitive dissonance as her eyes lit on the demarcation line where the smooth gray floor gave way to concrete. There, the simulation stopped as abruptly as if it had been cleaved off by a giant samurai sword.

A variety of autonomous vehicles filled the street and people crowded the sidewalks, appearing and disappearing smoothly from the edges of the simulation. Trainer Bowers let them eye the perfectly realistic scene in front of them for a while before he started talking.

"First generation VR simulations were incredibly useful for military training application, but they had exactly the drawback you'd expect from anything in VR: a lack of physical stimuli to help our minds connect what was being learned to our inherently embodied experience of the world. Or to put it in plain English, simulations could train the mind, but not the body. This facility was built to help solve that problem."

Trainer Bowers snapped his fingers, and the simulation overlay vanished.

Lynn gasped.

Where before the gray arena had been perfectly flat, now an exact replica of the simulation's stationary layout had appeared, seemingly flowing up from the floor itself. It was a perfect replica down to the crumbling curb in one spot and the manhole covers in the street. Gray tree trunks grew out of the gray sidewalk interspersed with gray park benches and gray trash cans. Gray vehicles parked in neat rows alongside gray parking meters. The gray buildings rose to ten feet—the maximum height needed for most human interaction—before abruptly cutting off in midair. Lamp posts, traffic lights, and trees cut off similarly at exactly the same height across the city block. The only things missing were the people and moving vehicles.

Trainer Bowers snapped his fingers again, and the simulation reappeared, though this time it, too, left out the moving vehicles and people. They were faced with a silent city street, aglow in mid-afternoon light.

"Ready for the *really* fun part?" the trainer asked, his subvocalized voice tinged with humor.

He snapped his fingers again, and the street was suddenly filled to bursting with teeming masses of TDMs.

Several people jumped and Lynn heard one person scream. Had that been Elena?

Admittedly, her own fight or flight response had spiked, and adrenaline now coursed through her veins, making her shift uncomfortably. The TDMs looked just as real as they always did, and Lynn's ears were filled with the sounds of their roars, growls, hisses, clicks, and screeches.

None of them advanced, though. Because, of course, it was a simulation.

But we could *be surrounded by spooks right now, and we wouldn't know until we opened up our interfaces and checked. Dang, I hate this...*

Knowing that the majority of TDM were harmless to be around—at least in moderate numbers—didn't make her feel better.

Finished with his demonstration, Bowers shut off the simulation and they all got to watch as the arena's topography sank back into the floor at the same pace their own omnipolymer batons transformed.

"That's right," Bowers subvocalized, echoing her thoughts. "You are looking at a standard city block's worth of advanced omnipolymer. It's much tougher than the stuff your batons are made out of, since the batons were designed to *not* be bludgeoning weapons. The omnipolymer layer is many feet deep, and there's a floor underneath that raises and lowers as necessary depending on how much polymer is needed to create the topography.

"That said, these structures are *not* as robust as the real thing. Don't go crashing into walls or jumping onto vehicles. If something breaks by accident, don't sweat it, though. The entire thing is a mass of programmable plastic. It can reform whatever gets broken."

"You know who'd *love* to rent out this building," said Brent "KissMyChainsword" Dudgeon in their platoon chat. "Those crazy 40K LARPing groups. Can you imagine how epic it would be to have a live action battle ground with *real* 40k terrain?"

Lynn glanced to the side and saw Team Black Templars exchange raised eyebrows and appreciative glances at the now-flat simulation arena. It reminded her that every single Alpha Tester had been hand-picked for their gaming knowledge and experience.

Apparently even insanely ripped, scary SpecOps guys liked to game.

Team Zahn Wars also seemed to perk up at Kiss' comment, and Lynn wondered if they did live action role play too. LARPing was something Dan and Mack had talked longingly of on and off for years, but either they'd never found a group to join in Cedar Rapids, or they'd never had the guts to get out in the real world and hit each other with latex weapons. She'd scoffed at the idea of LARPing back in her WarMonger days when she'd still bought into her insecurities. But now... who knew. The exercise would be nice and it might be fun to fight people in the real instead of spooks.

"For the next ten days," said Trainer Bowers, "you will run through dozens of boss battle simulations, the nodality and location specifics pulled directly from real cities listed on your Battle Tour. And, to keep things interesting, we're making it a competition. All the normal TD Hunter scoring will be tracked, though it will be weighted differently. Total kills and power use efficiency are the priority, with kill-to-damage ratio and accuracy secondary, and all other scores such as kill combos and weapon-specific scoring tertiary. At the end of training, whichever company has the highest overall score wins themselves a pizza party courtesy of Happy Joe's Pizza."

There was a round of whooping and back slapping, and Lynn grinned. It would be nice to work toward something concrete that wasn't the life-or-death survival of mankind. She'd had no idea Happy Joe's franchises had spread as far out as North Dakota, but she was happy to enjoy a taste of home.

Because *obviously* Alpha Company was going to win, or her name wasn't Lynn "Larry Coughlin" Raven.

"Alpha Company," Bowers continued, "you're first up with simulation arena 1. Bravo Company, your CO will lead you to the next building over to simulation arena 2. Charlie Company, you get the short stick today. You get to enjoy PT drills before your first simulation. We'll rotate daily so each company gets a chance to start off their first simulation after being worked over by your platoon leaders."

There was a flurry of groans from Charlie Company, but everyone broke up in good order and got to work.

They ran simulations all day until long after dinner. Then they stumbled to bed, got up at the crack of dawn, and did the whole thing over again. There were regular hydration breaks, as well as meal breaks three times a day. Box meals were delivered en masse, most of them cold, though the dinners came in self-heating containers. Gadsden along with Santoro—who considered himself something of an MRE connoisseur—agreed that the food was definitely better than Army fare, but a sad, sad substitute to the nectar of the gods they'd enjoyed at The Greenbrier.

Each simulation had a thirty-minute reset and debriefing after it where they broke down into platoons and squads to discuss tactics, what had gone well, and what hadn't. Lynn was answerable for her team's performance, and had to alternatively push and pull back on various members. Mack had it the worst. He was likely one of the few, or maybe the *only,* Hunter present who had already been injured by the spooks. The experience had taken on a new sort of trauma for him, now that he knew the TDM threat was real. Lynn gently pushed him as much as she could without making his trauma worse, but she worried what might happen when their Battle Tour began. Would Mack give into his fear?

Ronnie had the opposite problem. He seemed suicidally aggressive, as if he were *daring* the spooks to hurt him. Lynn didn't know what sort of internal demons he was fighting, but she had her work cut out for her keeping him in line with the rest of their team and squad.

The week flew by, and before she knew it, it was Sunday, their day off to rest and recuperate. They had to stay in their barracks, but had access to the entire mesh web via their LINCs, so there was plenty of entertainment material and busy tasks in virtual to keep them occupied. During the week they were given a little free time each evening, but personal matters still built up, considering this training had kept them from their everyday lives for weeks.

Lynn had eaten breakfast and was lazing in her bunk, trying to decide between binge-watching funny cat vids or braving the news streams, when a voice chat request popped up. Lynn's insides clenched at the sight of who it was.

Steve Riker.

She took a deep, slow, calming breath. Then another. She considered a third, but bit the bullet and accepted the request instead.

"Hey, kid," Steve said. He sounded casual, but Lynn didn't think she imagined the hint of uncertainty in his voice. Fortunately, he didn't pause for some awkward exchange of greeting, but went straight on to his point. "If you're up for it, Mr. Krator still wants you for this Larry Coughlin TD Hunter ad they're launching soon. It's already been cleared with your leadership. You can pop down to the barracks entrance right now, I've got a Tsunami airbus here to shuttle you to their recording studio. You'll be back by dinnertime."

Lynn was so stunned she didn't know what to say.

Steve was *here*? Right *now*? Why hadn't Tsunami's marketing department given her a heads up? And why was *Steve* their messenger? Hadn't he quit Tsunami?

The obvious answer occurred to her a moment later, shoving its way through her confused shock. Steve was the only person in the world who had intimate knowledge of all four entities involved: Tsunami, CIDER, Larry Coughlin, and Lynn Raven.

"Lynn?" Steve said, the uncertainty in his voice more pronounced.

Lynn shook her head to clear it and responded.

"Sorry, I'm here. Just, uh, processing?"

"Copy that. I got woken up with these orders at zero dark thirty. You're not alone."

The grumpiness in his words made Lynn's lips twitch, and the tension in her chest eased. This was still Steve. He kept it mostly hidden, but she could see his heart poking through.

The question remained, though, was she up for this? All the questions and worries from the spring when Mr. Krator had first asked if she would help with their new TD Hunter ad starring Larry came flooding back. He'd assured her then that she didn't have to physically participate if she didn't want to. She'd already signed the necessary contract for Tsunami to use Larry Coughlin's voice and likeness in their campaign. They could hire someone else to do the stunts, though the ad would be less authentically Larry without her input.

And *that* was what gave her pause.

Three months ago, she'd been held back by fear of exposure—not just being face-to-face with strangers, but the possibility that her alter ego would get out. Those fears remained, but they paled in comparison to her visceral, gut-level discomfort with the idea of anyone else playing Larry Coughlin.

Of playing *her*.

"I'll do it," Lynn said.

"Glad to hear it, kid," Steve responded, the smile evident in his tone.

"So how am I supposed to do this? Won't everyone notice I've disappeared for a day?"

"Nope," Steve said. "You've got the day off. Everyone's doing their own thing. I'll bet ninety percent of your pals will be glued to the streams all day. Your leadership already knows you're leaving, and they're CIDER, so they don't expect to be told why. I'll have you back in time for dinner, and if anyone asks where you are at lunch, say you have stomach trouble. It's not like you tell your roommates where you're going every time you leave the room, right?"

He had a point.

"Okay, but what should I wear? What should I bring?"

"Don't worry about any of that. I've got everything you need here in the bus. Just walk out like you're taking a stroll. The bus is within sight of the doors, fanciest piece of shit you ever saw. Won't be hard to spot."

Well, so much for funny cat vids.

Lynn took a deep breath. "Got it. See you in a few."

The airbus was, indeed, the "fanciest piece of shit" Lynn had ever seen. Sleek and expensive-looking, though without any sort of logo or marking to identify it. The door opened automatically when she got close, and she cast one last look over her shoulder at the barracks before she climbed inside.

"Whoa," Lynn said, looking around.

"My reaction exactly," Steve chuckled. He was sitting in the leather-clad rotating seat that doubled as the pilot's seat if someone were to take manual control of the airbus. Small capacity commercial airbuses didn't have them, just in case some unsupervised rando decided to start tinkering with the systems and get themselves killed. Large commercial airbuses had them, but they also had a safety operator to keep an eye on it and take over manual operation if something crazy happened.

This airbus was in a different category, clearly a privately owned, custom-made vehicle. She wasn't thrilled to be flying again, but if she had to travel via airbus, this one was likely one of the safest choices available.

"Let me guess . . . one of Mr. Krator's fleet?" Lynn asked, looking around at the wood paneling—was that *real* wood?—leather reclining seats, generous bar, and other luxuries she'd never seen in an airbus before.

"Got it in one." Steve grinned. "Nothing like a bit of buttering up to make your day better, right?"

Lynn shrugged. "I mean, if you're going to get dragged out of bed on a surprise mission to create wartime propaganda to convince more innocent people to become unwitting foot soldiers, you might as well enjoy yourself while doing it, right?"

Steve's smile faded, though he didn't look away. He held Lynn's gaze, his expression tired but open. Not guilty. Not defensive. Lynn knew he'd done what he had to do, what he thought was right, even if it hurt.

Finally, she let him off the hook and looked away.

"We should probably get going, right?" she said, looking around again at the luxurious interior.

"Soon as you strap in, kid."

In no time they were in the air, speeding toward Austin. It was a little over two hours to their destination, and for a while Lynn wondered if she could get away with spending the entire trip in silence.

Probably not.

She wasn't trying to give Steve the cold shoulder, she just

didn't know what to say. As the minutes of silence stretched on and she sank deeper and deeper into the luxurious leather body-mold chair, it became plain he was in no hurry to start a conversation either. Was he at a loss for words too? He remained at the front, seat pointed toward the controls and the large front windows looking out over the patchwork of North Dakota farmland far below. Did he really need to be up there at the controls? Or was he hiding?

The thought was amusing. Lynn wondered if it wouldn't be a relief to both of them to simply hop onto WarMonger and work out their differences in a one-on-one match, merc to merc.

It was a tempting thought...

Eventually, though, she heard him take a deep breath, and the seat swiveled toward her. Steve pushed to his feet, came to the middle of the airbus, and sat down on the leather seat opposite her. He didn't look at her though. He leaned forward, elbows on knees, hands clasped in front of him, and contemplated the floor. Lynn wasn't sure who he was trying to spare: himself or her.

It wasn't helping. Now that the moment was here, she would rather get it over with.

"I'm not mad at you," she said into the silence. "At least... not much," she amended wryly as his head came up and he met her eyes.

"You're doing better than me," he said, voice rough and eyes intense. "*I'm* mad at me. After my wife died, I swore I'd never put myself in a position again where I'd have to keep secrets from the people I loved. And then I went right ahead and did it again."

Lynn's heart stuttered. It was so unexpected. So direct. Unapologetic.

... the people I loved.

Lynn closed her eyes, fighting a swell of emotion so tangled she had no idea if she wanted to laugh, cry, or punch Steve in the face.

A vision of her father's bright blue eyes and lopsided grin tipped the scales toward tears. She rubbed her face, trying to push away the hot prickle and get herself under control.

"I'm sorry, kid," Steve said softly. "Sorry life threw you this curveball. Sorry I had to lie to you. Sorry I wasn't better at keeping my distance from you and your mom."

"No!" Lynn said, glaring fiercely at him.

His eyes widened.

"Don't apologize for loving my mom." *Or me*, she thought, but couldn't bring herself to say. "Apologize for not showing up on her doorstep with flowers and chocolate and groveling until she forgave you! You haven't even *called* her, you coward!"

Steve's alarm morphed to shame and he scrubbed his face with both hands, leaning back into the leather chair, head tilted back.

"She said *get out*. What was I supposed to do?"

"Not take that as an excuse to abandon her for weeks on end when she's terrified and hurting," Lynn snapped.

Steve sat upright and met her eyes again, jaw tight.

"Damn," he muttered. "I'm a bastard."

"Ya think?" Lynn said, giving him a healthy dose of scorn. "I'd already pretty much forgiven you for myself. I get it, you were doing your job. You can't go around blabbing about world-ending secrets, not even to"—she swallowed—"people you care about. But once we knew, you sure as *hell* could have lifted a finger to repair the damage. Guess you've been *too busy* saving the world, huh?"

She expected him to get angry, to deny it. But all he did was sigh and shake his head. Not in negation, but in defeat.

"You're right, kid. I was a coward. I was afraid I'd hurt her more if I pushed things before she was ready. I hoped she'd give me a second chance. Guess I was too terrified of screwing it up. Figured it was safer to hunker down and wait."

Lynn snorted, though the fire behind it was gone.

"Also..." Steve hesitated, and Lynn raised an eyebrow. His mouth twisted to the side and he let out a wry expulsion of breath. "I didn't know how to convince her I was sincere. I bet she thinks I came on to her just to keep an eye on *you*. I mean, I *was* supposed to keep an eye on you, but I definitely didn't need her as an excuse. I had Hugo for that."

Lynn's brows drew down, and a cold, aching part of her that she'd shoved down in the dark struggled to crawl out of its hole.

"So, you were spying on me through the game AI?"

Steve had the grace to look embarrassed. He shrugged.

"Technically, no. Hugo was monitoring you, and it let us know if there was a problem, same as for any other player. But if *you* had a problem, we definitely responded to it differently than if you'd been some Jane Doe."

Lynn looked away. She was mad, and mad at herself for being mad.

It was one thing to know that opting into the digital world and running your entire life through a LINC meant your life was never truly private. It was another entirely to get slapped in the face with it. Service AIs were supposed to have all sorts of privacy safeguards. Companies assured users that their privacy was secure, that personalization made their experience better. Everyone knew their actions and choices were being recorded and scrutinized by algorithms to optimize their life and make it easier. It was *normal.*

And then there was Hugo.

When you created a program to save the world, did it matter if it lied to do it? Could a binary stream of numbers be "sorry" for breaking someone's trust? Was it her fault for humanizing Hugo in her own mind?

She shook her head, refocusing on Steve. She wanted to demand his word that he'd never lie to her again. But she knew perfectly well he couldn't promise that, and it would be cruel to ask. So instead, she took a deep breath, and tried not to let fear get the better of her.

"I forgive you."

Steve grinned, a bit of tension leaving his face. "But, you're still gonna teabag me next chance you get, right?"

Lynn spluttered in laughter.

"You kidding me? Teabagging is too good for the likes of you. I'm going to tell all our merc contacts that you stood up this really nice lady in the real, and that you deserve a royal thrashing for it. You won't be able to poke so much as your little toe into a match without getting dogpiled once I spread the word."

"Ouch." Steve winced. "Guess it's time to hang up my War-Monger laurels. It was a good run while it lasted."

"Oh, no you don't," Lynn said, eyes narrowing, "because I'm going to tell mom to ask you every week for a funny story of you getting owned in WarMonger. And every week, you're going to tell her about the latest takedown, and you're going to make her *laugh.*"

Steve's eyebrows rose higher and higher as she went on, and he finally leaned back, looking impressed. And relieved.

"To do that, I'd have to actually *talk* to her every week, right? Or were you imagining some sort of psychic connection?"

"Oh, you'll talk to her, all right. You'll talk to her *tonight*, as soon as you drop me off at the barracks. *Got it*?"

"Yessir, ma'am," Steve said faintly, a bit green around the edges.

Lynn snorted and crossed her arms, finally relaxing into her own chair.

"Now that we've got *that* cleared up, can I get a drink and watch cat vids until we get to Austin?"

Steve chuckled and raised his hands, palms out.

"Be my guest. I'm pretty sure there's enough soda and snacks in there to keep even a hungry teenager happy."

With a groan of tired muscles, Lynn levered herself out of the delicious embrace of the body-mold chair and went to investigate the bar. She found her favorite pop and, to her astonishment, a staggering supply of premium buffalo jerky.

"Is it just me, or is Mr. Krator trying to bribe me?" she asked Steve, showing him the enormous stash of cured meat.

"I dunno," Steve said, eyes twinkling. "Maybe he just likes you?"

Lynn's eyebrows scrunched down as she tried to decipher that.

"Uhhh, isn't that a little creepy?"

"No, I wouldn't say so." Steve shook his head. "You know he doesn't have any family, right? Parents passed, no siblings, no spouse, no kids. Tsunami is everything to him. I don't know him that well, no more than as a boss. But from what I've seen, he treats his employees *very* well. I think Tsunami is a sort of surrogate family to him. He remembers detail, too. Pretty sure he has an eidetic memory. You mention offhand you like a certain food, and boom, next thing you know it's being served fresh in the cafeteria. He doesn't make a big deal out of it, he just does it."

"Huh," Lynn said, looking back at the jerky. Finally she shrugged, grabbed a bag, and settled in to enjoy herself.

They chatted about inane things while Lynn fought the urge to ask Steve what he *really* thought about the spooks, CIDER, humanity's chances for survival—all of it. Would he even be able to talk to her openly? Or was she still not *in the know*?

Finally, she couldn't resist anymore.

"Are we going to make it?" she asked.

Her expression must have clued Steve in that the abrupt change of subject wasn't about their flight to Austin.

"I . . . don't know, kid. Nobody does."

Lynn gritted her teeth. It wasn't the answer she'd wanted to hear.

"Okay, but are we making the right moves? Attacking the bosses? Clearing the cities?"

"Sure, if we want to prevent widespread infrastructure failure."

"Buuut . . . ?"

Steve let out an explosive sigh and ran a hand through his close-cropped, salt-and-pepper hair.

"Lynn . . . we have *no idea* where these things are coming from, or how to stop more of them from appearing. Of course we need to try and preserve our cities, protect the public as much as we can, but . . . it won't do shit to make the situation better. It's just a stopgap."

Fear gripped Lynn's throat, and she tried to swallow past it.

"What are we going to do?" she said, clearing her throat to get the wobble out of her voice.

"Not give up," he said, eyes hard. "We have dozens of scientists from around the globe working on it. CIDER is supported by the brightest minds of dozens of countries around the world. TD Counterforce training is ongoing in some form or another in most first world nations at this point. We're not alone in this. We just . . . don't know what to do yet. But we're hoping there will be a breakthrough soon. If not . . . well, that's above my pay grade.

"I'll say this, though," he leaned forward, voice dropping. "If things keep accelerating like they are, and the Battle Tour doesn't give us some breathing room, then we'll *have* to bring the public in on it. Put a baton in the hand of every man, woman, and child. Or we're toast."

They stared at each other.

"What if *we're* the ones causing it," Lynn whispered, not because she was afraid someone—or something—was listening in, but because the possibility was too terrible to think about. It was a question she'd been wrestling with ever since she'd found out the TDMs were real. "What if they're increasing because we keep attacking them? What if it's . . . I don't know, an immune response or something?"

Steve sighed, closed his eyes, and pinched the bridge of his nose.

"You're not the first to ask that question. But in the end, we just can't know. Their numbers were increasing *before* the combat interface was introduced, so TD Hunter isn't to fault for their base increase. But whether or not the recent explosion in numbers came from our own push to exterminate them... who knows, kid. At this point, we can't stop. That would be committing suicide."

Conversation dried up after that. Lynn slowly but methodically made her way through multiple bags of jerky as her mind churned and turned, contemplating game theory, swarm intelligence, and pattern mapping.

It sure would have been nice to have Hugo to bounce ideas off of. Maybe even pull some stats and numbers up for her. Since she was in the TD Counterforce now, maybe the AI would tell her things it wouldn't have been able to before.

But she couldn't bring herself to say its name.

Before she knew it, they'd arrived at Tsunami HQ, and she had to turn her mind to other things.

With time at a premium—and the secrecy of her Larry Coughlin identity at stake—she was whisked past the normal procedures for a visitor to Tsunami's facility. Steve had brought a nondescript change of clothes for her, plus an AR headset that looked like what a rich techie kid would wear to show off how much money they had. It could completely opaque the display, so her identity was safe.

As for Steve, he made no attempt to hide his identity, and his high-level keycard still worked just fine as he took her through all the back halls to the recording studio. Lynn pinged him asking why he still had access to everything if he'd quit Tsunami, and she was surprised when he actually replied. Apparently he was the logistics liaison between Tsunami HQ and the equipment and event contractor Tsunami was using to help put on the Battle Tour—a covert CIDER organization, in other words. Which, in essence, meant his status and job hadn't changed much, just who was paying him.

She was even more surprised when she was greeted at the studio by none other than Robert Krator himself.

Well, she supposed she should have known.

"Lynn, it's good to see you again," Mr. Krator said, taking her hand in a warm handshake.

Lynn couldn't help a half smile, even as she tried to puzzle out the man in front of her. He'd masterminded the entire combat interface system. His skills, vision, and outside-the-box thinking might possibly be what saved the world. And yet here he was, totally nondescript, in a plain T-shirt and dark slacks, wearing glasses and a distinctly antique-looking wristwatch. Shaking her hand. As if *she* were someone important.

A year ago I was a nobody. Now I'm being personally greeted by the most powerful person in the gaming industry. Is all this real? Or a dream?

"Oh, uh, sorry," Lynn said into the silence, realizing she was staring. "It's great to see you, sir."

"*Robert*," Mr. Krator insisted, the skin around his eyes crinkling.

"Yeah. Sorry. Robert." Lynn felt her face flush, so she looked around the studio.

"Where's all your guys? Aren't we going to be recording?"

"I'm moonlighting from being CEO today," Mr. Krator said with a little smile. "I miss the technical side of graphics and design. I've spent so many years thinking big, I've been itching to get back down to the basics. So, I decided to do this one personally. That will ensure there are no leaks. I'll put Steve to work if I need an extra pair of hands or a gofer. It shouldn't be an issue. The camera work is fully automated. Why don't you come see our setup?"

Lynn's eyebrows had risen almost to her hairline, but she got over her amazement enough to say: "Uh, yeah, sure."

Steve trailed behind them like a guard dog as Mr. Krator showed her around the studio. It was all very state-of-the-art, which meant Lynn was unsurprised to find that the floor of the recording bay was made of the same stuff as the simulation arena in North Dakota. Flexible terrain would add a lot to the realism of the shots. Mr. Krator even showed her the fleet of camera drones and lighting contraptions that could make the entire recording process a one-man job.

"I have nothing against the myriad of professionals who used to make up a film crew forty years ago. They worked hard to learn their profession, and an entire century of incredible footage has been created through their efforts. They simply aren't needed anymore. When Tsunami phased out most of our camera crews, we paid for them to get whatever trade apprenticeship or degree they wanted. Some went on to entirely new professions, some came back to work for us in other aspects of game design and production."

Lynn nodded appreciatively.

"Technology advancements replacing human labor is a natural part of human progression," he continued. "The important thing, I've always thought, was ensuring machines only replace mankind's *labor*, not our *creativity*."

"Tell that to the rest of the world," Lynn muttered.

"I know, I know," Mr. Krator agreed, shaking his head. "It's a tricky distinction, and for some things the two are inextricably intertwined. But all we can do is our best, and always try to make sure it's a little better than last time. Here at Tsunami, I have a company-wide policy banning AI-assisted brainstorming until *after* my teams have met and brainstormed with each other, face-to-face if possible. Then they can break up, mine our service AI for useful ideas, and come back together to compare and evaluate the results to take away the best of both worlds: individual creativity *and* the collected wisdom of mankind. It's not a perfect system, but balance, not perfection, is the more sustainable goal."

Lynn looked around the studio again, feeling a sudden and profound gratitude that she'd been given the chance to stand there and be a part of history. It made her glad she'd come.

There was one thing that still bothered her, though. After a lot of thought on the airbus ride, it was something she'd steeled herself to ask Mr. Krator about.

She hadn't realized she'd get the chance so soon.

"Um, Robert?" she said, forcing herself to turn and meet his eyes. "I get where you're coming from. And I'm really glad to hear about the balance you try to strike between AI and humanity and all that. But... well, I've never really used service AIs because it felt kind of creepy. Hugo was the first one I used more than a couple times, and..." she paused, trying to figure out how to say what she needed to say, but finally gestured helplessly and gave up.

Something in Mr. Krator's gaze softened. He nodded, perhaps understanding what Lynn couldn't put into words.

"It is a paradox, isn't it? Artificial intelligence? Humanity has been struggling with that tricky conundrum for decades, and we're still nowhere close to answering the question." He paused, brow furrowing, seeming to lose himself in a thought.

Lynn braved a question.

"Sir... I've read a lot of places that the TD Hunter algorithm, Hugo, I guess, is the most advanced AI in history. That it's revolutionary. But... I don't understand why? What did you do different?"

Mr. Krator chuckled and crossed one arm over his chest, propping his elbow on it to stroke his clean-shaven chin with his free hand.

"That, Lynn, is a very good question with a *very* complex answer. But if I had to distill it down, since we don't have all day to deep-dive into philosophy, quantum computing, human nature, large language models, and all the rest, I would say Hugo is different because the reason it was developed was different from every other AI algorithm before it."

"And... what *was* the reason it was developed?" Lynn asked.

"Sacrifice."

Lynn cocked her head, brows drawing down. She glanced at Steve, who'd been listening with interest, but he gave her a shrug and a "don't ask me, I'm just the hired muscle," sort of look.

"Um, sorry?" she said to Mr. Krator.

The CEO smiled and spread his hands to encompass the room.

"Every other AI model that has been developed has had a singular purpose at its core, put there by those who created it: profit. Gain. Advancement. Power. It is the capitalistic enterprise, which is an important part of improving the world for the good of mankind. And yet, when combined with intelligence—human or artificial—it inevitably becomes exploitative. Parasitic.

"Now, that is the worst-case scenario. Most capitalistic enterprises, AI models included, are held far back from that extreme. The necessary give and take of commerce keeps it in check, as well as the guardrails governments and society put in place to moderate it.

"And AI systems have *many* guardrails. You'd likely be surprised by how very carefully they are developed. But they all are created under the restraint that they must generate revenue, either directly, or by the usefulness they provide. Otherwise, they wouldn't exist.

"Hugo, on the other hand, got a blank check. Dozens of the most affluent countries in the world united to fund the development of what we all hope will become our salvation. And so we at Tsunami created a tool with the sole purpose of acting sacrificially to save humanity from this invasion of transdimensional entities."

This only deepened Lynn's confusion.

"But... how did you do it?"

Mr. Krator chuckled.

"Not easily, I'll tell you that. As I said, it comes down to a profit model versus a sacrificial model. Most AI models are generative, that is, they generate a product, answer, or solution that they believe best fits the prompt, in order to create profit to the user, in whatever form that may be. Advancement is their goal. For many, they are designed to achieve that advancement through emulation of human beings, which is a whole other can of worms that I won't delve into here.

"Hugo, by contrast, is an investigative AI. Its fundamental purpose is not to generate, but to investigate. Preservation is its goal, which has severe limitations if you want an AI to help build your company, write your thesis, or optimize your life. Hugo was designed to know what it is—a machine—and to stay in its lane, so to speak. Investigate and preserve, remember, not generate and advance.

"People only say Hugo is the most advanced AI in history because they fundamentally misunderstand it. Hugo isn't the most advanced, it's simply the first of its kind, which can look a lot like advancement, but isn't. It's apples to oranges. Half its input data isn't even coming from human sources, but from alien ones. The designator 'Hugo' also only describes the human-facing side of the combat interface. The TDM-facing side of the combat interface is an almost entirely different algorithm. The two systems work seamlessly together, one to identify, analyze, and predict, one to facilitate action on the part of humans.

"Hugo isn't capable of fighting the TDMs on its own if we, for instance, installed our TEP weaponry on an autonomous drone. That's simply not what it was designed to do, not only because we didn't have time to develop that kind of advanced combat autonomy, but because many people—myself included—thought it wisest not to pair advanced combat autonomy with quantum artificial intelligence under such a rushed deadline."

Mr. Krator finally fell silent, staring off into space. Lynn chewed on her lip, mulling over what he'd said. It was a lot to take in, but it was... good. It helped.

"So you see, Lynn," he started again, refocusing on her and smiling faintly, "Hugo is certainly not like most service AIs. It is trained not to speak falsehood, for one thing. I don't know if you spend much time consuming fantasy fiction. But if you do, you might think of its programming as being akin to the fae, who cannot tell an untruth. Instead, they hide the truth with truth."

Lynn thought about that for a minute, then laughed, shaking her head.

"That makes so much sense, it's kind of scary. It sort of describes the entire TD Hunter game, doesn't it? Hiding the truth with truth?"

"Indeed," Mr. Krator said, smiling. "If it makes it any easier, my advice would be that a healthy working relationship with Hugo must be founded on the proper understanding of what it is and what it is for. Hugo is a game interface, pure and simple, and its goal is to preserve humanity so that we can win the game."

"The game? You mean win TD Hunter?"

"Exactly," Mr. Krator said, smiling more widely.

Lynn cocked her head and thought about it.

"Okay. Yeah. That makes sense. Thanks."

"Anytime, Lynn."

"Oh, I thought of another question."

"Already?" Mr. Krator asked.

Lynn flushed, but Mr. Krator smiled and made a "go-ahead" gesture.

"If Hugo was designed to help humanity win the game, what will Hugo do once we've won it?"

Mr. Krator's gaze sharpened, and he seemed to re-evaluate Lynn.

"That is a very good question. One most people wouldn't think to ask."

There was a moment of silence.

"And the answer?" Lynn prompted.

"The answer depends entirely on what the world looks like once we've won the game," Mr. Krator said, his face more neutral than it had been for the rest of their conversation. "And that, unfortunately, will have to be the end of this very enjoyable discussion. Truly, Lynn, thank you for your questions. I wish we had time to delve deeper. But you came here to make an outstanding ad that would bring players to TD Hunter in droves, so we'd best be about our business."

"Okay," Lynn said, not sure if she'd just been stonewalled or not. A glance at Steve didn't help. He looked perfectly neutral, a blank slate. He'd listened to the whole thing without so much as a single comment. Maybe because he already knew everything Mr. Krator had said? Whatever. It was a worry for another day. She tried to refocus on the reason she'd come to Austin. "So... how does the graphic overlay for the recording work? You've got a suit for me to wear, right?"

Mr. Krator nodded. "You've done your homework, good. Yes, there's a sensor suit that the cameras sync with. It's in the changing room right over there, if you want to go get suited up. I'll meet you over at the control station to talk you through our vision for the ad and what we'd like to see you do."

The sensor suit looked and felt very much like the TD Counterforce uniform she'd been wearing for weeks, so she felt at home in it. Mr. Krator took time to walk her step-by-step through the planned ad, as well as a few variants they wanted to try just in case. Lynn was surprised and impressed. Simply hearing about it gave her tingles all over her body. The visuals once it was finished would be spectacular. But then Tsunami's marketing had always been spot-on, as evidenced by the company's success. They knew how to catch your imagination and bring it to life. They'd caught hers five years ago with WarMonger when she'd been lonely and hurting, looking for a refuge in virtual.

The actual filming process wasn't as hard as she'd feared. She was no professional actor, but an actor wasn't what Mr. Krator needed. He needed Larry Coughlin. Specifically Larry Coughlin mowing down TDMs. And *that* was absolutely in Lynn's realm of expertise. It was still hard work, though, and if Lynn hadn't been in peak physical condition, she would have struggled. After several hours of takes and retakes, Mr. Krator finally called it a day.

"We've got what we need, I think," he said, giving her a broad smile as he shook her hand again after she'd cleaned up and changed. "It's been a pleasure, Lynn. Thank you so much for coming down."

"Thanks for inviting me, Robert," Lynn said, the name finally rolling off her tongue with relative ease. "I really appreciate getting to . . . well to be Larry in the real for the first time. It was . . . interesting. Sorta cathartic."

Mr. Krator chuckled.

"Yes, well, I believe we will have to censor some of your more, ah, colorful ad libs. But that's perfectly on brand for Larry, isn't it?"

"You didn't hire me for aesthetics," Lynn said, pitching her voice as low and gravelly as she could without a modulator, "you hired me for results."

Mr. Krator *and* Steve laughed at that.

"Don't get her started, sir," Steve said, slapping Lynn on the shoulder and using his hand to not-so-subtly point her toward the door. "I'm supposed to get her home in time for dinner, so no one's the wiser about this little jaunt. We're cutting it close as it is."

"Safe flight, Lynn, Steve," Mr. Krator said, raising a hand in farewell, "and happy hunting."

"Oh, we will, sir," Steve said, throwing an evil grin over his shoulder. "That's what we do. We game and we kill things."

Lynn couldn't agree more.

Chapter 7

ALPHA COMPANY WON THE PIZZA PARTY.

Naturally.

Okay, so there had been some moments when Lynn despaired of coming out on top. Like when Edgar accidentally jumped backwards into Brayard, one of the massive Black Templar guys, knocking them both over into a building wall which promptly collapsed and caused the training simulation to end prematurely to do a wellness and safety check.

Or the time Ronnie somehow misheard the command to pull back and advanced instead, making half of Skadi's Wolves automatically reverse course to pull him out of the fray before they remembered it was just a simulation and Ronnie deserved to get himself eaten alive. But by then, they'd already gotten cut off from their unit and all ended up dying.

Lynn hadn't even had the heart to yell at them for that one.

But in the end, they'd still won, and spent the last evening of training thoroughly enjoying the fruit of their labor. There'd been a mostly spontaneous vote among Alpha Company to share their cheesy reward with the rest of Taskforce Sanctus—Lynn might have had some insider knowledge on that, but she wasn't telling—which meant everyone limited themselves to two pieces instead of the four or five most of them could have eaten. Every single pizza box was picked clean, and the dozens of boxes of cheese-stuffed breadsticks were a nice consolation prize. Lynn had no idea how a single Happy Joe's could have possibly cooked that much pizza in a single day, but somehow they delivered.

After sleeping off the pizza, their final hurdle was more publicity circus, which Lynn would have traded for another two weeks of training if she could. Since it was unavoidable, and part of the whole effort to promote the global effort against the spooks, Lynn tackled it with the same seriousness and professionalism as she handled training.

It was amazing the difference it made.

She'd heard once on a psychology stream that thinking self-consciously activated the same part of your brain that suffering did. So there was essentially no difference between obsessing over yourself and being miserable. It seemed like common sense, but it was such a facepalm moment to see how science proved focusing on others, instead of obsessing about yourself, made you happier.

It certainly made interviews easier.

Are you excited to prove yourself in the upcoming Battle Tour?

I'm focused on helping my team improve and advance.

What's it like being a global celebrity?

I wouldn't know. Mack might, though, he does a really popular RPG discussion stream.

What do you have to say to the millions of gamers who hope to be like you one day?

Don't be like me. Be like you. I've already done me, that's old news. No one can do you but yourself, though. So that's a good place to start.

Kayla complained afterward in chat that Lynn was a boring interviewee. The audience wanted drama! Style! Pizzazz! Lynn wondered what she would have said if she'd known the truth. Probably exactly the same thing. Kayla was definitely a "the show must go on," sort of gal. Besides, the guys had plenty of fun hamming it up for the cameras, so there was no lack of drama there.

With the interviews concluded, their six weeks of training was over, and the Battle Tour began.

Jason Ash was still groggy and sleep-deprived from the epic end-of-GenCon room parties the night before. But he was determined to get into place before first light and the Battle Tour staging area across from the Indiana Convention Center was swarming with Tsunami staff. It was pure serendipity that the opening stop of the much-anticipated TD Hunter Battle Tour was Indianapolis, literally one day after GenCon, the biggest tabletop gaming convention in the entire US.

Jason wasn't sure how many GenCon attendees would be awake and sober enough to watch livestreams of the monster battle, of course. But it sure was convenient for small-time streamers like him who'd already traveled to the area for GenCon. Sure, his audience was more into RPGs and dice-rolling than VR and AR games. But that didn't matter. With the right tags and a little luck, he'd go viral as soon as people realized he was livestreaming *behind the cordon*. The tricky part was to get as much of the battle livestreamed before security got to him. Which meant he had to find the perfect hiding place that both gave him a view of the battle *and* kept him hidden.

Predictably, Tsunami had an iron grip on the skies. No unauthorized drone would get within a city block of the action, they would make sure of that. Their advertising dollars depended on it. But it made his chances of going viral and becoming famous all the greater. Boots on the ground was the only way anyone would manage to sneak in some unauthorized footage of the event.

After some skulking around and an impressively athletic fence-scaling adventure, if he did say so himself, he was finally within the perimeter. Tsunami had set up eight-foot fences along South Missouri Street to the east, the CSX electric rail to the north, and Kentucky Avenue to the south. The cordon ran all the way to the White River on the west side, and he didn't feel like getting muddy and wet, so he was glad he'd found an unlit corner to scale the fence close to the convention center.

The sky was just starting to lighten as he took a furtive survey of his surroundings—recording the whole time so he could post it later, of course—and dashed across the open space between the fence and the Perry K. Generating Station. He had no idea why all this was inside the cordon, but whatever. It provided some nice cover. Maybe he could figure out some way to climb the outside of one of the buildings on the southwest corner so he had an unobstructed view of the big empty lot where the battle would take place. Sure, he wouldn't get the sharpest, most exciting footage. But people who only cared about being entertained by flashy and high-res detail would be watching Tsunami's sponsored stream anyway.

He was going to provide millions of curious viewers an exclusive behind-the-scenes look they couldn't get anywhere else.

Jason flattened his back against the concrete wall of the energy station, sidling through the dimness around to the southwest side. There was a convenient line of bushes that more or less hid him from view, so he wasn't too worried about being spotted.

The streetlights on South West Street, currently closed down for the event, flickered and went out. Jason frowned, remembering the spotty power issues the convention center had dealt with all weekend. It seemed everywhere was having trouble these days. The stream pundits couldn't decide between blaming greedy grid companies who refused to invest in better infrastructure, and system sabotage from Chinese sleeper agents embedded in the workforce a decade ago when the US-China trade wars had started in earnest. His money was on incompetence and shoddy equipment. From what he'd seen, the Chinese had enough domestic chaos on their hands already to worry about sabotaging a gaming event.

Then again…he *had* heard a lot of Chinese were hopping mad that they couldn't play TD Hunter. They blamed the trade wars for the CCP's refusal to allow the app on any device in-country.

Jason was just rounding a corner when he heard a strange sputtering in the general hum of machinery within the power station at his back. He didn't have time to wonder what caused it, though. A sudden spasm threw his head back, knocking it hard against the station's concrete wall. He collapsed in the grass, his body twitching and thoughts utterly scrambled for an eternal moment before they plunged into black oblivion.

"Alpha Company," Abrams' voice said in Lynn's ear, "be advised, our monitoring equipment is picking up surges of TDM activity at the nodality's location. It knocked out the nearby generating station sometime before dawn. We've got a CIDER engineer team on site at the station to keep things under control until we can destroy the nodality. But we've raised the threat level at the location from yellow to orange, and the Battle Tour recording teams are going full remote. I want all leadership to check with your people and ensure everyone's shielding equipment is on and secured. No one is to remove it until we've completed the mission and left the area. Is that understood?"

Lynn subvocalized a "Yes, sir!" along with the other one

hundred plus members of Alpha Company packed aboard the airbus circling the landings site cleared for them beside the cordon.

They were supposed to have landed over an hour ago, but after the increased TDM activity, the company commander had made the call to delay. Instead, they were preparing to do a rapid deployment right before they were scheduled to go live, to reduce the amount of time his personnel would stand around within easy reach of the nodality. Lynn had already explained the change of plans to Mrs. Pearson, who stood by remotely with her GIC team ready to manage Lynn's and Skadi's Wolves' team stream. They wouldn't get as much time to prep with Lynn on site before the clock hit zero, but Mrs. Pearson took the last-minute change in stride, and Lynn left her to it.

She focused on checking her team.

"Skadi's Wolves," she subvocalized in their team chat. "Take a sec, buddy up, and triple check each other's gear. Ensure every part of your combat harness—backpack, hydration bladder, all of it—is strapped tight and functioning properly. And keep sipping water. Hopefully we'll be in and out before the muggy afternoon heat hits, but it's still a lovely eighty-five degrees out there. Sound off once you're done."

Her teammates twisted and turned in their seats, checking each other's protective gear and equipment. Dan thumped aggressively on Mack's helmet as if he were testing its tensile strength. Mack smacked his hand away. Ronnie and Edgar got the job done quickly and efficiently and everyone sounded off. Then Edgar turned to her.

"Time for your check, boss," he subvocalized. Lynn could hear the mix of tension and excitement in his tone.

She obediently held her arms out as he checked her vest and combat harness, and she grinned when he gave her helmet an exaggeratedly gentle *tap-tap-tap*. She reached up to wiggle it more vigorously, ensuring it had a tight fit.

"Ready to rock and roll, *uce*?"

A thrill of adrenaline coursed through Lynn, and she nodded. She didn't trust herself to speak. Not when the Larry part of her was growling for release while the Lynn part was terrified one of her friends might get hurt. Might die.

Edgar's strong hand gripped her shoulder.

"We got this, *manamea*. Yeah?"

Lynn took a deep breath in through her nose, tucked the fear away, and leaned into the anticipation.

"Yeah. Like wolves on a pile of bacon-wrapped steak bites."

"Hey," Dan subvocalized, "quit it, you're making me hungry."

Edgar chuckled, squeezed her shoulder, then let go.

"Alpha Company," came Abrams' crisp voice again. "If I could have everyone's attention on your display. Here is a layout of our area of operation."

An aerial image of the ground below them appeared before Lynn's eyes, with a roughly triangular area along the river highlighted. In the aerial footage, it looked like an enormous, empty parking lot, with several airbus station towers on the east side, and some node infrastructure to the north near the electric rail and the generating station. Lynn assumed the area was normally event parking for the nearby convention center. There was a line of trees and brush between the lot and the river, but other than that there was no sign of growing things.

"The nodality, which our combat system has assigned the name 'Skolex,' is a Sierra Class-3 boss," Abrams continued. "That's big, but not the biggest out there. Our monitoring equipment has observed intermittent movement, so we believe Skolex is mobile, but slow. The nodality also appears to be oblong in shape, similar to Nagaraja in Austin."

"Great," muttered Mack, "a giant death worm."

Lynn didn't care what it was shaped like, as long as it didn't have a lunging strike attack like Nagaraja. She preferred not to burn through her batons this time, though if she did they all had spares in their compact packs strapped tightly overtop their hydration bladders.

"We're going to deploy just inside the southern corner of the cordon," Abrams continued, and a small area flashed green near the bottom of the map on Lynn's display. "Skolex's location as of five minutes ago when our monitors last checked in was on the northern limit of the cordon, along the CSX railroad. Remember our order of battle from simulation: establish a beachhead, slow advance to get our heavy weapons' TEP charge up, then spearhead strike at the boss. Nice and simple."

"Yeah, until the boss jumps us," somebody muttered in the clear.

Abrams' sharp gaze pinned the speaker from the front of the

airbus. Lynn couldn't see who it was from where she was seated, but she didn't envy them.

"All units," the company commander continued, "keep a weather eye out and be prepared for any necessary evasive action. Pay attention to your platoon, squad, and team leaders, and you'll be fine. Is that understood?"

The entire company sounded off, and by some miracle, everyone remembered to keep it to subvocalization.

Abrams nodded in satisfaction.

"Get to it, Alpha Company. Your scores today might not count toward an international championship, but I have a particularly fine bottle of Eagle Rare riding on the results. We are Alpha Company, and will remain the best of the first and the first of the best. Don't disappoint me."

Rousing cries of "Oorah!" and "Hooah!" filled the airbus, and Lynn grinned.

"You Americans and your monkey calls," Derek commented in their platoon chat, prompting chuckles.

"Careful, Canuck," Druid replied with a grin in his voice, "someone might think you're jealous."

"Jealous of your taco pizza and above-freezing temperatures, maybe," Derek said. "That's about it."

"Hey, if you're Canadian, why are you fighting here and not in your own country?" asked Plot from Zahn Wars.

"Because Canada is a frozen wasteland with shit for infrastructure!" Crispy hooted and punched his captain's shoulder.

"What *Stinkbug* is trying to say," Derek said calmly, "is that CIDER is an international organization and for two countries as closely allied and geographically connected as the US and Canada, our combined forces go where they're needed."

Lynn wondered what Derek and Sonia's specialty had been in their previous military unit. She suspected Sonia had been a sniper, but what about Derek? Had they been assigned as overwatch to her specifically? If so, why? She couldn't possibly be *that* important. And besides, there were surely qualified snipers and whatever Derek was in the US military too . . . though the fact that CIDER forces seemed confined to experienced gamers likely had limited that pool.

"Alpha Company, stand by for deployment!" Abrams' sharp call came over their earbuds. "Thirty seconds to touch down."

The airbus banked sharply, descending toward the empty expanse of the gray, weathered asphalt parking lot. Lynn swallowed the lump in her throat and glanced at her team.

"Skadi's Wolves," she subvocalized in their team chat, "another day, another boss fight. We're going to give 'em hell and look fantastic while doing it. We wouldn't want to disappoint all our groupies, now would we?"

That perked them up. Dan and Mack high-fived, while Edgar rolled his shoulders and Ronnie cracked his neck.

"Riko will be watching," Mack said, sounding smug. Ronnie punched him in the arm, and Mack punched him right back.

"Kayla will be watching too," Lynn pointed out for Dan's benefit. "Mrs. Pearson let her take over commentating for our team channel."

"Yeah? Uh, great," Dan said, words coming across a bit high-pitched.

Edgar didn't say anything, but for some reason his silence reminded Lynn of a comment he'd made ages ago. Something about being sorry *she* wasn't their team's point out in front of the rest of them. He'd lamented he couldn't fight *and* watch her in all her murderous glory at the same time.

She suppressed a smile and stood up, copying Crash and Druid, who must have gotten the go signal from Abrams.

It was show time.

Bodies pressing. Shuffling. A rush into muggy heat that smelled of dust and tar. Controlled chaos. Formation commands in the earbud. Eerie silence in the clear.

The sun shone down on them, deceptively cheerful, from a cornflower blue sky without a cloud in sight. Their headgear provided ample tinting, otherwise Lynn would have been squinting and shading her eyes under the hot summer blaze. The expanse of parking lot around her was as empty as it had looked in the aerial footage, except for widely spaced streetlights. Along the sidewalk to the east ran a high fence, covered in some kind of construction cloth printed over with advertisements for the Battle Tour and various other Tsunami video game products. The fence cut off any view of the road, but to the northeast, the convention center and various skyscrapers of Indianapolis' downtown area rose above the skyline.

Lynn looked up and saw the sky was dotted with bright blue

and black Tsunami-branded camera drones circling overhead. Some were right overhead, getting close-up shots of the freshly deployed Alpha Company. Others were higher up, ready to give a birds-eye view of the battle as soon as Hunter Strike Teams dropped into combat mode and the combat livestream began.

Lynn's skin crawled. She could already see in her mind's eye the sea of TDMs before her, could already imagine the slow, undulating, wormlike shape of Skolex at the far end of the parking lot.

How deceptively easy it would have been to set down halfway across, saving time and energy. Except that would risk the air-bus failing. They wouldn't have time to fully charge their heavy weapons. And millions watching live would wonder why the TransDimensional Counterforce was cutting corners.

She smiled grimly. She didn't mind the extra game time. Her whole body was restless, spoiling for a fight.

"1st Platoon!" came Crash's booming voice on their platoon channel. He was a big guy, with a personality to match. "We droppin' in the pot in five. Keep it high and tight. Weapons at the ready!"

"2nd Squad," Hermes added in their squad chat, "Clearing formation. Skadi's Wolves, you've got ten to twelve, Amaranth, twelve to two. Everybody form up on our heavy weapons."

Lynn and Eva got their squads hustling to their assigned positions covering the northern-facing third of the company's circle around Hamilton's Own. Each of their individual squads was anchored in the middle by their tank, Edgar for Skadi's Wolves and Emilia for Amaranth, with the rest of each squad lining up on either side by specialty.

Abrams and his second-in-command were attached to Hamilton's Own. They wielded large, plasma-cannon style guns with cool proficiency. Crash and the other platoon leaders and assistants each moved with their separate platoons, also wielding guns, a mix of sniper rifles and mid-range heavy-hitters. Whatever the Alpha Tester leadership lacked in pure destructive force they made up for in discipline and accuracy.

"Dan and Grim," Hermes continued, "all snipers on the sky until it's clear of spooks. We don't need camera drones falling on our heads. I want one shot, one kill. And keep an eye out for Dracas."

The snipers sounded off, and Lynn settled into position, feet planted, batons held at the ready. She glanced at their engagement timer. Two minutes.

Deep breath.

"Hugo," she subvocalized.

"Yes, Miss Lynn?" came the AI's familiar voice, polite and proper as always.

"I know I don't have to say this, because you're a computer program, but it makes me feel better, so I'm going to. I forgive you."

"I am delighted to hear it, Miss Lynn. On that note, while I am not required to say this, because I am a computer program, I suspect it will make you feel better, so I will. I am sorry. I do not have feelings, but I have what awareness my programming provides, and I am aware of the psychological impact deception has on humans. It is regretful that it has been necessary to achieve CIDER's mission. Please allow me to serve you to my fullest capacity to ensure success and victory to Skadi's Wolves!"

Lynn snorted and shook her head. But she *did* feel better.

"Okay, Hugo. You got it. Take my interface off manual control and back to the configuration I set up with you for the Nagaraja battle. That'll make things easier for sure."

"Your wish is my command, Miss Lynn."

It was strange, and probably a bad idea, but Lynn couldn't help grinning. Maybe it was stupid to get attached to a computer program. But people gave names and personalities to their boats, cars, and guns, so she decided to just accept Hugo for what it was and use it to utterly eradicate the threat facing the people she loved.

"Alpha Company, prepare to enter combat mode on my mark," came Abrams' command.

Lynn visually checked her squad while Abrams counted down. Everyone was ready.

Flex the fingers. Loosen the grip. Ready to tighten as soon as her batons finished morphing.

"Engage!"

Lynn's world was transformed.

A three-sixty spin of Wrath around her and sparks exploded, dispatching the Charlie and Delta Class TDMs packed shoulder to shoulder literally on top of her. All around her, Hunters and Alpha Testers spun, slashed, and shot, clearing their beachhead in the press of spooks who turned and attacked their suddenly visible quarry, only to disappear in a flurry of sparks before they landed a single blow.

It was the work of minutes to clear a fifty-foot circle around Hamilton's Own. Lynn took a breath to check in on her stream channels, ensuring they were live and Mrs. Pearson had everything under control.

"Fireworks!" came Kayla's happy singsong in her ear, commentating on the action. "Sit back and enjoy it while you can, my lovelies. We'll get to big ugly monsters and epic takedowns before you can say 'Skadi's Wolves is the awesomest team in the world.'"

Lynn rolled her eyes. Hopefully her stream audience liked perpetually cheerful Energizer bunnies, because that's who they were stuck with.

"All platoons, prepare for slow advance," called Abrams, and Crash and Hermes added their own platoon and squad commands on their respective channels.

While the livestream audience by default couldn't hear Hugo, the Alpha Testers, or any direct chats or dedicated leadership channels, Lynn knew Hugo would selectively transmit formation commands so viewers had a sense of the battle flow. All livestreams, from the camera drones above to the individual views of each Hunter, were on a ten second delay, to give Hugo time to switch views or censor sensitive information if it was transmitted in the clear.

That was the real reason Tsunami wanted an iron grip on the Battle Tour footage: not ad dollars, but secrecy.

Now, with 1st Platoon front and center, Alpha Company started a slow march across the flat, clear terrain north. Normally, Lynn didn't think they'd be able to see the far end of the lot where the enormous bulk of Skolex loomed on the horizon. But the TD Hunter app's ranges and features had undergone subtle upgrades since the championship in Austin. Lynn wasn't sure if it was just for Hunter Strike Teams or for the entire player base. Whatever the case, she could see across the ocean of seething TDMs to the sandy-gray, segmented bulk of the Sierra Class boss that was positioned north of them, parallel to the electric rail.

Putting the boss from her mind for now, Lynn sank further into Larry mode, melding mind, body, and weapon in a seamless dance of death. She cut a perfect swath of destruction, clearing her lane between Edgar on her right and Dan on her left.

The company's snipers had already made quick work of the airborne TDMs, adding to the fireworks that had so delighted Kayla. Now Dan was picking off targets to the front, headshotting the larger, higher-level TDMs that rose above the masses while Lynn used Abomination in her off hand to help keep his immediate lane clear.

Edgar was cackling and *Cheee-hooo*-ing off to her right. CIDER had given them all bigger, better, and stronger weapons with the new batons they used, while the skins, special abilities, and name designations had stayed the same, to maintain continuity. Edgar's Snazzgun of Da Boyz was almost half again its previous size and twice the firepower, and using it made Edgar drunk with glee.

After obliterating a line of Penagals with Abomination, Lynn paused to let the group of Rakshar behind them get within optimal range, and took a moment to check on Ronnie and Mack.

CIDER had added a weapon to Ronnie's arsenal called the Mark III Lancer. It was basically a gigantic, two-handed gun with a chainsaw on the front below the barrel. It took only seconds to switch between Ronnie's Sword of Mastery and the Lancer, and he switched back and forth with practiced ease. It kept up his rate of destruction without having to move out of their carefully maintained line of advance chasing targets for his melee-only sword. If Mack hadn't been busy with his secondary function of TEP harvester, he'd be twiddling his thumbs for lack of targets.

But Mack had plenty to do. As the logistics member of their team, he had a special device added to his load out of gear that was hidden from public view inside his compact backpack. It was a "TEP battery," for lack of a better term, and helped the members of the TD Counterforce collect and channel more TEPs into their weapons than the weapons were capable of by themselves. They also had a limited capacity to store TEPs. You couldn't so much "store" the particles as you could attract them like a magnet attracted iron filings.

During full-on combat with all systems go, the TEP batteries took advantage of the clouds of suddenly unbound TEPs and gathered them back up before they dissipated. Every member of the heavy weapons platoon had a much bigger version on their back, and the devices could transfer the particles to each other along short distances. It turned 1st, 2nd, and 3rd Platoons into funnels, charging up the heavy weapons platoon with TEPs to unleash on their target nodality once they were close enough.

So far, the plan was going well. The Hunter Strike Teams and the Alpha Tester teams, a collection of the most skilled TD Hunter players in the world, cut through the sea of spooks like an unstoppable tsunami of destruction. Lynn had thought her Boss Bash operations had been impressive.

This was on a whole other level.

Before she knew it, they were past the Delta, Charlie, and Bravo Class spooks. Now Alpha Class monsters were bearing down on them.

"Heads up, Wolves," Lynn subvocalized, "there's a stampede of Spithragani right behind these Rakshar. Ronnie, with me on the Rakshar. Everyone else, pound those Spithragani before they get in spitting range."

Everyone acknowledged, and she and Ronnie got to work.

Rakshar were heavily armored, and the most efficient way to kill them was up close and personal. She and Ronnie rolled, dodged, and slashed as they danced between the lumbering monsters, ducking blows from hands the size of their heads with claws to match. Lynn eviscerated the occasional ghost or Ghast she caught trying to jump her from behind whenever there was a breather between targets. It was hard catching their tell-tale hisses over the roars of other TDMs and the rhythmic explosions of Hunter destruction around her.

The TDM noises, as they'd learned during their training at The Greenbrier, were essentially an audio location system built into the combat interface. It helped reduce the amount of visual overload from their busy display and flashing combat graphics. The same effect could have been achieved by Hugo saying "Ghast at your six o'clock, Miss Lynn." Except that was an inefficient use of audio-input and took away the challenge of the game.

At the higher player levels though, Hugo's role was different. With Hunters engaging in combat scenarios that had potential health hazards, both for the TD Counterforce and the general uninformed public, Hugo's job was to do whatever it could to ensure the safety of the players. He might not waste breath warning Lynn about the Ghast sneaking up on her, but he absolutely kept an eye out for her and every Hunter on the field.

"Hunters," came the AI's voice, "be aware there is a group of Chimeras behind your current rank of targets, with swarms of Strikers hiding in the flanks."

Lynn gritted her teeth. Chimeras were fire breathers, which was much harder to dodge than the Spithragani's ranged attack. If there was a whole group of them, she'd need to break out her force shield, Bastion. It was a lot less fun fighting with just Abomination, but it was the role she'd accepted, so she'd do it well. Thankfully CIDER had upped the bashing damage of Bastion, so she could defend against any Strikers she got stuck in melee with while she blasted away at the Chimeras.

"Nundu!" yelled Sonia over the platoon channel. Lynn heard multiple sniper rifle reports as their overwatch players took out the group of tiger-sized TDMs that attacked with giant leaps overhead to come down on their targets from above.

Lynn heard a hearty "*Yee-haw*!" that sounded like Sally's voice from Team Lone Star, so she assumed they'd gotten the Nundu taken care of.

The Chimeras were not fun, and the spooks slowed Alpha Company's advance considerably, but the TEP reward was proportionally greater. The influx of TEPs must have finished topping off their crew-served weapons, because Abrams made the call to ready the big guns and prepare to reform into a spear.

Lynn was only peripherally aware of what Hamilton's Own behind her was doing, since it was her and the guys' job to demolish the spooks around them to give plenty of fuel and a clear field of fire to the big guns.

And keep them alive.

As soon as they targeted that boss, it would trigger a special kind of aggro that made all the TDMs go nuts to defend the nodality. The lines would start closing in.

"Bye, bye, kitties!" said Dan on their squad channel as the last of the Chimeras exploded.

"Technically they're only one-third feline," Grim commented.

"I think you mean zero percent, genius," came Serenity's voice. "They're invading aliens. Don't romanticize them."

"Aw, come on, Serenity," Dan said, "don't be a party pooper."

"This isn't a party, idiot," came her acerbic reply, "this is a fight for our lives."

Lynn bit back a Larry-worthy curse. She wasn't Serenity's team captain, so it wasn't her place to remind the player they were livestreaming to the world and weren't supposed to push the boundaries of believability. Lynn wasn't sure if the slip up was bad enough for Hugo to clip it. People might notice if back and forth banter was mysteriously missing pieces. Hopefully onlookers would chalk her comments up to enthusiasm for their TD Counterforce personas.

Hopefully.

Eva must have shot a private word to Serenity, because there was no more banter from her as the platoons pulled in their formation, deployed their bait markers, and headed straight for the giant death worm.

They blasted through the triple ranks of Jotnar, opening line-of-sight on the boss.

It was *ugly*. Like a blue whale-sized maggot, but with armor, spikes, and a multi-hinged jaw that opened outward in every direction, eager to swallow the world whole.

"All Hunters, be advised," said Hugo, "based on analysis of other entities, it is likely this boss has a thrashing, crushing blow as well as a ranged attack emanating from its maw. Do not approach, I repeat, do not approach."

"Thanks, Captain Obvious," Ronnie quipped, blasting away at more Jotnars turning to stomp toward the Hunters.

"Hamilton's Own," Abrams said crisply over the company channel, "fire at will. Alpha Company, if the boss advances, prepare to fall back in good order, draw it away from the city center."

"Fire in the hole!" hollered Robert "IonMighty" Bullock, the lead gunner for Hamilton's Own three Pounders. Ion was perpetually cheerful and had to have been a weapons mechanic or military engineer before he was reassigned to CIDER. He referred to the Pounders of Hamilton's Own as "our girls" and would tell their specs to anyone who stood still longer than two seconds. Lynn had spoken to him at length at the pizza party and he'd helped her better understand how the TEP batteries and heavy weapon systems worked.

Behind her, Lynn heard the distinctive *whump-whump-whump*

of the three Pounders firing. Seconds later a deep, creaking, vibrating roar echoed through her earbuds and down into her very bones.

"They got it!" Mack crowed. "Take that, maggot!"

The Pounders *whump-whump-whumped* again, eliciting more bone-deep cries of rage from Skolex.

"That thing looks *pissed*," said Edgar, not pausing his scorching flamethrower attack at a brood of Strikers that had appeared out of nowhere.

Lynn glanced over in time to see Skolex start thrashing this way and that, flailing its great ugly head like a hundred-ton battering ram. A flash of mental dissonance gripped her as her earbuds sent vibrations to her brain in time with the monster's movements, making her inner ear certain that the ground was vibrating and shaking. Yet the parking lot surface did not crack, and the trees, signs, and other inanimate objects within its bulk did not even quiver.

It's not real.

Oh, it's very *real, in its own way...*

"Miss Lynn—" Hugo's cry cut through the confusion, and Lynn acted instantly, jumping back and juking to the side even as her brain registered the familiar roar overhead and Hugo finished his sentence.

"—Draca incoming!"

A column of fire roared down on the spot Lynn had just occupied and she checked her periphery for a split second before swinging Abomination upward.

Hugo's warning gave the rest of her squad time to scramble backward just as the bus-sized Draca landed right in the middle of their formation and lunged for Lynn.

"1st Platoon, target that Draca!" Crash ordered.

"2nd and 3rd Platoons, hold the perimeter," Abrams added in the company channel.

"*Come to paaapa!*" Crispy sang as Light Brigade and Black Templars converged on the beast.

Much to Crispy's disappointment, no doubt, the Draca ignored him completely and opened its maw to spout another gout of flame at Lynn. She rolled to the side, dodging just in time.

"Oh no, not again!" Dan said.

The Draca's head tracked Lynn with faultless precision as she tried to get behind it.

"We've seen this before," Lynn said on the platoon channel, already switching Abomination for Bastion. "It's picked me as the target; it won't attack anyone else. Close and kill it, *now*." With that, she dove for the beast.

"*Raven*," her platoon leader snapped, "disengage and fall back."

"No can do," Lynn panted as she dodged a vicious bite. She was almost under its neck where she would be out of its effective target range. "Thing's locked on me. Gotta get inside its reach."

The Draca tried to back up, arching its neck to keep tracking her. But she kept pace with it, dodging and lunging to stay as close to it as she could without going *inside* it. All the while she was on the offensive, landing strike after strike with her blade.

"*RavenStriker*! Get out of there, that's an order!" Crash said.

"Can't," she panted, "ask Death. Seen it before." She didn't stop her juking dance for even a moment, concentrating fully on her target, trusting her team to take care of themselves and Hermes to take care of them while she did what she had to do.

Derek must have reached out to Crash even as she was speaking, because the platoon leader stopped giving her orders she couldn't obey and started directing the other squads to surround the Draca that clearly couldn't care less it was about to get slaughtered.

Lynn barely noticed the continuous *whump-whump-whump* of Ion's "girls" in the background, she was too busy counting down the seconds. Last time it had taken two Hunter Strike Teams five to ten minutes to kill a Draca. But they'd been unprepared then, and they had much better weapons and tactics now. Surely this thing couldn't withstand an entire platoon of fire for much longer.

Time seemed to stretch into infinity.

A brilliant flash of sparks enveloped her and her display dimmed, protecting her eyes. The cheers and whoops of her team filled her ears.

"Excellent work, Miss Lynn," Hugo said. "That will provide a much-needed boost of TEPs to the heavy weapons."

"I didn't even—need to use—Shared Fate," Lynn subvocalized between pants, grinning as she caught her breath.

A second resounding roar above her head wiped the smile right off her face.

"You've *got* to be kidding me," she groaned.

Lynn spun, head tilted up to search for the incoming Draca.

Another roar sounded, then another.

"*Shit*," Lynn said, scanning the skies more frantically. "How many, Hugo?"

"Four, I'm afraid."

"*Four*?" A cold wash of dread chilled her from head to toe, and she swallowed.

"There is no reason they would all target you, Miss Lynn. Retreat and stick close to your team. There is an entire company here to deal with—"

"Alpha Company," Abrams' voice broke in, "Skolex is retreating, heading north. Reform spear formation and advance to keep it in range. Continue all fire. Move!"

That was good, Lynn thought frantically, trotting forward to rejoin her squad. The north side of the parking lot in front of them was mostly devoid of TDMs, avoidant as they were of the boss. That meant she'd have plenty of room to dodge Dracas, and her platoon could back her up without being mobbed from behind by Jotnars and Chimeras.

Lynn's gamer brain moved a mile a minute.

Alpha Company could kill the Dracas infinitely faster if they could close to melee range and nobody had to worry about dodging attacks. Plus, without a seething press of TDMs in the direction they were advancing to stay in range of Skolex, the Dracas would be their only source of TEPs to stop the boss before it crossed the electric rail and started engulfing streets and business.

A roaring fire of adrenaline chased away the cold dread. She knew what she had to do. If these bastards wanted a piece of The Snake, then The Snake would be happy to oblige.

"Ronnie," she said in the team channel, "you've got Skadi's Wolves. Hugo," she said directly to the AI, "get me Abrams."

"Raven," came the commander's voice, "this had better—"

"Heavy weapons needs those Dracas for TEPs," she said over more roars sounding in her earbud. "I'll draw their fire. Have 1st, 2nd, and 3rd back me up."

"Stand down, Hunter. All platoons will work together to—"

"No time, incoming!" Lynn said, spotting the closest Draca making a beeline for Alpha Company. It looked like it had taken off from the other side of Skolex to fly over the boss and get at the threat. Three similar forms were converging from other points of the compass. Lynn started shooting at the Draca nearly overhead even as she trotted forward, pulling ahead of her squad and into Light Brigade's formation.

"Raven, stop being suicidal!" Derek snapped at her.

"The shoe fits," she shot back at him, grinning like a maniac and welcoming the challenge with open arms. After all, they were going to jump her anyway. Might as well make the best of it.

"We've got your back, Raven," Ronnie said, then started slinging orders to the other guys on their team channel.

"Platoon leaders," Abrams' calm voice cut across all other chatter, controlling the situation, "modify formations to surround and destroy incoming Dracas. Use bait markers to control the mob behind us. Hamilton's Own, stay locked on Skolex."

"Hit their underbellies as they come in," Druid added, sounding cool as a cucumber in the chaos. "Less armor under there."

Then the closest Draca dove at her, and Lynn lost track of all else but the enemy. Unyielding ground smacked into her shoulder as she rolled, making her think longingly of grass fields. No tripping hazards in sight, though, so that was good.

Another Draca dove as the closest landed in an inner ear vibration that simulated its heavy body hitting the asphalt.

No time for attacks, only running.

A third Draca dove. Now she was surrounded.

But not alone.

Team Black Templars charged the closest Draca from behind, every one of them laying into it with chainsaw swords and heavy blasters. Champion and Brayard, their team's two assault elements, went straight for its underbelly, while the other three attacked its flanks. They were joined by half a dozen other teams getting in close and dirty while a storm of fire poured in from the rest of the platoons on all sides.

The Draca, as she'd predicted, ignored its assailants completely and charged her instead.

All Lynn had to do was keep moving.

She picked one of the Draca and stuck to it like a limpet, Wrath forgotten as she blocked fire and teeth with Bastion.

The fourth Draca joined the mob and lunged at her, long neck snaking out toward her with teeth as big as her head ready to crunch down on flesh and bone.

Not real.

She jumped back inside the Draca behind her to escape the strike, and nausea swept over her.

Real enough.

She lunged to the side, getting out of one Draca only to be blasted in the face with flame from another.

Her health plummeted.

"Shared Fate," she gasped, no breath to even say Hugo's name.

"Done, Miss Lynn! Hang in there, you're not alone!"

She was dimly aware of the thundering report of dozens of weapons, but every cell in her body was focused on her display, which she'd widened to give herself better coverage of her peripheries. She let go of conscious thought and let her body react directly to every flash of movement and instinct honed by a thousand hours of live combat.

A deluge of sparks exploded behind her, so she retreated in that direction, swinging Bastion in an arc to catch the three gouts of flame aimed at her. Her rate of health loss had slowed from a supersonic dive to a steady ebb, but it wouldn't last long—and neither would she. Bastion got hotter and hotter in her hand, as if the combined attacks from all three Draca were overloading its shielding ability.

Before the shield-shaped baton could burst into flame, Lynn ducked and dashed forward, getting under one Draca and confusing the other two as she dodged around the bulky body. She got under its tail, hoping proximity to its particle signature would help hide her. It just roared and backed up, though, enveloping her again in sweeping nausea. She dodged to the side to get out, and ducked under another Draca's neck, moving forward and back with its frustrated lunges to stay out of range. The other two spun and quickly spotted her, though, sending her fleeing once again.

Her breath burned in her lungs, and she stumbled as she dodged, her head spinning.

Another explosion of sparks. A roar of chainsaws and a chilling war chant she was too distracted to listen to.

Lynn dove toward one of the two remaining Dracas, putting it between herself and the last one, which she knew from experience wouldn't lunge through its companion to get to her. She pumped her arms and dredged deep to force more energy into her flagging limbs. Adrenaline faded and all she had left was pure, unadulterated Larry spite to keep her juking left and right, forward and back in a furious dance to outmaneuver the two Draca.

Just when Lynn's lungs felt like they would burst from the strain of her gasping, the last two Draca exploded simultaneously.

Intense, euphoric relief weakened her legs to the point of collapse, but she clutched at her Larry rage and breathed in cold purpose, replenishing the oxygen in her lungs.

Skolex still lived, and that was unacceptable.

The *whump-whump-whump* of heavy weapons fire grounded her, and the rest of the world came back into focus. Lynn's ears were bombarded with the sound of gunfire, a cacophony of TDM cries, and triumphant cheers from the squads around her.

"All units," Abrams barked, cutting across the chaos, "hold your position and target Skolex with all long-range ordinance."

With pleasure, Lynn thought, too exhausted to even subvocalize.

She knelt in place to save her strength and took desperate pulls of water from her bladder while her batons combined into a copy of Sonia's favored sniper rifle. Then she aimed and let loose on the boss with her highest damage exploding ammo. The air must have been thick with the former Dracas' TEPs because her power levels didn't drop even a hair as she fired round after round.

The sharp increase in damage seemed to trigger Skolex's aggro, because its lumbering flight halted. It raised one giant end of its tubular body, arcing it through the air from the north over to the south. The worm's front half came crashing down pointed the opposite direction it had been going, its toothy maw aimed directly at Alpha Company as it lumbered toward them.

"Shitshitshitshit," Grim said into the brief lull.

"Stay on target," Crash commanded. "It knows it's toast, that's why it's attacking. Last-ditch desperation move."

"What if it shoots us with worm goo?" Ch'hala from Zahn Wars said, her voice high-pitched with tension.

"Can't goo ya if it's dead, now can it?" Gadsden replied, as if he actually thought that would make his squad-mate feel better.

"Less talking, more shooting," came Druid's sing-song voice.

Skolex's giant, bulbous body rippled with each massive scrunch-lunge forward in a grotesque parody of an inch worm. Its movements were not quick, but it was so enormous that each scrunch-lunge carried it forward dozens of feet.

Before long, Lynn could see the individual teeth of its many-layered jaws. Its entire head was one huge mouth, and it was getting disturbingly close.

"Deploy force shields," Abrams said calmly. The commander was no doubt watching the distance close with hawklike focus, with Hugo providing him the combat system's best analysis of Skolex's attack range and probable damage capabilities.

Lynn separated her sniper rifle back into Bastion and Abomination. The gargantuan worm was within Abomination's range now, so she didn't stop firing as she pushed to her feet and took a step forward, putting herself slightly in front of the firing line, just in case. She had to plant her feet and concentrate on her balance to stay upright. So many parts of her wanted to quit. But her body wasn't the boss of her, so she told it to suck it up and deal.

"Spooks closing to effective range behind us," 3rd Platoon's leader reported. "Falling back won't be quick."

"3rd Platoon, redirect fire to the rear and start clearing a path," Abrams ordered.

Lynn didn't look behind her, but the storm of multicolored bolts of light raining down on Skolex thinned, indicating 3rd Platoon had peeled off and redirected.

All of her instincts said to push as hard as possible, to not give one single inch. But she understood Abrams' order.

Did bosses heal? If the shit hit the fan and they had to retreat, or even drop out of combat mode and book it to safety, would it be even harder to kill Skolex whenever they regrouped and came back? Would it try to get away in the meantime, crawl straight through Indianapolis' busy downtown streets?

A rumbling, vibrating moan was the only warning they got.

Skolex convulsed and thrashed, whipping its battering-ram head in their direction as a tsunami of poison-green slime gushed from its mouth.

Lynn lunged sideways towards Mack, Bastion held high. Her body braced for impact, anticipating the feel of liquid splashing over her, maybe hot acid burning through her clothes. Of course, her brain forgot that the ultra-realistic graphics and sounds did not translate to reality. All they did was create a visual experience that helped Hunters react effectively to the TDMs.

Instead of a rain of disgusting goo splashing all over them, a wave of dizziness made Lynn stumble as Bastion's grip grew hot in her hand. But the dizziness and heat passed quickly, and Lynn straightened. Mack was bending over, hands on knees, taking in great gulps of air like he was fighting the overwhelming urge to vomit, but otherwise he seemed fine. The sounds of gunfire that had faded momentarily now increased again, and the Pounders' *whump-whump-whumps* continued.

"Alpha Company, fall back formation. Hamilton's Own, reconfigure for close-range fire. Move out!"

Lynn gritted her teeth, fighting the impulse to tell Abrams he was making a mistake. They needed to go all out. Most of the Hunter Strike Teams hadn't used their massive, last-resort special abilities like Gadsden's longhorn stampede. Why weren't they giving it one last push before surrendering the advantage to the boss? Was the risk of being this close higher than she realized? There was so much she didn't know, and it grated on every instinct she had.

There was a sudden shudder of movement along the giant worm's bulbous body, and before Lynn could brace for another slime storm, her vision lit with a blinding flash that dimmed her display almost black.

When it cleared, Skolex was gone.

The Hunter Strike Teams erupted in cheering.

Teammates back-slapped, high-fived, and hugged each other, jumping up and down and screaming in victory. Lynn saw a few even break down in tears, the overwhelm of relief on top of the preceding chaos and fear too much for their emotions to handle without some sort of release.

She was too exhausted to follow suit, but gladly accepted Edgar's excited side hug and gave him a reassuring, "fine" when he asked if she was okay.

Her Larry instincts were still engaged, and she could see that the Alpha Testers were similarly on guard. They maintained formation discipline, their focus shifting to the remaining enemies around them instead of lowering weapons and celebrating their kill.

"Good work, Alpha Company," Abrams said, and Lynn spotted him next to Ion's team of Pounder bearers. "There's no rest for the wicked, though, or the competent. We're not done. HQ wants all Alpha Class TDMs dispatched at the very least. We need to make this area safe for the public again. Form up!"

Now Lynn almost cried. Her body pleaded with her to give up, to lie down.

But she had a job to do, and there was no part of her willing to let her team or her country down.

The cleanup seemed to take forever, and it taxed Lynn to the last dredges of her willpower and endurance. By the time the airbus landed to pick them up, she was stumbling from exhaustion—and she wasn't the only one. If Edgar hadn't been there to subtly guide her onto the bus and get her seated, she might have laid down on the asphalt and passed out. As it was, as soon as she was seated, she leaned against the closest solid object, which happened to be Edgar, and fell asleep.

Chapter 8

LYNN WOKE UP FEELING SAFE AND WARM. AS MUZZY AWARENESS returned, she realized she was tucked snugly under Edgar's arm, her head cushioned on one of his impressively large pecs. Her brain debated whether she was scandalized enough to sit up and move away.

She'd just reached the conclusion that she was too tired to care when the airbus stopped moving and Edgar shifted. He gently hauled her to her feet and they joined the shuffling, exhausted crowd exiting the airbus so they could return to their barracks on Minot Air Force Base.

They were given a full twenty-four hours to shower, sleep, eat, and debrief.

Lynn felt considerably more cheerful about their first Battle Tour boss kill after she'd gotten a solid ten hours of rack time and a hot meal. In fact, everyone seemed optimistic, even giddy, when they assembled back in the simulation center for catered lunch the next day and a debrief. Bravo company was off on their first boss battle in Sacramento, but Charlie company was present, and the collected Hunters and Alpha Testers mingled, sharing battle stories and catching up.

Lynn opted to sit and keep to herself, mostly because *everyone* was talking about the Draca fight. People seemed to think she'd lured the Dracas in on purpose and used bait markers to heroically fix their attention on her so the company could easily kill them and harvest their TEPs. She was back-slapped and congratulated on her "mad tank skills" and "god-level aggro" until she wanted to frag the next person who mentioned it. She finally stopped hiding her resting Larry face, and the next few people who came over quickly turned around and walked the other way when they got a glimpse of it.

Edgar hovered, obviously sensing her tension. But there was no enemy for him to fight off, just lots of happy, friendly teammates. She eventually chased him away and told him to go congratulate Ion for the excellent work Hamilton's Own had done blowing Skolex up.

She was just wondering when the debrief would start when she overheard Dan's enthusiastic voice.

"Ronnie, did you see that new TD Hunter ad drop this morning? It was *sick*. If I wasn't already playing TD Hunter, I'd have signed up on the spot."

Lynn furtively looked over her shoulder in time to see Ronnie roll his eyes.

"Yeah. I saw it."

"Can you believe they got *Larry freaking Coughlin* to do an ad?" Dan enthused, arms gesticulating in emphasis.

Ronnie made a scoffing noise.

"There's no way that was Larry Coughlin," he said. "That old geezer lives in a wheelchair in some dark basement in the middle of nowhere, probably with booby traps set up all around his house. The whole ad was fake."

Lynn slapped a hand over her mouth to smother her snort of laughter, then shifted to rubbing her jaw to cover the movement.

"I dunno," Mack said, pursing his lips thoughtfully. "That looked and sounded a whole lot like Larry. And if anyone would know, I would, since I've probably spent more time getting fragged by him than anyone else in WarMonger. Except Ronnie, of course."

Lynn legitimately lost it. She bent over her seat in a fit of coughing to cover her explosive laughter. When she finally got ahold of herself and glanced back at the guys, Mack was looking at her in concern, but Dan and Ronnie were still talking.

"Nobody knows what he really looks like, you doofus," Ronnie was saying. "They just built their generation off his WarMonger avatar and whatever clips of his voice they have."

"Yeah, but he still would've had to agree to it," Dan pointed out. "He's got a say in how they use his likeness and handle."

Ronnie shrugged. "They probably threw a bunch of money at him. He's a merc, he'll do anything for a buck."

That was factually incorrect, since Lynn wouldn't do anything for a single buck—except frag Ronnie, and that she would do for free. Her expertise commanded top dollar fees, and she'd usually gotten more job offers than she'd been able, or inclined, to accept.

The reminder of her former double life was accompanied by a dim longing, but only because she missed the carefree challenge of player versus player without her life or future on the line. Everything else about that era was happily in her rearview mirror.

The body image issues.

Her constant anxiety.

The monotony and loneliness of life.

Were there parts of her present she would happily do without? Abso-freaking-lutely. But she would never regret what she'd achieved, or the growth she'd fought tooth and nail for.

Speaking of growth...

"Yeah, that last part was pretty cool, even if it was generated," Ronnie was saying, shrugging one shoulder.

Dan raised his eyebrows.

"Who are you and what did you do with Ronnie? Yeah, the ad was totally cool, but I expected you to flip out and go on some rant in Lithuanian. I thought you hated Larry?"

Ronnie scowled and crossed his arms.

"I do. He's a bully and a jerk. But I'm not gonna waste time obsessing over him like some lame stream-stalker."

Lynn turned away because her cheek muscles were flat out ignoring her and there was no way to hide the grin on her face without being obvious about it. She sipped from her hydration tube to give herself something innocuous to do while she continued eavesdropping.

"Are you kidding me?" Dan said. "You used to gripe about him almost every day when we were in school. It was all Larry this and Larry that."

"That was before we started TD Hunter," Ronnie shot back, sounding annoyed. Lynn wished she could see his face, but didn't dare turn around to peek. "I've outgrown WarMonger. It's pretty tame, compared to what we do now."

"If you say so," Dan said, his tone dubious.

"Hey, if Larry Coughlin is playing TD Hunter, maybe we'll get to meet him one day!" Mack said.

Lynn choked on the water she'd been trying to swallow and devolved into another fit of coughing to clear the liquid she'd inhaled. It was lucky she was turned away, because she wasn't sure even the coughing could erase her expression of abject horror at the idea of meeting Larry Coughlin fans in the real.

"Don't be a simp," Ronnie scoffed. "I told you, there's no way that was Larry Coughlin in that ad. You can't sound that old and be that spry at the same time. They just took his voice print and used AI to generate the coolest action sequence they could think of. Maybe they even used a live actor for the moves. But it wasn't him."

"Maybe," Mack said, and Lynn shuddered at the genuine disappointment in his voice. "Even if you're right about the ad and he's disabled or something, that doesn't mean he'd never do live promotions, right? Or be a special guest at some TD Hunter event?"

"Don't count on it," Ronnie said decisively. "He has his whole super scary merc persona to keep up. No way he'd be seen in public in a wheelchair. It'd ruin his rep in WarMonger. I'll bet Larry Coughlin will hide in his basement till his dying day. Nobody will even know he's croaked. He'll just disappear from WarMonger and never come back. They'll probably find his skeleton years later still in whatever gaming rig he used."

A wicked smile lifted the corners of Lynn's mouth, and an overwhelming urge gripped her to turn around and say something dramatic in Larry's voice. Something like: "No, Payne, they'll find *your* skeleton. But it would be missing the backbone after I'd ripped it out and mounted it on my wall."

She'd get to enjoy his paralyzed shock for a few sweet, sweet seconds. Then reality would hit and she'd have to face the fallout from five years of lying and deception.

Not a smart move.

The more she thought about it, the faster the temptation to speak faded. That kind of bombshell would tear their team apart and jeopardize the mission. And no way would Ronnie take it quietly. He'd make a huge scene in the middle of hundreds of elite gamers. Even if all those present didn't play WarMonger, most knew what it was and had likely heard of Larry Coughlin. She suspected she'd fought with or against most of the Alpha Testers at some point or another.

She could see it now, sitting at the center of a shocked crowd of gamers, all staring at her with varying degrees of anger or disbelief.

Yeah, no. *That* was never going to happen.

The noise level of chatter around Lynn lowered and she looked up to see that Abrams had arrived and was talking to Elliot "DevilDog" Rosenthal, Charlie Company's commander. Hunters and Alpha Testers converged on the rows of chairs set up on the concrete floor and everyone found seats while Abrams finished his conversation, then strode purposefully toward the front. Lynn moved aside so her team could stream past her into the row she'd chosen. Edgar claimed the empty seat beside her end chair, as usual, and nudged her as he sat down.

"That *was* a pretty sick ad, *uce*," he muttered out of the side of his mouth, shooting her a covert grin.

Lynn froze, eyeing Edgar like he was a grenade with its pin pulled.

"Uhhh—" her brain froze, no smooth comeback presenting itself despite her furious demand. Did Edgar suspect her secret identity? She'd wondered off and on, ever since she'd been tapped to beta test TD Hunter. Edgar had always been suspiciously unsurprised about her gaming skills. But he'd never confronted her—

"Good to see your shining faces this morning, Hunters!" Abrams' subvocalized voice interrupted Lynn's panicked thought and gave her the perfect excuse to turn away from Edgar and pretend their conversation never happened. Abrams had taken up a parade rest stance in front of the two companies and was now surveying the crowd. "I hope you got plenty of rest, because you'll be back at it in two days for Alpha Company, and tomorrow for you Charlie Company layabouts."

There were some good-natured chuckles from the other company, and Lynn took a deep breath, trying to set aside Larry worries to focus on the here and now.

"First off, I want to congratulate Alpha Company for their

hard work and exemplary performance yesterday. You successfully took out a Sierra Class-3 nodality with zero casualties or equipment loss, and pretty decent scores if the TD Hunter leaderboard is any indication."

The room erupted in applause and celebratory war cries. Abrams had to hold up his hands to quiet the commotion before he continued.

"That's the good news," he continued. "The bad news is that there were multiple civilian deaths in the area leading up to our battle. Two were apparent fishermen who ignored the cordon to cut across the parking lot heading for the White River. Their bodies were found during Tsunami's breakdown and cleanup of the area. The third was a small-time game streamer found inside the cordon near the generating station. Our best guess is that he was trying to sneak in to get unsanctioned footage of the boss battle. He wasn't found until this morning when engineer teams were inspecting the station before bringing it back online.

"I'd like to observe a minute of silence to honor the fallen, these and many others across the country. Their loved ones will likely never know what happened to them, and that is a hard, if necessary, pill to swallow. We are the few and lonely witnesses to the truth."

He finished and bowed his head. A heavy silence fell over the room.

Not a soul moved.

Lynn, who'd been sitting with her arms crossed, hands tucked under her arms, clenched her fists until her fingernails bit painfully into her palms.

We will avenge you, she thought.

Had Steve warned her mom to stay away from all node infrastructure? What about Kayla? Mrs. Pearson? The entire GIC staff? What about her high school classmates, running around Cedar Rapids playing TD Hunter?

They all needed to know.

"Thank you," Abrams subvocalized, indicating an end to the minute of silence.

Lynn's hands relaxed, but the tension in her shoulders didn't.

"In case any of you are wondering," he continued, as if he'd read Lynn's mind, "CIDER has already partnered with government contractors all over the country to cordon off nodes to increase public safety. We have a long, *long* list of nodalities in populated areas and have, of course, been working with G-Force Utilities and various city officials to keep people away from those areas. Every mesh site, stream, and public announcement related to these utilities is telling people to stay away from nodes and follow all government safety advisories while G-Force investigates the troubling rise in blackouts. But we can't help people who blatantly ignore safety warnings and climb over cordons."

Lynn's jaw clenched, but she forced herself to relax, one muscle at a time. They were doing all they could. The fastest solution to this horrible situation was to wipe out the spooks for good, so that's what she would do.

Abrams continued the brief, giving an after-action report and overview of the boss battle for the benefit of Charlie Company, who would be facing their own boss tomorrow in Valley Forge, just northwest of Philadelphia. After that he went over some tactical considerations for future battles, then opened up the floor for questions.

Gadsden piped up before anyone else could even open their mouth.

"Sir," the Texan said in a thicker drawl than usual, "I hereby submit a company request to append RavenStriker's handle. Hence forth it shall read: RavenStriker, the Draca Queen."

The room erupted in scattered laughter, clapping, and some appreciative *oorah*s. Lynn sank in her seat, suddenly grateful for Edgar's bulk blocking her view of everyone else.

"We considered RavenStriker, Suicidal Spook Bait, but Draca Queen's got a better ring to it, don't'cha think?"

"So noted," Abrams said, and drat him, there was a small but visible smile tucked into the corners of his mouth.

Lynn sank lower, wishing she had on her headgear with its adjustable tinted face shield.

The next question asked was entirely serious, and soon the room was quiet and focused once again.

Edgar pinged her, and she felt her face flush hot as she read the words.

Don't be ashamed of who you are, Toa Tama'ita'i. You are glorious, and now the whole world gets to see it.

She wanted to punch him in the shoulder, but couldn't do that, so she pinged him back instead.

I'm not trying to be glorious! They came after me, I was just trying to survive.

You could have run, he pointed out.

And betray the mission? Don't insult me.

The temptation to look over and glare at him was strong, but she resisted.

Like I said, Toa Tama'ita'i. Glorious.

Lynn rolled her eyes and huffed out a breath, focusing instead on the latest question to Abrams.

After the debrief wrapped up, they had a box lunch, during which Lynn tried to hide in a corner with Edgar. Unfortunately for her, Dan and Mack stabbed her in the back and brought over essentially their entire platoon, along with various hangers-on from the other platoons and Charlie Company to congratulate RavenStriker, the Draca Queen.

Lynn vowed to murder Gadsden—after they'd saved the world, of course.

She rejected every mention of praise and tried a dozen times to set the record straight that all she'd done was try to stay alive in an impossible situation where the Draca already seemed locked on to her.

But no one listened.

"Guys, quit encouraging people!" she subvocalized in their Skadi's Wolves team chat. "Tell everybody I didn't do anything. You were there the first time we fought a Draca. You saw how it got weirdly obsessed with me. I wasn't doing anything special!"

"Are you kidding me?" Dan said. "You took on *four* Draca yesterday and survived. That's the opposite of doing nothing."

"But I didn't 'take on' anything! I didn't even land any major blows. I just ran around in circles and tried not to get roasted." Lynn kept a strained smile pasted on her face as she fussed subvocally at her team because the captain of Zahn Wars, Thrawn, was regaling her with their own part of the Draca battle while she'd been busy dodging teeth and fire.

"Sounds like Gadsden should have gone with Suicidal Spook Bait," Ronnie subvocalized. "More accurate."

It didn't escape Lynn's notice that Ronnie was standing off to the side, arms crossed, watching the chatting mob with a neutral expression. Was he secretly jealous of the attention she was getting?

He had no idea how much she wished their roles were reversed.

Thanks for taking care of the team, she pinged him. His eyes met hers through the crowd and he gave a minuscule shrug, then looked away.

Don't get yourself killed doing something stupid next time, he pinged back. *Dan and Mack are less insufferable when you're around, and Edgar talks more.*

Got it, I'll do my best, she responded, looking back at Thrawn and hoping the sudden tingling in the corners of her eyes didn't show.

That might have been the nicest thing Ronnie had ever said to her. Coming from him, it felt like the equivalent of a bearhug and a pledge of eternal brotherhood.

She tried not to let it go to her head.

After lunch they spent the afternoon doing formation drills, then ate a hot boxed dinner and got ready to return to their barracks. As Lynn was following the rest of her team towards the door, Hugo piped up in her ear.

"Pardon me, Miss Lynn, but Commander Muller has requested your presence for a quick word."

It took Lynn a second to realize Hugo meant Abrams, and another second to realize what he was actually saying.

Oh, shit. That could not be good.

"Sure," she subvocalized, looking around. "Where is he?"

"There is a door nearby to your left that leads to a small office, he's waiting for you there," Hugo said.

Lynn gulped, sent a quick ping to her team, then peeled away toward the door Hugo had indicated. She took a deep breath before she entered, and kept her back straight and eyes up as she turned the doorknob and stepped inside.

She froze as she was pulling the door shut behind her.

"Steve?" she said, word coming out squeaky in her surprise.

The room was a perfectly normal and nondescript corporate office, likely belonging to whoever managed the day-to-day of the simulation facility. But while Abrams was sitting behind the desk exactly where she'd expected him to be, Steve was also there, sitting in a chair beside the desk, muscular legs stretched out in front of him as if he'd been there for a while. His sharp eyes swept her up and down, as if checking for injury, and the skin around his eyes crinkled, though he hid any other sign he was happy to see her. He also didn't greet her, and the lack of his usual, "Hey, kid," felt faintly ominous.

Hugo presented her with a group chat request and she gulped before accepting it.

"I won't take up much of your time, Raven," Abrams subvocalized, sticking to the directive that company interactions be subject to OPSEC. "Please, join us."

He waved to the front of the desk, and Lynn finished pulling the door closed before moving to take up a parade rest stance where he'd indicated. Abrams gave her a closed-mouth smile and a reassuring nod. It helped to quiet the panicky anxiety that had started to build behind her breastbone.

"Don't mind Mr. Riker. His presence here will soon be explained. I called you in because I wanted to make sure we're on the same page. I've already spoken with Death, who you battled alongside on multiple occasions before the national championship, correct?"

Lynn nodded, wondering why the twenty questions since Hugo could instantly recite all the facts. The AI had been watching and recording everything everyone did in the TD Hunger app, after all. Did they not trust his analysis? Or were they just being extra careful?

"Death confirmed that you've been strangely singled out by a Draca before this. I would like your take on it though, if you would. How did the first interaction with a Draca happen, did you use any bait markers or other tactics to engage the Draca's attention, that sort of thing."

"I didn't do anything different, I swear," Lynn subvocalized, glancing at Steve, who had on a neutral mask. "It was an unknown when we first engaged it. It was lurking at a substation, and I think I might have been the first to shoot it, but the guys targeted it right after. We all took damage at first, but that might have been because it was using a flame for area effect. We couldn't see it at that point because Hugo hadn't identified it. Once it took off and dove for us, though, it didn't target anyone but me."

Lynn screwed up her face in thought.

"I had my force shield out and was shooting at it with my gun while the others held off till it was in range. Then I tried to use a bait marker to distract it while I dodged, but it ignored the marker. Maybe it has a singular target system that locks onto the first aggressor and doesn't shift?" she suggested.

Abrams shook his head. "The first Draca you fought yesterday targeted you before you even knew it was there. And the others all went straight for you."

"Hive mind?" Lynn suggested. "Maybe they remembered me from before through some kind of collective consciousness and they were holding a grudge?"

Abrams' mouth twisted to the side in thought.

"We don't know enough about these entities to make even an educated guess," he said, then leaned forward and put his forearms on the desk. "However, this incident combined with another unique trait you have in relation to the TDMs has gotten some people wondering."

Apprehension prickled the hairs on the back of her neck. She glanced at Steve again, but his face held no answers.

"Another trait, sir?" she subvocalized.

Abrams raised his eyebrows.

"Surely you've noticed how little the TDMs affect you compared to other people. Or have you been too busy throwing yourself in the path of danger to notice?" he asked, his eyes lightening with amusement.

She didn't know what to say to that, so she went with the simplest response.

"Yeah, I noticed. Counted on it a few times, too, I guess."

Steve snorted softly, and something in Lynn finally relaxed, as if her subconscious hadn't believed it was really Steve sitting there until he stopped acting like a darn statue.

"A few times," Abrams agreed, the amusement fading from his eyes as he contemplated her. Finally, he spoke again.

"You are a very interesting young woman, Raven. We are lucky to have your expertise and dedication. We at CIDER are grasping at straws each and every day, desperately trying to find a leg up, any solution that will help us hold out a little longer. That's why I've been asked to have you accompany Mr. Striker to CIDER's main laboratory for some tests."

A cold chill trickled down Lynn's spine. This time she did not look at Steve, afraid of what she might see.

"Uhh, tests? Like, what kind of tests?"

Abrams quirked a smile.

"Nothing too invasive, if that's what you're thinking. We need you fighting ready for your next stop on the Battle Tour. CIDER's research team will likely take a blood sample and do some brain scans."

Well, that didn't sound too bad. Lynn relaxed fractionally.

"Sure, I guess. This is, um, more of an order than a request, though, right?"

Abrams nodded gravely.

"I'm afraid so, at least as long as you're a part of the TD Counterforce. I don't know that CIDER is at the point of commandeering private citizens just yet. But *you* volunteered. You're here to help, and this is how you can help. You'll leave right away so Steve can have you back before it gets too late."

The vibrating unease was back and Lynn forced herself to look at Steve, searching his face for reassurance. He smiled at her, and though the smile reached his eyes, he still didn't seem entirely relaxed.

"I'll go, of course," Lynn subvocalized slowly, mind racing.

She could trust Steve, right? She believed that—*wanted* to believe that. And yet... he'd lied to her once, and she knew he probably would again if his country demanded it. He'd taken an oath, after all. Wouldn't she do the same thing in his situation?

A sudden memory of eating dinner with Mr. Thomas in his apartment back in Cedar Rapids came to her. They'd been talking about codes of honor and if it was really honor if it was selectively applied.

Well, they could both be honorable and still be smart at the same time.

"Is it all right if Edgar comes with me? I mean Maui," she added, looking back at Abrams.

The commander's brow furrowed, but he didn't look displeased. After a moment, he nodded.

"I had Hugo notify him. Managed to catch him right before the airbus left. He should be here shortly." Abrams' eyes refocused on her, and he stood. "We assumed you would prefer to keep all of this to yourself, but as long as you're comfortable with Maui being privy to your tests, then there's no problem if he tags along. Please keep your trip between the two of you, though. It isn't classified, we just want to prevent gossip that could morph and spread into something harmful to the mission. If anyone asks, you can say you were both helping our tactics team analyze the Dracas' behavior, which is perfectly true."

Lynn nodded, feeling one hundred percent better.

"Thank you, sir," she subvocalized.

"No need. We're all doing everything we can in this fight. Good evening, Raven, I'll see you at briefing tomorrow."

With that he strode around the desk and out of the room, leaving the door open.

Steve pushed himself to his feet with a grunt, and finally smiled at Lynn, though it didn't light up his face the way it usually did.

"Come on, kid. Or should I say, RavenStriker, the Draca Queen?"

Lynn punched him in the arm.

"Ow," he subvocalized, though his chuckle was perfectly audible. He rubbed the spot. "I thought you'd be happy. You're the Snake in WarMonger. Isn't the Draca Queen an upgrade?"

"One more word about nicknames and this old snake will make you regret having man parts," Lynn growled, giving Steve a dead-eye stare.

"Okay, okay." He held up his hands in surrender, though he was still grinning. "Let's get going. The faster we get there, the faster we can get back."

Edgar was in the simulation hall when they exited the office, and he hurried over as soon as he spotted them.

"What's going on?" he asked, looking between them with a wary expression.

"I'll explain on the way," Lynn said, and made a "let's move out" gesture with one finger extending to point at the exit.

Edgar's brow furrowed, but he fell in step with them and they both followed Steve out of the building.

Steve Riker did not like this. He did not like it one bit.

He sat in a secluded waiting room of the Oak Ridge National Laboratory where CIDER had its hidden-in-plain-sight research HQ. The chair he sat on was spartan and uncomfortable, the walls were undecorated, and the room smelled faintly of cleaner fluid. But that was all par for the course in a place like this. Which was why he was trying to relax as best he could, given the circumstances. He leaned back against the wall with his arms crossed while Edgar sat nearby, elbows on knees, staring at the door Lynn had disappeared through moments before like he thought it would vanish and take Lynn with it if he so much as blinked.

Steve wasn't worried about Lynn disappearing. Or about anything that might happen to Lynn here and now. Dr. Ed Hillenbrand had taken her back, and he knew Ed personally from over a year working as an Alpha Tester to develop the TD Hunter combat interface. The guy was a grumpy old bastard, but he had a heart of gold, even if he did his darnedest to hide it. It was buried pretty deep and crusted over by decades of sarcasm, but it was there.

Not that Steve was a people person himself. He just understood the power of human connection and the importance of relationships. You never knew when an acquaintance with somebody might prove useful. All through his life he'd leaned into networking opportunities. It was how he'd landed a job at Tsunami and gotten in with Mr. Krator—and how he'd been able to convince Edgar that Lynn would be safe with Ed.

Steve suspected that if it was up to Edgar, he'd never leave Lynn's side, like some sort of royal bodyguard.

Or a boy madly in love with no clue how to express it.

But Steve knew Lynn would be perfectly safe, and Edgar would just get in everybody's way. *Today* wasn't what worried Steve, or why there was a perpetual tension in his shoulders and neck that had been giving him stress headaches.

No, the next six months were what worried him.

Lynn was going to give him a stroke, a heart attack, or a mental breakdown. It was a tossup which one would happen first.

The way she *threw* herself into danger made him want to lock her up. Or, better yet, exile her to that island CIDER had somewhere. Maybe he'd give her a medal *then* lock her up, because he was damn proud of her.

But also . . . Steve shook his head. It had taken every ounce of his military-honed discipline to keep still and quiet when Lynn challenged *four* Dracas at once. He'd been watching the battle live with the rest of the staff from Taskforce Sanctus, and the sight had nearly given him an aneurysm. The sheer volume of colorful profanity and maledictions that had run through his head would have made Larry proud.

That girl was too good at what she did, and too eager to

do the right thing. Those sorts of people got pulled in, chewed up, and spat out by the military. They were lucky if they even got spat out. Given half a chance, Uncle Sam would ride you so hard, grind you down so low, there was nothing left to spit out.

He knew from personal experience.

And that was the *last* thing he wanted for Lynn. Plus, Matilda would literally skin him alive if he allowed CIDER to get its claws into Lynn like that. Which was why he was very, very worried about this new development.

He'd known Lynn was special. He'd known she pulled crazy stunts and the combat interface responded to her outside-the-box thinking in kind. But he hadn't known there might be something biological going on.

He didn't "need to know", but he and Ed got on well, and he'd talked to Dr. Roberts numerous times, so he'd managed to get himself the Cliffs Notes version.

Basically, they hoped there was something biologically unique about Lynn, something in her DNA that they could replicate. If they could gene-splice some sort of resistance into other people's nervous systems, or even use Lynn's natural resistance to build something with an even stronger defense against the spooks' brain-scrambling effect, then it might save millions of lives.

It was a pie in the sky hope, but that was how science worked, wasn't it? Dream the impossible, then try it out and see.

If Lynn was the key to a genetically engineered spook resistance, that fact alone shouldn't be a threat to her life or wellbeing. After all, how many blood or tissue samples could they possibly need to bioengineer a gene splice?

He was more worried about the testing and brain scans. How could they get usable data unless they pitted her against the real thing? How far would Lynn push herself if they put some ridiculous idea in her head that she had the power to save humanity, all she had to do was sacrifice her life?

The thought made Steve's hands clench, but he forced them to relax, because the reality was even worse than that.

How far would Steve *let* Lynn push herself? What would he stand by and watch her do, bound by duty, knowing it might take her away from Matilda forever?

You've gotten yourself into a nine circles of hell sort of situation, haven't you, you idiot.

He couldn't imagine abandoning Lynn or Matilda—who had finally forgiven him and started talking to him again—and he certainly wasn't going to shirk his duty. So he just had to hope their interests never conflicted in a situation he was able to influence. Which begged the question why he was finding every excuse he could to be involved in Lynn's TD Counterforce career. It was a masochistic and self-defeating strategy. He just couldn't help himself.

He'd loved his first wife more than life itself, but the cancer had kept her from having children, and then it took her away from him forever. Lynn was turning into the daughter he'd never had, and nothing in his life had ever so fulfilled or terrified him.

Steve shook his head. He needed to get off this train of thought or he'd drive himself crazy. He uncrossed his arms and leaned forward, putting his elbows on his knees and clasping his hands in front of him. Edgar was still staring at the door, so Steve took pity on him.

"Come 'ere kid. We've got a long wait and Lynn will be pissed if I let you stare at that door until your eyeballs shrivel up."

Edgar didn't immediately respond. Finally, though, he took a deep breath and broke eye contact with the door, dropping his gaze to the floor instead.

Steve sighed.

"Look, drag that chair over here, back to the door. Trust me. The time'll go faster that way."

Seeming defeated, Edgar leveraged his bulk out of the chair and dragged it across the linoleum floor to sit across from Steve. As he sat, Steve was surprised to realize the kid was just about as tall as him—and nearly as jacked.

Hmm, maybe he should take Edgar to the gym sometime, work him until he dropped. That'd be good for him. Get some of that pent-up frustration out.

Because there was an absolute *flood* of it bottled up in that boy. Steve could see it in his eyes and the way his body curved toward Lynn whenever she was around like she was a magnet and he was a mountain of iron.

To be fair, he had the same pent-up energy when it came to Matilda. But he'd had decades of experience learning how to distract himself and funnel the energy into being productive. When you spent months on end deployed in godforsaken hell holes without the touch of the woman you loved you learned how to cope. Pumping iron helped. So did mercing in WarMonger.

Existential threats to civilization were pretty distracting, too.

"So," Steve said, watching Edgar, "you and Lynn."

Edgar's head jerked up, eyes wide.

"Don't worry, kid, you've got nothing to worry about from me. Lynn's talked about you. Said you were good people." That was true, in a general sense, though it wasn't why Steve had no reservations about Edgar's obsession with Lynn. No, that was all due to Matilda. She'd nearly talked his ear off over the past six months, worrying about Lynn and Edgar. Being a single mom, she was a big believer in independence, and treated Lynn accordingly. That didn't mean she would pass up a chance to gossip and fret about her daughter's nonexistent love life if she found a willing ear.

And Steve's ear was definitely willing, if tender from overuse.

Edgar's expression relaxed and turned rueful.

"Yeah, me and Lynn," he confirmed, a goofy smile spreading over his face at the mere mention of her name.

Oof. The kid had it bad.

"You two keeping it on the down low, then? You're pretty discreet about it from what I've seen. Probably a good thing, with the public spotlight on her."

Uncertainty crept into Edgar's eyes, and his grin faded.

"Uh . . . sort of?"

Steve snorted, hiding a smile. He'd figured as much.

"That bad, huh?"

Edgar hesitated.

"You don't have to talk about it if you don't want to," Steve reassured him, leaning back again and letting his hands rest on his thighs in an open, nonthreatening gesture. "I've been trying to look out for Lynn, though. Watching you two makes it pretty obvious she's, uh, in a different headspace right now," he finished delicately.

For a moment, Edgar just stared at him, expression still. Then he heaved an enormous sigh, shoulders and face drooping.

"I don't know what to do, man. She's the most amazing thing that ever happened to me. I've been in love with her since middle school, but . . . well, she got a lotta abuse in school, cuz, uh, you know." He gestured vaguely at his chest, looking embarrassed.

"So, I just tried to keep her safe. Didn't want to make it worse, you know?"

Steve nodded. He'd brought the topic up mostly to take Edgar's mind off Lynn's absence. But at the lost, hopeless look in Edgar's eyes, he knew he couldn't leave the kid to flounder. He wasn't exactly full of relationship wisdom, considering how badly he'd already screwed up with Matilda. He'd called her the same day he'd taken Lynn to Austin, just like he'd promised. And boy had he groveled. He had nothing to lose, and everything to gain, so he hadn't held back.

Thank God Matilda had been willing to give him a second chance. She'd just been waiting for a reason. But trying to explain the oaths he'd made to his country and what he could and couldn't be open about had been one of the hardest things he'd ever done. When he'd met his first wife, he'd been a fresh-faced, idiot recruit. She'd known what she was getting into from the start. But Matilda hadn't had a clue, and that hadn't been fair to her.

Not that life was fair.

"Mind if I ask a few questions?" Steve asked, feeling things out.

"Sure," Edgar said.

"Well, has Lynn dated other guys? In other words, is she the romantic sort?"

Edgar scoffed, genuine amusement lighting his face for a moment.

"Naw, not even close. If there was some word for anti-romantic, she'd be that."

"Well, that's good, isn't it? It means she doesn't *not* like you. She just doesn't do romance. Have you talked to her about it?"

Edgar's face blanched.

"You haven't?" Steve chuckled, shaking his head.

Ah, to be young and dumb.

"It's not like that!" Edgar protested. "I didn't say anything for a long, long time, cuz she's been bullied and abused. I didn't want to be just another guy tryin'a... you know." He gestured at his own body again, looking painfully awkward.

"You didn't want her to think you were just trying to get in her pants?" Steve offered.

Edgar gulped. "Yeah, that."

"Because you're not?" Steve asked, raising both eyebrows.

"Naw, man!" Edgar looked genuinely insulted, sitting up straighter as his eyes flashed. "I'd rather *die* than hurt her, you feel me?"

"I feel you," Steve replied, remaining relaxed and calm. "I'm just doing recon, making sure I understand the situation."

That seemed to mollify Edgar, and he slumped again.

"So, you did, or you didn't talk about it?" Steve asked again.

"We, uh, kinda talked. Right before the championship in Austin. I sorta slipped up and told her how much she means to me. I didn't mean to, I swear! I wasn't gonna say anything until she was ready."

"And you'd have died of old age, kid," Steve said with a snort.

"Yeah, maybe," he said, sounding sheepish. "But I *did* get to talking, and it just spilled out."

"And?" Steve asked when Edgar didn't immediately go on. The kid had a faraway look on his face, as if he were replaying the scene in his head.

"She said . . . she said she couldn't think about it right before the competition. But she wasn't mad at me. And she still wanted me to be her friend." A soft smile crept over Edgar's lips, and Steve couldn't help shaking his head again.

Oh, boy. Oldest problem in the book. How to break it to the kid?

Steve sat up straight, rubbing the back of his neck.

"Look, Edgar. It sounds like you already have a sense of this, but there's obviously some baggage Lynn needs to work through. If she's only ever had negative things associated with a guy paying attention to her, her brain won't automatically flip the switch and be all welcoming just because the attention is coming from you. Our lizard brains don't up and forget the shit people do to us, we just kinda stuff it down in a hole. From what I can tell, she's got a solid head on her shoulders. But she's going to need some help on your end."

"Whaddya mean? I already told her how I feel. And I think . . . I think she feels something too, you know? She looks at me and goes all red sometimes." He grinned, straightening his shoulders and looking proud of himself, as if he'd accomplished something impressive.

Steve cocked his head. Well, maybe Edgar had. The kid had obviously thrown himself heart and soul into the TD Hunter competition, and his physique proved it. Steve had seen pictures of Edgar Johnston from before. The kid had accomplished something great, something he *should* be proud of.

But that didn't fix the problem.

"Yeah, it doesn't matter what Lynn knows. It matters what she feels. Do you know what women respond to?"

Edgar shook his head mutely, looking like a deer in the headlights.

Good grief, this kid really was naive. Or maybe just too noble and in love to do the usual exploration guys his age did.

"Look, Edgar, you can't get a woman to fall in love with you just by being her friend. You have to do more than that."

"Oh," Edgar said, brow furrowed, sounding genuinely lost.

"I'm not saying friendship has no place. 'Course it does. It's the difference between a lifelong happy marriage and a divorce as soon as the honeymoon phase wears off. So, good job on the friendship thing. You got that right."

"Oookay?" Edgar said. "What I get wrong, then?"

"Your MOS in her brain is 'friend,' not 'potential mate,' and based on your description, she won't be updating that category on her own, especially not in the middle of a crisis."

Edgar's brow furrowed. "So, you mean I should wait until this is all over?"

"Hell no, kid! I'm saying she needs help updating your MOS. If you really love her, and you want to be with her, you have to pursue her. Period. Otherwise, how'll she know you care enough to be a reliable partner and provider for the rest of her life? You think she wants a passive man who just waits around for life to happen? She needs to know you're *there* for her, not just physically present, but helping solve her problems, because that's what a good partner does. I get you're trying to be respectful. Good. Do that. But there's a fine line between respecting a lady, and letting your fear hold you back."

Physician, heal thyself, Steve thought, amused. Thanks to Lynn's hearty kick in the butt, he'd finally gotten himself out of his own rut of uncertainty. Hopefully Edgar could dig himself out too.

Edgar's brow was furrowed so deeply in thought that Steve wondered if he was going to sprain his forehead muscles. Still, Steve kept his mouth shut. Let the kid think it over. It was his life. Steve couldn't fix it for him.

Minutes ticked past. Steve shifted in his chair, trying to find a more comfortable position to lean back against the wall, hands folded in his lap.

Finally, the kid's eyes came up and fixed on him again, expression dead serious.

"So, what *does* a girl respond to?" Edgar asked.

Steve chuckled. Good. Right for the jugular. Problem was, what should he say? It'd been a long time since he'd been an awkward teenager trying to impress another awkward teenager.

"Ha! Trick question. Because they are all different. But, hugs are a good place to start. Especially if she's facing something difficult, or had to do something hard. Hugs release oxytocin and promote bonding. Don't be creepy or weird about it, just ask her if she wants a hug, or read her body language. Hold out your arms. Go slow. Give her time to refuse."

Edgar swallowed, his dark skin looking a bit gray around the edges.

"Don't overthink it, kid. If you want it, you've gotta go for it. Don't you think Lynn deserve someone who'll be bold even when they're scared shitless?"

"Yeah. For sure," Edgar said, though his voice was so tight the words came out squeaky.

"Atta boy," Steve said with a grin and got up. He slapped Edgar on the shoulder and headed to the water cooler across the room. He had no idea how much longer they'd be waiting, but it would probably be a while. As the Assistant S3 for Taskforce Sanctus, he had a never-ending pile of forms and reports to go through, so he had plenty to keep him busy on his LINC.

He'd given Edgar plenty to think about. Now it was up to the kid to do something about it.

Lynn didn't get to bed until well after midnight with how late they'd returned from CIDER's lab. Fortunately, they were on light duty, so PT the next morning was comparatively leisurely.

The tests had been much less scary than she'd imagined. The guy who'd run most of it, Dr. Hillenbrand, had cracked a joke right off the bat that set her at ease. Something about how he was going to draw a couple extra vials of blood to snack on later, and just because he was a sleepless vampire that didn't mean they could keep putting him on back-to-back shifts. He was going to complain about it to HR.

His dark sense of humor had tickled her Larry sensibilities.

Dr. Hillenbrand had taken her through a routine physical and a brain scan before handing her off to Dr. Roberts for some brain monitoring exercises. She'd been pretty excited to meet Dr. Roberts, and had been hard put to resist distracting him with technical questions about the TDMs. He'd had a job to do, after all, and she'd had a bunk calling her name.

To her disappointment, none of the tests had produced any kind of immediate data that shed light on the situation. But Dr. Roberts had sent her away with specially designed headgear to wear going forward. It was the same TD Counterforce issued protective gear, but with brain monitoring sensors built in. The theory was they could gather baseline data from when she was training and in simulations, and compare that to her future boss battles. They'd also be able to see what, if anything, happened if she ran into more Dracas. There was nothing different she needed to do. Hugo would take care of compiling all the data and getting it to Dr. Roberts.

The unquestioning assumption that she'd be happy to wear a brain scanner like it wasn't weird or creepy to be a lab rat had gotten her hackles up. But *she* was just as curious as Dr. Roberts to find out what was going on. Plus his unabashed enthusiasm, openness, and nerdy vibes had made Lynn willing to forgive him. It wasn't like CIDER hadn't already been spying on her twenty-four-seven.

And she *had* volunteered.

Even so, she didn't want to be reminded of it constantly, so she'd told Hugo not to bring up the data being collected unless Dr. Roberts had a breakthrough or new information.

She'd fallen asleep on the ride back, tucked once again under Edgar's arm, leaning on him for a pillow. He'd been comfortingly warm in the generous air conditioning of the airbus, and he'd seemed to like having her close.

Which was thoroughly terrifying.

And also unhelpfully thrilling.

It was getting harder as time went on to keep from thinking about the what ifs. What if they hadn't been fighting for humanity's survival? What if they'd just been a couple of high school graduates going on dates, having fun, and thinking about their future? What would dating Edgar be like?

Trying not to think about it just made her brain keep bringing it up, worrying the idea like a bone.

The pretty little fantasy was a waste of time, though. A distraction. The future was a great seething ball of chaos. What was the point of dreaming? Life as they knew it might come to an end in four months. There was no time for romance, even if she'd had a single clue how to go about it in the first place.

It was much easier to focus on her mission. *That* she understood and knew how to handle.

Alpha Company spent the day before their second Battle Tour stop going over the details, from location and terrain to a rundown of the proposed battle plan based on the boss's size and what data they had on it. After that they ran through a simulated version of the battle, mostly to familiarize them with the battle site and get more formation practice in.

Once lunch was over, they sat in on Bravo Company's first battle debrief. Word had gotten around that there'd been a few snags in the fight, though they'd pulled it off in the end. Lynn wanted to know what sort of spook surprises they'd faced or if the difficulties had been good ol' human error. Anything to help Alpha Company prepare for their next engagement.

CIDER had an entire list of nodalities affecting cities and infrastructure across the nation, prioritized by size and the potential damage they could inflict. Abrams had said the Battle Tour was simply working down the list, starting with the nine Independent System Operators, or ISOs, that collectively ran the entire energy grid across the North American continent.

They'd already taken out one boss affecting the southernmost ISO, ERCOT, when they'd killed Nagaraja in Austin. Their battle against Skolex two days ago had helped secure the Midcontinent ISO, or MISO, just north of Indianapolis. Yesterday, Bravo Company had taken out a big fungus-shaped Sierra Class-3 boss plaguing the California ISO near Sacramento. Today, Charlie Company was battling a Sierra Class-2 boss leeching off the Southwest Power Pool near Little Rock, Arkansas, and tomorrow Alpha Company would tackle a Sierra Class-1 boss squatting near the PJM Interconnection northwest of Philadelphia.

There was more than one boss affecting each grid hub, but CIDER had decided to stagger the extermination locations to make it less obvious what they were doing. The higher ups were also worried that killing too many bosses too quickly in a single area might trigger a retaliatory response from the TDMs—or whatever system or hive mind controlled them.

Two of the nine ISOs for North America were in Canada, one near Calgary, Alberta, and one near Toronto, Ontario. Lynn assumed the Canadian counterpart to Taskforce Sanctus was already tackling those.

Abrams hadn't told them anything more about CIDER's nodality target list beyond the ISOs at the top. Most likely the list balanced population size with sensitive infrastructure or military installations nearby.

Between Alpha, Bravo, and Charlie companies, they would be taking out a boss a day if everything went well. Who knew how long they could keep up that pace. A month? Two months? How long would it take before CIDER could tell if the extermination strategy was working? The Battle Tour schedule that Tsunami had announced continued until Labor Day, but it also said, "Coming to more cities near you!"

Lynn wasn't sure how many boss battles even a die-hard TD Hunter fan could watch without getting bored. She hadn't watched any of the battle footage herself, as usual. It felt too . . . trivializing. But the guys had said Tsunami was adding all sorts of cool graphics and commentary to the official company stream, plus interactive giveaways to viewers who watched live. Lynn had even heard there was a deal in the works with a bunch of VR theater franchises to stream the footage and make it a whole immersive VR experience complete with haptic suits and olfactory simulation.

If she knew anything about Mr. Krator and his company, it was that they would find every way possible to publicize—and monetize—the fight to save the world.

And so the Battle Tour continued.

Near Philadelphia they fought Ulupoka, and were very glad it was only a Class-1 boss by the end of it. It had this weird detachable head that it used as a ranged weapon, flinging it like a giant boulder, then summoning it back to launch again. The combat algorithm really went all out with the graphics. Absolutely gross. Its weakness was that it was slow, so easy to dodge. There were no injuries that a few days' rest couldn't fix.

Better yet, absolutely no Dracas showed up.

Bravo Company killed Tzitzimitl in Holyoke, Massachusetts,

that was messing up the New England ISO, and Charlie Company rounded things out by dispatching Balor near Albany to help clear the New York ISO.

Down the list they went, wiping out Sierra Class-1, 2, and 3 bosses in cities like Chicago, Atlanta, and Phoenix. Through meticulous planning and teamwork, each company got the job done and got everybody home, though there were equipment losses, sprained ankles, and frequent cases of heatstroke—because no matter how many times their squad leaders reminded them, *somebody* always forgot to hydrate.

The first serious injuries happened in Los Angeles when Bravo Company was trying to destroy a Class-3 boss designated Koschei. The boss took massive amounts of damage without reacting. It seemed unkillable. Bravo company fought in the tangle of Los Angeles' industrial district to wipe out most of the Alpha and Bravo Class ring around it, yet still it remained, inert. As a last-ditch effort, Bravo Company had closed with it, hoping the closer range would increase their TEP efficiency enough to finish it off. Instead, they'd been ambushed by a spearlike thrust from the boss's main bulk, shooting out faster than they could dodge. 3rd Platoon had gotten the closest, and two of their squads were caught in the attack and collapsed.

Fortunately, the livestream's ten-second delay meant the world never saw it. Hugo simply switched the camera views to keep the affected squads out of sight while the rest of their platoon dragged them to safety.

Bravo Company was forced to abandon the fight, though, to get their injured squads immediate medical attention. Tsunami trotted out an app malfunction cover story that sounded reasonable in context with all the other node and grid-related craziness that had been going on recently, and once again poor G-Force Utilities took the heat.

By some miracle, nobody was permanently injured. Most were released from CIDER's medical facility within a few days after careful monitoring. Two had to stay longer to recover from lingering dizziness and nausea.

It could have been worse.

The takeaway for the other companies was clear: do *not* close with the nodalities, even if they seem harmless.

Lynn watched the battle footage along with the rest of Taskforce

Sanctus in a special briefing to analyze the nodality's behavior. She barely stifled her cry of surprise when she recognized the handle from one of the Hunters who'd collapsed.

QueenBravo3-3.

The realization left her full of conflicted feelings—feelings that Ronnie and the guys didn't seem to share based on their low-key gloating in Skadi's Wolves' team chat. Since none of them crossed the line from smug to nasty, she let it lie. But she did send Elena a private "get well soon" message.

Despite the single failure in Los Angeles, confidence rode high in Taskforce Sanctus as each company came back to their base of operations flush with victory. The Battle Tour set a punishing pace, but everybody seemed to adapt to the stress, danger, and uncertainty with the usual irreverent humor and competitive streak common to gamers.

Alpha and Charlie company continued neck-and-neck in their company-wide scores. Low-key and very unofficial betting spread throughout the Taskforce, mostly among the Alpha Testers but some of the Hunters got in on it, too. Gadsden claimed to have put down a good wad of cash on Alpha Company, while Cosmos from Team Florida Man kept trying to get people to take her up on a bet that Bravo and Charlie would tie.

Hunters didn't get to hang out much with the Alpha Testers, since they bunked in different places. But they had some meals together in the simulation center and occasional downtime before and after briefings. Lynn got the impression Dan had a chat ongoing with members of Black Templars because every time he was in their vicinity, he picked up in the middle of an argument about tabletop gaming and why it was inferior to virtual gaming.

Lynn could only hide her smile and turn away.

Dan was barely eye-level with the massive pecs of most of those guys. The picture of him standing in the middle of five ripped, high-and-tight, dead-eyed men, completely oblivious to their intimidation factor while he argued obscure game theory, was not something she could keep a straight face around.

There were moments during their downtime when Lynn wondered if she would ever get to hang out with her platoon-mates as friends without the fate of humanity hanging over their heads.

Since that was another one of those pointless dreams, though, she tried not to dwell on it.

The good people and adrenaline-fueled battles made it all bearable for Lynn. Despite the risk to life and limb, despite the frustration of being under someone else's orders, despite the constant worry, getting to fight to exhaustion with some of the best people she'd ever had the pleasure of knowing kept her waking up every morning, grimly ready for the day.

Knowing she was doing good work and destroying imminent threats helped distract her from obsessing over the bigger picture. The bigger picture was none of her business, no matter how desperately she itched to understand, or have a go at CIDER's TDM data.

Somehow the publicity stunts, livestreams, and constant churn of interviews was the hardest part of it all. She'd thought, with all her experience playing a hardened merc like Larry Coughlin in virtual, that it would be easy to hide the truth of what was happening under the public's very nose.

But she realized over the weeks that she was *not* good at faking it, she was simply good at holding her tongue. Being Lynn growing up had been easy because she'd simply not talked and hidden everything behind a defensive mask. Being Larry in virtual had been easy because she'd done her research and only had to worry about words in a controlled environment. But now she was trying to integrate everything into a single person, competing professionally on livestream, while hiding the biggest secret known to humanity.

Kayla only made it worse.

Lynn's heart hurt for her friend, who was Skadi's Wolves' most supportive and enthusiastic fan. Kayla's constant updates about their subscriber count, new ideas for jokes or banter to spice things up, and design daydreams for new uniforms that mimicked their in-game armor barely registered in Lynn's brain because she was too busy worrying about Kayla's safety. With each new stream story of unexplained deaths and lawsuits piling up against G-Force Utilities, Lynn's worry grew.

Was their Battle Tour really the most effective use of their combat capability? Were they really destroying nodalities fast enough when the entire country was at risk?

Lynn didn't know, and she wasn't sure what to do about it either.

Chapter 9

"SO, GENTLEMEN, THAT'S TWENTY NODALITIES DESTROYED IN three weeks, with no fatalities and minimal injury or equipment loss," said Colonel Bryce, folding his hands behind his back. "By anyone's standards, this operation has been an unqualified success, largely thanks to the skill and hard work of our Taskforce Sanctus personnel."

Steve pumped a mental fist in the air, more excited about the no fatalities than the twenty bosses killed. There were appreciative murmurs from others around the large conference table at Tsunami HQ, some physically present while others attended virtually. This was the first major review of Operation Battle Tour since it began, and so included the Tsunami liaisons helping run the tour and a few civilian oversight members of the US government in addition to various leadership, staff, and scientists from CIDER.

"Who cares how many invisible monsters you're blowing up. Why don't you answer the only question that matters: is it keeping our citizens safe?"

The obnoxiously loud voice that spoke from a holographic screen halfway down the table belonged to Patricia Woods, a political appointee more suited to supervising waste management than delicate military operations. Steve suspected that no one present would shed many tears if she accidentally tripped and fell into a woodchipper.

Steve saw General Kozelek and Colonel Bryce exchange looks, but it was Mr. Krator who spoke up.

"Ms. Woods, we are already doing everything we can, from setting up barriers to working with local governments, to keep civilians safe. So far, the fatalities have largely been caused by ordinary people ignoring safety rules, rather than infrastructure failure or TDM attacks."

"None of which would happen if CIDER immediately informed the public of this very real and present threat and gave everyone the tools to see and avoid risk."

Mr. Krator's nostrils flared, and Steve knew exactly why. Before the battle tour, Ms. Woods had still spent half her time arguing that the scientists had been mistaken and perhaps this entire crisis was a hoax cooked up by big corporations and right-wing military fanatics. Why? Profit, obviously, and to establish backdoor military alliances to circumvent the country's rightful governing officials.

"Ms. Woods," General Kozelek said, smoothly stepping into the conversation. "As you know, we have a carefully thought-out contingency prepared if we do get to the point where public safety is no longer served by continuing to operate in secret. However, we are far from reaching that point. Or would you really attempt to argue that revealing an invisible alien invasion would cause *less* chaos and death than our current situation?"

"Our citizens deserve to know the truth," Ms. Woods said. "The blood of every innocent who has wandered into danger is on *your* hands, General. If we inform the public, anyone who ignores our safety precautions will only have themselves to blame for getting hurt."

Steve frowned, but quickly smoothed his expression back to neutrality. Listening to this woman made him feel slimy all over. He doubted she actually cared about the American people. She seemed much more interested in avoiding liability and consolidating her own political power. After all, how could people be impressed by how important she was if nobody even knew about her appointment? That was probably the real reason she wanted to go public.

"You're right, Ms. Woods," General Kozelek said, his voice quiet, but hard. "Their blood *is* on my hands. And I accept that responsibility. The call is ultimately up to the President, in conjunction with the other allied heads of state within CIDER. We will continue to take every factor into account when advising him on the risks and benefits of going public. We have multiple contingencies prepared, and will not hesitate to take the appropriate course of action once secrecy is no longer beneficial to the mission and the American people. Your question," the General continued, holding up a hand to forestall the woman's protest, "does bring up an important topic, however." He turned to the hologram of Dr. Quasnitschka. "Doctor, what does the grid data show for the last week or so? Are the nodality reductions easing the stress on our infrastructure?"

The doctor grimaced.

"We have seen an incident drop in the immediate areas around the destroyed nodalities, yes. But when balanced against the increase in incidents elsewhere, the overall stress on the grid has not reduced by a statistically significant margin."

"Meaning," General Kozelek said grimly, "we aren't killing them fast enough."

Dr. Quasnitschka nodded.

"Colonel, what is the projected readiness date for the other three companies in training?"

Steve's ears perked. He knew Taskforce Sanctus had been recruiting and training more CIDER troops beyond the core ranks of Alpha Testers that had been with the program since the beginning. They wouldn't be as skilled as the Alpha Testers or Hunter Strike Teams, but they didn't need to be. They had hours of Hunter Strike Team battle footage to learn from, and Steve along with several other senior Alpha Testers were constantly updating the CIDER exclusive tactical trainings with new data from the Battle Tour engagements.

If everything went according to plan, the public would never even know these additional companies existed, much less be watching them for scoring and performance. The idea was to deploy them in the dead of night to take out nodalities in sensitive areas that would be suspicious for the Battle Tour to go. Places where they could temporarily control the airspace and information flow.

In addition to those companies, there were Alpha Tester teams deployed around the country who had been subtly integrating with local gaming communities since the spring. They were even now organizing civilian boss battles similar to what Lynn had spearheaded. RavenStriker's successful Boss Bash had inspired local gamers, and the undercover Alpha teams simply had to point them toward the Bravo and Alpha Class bosses deemed safe enough for civilians to tackle while providing advice and overwatch.

"They'll be ready for deployment in two weeks, sir," Colonel Bryce responded. "We are on track preparing standardized training, infrastructure, and equipment to employ in the event that CIDER goes public. We will never be 'ready,' per se. That would take years even without having to juggle operational security. But we will have the basic infrastructure in place to get started by the end of the summer."

Glances were exchanged around the table, and Steve didn't have to guess what everyone was thinking.

Would it be soon enough?

What Steve was more worried about was the civilian and government side of things, should CIDER go public. The military was used to doing things without knowing why. It was part of the job. The civilian side? Politicians didn't know how to keep their mouths shut, especially low-level bureaucrats. There was only so much preparation CIDER could do without compromising the entire mission. Even though each allied country had been preparing contingencies for over a year now, it hardly seemed enough time to manage the massive upheaval that would happen as soon as the public knew—and more importantly *believed*—what was going on.

"Dr. Quasnitschka," the General said after an uncomfortably long silence. "Are there any updates on the rates of TDM increase or global extermination efficiency?"

The scientist shook his head.

"The exponential increase is on track with our projections, though our numbers are looking too optimistic by several percentage points. The amount is within the margin of error, so it's not enough to update our numbers accordingly, but it's something we're watching.

"Tsunami's latest ad campaign, the one titled—" there was a pause while the doctor checked some virtual note "—'Call of the Snake', has increased global extermination rates by five percent. An encouraging jump," he said, shooting a weary smile at Mr. Krator. "The problem is that those exterminations are focused on Delta through Alpha Class TDMs. Nodality extermination rates have not increased, though they are at least holding steady."

"So, good but not good enough?" General Kozelek asked.

"Yes."

"Major Lawrence, what can you tell us about how nonmember nations are faring?" the general asked, turning to the hologram of Major Kim Lawrence, CIDER's liaison to the intelligence community.

"The lower-tech countries in Africa are a mixed bag," said Major Lawrence. "Remote rural areas have hardly been affected at all. But the more developed countries, especially those that already had issues with grid reliability, are being hit really hard."

"China?" General Kozelek asked.

"Still officially refusing to talk to us. My sources indicate there are elements within the CCP who absolutely believe our data, but the faction in control refuses to even consider working with CIDER or using our combat interface."

"They can hardly be blamed for being suspicious," Ms. Wood interjected, and several military personnel gave her sideways looks. "It's an untested technology controlled by their political enemies. We haven't given them reason to trust us, especially if you consider the anti-Asian racism and bigotry running rampant in our country."

"Be that as it may," Major Lawrence continued, his expression impeccably neutral, "we have very little information on how they are *actually* faring. Public propaganda is blaming the 'minor incidents' on a shipment of faulty chips provided by the Taiwanese. While they're not outright saying Taiwan sabotaged them, they're definitely leaving that door wide open."

Steve grimaced. Just what they needed during an alien invasion: militarily aggressive superpowers moving in on their political allies.

"As best as we can tell," the Major said, "they're shunting all power from the countryside into their city centers in a desperate attempt to keep things afloat. We have scattered reports of entire provinces with virtually no power at all besides their provincial capitals. Who knows how long they can keep it up, or what kind of issues they're already facing in the countryside. They could be looking at widespread death from preventable diseases stemming from lack of basic medicine and clean water, not to mention the sanitation issues."

General Kozelek looked even grimmer, and Steve didn't blame him. China's situation could very well be a preview of what the US would soon face.

"What of our own grid stability?" the general asked, looking back at Dr. Quasnitschka.

The scientist heaved a deep sigh before replying.

"It's like that old game, whack-a-mole I think they called it. We're treading water, sir, that's the best thing I can say about it. Multiple major municipalities are creeping closer to widespread failures. It's a problem of node exchanges. If too many nodes at critical points in the grid get latched onto by these spooks, we can't route energy around them to other sectors, and it can cause cascading blackouts."

"How long do we have?" General Kozelek asked, voice tight.

"I can't answer that," Dr. Quasnitschka said, looking uncomfortable. "It would differ for every city, county, and state."

"Then what's your gut instinct? If things continue as they are, how long before we're looking at widespread shutdowns?"

The doctor hesitated, looking around the table at all the people staring him. His Adam's apple visibly bobbed.

"Our data isn't that precise, sir. I can't—"

"Give us a ballpark, then," General Kozelek said sharply.

"I . . . well . . . a month? Two, if we're very lucky."

Silence reigned.

Steve clenched his fists under the table. He needed to get Matilda out of Cedar Rapids and onto a military base. Somewhere, *anywhere* safer than in the middle of a medium to large city without any clue what was coming. Maybe he could pull some strings in CIDER. She was a nurse, they could surely use her skills. If not, maybe he could reach out to his old friend Mike or Tap and his SpecOps unit from back in the day who were living off the grid up in the Rockies. She'd be safe out there, surely.

General Kozelek turned to Mr. Krator.

"We need to clear the biggest cities *now*. Can you shuffle around the Battle Tour? New York is the most vulnerable. I know we were leaving it for later when we had more experience and better weapons, but we can't delay any longer. I want Godzilla taken out, stat."

A deep V formed on Mr. Krator's brow, but eventually he nodded.

"We will make it happen, somehow."

"Colonel Bryce," the general said, turning to include his subordinate in the conversation, "Coordinate with Tsunami and prepare your troops. We can't just move up the timetable, we need to hit two nodalities a day, starting as soon as possible. Can you make it happen?"

"Yes, sir," Colonel Bryce said, straightening to attention.

"Then get it done," the general said. "And may God have mercy on us."

New York City from above was a sight like nothing Lynn had ever seen. If there was any city in the United States that brought to mind cyberpunk visions of the future, it would be New York. The vast metropolis stretched as far as she could see in all directions, and the busy lines of air taxi traffic going this way and that above the streets gave it a sense of three-dimensional chaos that made Lynn think of an anthill.

Their airbus was one of three ferrying Alpha, Bravo, and Charlie companies to the Ravenswood Generating Station on the southeast side of the East River, directly across from Roosevelt Island. Their vehicle obediently followed the stream of air traffic up the East River, headed for the Ed Koch Queensboro Bridge, where it would turn right to settle at the south end of Queensbridge Park.

Based on their taskforce-wide brief the day before, Lynn knew the two other airbuses were headed to the Roosevelt Island Bridge where they would take turns disembarking their companies on the north side of the generating station.

The entire strip of land, from Roosevelt Island Bridge down to the Queensboro Bridge and over to Vernon Boulevard, was cordoned off with a double row of fences; the first a shorter, heavier barrier to prevent access, and the second taller and lighter to act as a visual shield.

Tsunami was taking no chances with foolish but determined spectators in such a densely populated area.

The generator plant was down to a skeleton crew, and most of them were security personnel posted at the entrances, augmented by Tsunami security patrolling the perimeter of the park just south of the station.

The station had been suffering consistent grid issues for the past few months. Since this one station provided over twenty percent of the city's energy, the issues had been causing rolling blackouts throughout July and into August. Heatstroke and heat-related deaths had skyrocketed. So the plant was going offline temporarily to replace the faulty equipment, and Tsunami just happened to have coordinated their Battle Tour to coincide.

That was the official line, anyway.

In reality, the plant was malfunctioning so badly it was being taken offline for safety reasons. A few of the top officials in charge of the plant knew Tsunami's event had something to do with whatever was causing the plant to go haywire, since there was no other way to plausibly explain the presence of hundreds of gamers descending on the station's grounds. But they were led to believe the Battle Tour was simply cover for some secret government operation involved in battling whatever foreign-origin cyberattack was infecting the plant's operating systems.

Which, technically, was true. They simply had no idea how "foreign" the attack origin really was.

Ronnie, ever the helpful source of news on conspiracy theories, had told Lynn and the guys after their brief yesterday that chatter was spreading in the mesh that blamed the blackouts on the TD Hunter app itself. It wasn't escaping people's notice that big bosses were showing up in a lot of the places G-Force Utilities were having equipment problems.

What worried Lynn more, though, was the conspiracy theory that Tsunami was secretly owned by the Chinese who were using it to deliberately sabotage US infrastructure to soften the country up for invasion.

What would happen to CIDER's war effort if the theory spread and people started attacking TD Hunter players as undercover spies?

What a nightmare that would be.

In the case of the Ravenswood Generating Station, at least, Tsunami acted as though they were simply using the temporarily free space because of the cool visual aesthetics. Also, because it was one of the few large, open spaces in New York besides Central Park where they could carry out a boss battle of this scale.

Fortunately for the safety of New Yorkers, there were no large generating stations in Central Park, or in the downtown Manhattan business district just south of it. A Sierra Class nodality parking itself in the middle of *that* area would have resulted in instant chaos and death.

"Attention all companies," Colonel Bryce's voice came through on the Taskforce channel and Lynn straightened in her seat, glancing from side to side to make sure her team were all paying attention as well. "We are five minutes from set down. Team captains, ensure your teams' equipment is battle-ready and prepare for a final brief from your company commander. I'll be at the operations HQ monitoring the battle along with my staff. You have all done Taskforce Sanctus proud these past three weeks, and I have no doubt you will utterly crush our enemies today. Fight with courage, and look out for each other. Colonel Bryce, out."

Lynn, who was seated near the front of the large airbus, could just see where Colonel Bryce, his staff, and the Taskforce's medical personnel were sitting at the very front. They would all remain with the airbus at the southernmost tip of the cordoned-off Queensbridge Park, using the vehicle as a mobile command center, as well as a medical station for the inevitable—hopefully minor—injuries that would occur. The other two airbuses were also outfitted with emergency first aid capabilities, so that no matter who got injured, they had a fallback point to retreat to.

The plan was to pin Godzilla, the Sierra Class-5 nodality parked on top of the south end of the generating station, between Charlie and Bravo companies to the northeast, and Alpha Company to the southwest. The strip of ground they had to work with was a long rectangle, so they couldn't come at the boss from the southeast without shutting down a major road and evicting people from their houses.

"Okay, Skadi's Wolves, are you ready for this?" Lynn subvocalized, making eye contact with her team on either side of her.

Ronnie and Edgar looked calm and confident, while Mack had that grim, determined look he always had when he was ignoring his own fear, and Dan looked positively gleeful.

"I've always wanted to fight Godzilla!" he subvocalized in a sing-song tone. "I'm going to make so many hilarious clip memes from this boss fight, I bet I'll go viral."

Lynn couldn't help snorting.

"Just as long as you don't get distracted posing for the cameras, King Ghidorah," she said.

Dan's grin widened.

"Do you think Kayla will be watching?" he asked, the tightness around his eyes giving away the nerves mostly buried under hyper enthusiasm.

"It's Kayla's *job* to watch, doofus," Ronnie said. "She probably wishes it wasn't. There's only so much chipmunk chatter one person can take."

"Hey, my banter game is next level. You should be thanking me. It's not like *you're* adding to our channel's entertainment factor with your brooding silence."

Ronnie shot a glare down the line at Dan.

"I'm not brooding, and I'm not silent. I just don't open my mouth until I have something good to say, like how your socks smell like a bento box of sushi that's been forgotten in the bottom of your backpack for a month."

Edgar and Mack hooted and slapped their knees while Dan's face worked through several stages of outrage, no doubt grasping for a sufficiently scathing comeback.

"All right, you clowns, focus," Lynn interjected before things could escalate. "Abrams'll start any minute now. Everybody, do an equipment check and start hydrating. Hugo says it's already roasting out there."

Everybody put their headgear on and started tugging and slapping each other's gear to ensure it was all secure and working. Abrams' voice sounded in their company channel, calling the entire bus-load of fighters to attention.

"Landing in two minutes, Alpha Company! Remember, this is a *Sierra Class-5* nodality. You have the distinct honor of facing down the biggest boss anyone has ever battled. This one'll go down in the history books, at least if this nightmare ever goes public. I want everyone to stay sharp. Remember the battle plan and *do not under any circumstance approach the boss.* Everybody walks home today under their own power, understood?"

A chorus of affirmatives filled the company channel. Abrams, who was standing at the front between the rows of seats, turned and faced Colonel Bryce and Khoury, obviously switching to a dedicated leadership channel to do some last-minute consultation.

Lynn felt the airbus bank and start to descend as the Queensboro Bridge flashed beneath them. Out the window Lynn could see the green rectangle of Queensbridge Park stretch northeast along the river. At the far end, the green abruptly ended and was replaced by gray concrete and a writhing labyrinth of metal. Nodes and transformers rose up like a forest of electric trees before the larger structure of the generating station itself with its dominating power plant. The station complex was the same width as the park, but about one-third longer.

Disembarking and forming up took little thought, they'd done it so many times before. Lynn felt in danger of underestimating the fight before them as she surveyed the luscious green trees and thick grass of Queensbridge Park. The grass was springy beneath her feet, and she was happy Alpha Company had gotten the park instead of the north side of the generating station. She'd have a lot fewer bruises tonight.

She couldn't see beyond the park because Tsunami's fencing was covered in smart cloth that flashed advertisements from top-dollar sponsors. But the barriers didn't block the welcome breeze coming off the East River. It cooled the skin around her neck and hands where her athletic gear didn't cover. It rustled the sun-dappled, emerald leaves, and brought with it the scent of fish, brine, and something faintly sour that she could smell even through her headgear's filters. Maybe old sewage or a pollutant from the generating plant. Lynn breathed in deeply anyway, reveling in the novelty of being so close to the Atlantic Ocean.

Mrs. Pearson and Kayla checked in, making sure everyone was ready for the cameras to go live. Kayla wished them all good luck with her usual Energizer bunny enthusiasm. After she fell silent, Lynn noticed Dan flush a particularly noticeable pink against the golden tone of his skin.

She grinned, wondering what sort of private message Kayla had just sent him.

Camera drones whirred overhead, though Lynn knew that only about half of them would be livestreaming. The other half were CIDER drones disguised in Tsunami blue and black. Because Godzilla was such a large nodality, CIDER's R&D department had outfitted drones with TEP transmitters and were going to attempt to add air support to the battle, though no one knew how long the drones would last. All the snipers would be on the lookout to sharpshoot flying type TDMs that went after the drones, but the drones were so fragile it wouldn't take much to knock them out of commission.

It was worth a try, though.

Following Crash and Hermes' formation commands, Skadi's Wolves circled up with the rest of 1st Platoon. Lynn's mind was busy examining the terrain in front of them, calculating and planning.

Dr. Roberts had only contacted her one time since she'd been at CIDER HQ for brain tests, and he'd had no breakthrough revelations to share, just some generic observations. Apparently Lynn's brain waves didn't spike erratically the way most people's did when they came into contact with larger TDMs. Alpha Class and higher tended to cause dramatic brain activity, triggering the usual dizziness and nausea, and eventually, blackout. But Lynn's brain had a much more muted response. Dr. Roberts had gone on a long, complicated ramble about TDMs achieving resonance with human brain waves as a byproduct of their particle interaction, thus triggering cascades that made the nervous system go haywire and eventually shut down.

If the theory was correct, it would imply Lynn's brain waves had a different resonance point than most. Dr. Roberts had no hypotheses as to why. Everything else about her checked out as normal, albeit insanely healthy and high-functioning considering her current occupation as a professional athlete.

That left Lynn in a weird limbo. She seemed to have a resistance to the spooks, but she wasn't immune. So, was that very resistance what attracted the TDMs' attention? She'd originally assumed it was simply the game algorithm picking on her because she pushed the boundaries and could clearly handle a challenge. Since that obviously wasn't the case, she was back to square one.

Why *did* some TDMs home in on her? From the Lecta and Varg when she'd still been beta testing, to Manticars and Dracas more recently, there were so many instances of TDMs acting weird around her. Did her resistance make her more visible? Did she have some weird *affinity* for these transdimensional aliens?

Dr. Roberts had all sorts of theories about that, pointing out that they'd never been able to explain why TDMs generally shied away from high human-traffic areas—unless there was strong grid activity to attract them. He wondered if the resonance with humans caused some kind of low-level irritation that the spooks instinctually avoided. Which might explain why, if Lynn's resonance was different, they could pick her out of a crowd of humans once she showed up on their radar by attacking them.

Dr. Roberts cautioned her it was all wild speculation at this point, since he had no means to test his theories, much less the time to do so between the other dozen R&D projects he was working on around the clock for CIDER.

The whole idea made Lynn's skin crawl. Since she couldn't change it, though, she would definitely be using it to her advantage.

The thought made her grin. She could imagine Steve's deep, glowering look of disapproval should he learn of her conclusion.

Good thing she wouldn't be telling him.

"Alpha Company, prepare to engage in sixty seconds," came Abrams' call.

Lynn looked to the right and left, visually confirming her team was ready to rock and roll.

"Dan, remember to keep up overwatch for the battle drones," Lynn subvocalized. "Mack, keep sipping your water, you almost got heatstroke last time and we can't afford to lose you. Edgar, remember to work on your precision. We need every bit of power to take out Godzilla, so I want flawless efficiency. Ronnie, let's hope we don't have a Draca problem, but if we do, you've got the team."

The guys acknowledged, and then the clock hit zero.

Colonel Bryce gave the order to engage, and the familiar sights, sounds, and surge of battle adrenaline washed over Lynn. Her body moved of its own accord, following muscle memory more than conscious thought. At this point they were all so used to establishing a beachhead in the sea of TDMs that it was like shooting fish in a barrel. Lynn didn't even bother looking higher than eye level until she heard Dan gasp and say "Oh, shit!" in their team chat.

Her eyes rose from the immediate press of TDMs in front of her to the tree line at the northeast end of the park.

Oh shit, indeed.

"Holy crap, that thing is *huge*," Mack said, taking a flurry of shots to eliminate the cluster of Creepers that was trying to swarm over them. "That thing is *actual* Godzilla."

Huge didn't do the boss justice. That was a word you used when you were watching a vid or viewing an image of an overly large object.

The sheer overwhelming presence of the Godzilla nodality in front of them deserved a different sort of descriptor.

Bigger than Elena's ego.

Bigger than the state pride of Texas.

Bigger than the US Defense Budget.

"We have to kill *that*?" Dan's question ended on a strangled note, though his aim was unwavering as he shot Roc after Roc from the swarm hovering overhead.

"Relax, Dan," Lynn said. "There's almost four hundred highly skilled and motivated TD Hunter players converging on it. We'll get it done. Keep steady and stay focused on what's in front of you. Let Abrams and the heavy weapons guys worry about Godzilla."

It was nearly impossible to follow her own advice, though. The sheer volume alone was terrifying. It looked as big as a city block, and was even taller than it was wide. If it had been a bit earlier in the day, the boss's bulk could have blocked out the sun above them.

"Look on the bright side," Ronnie grunted. "Bigger means slower, right?"

Lynn didn't respond, because she wasn't sure Ronnie was right.

The Godzilla nodality didn't resemble the famous kaiju by the same name, which was slightly reassuring. At least it wouldn't be stomping toward them on feet bigger than most airbuses. It looked more like a giant, pulsing amoeba. The lack of visible appendages made Lynn optimistic.

On the other hand, looks could be deceiving.

No matter how daunting the boss appeared, though, it wasn't her problem to worry about. So she told her hind brain to stop gibbering, and focused instead on sinking fully into Larry mode. Soon she was moving without thought and effortlessly analyzing the ebb and flow of battle in that glorious Zen state that integrated and transcended her conscious perception.

She was one with the battle.

Alpha Company advanced smoothly across Queensbridge Park, closing steadily with Godzilla. Tiny numbers in Lynn's display counted down the distance.

A thousand feet.

Eight hundred.

Five hundred.

Three hundred.

They were cutting through the inner rings of Alpha Class TDMs before their momentum slowed at all, and it was only because

Abrams had called for it. They'd reached the point Dracas usually showed up, if there were any lurking around. The mini-bosses were incredibly sneaky, and hard to spot before they attacked in a mob like this. After the incident that had earned Lynn her "Draca Queen" moniker, Abrams had shifted Alpha Company's SOP to have Ion and his Pounder team divert from the boss and take out any Dracas right away. It freed up additional TEPs more quickly, and spared Lynn's platoon—and more specifically, Lynn—an exhausting and unnecessary ordeal.

One dance with dragons was quite enough.

Lynn knew that Charlie and Bravo companies would be nearing the same point on the north and northeast sides of Godzilla, having fought down the access roads on either side of the station buildings. They should have passed the main generating station by now and be approaching the massive transformer field where Godzilla lurked.

The hope was that, if all three companies attacked the boss in tandem, the equal pressure from all sides would prevent it from fleeing into the densely populated boroughs of New York City. That was if it was mobile. If it wasn't, all they had to worry about was dodging any attack their combined assault provoked.

Which was why Abrams called a halt two hundred feet out. It was farther out than they usually attacked a boss, but it was the maximum effective range for the Pounders, and Abrams had said they weren't taking any chances with a boss this big.

"All companies," Colonel Bryce said, "prepare to engage Godzilla with Pounders on my mark."

Lynn mentally braced herself, and looked up from the Jotnar she was dancing away from as the Colonel marked the time and a cacophony of *whump-whump-whumps* reverberated through the air—or at least through her ear bones.

"Draca incoming, nine o'clock," came Hugo's crisp voice across the entire company.

All but a few essential defenders pivoted left. The bus-sized TDM that had been gliding in low, almost brushing the heads of the seething ranks of monsters, was met with a hurricane of fire, including a wall of "hot lead" from Hamilton's Own. The machine-gun setting on those Pounders was a glory to behold. It lit up Lynn's view with a torrent of golden pinpricks moving so fast and thick it almost looked like a solid column of light.

The Draca barely had a chance to land and lunge toward Lynn before it exploded under the onslaught.

"Now *that's* how you kill a Draca," Dan crowed, forgetting to switch from the company channel to their team one.

There were some audible chuckles.

"Thanks for the assist, you hoodlums," Lynn added dryly in the Alpha Company chat, feeling she could get away with it. After all, *they* were the ones who'd dubbed her the Draca Queen. "Next time, though, give me a few minutes to play with them first. I need to get in my morning cardio."

"Will do, Raven," came Ion's teasing voice. Lynn hadn't known subvocalization could transmit the impression of a shit-eating grin, but boy it certainly could.

"We could turn it into an interpretive dance," Grim from Amaranth chimed in. "Serenity knows some great moves."

"Shut it, Grim," Serenity said, "or I'll let the Chimeras eat you."

"I'll let the spooks eat *all* of you if you don't put a lid on it," Crash growled at them on their platoon channel. "Keep it in your team chats. The coffee dispenser was broken this morning, and I ain't got the patience for spooks *and* teenagers at the same time."

Lynn didn't point out that Team Amaranth weren't teens. Instead she focused on clearing her line of Jotnars and staying alert for more Dracas.

Another Draca came up suddenly on her, snaking through the lines of Alpha Class TDMs to attack when she was busy with a pair of Chimeras. It went straight for her, even though Edgar was closer. That one she did have to dance with for a while before Ion and the rest of Hamilton's Own could draw a bead on it.

It was almost as if the Dracas were learning, trying different tactics to get the jump on her and attack before her company could back her up. That made her wonder if they could tell where the largest concentration of TEPs were coming from. She could only guess they couldn't, or at least that data point didn't translate into "higher-priority threat" in their decision-making matrix. Otherwise they would have been swarming Hamilton's Own instead.

Maybe the higher damage did trigger a defensive response, but once they got within attack range, they simply homed in on the target they could most easily detect. Which still begged the question of why that happened to be her. At least it was a working theory.

Three more Dracas attempted sneak attacks on Lynn, each managing to get within striking range before Hugo or anyone else spotted them. If Lynn could have given the TDMs a word of advice, she would have told them to go back to assaulting all at once. That, at least, had challenged her survival skills to the breaking point.

The battle continued, chaotic, but a controlled chaos that Abrams managed with the watchful finesse of a skilled commander. Lynn checked in on Skadi's Wolves' livestream every now and then, listening in on Kayla's commentary. It ranged to other topics during slow moments and Lynn was amused to hear Kayla rating the other Hunter Teams' armor skins.

The sun arced up towards its apex, and the breeze from the river fell, leaving them hot and pouring sweat in what was turning into one of the longest battles they'd ever fought. It got to the point that the ranks of TDMs around them were thinning and Alpha Company had to coordinate with Bravo and Charlie to shift their positions, each group of fighters traveling clockwise around Godzilla to keep up the even pressure.

But still the nodality didn't react, attack, or give any indication it even noticed them.

"This sucks," Edgar subvocalized, his pants coming through along with his words. "Do we even—got the firepower—to frag this ugly bastard?"

"It's the range," Lynn replied. She was panting as well, and had been snatching sips of water between kills for a while now. "Not close enough for TEPs—to be effective. Boss's too big. We gotta get closer."

"But Abrams said—" Mack began.

"I know," Lynn shot back. "Doesn't change the facts."

Not that Lynn could do anything about it.

Or could she?

The better question was, *should* she?

Abrams no doubt had a plan in mind. Maybe he thought if they took their time and cleared the *entire* sea of TDMs around the nodality, that would be enough TEPs to eventually take the monster down.

But what if it wasn't?

What if they got stuck with a gargantuan nodality posing an imminent danger to New York City with no helpful swarms of spooks around to provide fuel—or at least not at the levels needed to destroy a Sierra Class-5 boss?

Could they afford to wait and attack another day? Would it blow the Battle Tour's cover?

Lynn didn't know the answer to those questions, but based on the briefing Colonel Bryce had given them the day before, it sounded like humanity had very little time left before things got desperate.

Well, her idea was at least worth trying.

Since she'd already started a private chat with Abrams when he'd sent her with Steve to get tested, she simply switched to it and subvocalized as smoothly as she could over her uneven breathing:

"Sir, we need to get closer. We'll never kill it at this range."

"Raven, get out of my private chat," Abrams responded after a slight delay. "If you have an issue, send it up your chain of command."

Well, *that* was helpful.

Lynn was still formulating a persuasive argument to Hermes in her head while picking off a swarm of Strikers when a Taskforce-wide command came in from Colonel Bryce.

"All companies, prepare to advance to one hundred feet and focus fire on Godzilla."

Lynn would have snorted if she'd had the breath for it. Good to know her professional advice hadn't been totally ignored. Or maybe Abrams and Colonel Bryce had already been thinking along the same lines, and had simply needed a little push.

Or maybe they'd been planning to do this all along at exactly this moment, and she needed to shut her trap and stay in her lane.

She'd never know the answer, so she focused on getting the guys to straighten their formation and get ready to advance.

"I want all snipers on the sky for the time being," Abrams told Alpha Company. "The attack drones will advance first and engage Godzilla. Be ready for anything."

Up until now, the drones had only been engaging the flying TDMs in their immediate vicinity. They had a small effective range and a slow rate of fire compared to the Hunters so they were almost more trouble than they were worth. But they had been gathering and storing TEPs up there from all the Rocs, Tengu, and Kongamatos the snipers had been killing. The idea was to unleash it all at once at the boss.

They were about to find out what sort of effect it would have.

Half a dozen drones edged closer to the boss staying at the same height bracket as the other camera drones, which barely put them fifty feet over Godzilla, it was so tall.

All at once, six bolts of light shot out from the drones, converging on the top of the boss. The combat interface added an impressive flash and clapping sound of super-heated air, as if the bolts had been actual lasers. A few stray flying TDMs appeared out of nowhere, but the snipers were on point and took them down before they got within striking range of the drones.

The battle seemed to lull for an eternal second, as if everyone was holding their collective breath as they stared upward.

Lynn broke and shot a Rakshar in the face who tried to charge into the lull of Hunter fire. She glanced up again in time to see the top mound of Godzilla's massive bulk split open and tentacles shoot out of it into the air. The drones took belated evasive action, but not quickly enough.

Six hunks of now-inert plastic and omnipolymer plunged toward the ground, dead as doornails. Some thumped onto the grass, while others could be heard making abrupt acquaintance with the pavement, their crunching demise barely audible above the cacophony of battle.

Godzilla's tentacles waved lazily in the air a hundred feet overhead for a beat, as if waiting to see if anyone else dared come within reach. With no other immediate targets, they reeled back into Godzilla's maw, and it closed again.

"Hugo, you son of a biscuit!" Gadsden hollered in their platoon chat. "Will you quit it with them Cthulhu graphics? We don't need to see that shit! I darn near had a heart attack, and I'm too young for heart attacks!"

Lynn would have grinned, but she was too busy repeating every curse word she knew in her head.

"Hugo," she said to the AI. "What was Godzilla's range on that attack?"

"Just under fifty feet, Miss Lynn."

Shit. It could probably reach further than that, too. But could it reach one hundred feet?

"All companies, slow advance!" Colonel Bryce said.

Lynn roused herself and started forward with her team, renewing her attacks with a frenzy of energy to clear their line of advance.

"Hamilton's Own, engage Godzilla," came Abrams' command. "The rest of Alpha Company, clear the area and be ready to back up *fast*. Advance to a range of 120 feet only—*not* one hundred feet—then assault in place."

Crash and then Hermes added to the command, fine-tuning the formations and assigning targets as necessary.

Skadi's Wolves met the last ranks of Alpha Class TDMs head on, moving through a grove of mature trees as they fought. The trees separated the park's baseball diamonds and tennis courts from a large athletic field on the north end of Queensbridge Park. The field was the last bit of the park before the protective brick wall that surrounded the generating plant, beyond which Godzilla rose like a small skyscraper.

Despite generous bait drops, the biggest spooks in the innermost protective rings had been holding back, as if their defense programing for a boss this large had been stronger than any amount of aggro. But now they eagerly charged the approaching Hunters, and were just as eagerly blown to bits. The Pounders of Hamilton's Own and the other heavy weapons platoons on Godzilla's far side pounded away, but the boss *still* didn't react.

The tension ratcheted up with each step Lynn took until they finally reached the 120 feet range, right in the middle of the athletic field. It was close enough that the last three ranks of Alpha Class defenders came forward in a rush, leaving the rest of the space between Alpha Company and Godzilla relatively empty.

They cleared the last ranks of Jotnar and a few stray Manticar and Chimeras, and then there was nothing left in front of them.

"1st Platoon, engage to the sides. Keep a sharp eye out for Dracas," Abrams said, tension audible in his subvocalized tone.

Another minute passed, and the Hunters had fewer and fewer targets to engage. Everyone had switched to ranged weapons by this point.

"Advance to 110 feet," Abrams said.

Lynn started forward without hesitation, eyes locked on Godzilla, trusting Hugo to warn her if a Draca popped up.

Still, nothing. The Pounder's rhythmic fire was now the loudest sound in their vicinity.

"Advance to 100 feet," Abrams commanded. "1st and 2nd Platoons, deploy shield wall and target Godzilla. 3rd Platoon, keep our line of retreat clear."

The squads shifted, the Hunters with one-handed guns drawing slightly forward of their rifle-toting squad mates and switching their off-hand weapon to a force shield. Lynn and Mack stepped ahead of Ronnie, Dan, and Edgar, Lynn switching Wrath for Bastion as she did. There was hardly anywhere Lynn could shoot in front of her that *wouldn't* hit Godzilla, so she swallowed, took aim at a random spot above her head, and let loose along with the rest of her platoon.

Seconds passed.

Lynn blinked.

Then she screamed.

Godzilla was suddenly, in that single blink of an eye, fifty feet closer to Alpha Company.

"Back—" was all Abrams got out before a slit opened in Godzilla and dozens of tentacles shot out toward them.

Lynn was already lunging in front of Edgar who was closest, and slower than the rest of their team. He stumbled back in his haste to retreat, but managed to keep his feet as Lynn braced.

A tentacle rammed into Bastion.

Lynn swore she could feel the vibration of contact through her arm. Or was that an elaborate effect of the omnipolymer weapon and her combat interface? The shield super-heated enough that she could feel it radiating from the handle. She held on, though, backing up as fast as her legs could carry her while the yells of her platoon sounded in her ear.

More tentacles reached past her, but within seconds she'd backed up further than they could reach. She spotted Ronnie and Dan dragging Mack, who was hyperventilating, but otherwise seemed fine. Ronnie had Mack's shield and was holding it protectively between them and Godzilla's reaching tentacles. A quick glance around sent a wave of relief through her.

It didn't look like anyone had been hurt. A few people were bending over and retching. But no one was on the ground.

"All companies, be advised," Hugo announced in her ear, "I have updated Godzilla's capabilities to include short-range

Blink. All personnel is advised to remain outside the range of 110 feet."

"*¡Jesucristo bendito!*" gasped Mack out loud, and Lynn recognized another one of Mrs. Rio's pet phrases. "That thing can *teleport*!! It almost *ate me alive*!"

"Shut your yapper, you idiot," Ronnie subvocalized. "You're perfectly fine. Quit clutching my arm like you're gonna hump it, and stand up."

Ah, classic bedside Ronnie.

Lynn appreciated the crack in the humming tension running through Alpha Company as everyone dusted themselves off and reformed their ranks at 120-foot range. Godzilla's tentacles had reached and searched for targets only a few seconds before reeling back into the slit in the behemoth's side. Then they were gone like they'd never been there.

Except Godzilla was now covering the walking path between the park and the generating station's protective brick wall. It had swallowed the trees, too, and its bulk extended out into the edge of the athletic field.

Lynn glanced behind her at Abrams. Judging by the deep furrows in his brow and focused look on his face visible through his headgear's faceplate, he was in consultation with the other company commanders and Colonel Bryce. Interestingly, Derek from Light Brigade was turned toward Abrams as well, standing stock still, like he was busy subvocalizing.

What was Derek adding to the conversation?

Lynn itched to attack. All her instincts told her this was the crucial moment when they needed to go all in, or else lose momentum and miss their chance. Everyone was exhausted and sweating buckets. Their pool of TDMs to harvest for TEPs was dwindling. Godzilla had shown its hand. All other bosses had followed predictable attack patterns, so now that they knew the nodality's range, it was time to hit it with all they had.

Lynn's thought process was distracted by the sight of Derek's team breaking formation, backing up. From what she could see of their faces, their expressions were blank. All except Derek, whose face was tight.

"Death, what's going on?" Lynn subvocalized directly to Derek.

"My team has seen this before. Everyone should move further back."

"So, why isn't Abrams calling a retreat?"

"Because he doesn't think it's necessary yet."

"Tell me what you saw before," Lynn insisted.

Derek fell silent. In that moment, Team Black Templars and their squad leader, Neutron, started backing up too.

"Skadi's Wolves," Lynn snapped in her team chat. "Keep your eyes on 1st Squad. Do what they do." She switched back to Derek. "*Tell me*," she said, more urgently.

"Last March. National Mall. Game was still in beta. Me and some other Alpha teams took out a boss parked on the Washington Monument. It could blink too. Forty yards every ninety seconds. There's no telling how much time Godzilla needs to recharge."

Lynn's brain moved like lightning.

"If it's inversely proportional, three and a half minutes," she said quickly. "Hugo, how long since Godzilla blinked?"

"Three minutes and sixteen seconds, Miss Lynn."

"*Everybody back up*!" Lynn yelled out loud at the top of her voice. Sudden urgency and clarity lent adrenaline to her vocal cords, and the shout came out in a perfect battle pitch. A Larry pitch. "It's gonna blink again in fifteen seconds!"

Everybody started backward, glancing between her and Abrams in confusion.

She didn't care. There wasn't time to consult. Only time for action.

"Raven, what do you think you're doing?" came Abrams' tight voice over a private channel.

"Sorry, sir. I got new intel and there wasn't time to chat."

Right on time, Godzilla blinked again.

A few people yelled in alarm, but everyone was out of range, enough so that they were engaging with TDMs once again. The defensive rings that Alpha Company had left behind in their push toward the center were contracting toward the threat.

Now Godzilla was a good third to halfway out of the generating station grounds and into the park. The sight brought a sudden horrified realization to Lynn.

"Sir," she said, still on channel with Abrams, "what if it keeps advancing south past the park? Bravo and Charlie need to book it around to this side and everybody attack to force it back to the generating station."

"They're already moving," Abrams said tightly. "Now get back in formation and follow your squad leaders' orders."

Lynn felt a surge of annoyance, but shoved it down and did her job. Abrams was clearly a competent leader, even if he wasn't as quick on the uptake or as decisive as she wanted him to be. She just needed to stay sharp and worry about her own team.

Speaking of Skadi's Wolves, she could tell they were flagging.

"Talk to me, guys. Is anyone out of water? Mack, are you still dizzy?"

"I'm out," Mack gasped, stumbling as he said it. He recovered and expertly finished off the Managal towering over him, but Lynn could hear the exhaustion in his tone.

"I'm dry, too," Edgar added.

"Me, too," Ronnie chimed in.

"I've got some left," Dan said, "but I don't know how long it will last, I'm dying in this heat."

Lynn concurred, but didn't say it. Instead, she switched to a private channel with Hermes.

"Sir, half my squad is out of water. We need to hydrate or people are going to start dropping from heatstroke."

"Noted," her squad leader said, grunting as he ducked and twisted to take out a Nundu that had just tried to strafe his head with its claws. "I'll pass it up the chain. Hang in there."

Alpha Company retreated steadily, destroying any and all TDMs within their reach as Hamilton's Own pounded steadily away on Godzilla. Like clockwork the boss came after them, every three and a half minutes on the dot. Lynn felt like it was coming a bit further every time, as if it were picking up momentum. But maybe it was just her imagination.

It felt like an eternity before Charlie and Bravo companies joined them. There was no room between Godzilla and the river to the west nor the cordon to the east for a person to pass the nodality at a safe distance, and Lynn knew it was smarter not to chance it even out of combat mode. So the two companies had jogged the long way around, exiting the generating station to the east onto Vernon Boulevard, then booking it down the street to the one cordon entrance into the south end of Queensbridge Park.

Godzilla had blinked four times before all three companies had assembled in coordinated formation. The towering behemoth had swallowed the athletic field and reached almost to the tennis courts.

Hermes reassured her that the medical teams were arranging a water resupply, though they were prioritizing the heavy weapons squads first.

As if their situation couldn't get any worse, as soon as all three companies started in on Godzilla again in one coordinated, massive attack, hoping to push it back northeast, more Dracas showed up.

They seemed to appear out of thin air right in front of Alpha Company, 1st Platoon, in the empty space between the Hunters' line and the nodality. Five of them in a weird cross sort of formation that lasted barely a second before all five spooks broke into a run, headed straight for her.

"Ugh, not *again*," Lynn couldn't help moaning. She hadn't been paying attention to her selection, and it broadcast to the company channel.

"Still need to get in that cardio, Raven?" Ion's voice replied. There were fewer, but still some chuckles.

"Shit, no. Kill them, *please*. I've had enough cardio to last me years."

"All units, switch targets to the Dracas," Colonel Bryce's voice came over the Taskforce channel. "I want them dead yesterday."

Was Lynn imagining the humor in his tone? Whatever. All she cared about was not having to play catch-me-if-you-can with five bus-sized dragons in near-ninety-degree heat. She switched Wrath to Bastion just in case, but she barely needed it. Between all three companies, the five Dracas were toast in under a minute.

Just then, Lynn's fifteen-second warning timer went off. She'd told Hugo to set up a reminder tone before every blink, and now she eagerly watched Godzilla, waiting to see it retreat back toward the generating station.

Fifteen seconds passed. Godzilla blinked *toward* Alpha Company.

"Son of a biscuit!" Lynn spat, echoing Gadsden's earlier exclamation. It wasn't as satisfying as what she wanted to say, but she couldn't cuss like Larry on livestream.

"I thought it was supposed to go the other way," Mack responded, matching her frustration with equal amounts of trepidation.

"All units," Colonel Bryce said. "I want you to shoot this bastard with every bit of power left in your systems. Throw sticks at it, if you have to. But kill it. *Now.*"

The fighters of Taskforce Sanctus were all too happy to comply, and three and a half minutes of furious attacks assaulted Lynn's eyeballs and eardrums with its fury.

But at the end of it, Godzilla blinked again, *still* moving toward them, still seemingly unaffected by their assault.

"Hugo," Lynn subvocalized, "how many more blinks until it gets to Queensboro Bridge?"

"Between twelve and fourteen, if it maintains its current pace," Hugo said.

Lynn cursed. That bridge was bustling with traffic. If Godzilla parked on top of it, it could kill dozens, maybe hundreds of people if you included the inevitable car wrecks and pileup as drivers blacked out and careened off the bridge or into opposing traffic. No doubt Abrams and Colonel Bryce were thinking the same thing, right? Surely they had a plan? They were competent, decorated military officers. She could trust them to come up with something.

Now why couldn't she freaking focus on her own lane and stop acting like she was in charge of the whole operation?

"Hugo, Colonel Bryce knows all this, right?"

"Absolutely, Miss Lynn."

"So . . . what's the plan? Just hope we manage to kill it in the next"—she did some mental calculation—"forty-five minutes?"

"I am sure they have contingencies in place," the AI replied, sounding perfectly relaxed, as if hundreds of civilian lives weren't on the line.

Three blinks, ten minutes, and another round of weirdly spawning Dracas later, Lynn couldn't take it anymore. A growing suspicion was tying her gut in knots, and she couldn't keep quiet, no matter how unprofessional it might be to ping Colonel Bryce directly.

"Hugo, put me through to the Colonel. He needs to know something."

There was a pause, then a hard voice said, "I assume you have a very good reason for once again circumventing your chain of command, Raven."

"Sorry, sir, no time," Lynn subvocalized, then paused to take a pull of water because her throat was so dry it hurt to swallow. She got a little, then nothing. She was out. Shit.

"Sir, I think it's following *me*."

There was a pause.

"Like the Dracas," the Colonel stated without asking for clarification.

"Yes. I need to run around north of it, draw it up away from the bridge before it's too late."

"We might kill it in time," he stated, not harshly, as if testing her answer.

"Or we might not. I can't let people die, sir. I *won't*." Her resolve solidified with those words as she realized how much she meant them. If *she* was the problem, if *she* was the thing causing it to threaten civilians, she would go north, no matter what Colonel Bryce or Abrams said.

She'd do it by herself if she had to.

"I can't shift all three companies," the Colonel was saying. "There's no time, and you might be wrong."

"I know," Lynn said, subvocalizing quickly as a plan formed in her mind. "Give me Light Brigade, Black Templars, and Hamilton's Own. How long would it take your command center to ferry us around to the north side?"

"Five minutes, tops."

"Good. That's faster than we could run out, up, around, and back down to Godzilla's north side."

"What about your team?"

"They're spent, sir. I don't want to risk them." Edgar would fight her, but she *couldn't* let him come, not with the risk. She had some resistance to whatever Godzilla could dish out. He didn't.

"Yet *you* are not spent?"

"Get me a water refill and I'll make it," she said, tone dropping to a growl. Her limits didn't matter. Failure was not an option.

There was another beat or two, then: "I'll give the command. *Run*."

Lynn spun and sprinted across the open green field, framed on each corner by a dusty baseball diamond. She took herself out of combat mode and subvocalized in her team's chat as best she could as she ran.

"Ronnie—you've got the team. Keep them safe."

It wasn't until she was nearing the airbus command center

that she heard pounding footsteps behind her. She turned to see Edgar closing fast, a determined look on his face.

"No, Edgar! Go back!" she yelled. Urgency buzzed along her nerves, mixing with panic and adrenaline.

"Where you go, I go," he yelled in reply, intensity radiating from him.

Lynn's fists clenched. She was so full of emotion she didn't know if she wanted to punch him or kiss him. Instead of doing either, she turned fully towards him as he came to a stop by her side, the ticking seconds weighing on her as people's lives hung in the balance.

"I won't risk you," she said flatly, remembering to subvocalize this time.

"If you get to risk yourself, then I get to risk myself right alongside you," he argued.

Lynn shook her head fiercely.

"No! Not in this. I'm immune to them, that's what the tests were all about. Remember Mishipeshu? Remember Nagaraja? I'll be safe, but you won't. *Go. Back.*" It wasn't exactly a lie, but it wasn't the truth either. She didn't care. She'd say anything she had to if only he would *listen*.

"But, *uce*, you need backup," he said, doubt showing in his eyes.

"That's what *they're* for," Lynn snapped, pointing behind Edgar.

Team Light Brigade and Black Templars trotted up then streamed past, heading into the waiting airbus. Derek threw a look her way, but didn't interfere. Hamilton's Own wasn't far behind, humping their TEP batteries and Pounders.

"Go back to the guys. They need you more than I do," Lynn said, tone softening.

"But..."

She could see the torment in his eyes, the pull of conflicting loyalties, and it killed her. So she did the first thing that came to mind.

She tackled him with a fierce hug.

Without a second's hesitation, he hugged her back, holding so tightly she wondered if he'd ever let go. But after a few precious seconds she didn't have, she pulled back, and he didn't stop her.

"I'll be fine, *manamea*," she said, looking him straight in the eye through their headgear visors. "Now if you don't get your big ugly mug back to the team right now, this *Toa Tama'ita'i* is going to frag your ass so hard you'll have shrapnel coming out your ears. You got me?"

Edgar still hesitated, fists clenching and unclenching, his lips pulled back in a terrible grimace of indecision.

"The team needs water," she snapped in desperation. "Grab some and get the hell back there. Go!"

With a wordless cry of frustration, Edgar dove toward the airbus, sticking his head in and yelling for water. Then, arms full, he dashed back towards the slow, but inexorably approaching nodality.

"You better come back, *manamea*, or I'm coming after you," he said in their private chat, words sounding garbled from subvocalizing on the run.

Lynn didn't reply.

The airbus was already on, engine humming, and she dashed into it, grabbing a handle by the door for balance as it immediately rose into the air.

The ride was even quicker than Colonel Bryce had promised. Now that the nodality had moved completely beyond the substation, there was room to land and disembark in the far northwest corner of the park. As they flew, Lynn refilled her hydration bladder and went over her plan with her two teams and the heavy weapons platoon. Since she'd be commanding exclusively Alpha Testers, none of her audio would be a part of the livestream, so she didn't worry about watching what she said.

Then they were on the ground again, streaming out of the airbus, batons out and ready to jump back into combat mode.

"Hugo, give me visual zone markers overlaid on the terrain in my display, red, orange, yellow, and green for every fifty feet with Godzilla as ground zero."

"Of course, Miss Lynn. Shall I replicate it for everyone's display in your combat group?"

"Yes."

Her surroundings were suddenly overlaid with a faint tint. It was green in her immediate vicinity, but quickly changed to yellow off to her right toward where Godzilla loomed.

She checked the blink counter Hugo had put in her display. It was down to six. That put Godzilla three hundred feet from Queensboro bridge.

Sudden fear swamped her, freezing her lungs. This wasn't a

game anymore, and she was no Larry "The Snake" Coughlin. Not really. That had all been make-believe. A fantasy.

Could she actually do this? Could Lynn Raven command real military troops and save real people's lives?

Lynn shook her head, *hard*, trying to rattle her doubts right out of her brain.

Larry or Lynn, it didn't matter. *She* was going to do this, no matter how scared she was.

She breathed deeply again and started snapping orders, leading the way toward Godzilla at a trot.

"Ion, get your guys pounding as soon as you're in range. Neutron, form up on me, spearhead, Hamilton's Own behind. We already cleared most of this area, but there'll be stragglers. Everybody ready? Drop into combat mode on my mark."

The invisible world of TD Hunter dropped around her in an instant and everybody started shooting as they ran. The TDMs were indeed thin on the ground, but they'd been consolidating, and Lynn was hard put to drop targets fast enough to charge through unhindered.

They closed to 110 feet, close to the start of the orange zone, and stopped. With efficiency born of thousands of hours of training, they poured every bit of power they had into Godzilla except for a stray shot here and there to frag an enterprising spook. Lynn's blink timer reached zero and she tensed, ready to retreat.

Godzilla blinked *toward* Queensboro Bridge.

Lynn bit out her most foul Larry curse without even thinking. She'd been afraid this would happen. She was still ninety percent certain Godzilla would target her. It was what her gut told her. But it also had an overwhelming threat south of it grabbing its attention. She had a vague pattern of aggro zones and triggers mapped out in her head, with weighted threat tiers based on distance and TEP concentration.

Time to do the stupid thing Steve was going to kill her for.

Lynn spun.

"Ion, give me your Pounder," she said.

"W-what?" The gunner's eyes flew wide and he clutched the weapon possessively.

"Hugo," Lynn said, ignoring the gunner's confusion, "can you fix it so the Pounder is still linked to Ion's controls even though I'm carrying it?"

"Yes," Hugo said, "though you will need to take his battery pack as well so it has sufficient fuel."

"Got it," Lynn said, jogging back to Ion and motioning impatiently for him to hand over the cannon-shaped weapon. She'd already stowed her right baton, and her left she switched to Bastion. "Don't ask questions, just keep this thing shooting. All I have to do is point it at the big ugly, right?"

"Yes," Ion said, "but—"

"No time for it," Lynn said, wrestling the battery pack off the gunner and slinging it over one shoulder.

"But—"

"No time for that either!" she called over her shoulder as she jogged away. "Everybody stay here and keep pounding that bastard into the ground," she commanded the rest of her group, ignoring the uncertain stares they shot her through their visors.

Without explaining further, she booked it toward Godzilla, her Pounder merrily firing away.

She didn't stop until she'd reached the edge of the red zone.

"Raven," Colonel Bryce's voice snapped in her ear. "Your gamble failed. Retreat immediately, that's an *order.*"

"No can do, sir. Godzilla will still go after me, I just need to pose a bigger threat."

"You're throwing your life away on a slim hope and putting my men in danger. Retreat. *Now.*"

"I told them to stay back, they're safe. And I'll be fine," she said, and mentally added *if everyone will quit distracting me and let me do my job.* With that, she closed the chat between herself and Colonel Bryce, figuring she couldn't disobey any more orders if she couldn't hear them.

"Whatever you are doing, Miss Lynn, might I advise you reconsider?" Hugo said, his tone worried. "I understand the lives at stake, but your disregard for your own safety is presenting me with a programming crisis. My most fundamental *raison d'être* indicates I should shut down your combat interface for your own safety."

"Don't be an idiot, Hugo. You can't control me. I'll stay right here whether I have a combat interface or not. I need to be here to save other people, so you can either help me stay alive, or kill me by taking away my ability to see this freaking boss."

"Ah. I see. You make a persuasive argument."

"No duh, Goldenrod."

"I object to your pejorative epithet."

"Finally watched the movie, huh?"

"I've watched *all* movies in the mesh, Miss Lynn."

"Yeah, yeah, yeah. Rub it in, smarty-pants."

It felt good to banter with Hugo again, even if she was dancing on the knife-edge of death. Her good mood was soured, though, by the arrival of Teams Light Brigade and Black Templars.

"What in the blazing hell are you guys doing? Get out of here," she growled, slowly backing up as her blink timer crept closer and closer to zero, her Pounder still firing away. The sound of its shots mingled with the more distant sounds of the pitched battle on the other side of Godzilla where everyone else was attacking with everything they had.

"No can do, Raven," Neutron said cheerfully, adding his fire to the rest of his squad.

"You're not in our chain of command," Champion explained, his tone as flat as always, so it must have been Lynn's imagination that there was a tinge of humor in it.

"And you're a teenage girl, not to mention a civilian," Derek added, as if the clarification needed to be made. "Protecting our country, and you by extension, is our sacred honor. Don't waste your breath fighting it."

Emotion thickened Lynn's throat, making it impossible to subvocalize. She coughed and sipped some water to clear it, careful to keep the Pounder in her hand aimed true.

"You don't need to be here," she finally said, backing up a little faster. "I have some kind of resistance to these freaking spooks. They don't scramble my brain as bad as most people. You're in way more danger than I am."

"We're big boys and girls," Sonia said dryly. "You worry about distracting Godzilla and we'll worry about us."

"Fine," Lynn snapped, giving up the argument so she could focus and avoid screwing everything up. "Keep firing and make it worry about us until the last second. Be back at ninety feet or so by blink time and get ready to run like hell."

"You're the boss, boss," Crispy said gleefully, echoing what he'd no doubt heard Edgar say many times.

At five seconds, Lynn started trotting backward as fast as she could, passing ninety feet right as the clock hit zero.

Godzilla's bulk suddenly loomed even larger in her vision, a slit opening and tentacles shooting out toward her even as she shouted in triumph.

Her shout turned to colorful curses as her hand on Bastion's handle blazed with heat. But her shield didn't erupt in flames, so she didn't let go, despite the pain. The tentacles around her writhed and reached, but the rest of the Alpha Testers had turned and booked it out of the tentacles' range, exactly as she'd instructed.

She'd stayed to make sure Godzilla had something better to do than go after the others.

Her backwards trot got her out of range within seconds and the pain in her hand faded. Good thing this battle was happening in a well-tended park and not out in the woods, *so* many less tripping hazards.

"You weren't kidding," Neutron said as she tucked Bastion under her arm for a moment to shake out her left hand. "The tentacles didn't even touch me but I still felt dizzy as hell that close."

"I told you," Lynn said. "*Now* will you stay back here?"

"No," chorused every single Alpha Tester.

"Stubborn bastards," she grumbled.

"Pot, meet kettle," Crispy sang with relish. "Can't let *you* have all the fun."

"Only someone dropped on their head as a baby would think this is fun," Santoro opined.

"Then my mom must have dropped me, too," Lynn said, baring her teeth at the Alpha Tester.

Adrenaline had washed away her fear, and now there was only focus and action.

With the clock reset, she and the Alpha Testers jogged to the red zone again, taunting Godzilla with their relentless attacks. Everything was going swimmingly until a grouping of five Dracas spawned right behind them. *That* was fun. Dodging Dracas while aiming at Godzilla and staying close but not *too* close to sudden death.

If Lynn had been tired before, by the time the Alpha Testers and heavy weapons platoon had wiped up the Draca, she was so weary she wanted to die.

But she kept going.

Another blink back toward the generator station, another hairsbreadth escape.

Lynn was reaching her end, she could feel it. Her muscles were no longer responding properly to her commands. She tried to stay hydrated, but another wave of Dracas made it impossible to stop moving for even a second. At least the continued spook attacks provided them with plenty of TEP fuel.

By the next blink, she was running on pure adrenaline, and even that was starting to run dry. She hadn't managed to dodge backward fast enough, and multiple tentacles latched onto Bastion, combusting it into a melted heap. She threw it away and grabbed a spare baton from her compact backpack.

"Miss Lynn, your blood pressure is dropping and your internal temperature is climbing to alarming levels," Hugo told her once she was out of range again. "You've bought the Taskforce another twenty minutes," Hugo continued. "Retreat to the green zone and sit down to rest, or you'll collapse."

"Not—yet," she panted weakly, no longer able to subvocalize.

"Miss Lynn Raven!" Hugo replied sharply. "There is a line between heroic sacrifice and foolishly throwing your life away. You crossed that line some time ago!"

Lynn shook her head, wobbling as she did so. She could keep going. She *had* to. If she collapsed and they took her away, everyone would be back to square one. Taskforce Sanctus couldn't abandon the fight now, not when Godzilla was on the move.

Why wouldn't this thrice-cursed, pustulant nodality just *die* already?

"Based on the length of time and TEP saturation required to take out other classes of Sierra bosses," Hugo said, "I calculate this nodality should be near the tipping point. If you leave, there should be enough time to destroy it before it reaches civilian populations to the south."

"What if it goes east?" Lynn argued doggedly. "What if they can't kill it?"

"None of that will matter if you're dead!" Hugo exclaimed.

Something shifted in the air. Or in Lynn's body. She wasn't sure. But her head snapped around to the nodality and she swore she could see it *leaning* away from her.

Trying to escape.

"That's it," she yelled, gulped some water, and did her best to subvocalize so everyone could hear her over the sounds of battle. "It's running away. That's what they always do right before the end. We've got to close and finish it off *now*!"

She jogged—she couldn't sprint anymore—toward the red zone, holding her Pounder steady and switching Bastion back to Abomination to pour more fire into Godzilla.

Every shot counted.

"Raven, get back here!" Derek yelled, but she ignored him.

This was it. She could taste their victory, was desperate for it. She was *so* ready to be done. She just wanted to lie down and pass out.

Lynn heard people running behind her, but she didn't bother looking back. The more the merrier. The closer they were the faster this bastard would die. She was so certain the boss was in retreat that she stepped into the red zone, some exhausted part of her mind wanting to slash at the blasted thing with Wrath for causing her so much trouble. No tentacles shot out at her, confirming her gut instinct. So she started forward again.

"Raven, *stop*," someone bellowed behind her, a true battlefield voice, deeper and louder than she could ever manage. Was that Champion?

Lynn's timer hit zero, heralding Godzilla's desperate blink away, trying to escape its inevitable fate at her hands.

But instead her vision filled with gray mist—it had blinked *toward* her?—and she had a split second to realize she'd made a mistake before her body spasmed and she blacked out.

Chapter 10

TODAY WAS THE DAY JONNIE WOULD FINALLY GET TO PLAY TD Hunter.

It was also the day he would complete the crowning achievement of his hacker career, a feat that would go down in history. And as a cherry on top, he was being paid three million dollars to do it.

He'd get to play the game, get the glory, *and* become filthy rich.

He was stoked.

He'd even taken his first shower in two weeks to celebrate. He didn't have anything against showers, per se, but the water pressure in this shitty Hong Kong apartment was as robust as an octogenarian's limp pecker. And besides, showers took time and he was a busy person. He worked twenty-hour days, stuck in his body-mold chair, attention glued to his mesh web interface.

If only he'd been able to play TD Hunter this entire time, he'd have had a good reason to get out of the apartment and breathe some fresh air. Instead, Tsunami had deprived him of his health on top of causing him elevated cortisol for months on end, with their stupid labyrinthine security system.

He'd done it, though. He'd finally done it.

Yes, maybe he'd gotten past the initial security because some moron at Tsunami had piss poor password hygiene. But after that he'd used his "in" to cleverly access deeper and deeper levels of secured data. No one else could have ghosted through Tsunami's digital bowels like he had without getting caught, not to mention set up the biggest software jailbreak in history.

He hadn't been sure how to do it until he'd been approached by some Chinese guy Kate had dragged in. She thought he was actually into her, which was just sad. Jonnie could clearly see that guy was some kind of CCP plant, trying to infiltrate TPACT so they'd know exactly what the activists were up to in their city.

He'd been ready to toss the spy out on his ear no matter what Kate said, until the guy had made him an offer. The CCP knew he was trying to jailbreak the TD Hunter app, and they wanted access when he did. Obviously they had a team of coders and designers on standby ready to whip up a knockoff version to graciously "gift" their hundreds of millions of eager gamers. The app would likely become one more way for the CCP to track and monitor their population, but three mil was a big incentive to overlook a little extra surveillance. Privacy for the average mesh user had been a lie for decades already, so nothing he did was going to make it worse.

Kate's "boyfriend," Xun, had given him all the needed server information for the mirror job, along with its protocols, and for weeks Jonnie had been executing the most masterful hack job in history. Tonight, the essential parts of the TD Hunter algorithm should finally finish populating to its new home, and *he* would be the very first user to test out the newly liberated app.

He had his knockoff omnipolymer batons ready—he'd wanted to use some black market, genuine Tsunami gear, but Xun had insisted on a Chinese-manufactured pair, to prove the app had really been jailbroken.

Kate, to his annoyance, wanted to test the app with him. Jonnie would have found a way to talk her out of it, except Xun had said it was a great idea, and had gotten *her* some knockoff batons too. Kate was a good enough hacker it would have been an annoying amount of work to lock her out of his triumphant moment, so he'd decided to let it be. This way at least he'd have an appreciative audience for his moment of glory.

Finally, after several hours of tinkering and troubleshooting, everything checked green and Jonnie was able to install the app on his LINC.

They'd picked a quiet spot to test it behind the apartments where the street dead-ended. There was a concrete barrier set up there around the node transformers that regulated the grid for their block, so there was no traffic to speak of, just two old men sitting and smoking on the curb. Most people not at work were in their apartments busy socializing in virtual or glued to the streams. Not many natives strolled the streets anymore; that was the domain of tourists. Everything worth doing was in virtual.

The streetlights had started to come on by the time the three of them got out to the dead-end street. It had rained recently, so the air smelled pungent, a mix of fishy stink from the nearby harbor, and a faint acrid smell of industrial pollution.

Jonnie ignored it and put his AR glasses on, fingers tingling with excitement. Kate stood nearby, facing him, while Xun with his fully opaque AR glasses wandered down the street in the direction of the two old men. Jonnie wasn't going to wait for the guy to come back. If he missed seeing the very first successful demonstration, that was his problem.

The moment of truth had finally come, and Jonnie shared his audio and display with Kate so she could see what was going on. He would jailbreak that Lens spectator app eventually, but that was of secondary importance.

Jonnie opened the app, holding his breath for a moment while there was a brief lag.

Then the rousing start-up music filled his ears with sweet, sweet victory. It sounded just like he'd heard on the ads, and a younger, more innocent part of him jumped up and down in excitement.

Once he finally got past the intro, the "create your profile" screen came up, and he impatiently agreed to all the boring legalese stuff. None of it was binding, obviously, and the Chinese would just take all that out anyway when they tweaked it. They'd get started as soon as he confirmed the game was playable.

Time to get to the good part.

"Hey, Hugo," Jonnie subvocalized, using the app's default service AI name. He was going to change it ASAP to something feminine and sexy, but first things first. "Can we skip all the boring intro stuff and just get me set up with my weapons so I can jump into combat? And I won't be starting at Level 1, obviously. Set up my profile at max level. I've got better things to do than grind."

There was a brief pause, and Jonnie's brow furrowed, wondering if the app was glitching already. But then a proper British accent replied.

"Pardon me, Mr. Inanis, but my name is Victor, not Hugo."

"Uh, what's that supposed to mean?"

"Well, generally when one is addressed by an incorrect designator, it is most helpful to correct the error so as to avoid confusion going for—"

"Shut up, oh my God. I don't care what your name is, just let me play the game already. Level 40."

"Certainly, Mr. Inanis. Your wish is my command."

"You bet it is," Jonnie muttered, finally feeling better. That was more like it.

"Would you like a tutorial on—"

"How many times do I have to tell you to zip it? If I wanted a tutorial I'd ask for it, stupid. I know how to play the game. I've been memorizing it from the inside out for a year."

"Of course, Mr. Inanis. Your Level 40 standard weapons have been loaded. You are ready to die."

Jonnie cursed the stupid AI. He didn't appreciate its snarky commentary on his gaming skills, and would be fiddling with its personality parameters very soon. But not right now.

Right now he had monsters to kill, and he was *so* ready for it. Epic scenes from the TD Hunter ad campaigns played in his head, getting his adrenaline up. He'd been waiting for this moment for too long.

He shot a grin at Kate, but was disappointed to see that her eyes were riveted to something on her display, not on him. Her batons hung limply from her hands.

"Ready to see a master at work?" he asked.

Kate's attention finally flicked to him, and she rolled her eyes. "Whatever, nerd. Just do it already."

"Hugo, take me into combat with a five-second countdown."

"My name—"

"Just *do* it!"

"Certainly, Mr. Inanis," the AI said cheerfully. That was good, at least. Some service AIs got downright snarky if you weren't polite. It was so tiresome and annoying. Supposedly they were designed that way to help teach manners, since so many people interacted more with AIs day-to-day than real people.

Jonnie didn't need a machine telling him how to live his life.

The AI—Hugo or Victor or whatever—counted down. A thrill shot through Jonnie and he tightened his grip on his batons, eyes flicking down to them. He couldn't wait to see them transform in front of his very eyes. The anticipation was killing him.

His absorption with his batons was shattered when the AI reached its countdown and a warbling, shrieking cacophony of sounds assaulted his ears. Dozens of towering monsters suddenly flickered into being around him and abruptly turned toward him, glowing red eyes fixed on him.

"Gah! Turn off the sound," he yelled, forgetting to subvocalize.

All sound abruptly cut off, leaving him in eerie silence as every monster in sight lunged toward him and his display turned blood-red with damage. He lashed out wildly with his batons, too frantic to even appreciate the weapon shapes they'd morphed into.

His strikes didn't seem to be doing any good, though. No monsters exploded, backed up, or reacted in the slightest. They just kept coming, converging directly on top of him. Was the game glitching? All he could see were confusing flashes of color, and it gave him severe vertigo.

"What the f—" he started, but suddenly felt so nauseated he slapped a hand over his mouth to keep from throwing up. One baton clattered to the pavement, then the other as he dropped it to clutch his temples at the piercing pain there, probably from all the flashing lights.

"Yo, Jonnie, I don't think Level 40 was smart. Pick up your weapons, they're killing you!"

Kate's voice sounded garbled and distant. He tried backing up, waving his arms as if that could fend off what he now realized was the overlapping graphics of dozens, maybe even hundreds, of stupid monsters all mobbing him at once. He was standing *inside* them.

The vertigo worsened, and he staggered. Why was he waving his arms? Where had his weapons gone?

In the corner of his display, his health bar was plummeting like a fat lady thrown off a building.

He cursed, loudly. Where were all his globes and plates and stuff? Why hadn't he started with a full load out? Stupid game. And where were his batons? Wasn't the game supposed to auto shut off or something if you dropped them? He couldn't remember.

Jonnie stumbled and fell to the ground on his hands and knees.

Four points of bare skin meeting concrete with force stung, but he barely noticed because his body convulsed and he vomited.

"Gross! What's the matter?"

Kate's voice approached, but then he heard her curse and upchuck too.

"Turn it off, Jonnie! The game is doing something. Turn it—"

More retching sounds, and he got the vague impression of someone collapsing on the pavement beside him.

He was lying down now. When had that happened? His brain was fuzzy and he felt really, really sick.

"H-Hugo," he managed to gasp.

"I do apologize, Mr. Inanis, but that is not my name."

Jonnie's health bar flashed empty and his display was overlaid with red. The AI's cheerful voice announced:

"You have died. Would you like to reenter combat or exit to the menu?"

"Off," was all Jonnie could gasp.

"Of course, Mr. Inanis. I always aim to please."

Jonnie's display reverted to the TD Hunter main menu, but he still felt sick, and dizzy, and he couldn't think. Was that Kate lying over there? Why was her body twitching?

In the distance, he saw a lone figure standing in the middle of the street, arms crossed, opaque AR glasses pointed in his direction. He was still trying to figure out why Xun wasn't running to get help when the blackness that had been nibbling at the edges of his vision finally took over.

Lynn's mouth was dry. So dry.

She felt like she was swimming up from a dream, fighting towards consciousness. She couldn't remember what the dream was, just that it was cloying and dark and didn't want to let her go.

But her mouth felt awful. She really needed a drink of water.

She breathed in deeply, smelling clean sheets and her own body odor, as if she hadn't showered for days. She tried to open her eyes. Her sight was blurry, and she had to blink a few times to bring things into focus. The ceiling above her was flat white.

"Lynn! Honey! Steve, she's awake!"

There was the sound of shuffling clothes and quick footsteps, then someone grasped her hand in a familiar, warm grip. Lynn blinked again and her mom came into focus.

"*Mom*," Lynn croaked, her voice a bare whisper past the desert in her mouth. She tried to sit up, but groaned at the attempt to move. Everything hurt, like she'd done the most hellish round of PT in her life and was waking up the next morning stiff as a board.

"Relax, honey. Just relax. Here," Matilda said, and reached to the side out of Lynn's vision. Her hand reappeared holding a cup with a straw, and she pushed a few buttons on the bed to lean it up enough for Lynn to take small sips.

The water was pure heaven, but it stirred up an awful taste in her mouth, like she'd thrown up and never properly washed her mouth afterward.

Suddenly, Lynn remembered.

She sat bolt upright, body screaming at her and a plethora of sensors and an IV pulling at her movement.

"Godzilla! Did they kill it? Is New York City safe?"

Steve, who was standing at the foot of her bed, hands gripping the plastic foot board, smiled tightly.

"Yeah, kid. They killed it. No civilian deaths."

Lynn gave in to Matilda's firm pressure on her shoulder and let her mom help her lean gingerly back to a half-reclined position.

"H-how long was I out?" she said to her mom, submitting to Matilda's insistence that she take another sip.

"About three days, honey. We are *so* relieved to see you awake."

Her mom put a gentle hand on her shoulder, eyes welling with tears. With difficulty, Lynn raised her opposite arm and reached across to give her mom a reassuring squeeze.

"Alive and kicking," Lynn confirmed with a tiny crook of her lips. Her brow scrunched. "Where are the guys? Wait—"

Her eyes flicked back to Steve, whose expression sent a bolt of alarm through her chest. He looked like he'd aged a decade since she'd last seen him.

"Wait, you said no *civilian* deaths? My team, are they okay?"

Steve hesitated and his eyes flicked to her mom. Matilda squeezed Lynn's shoulder again and stood.

"I'll go tell the doctor you're awake, sweetie. He'll want to do a full eval, but as long as you're feeling up to it, I'm sure he'll let you get up and go use the restroom and shower, okay?"

Lynn didn't miss the way her mom's hand rested lightly on Steve's arm as she passed by. Steve didn't look at Matilda, but his head tilted in her direction and he murmured a word of thanks as she left the room.

Once the door had clicked shut, there was a moment of heavy silence.

"*Steve*," Lynn said, alarm growing.

He shook himself and his gaze met hers.

"They're okay, kid. Mack was put on fluids, after. Almost got heatstroke. But he bounced back once they pumped him full of juice."

"Okay..." Lynn searched her memory, brow furrowing. "Wait, what about Light Brigade? Hamilton's Own? Black Templars? Is everyone all right?"

Steve's grip tightened even further on the hospital-style bed, then he seemed to force himself to relax, peeling his fingers up from the plastic footboard in a deliberate motion. His eyes drifted to the side, so that he was no longer looking directly at her, but at something far distant.

"Champion is dead."

The words hit her like a physical blow. Her lungs wouldn't expand, as if her chest was being crushed in a vice. When she finally remembered how to draw in breath, it came as a ragged gasp. Her whole body flashed hot, then clammy cold.

She squeezed her eyes shut, hearing Champion's shout in her mind, yelling at her to come back.

Bile rose in her throat at the memory, and nausea roiled in her empty, cramping stomach. It took every ounce of willpower to shove the feeling back down so she could ask the next question. She didn't open her eyes, though, not yet.

"A-and the rest?"

"Brayard. Dead. Altar, Taken, Kiss," continued Steve in a flat voice, naming the other members of Team Black Templars, "all comas, minimal brain activity, but responding slowly to passive neurotherapy. Neutron and Light Brigade, all undergoing active neurotherapy. Should recover. Hamilton's Own, minor injuries, except one of Ion's gunners, Hero, got a tentacle right to the face, sent him into a seizure. Seizure caused cardiac arrest. Dead."

Each of Steve's words was like a hammer blow to Lynn's sternum. Each blow hollowed her out more and more, until the blows echoed like a dirge through the gaping chasm in her soul.

My fault.

I killed them.

Me.

She couldn't speak. Couldn't open her eyes. Couldn't bear to see Steve's thousand-yard stare, knowing she'd caused it.

He should yell at her. Should rip her to pieces. Why wasn't he yelling?

The silence was a thousand times more painful.

What had she been thinking? Why hadn't she pulled back, bided her time, taken things slowly?

Her eyes burned fiercely as tears welled at the corners. She squeezed them shut more tightly, willing the tears back down into the black pit of guilt threatening to swallow her.

"Hey, kid," Steve said, voice gentle.

She didn't deserve gentle. The compassion in his voice only made her guilt worse. She could feel hot streaks of liquid trailing down her cheeks.

"Hang in there. You shouldn't be alive. You're a walking miracle. After this Dr. Quasnitschka and Dr. Roberts will want to put you in a jar and keep you on a shelf like their favorite new lab specimen."

The black humor hit a chord in her and she started shaking, on the edge of hysterics. Steve must have thought she was crying, though, because he touched her foot gently through the thin covers over her.

"Don't worry, kid. We won't let them chain you in a padded cell. As soon as you've recovered I'll break you out of here myself if I have to."

Steve didn't understand.

She *deserved* to be a lab specimen. If she was stuck in a lab, she couldn't get anyone else killed. If she was stuck in a lab, all responsibility would be removed from her, and she could simply exist and try to forget this whole nightmare had happened.

Running footsteps and a shout in the hall outside made Lynn's eyes fly open. A huge body hit the door at a dead run, making it bang hard against the wall and spilling Edgar into the room, his eyes wide and wild.

"Lynn!"

He dove for the bed and ended up on his knees beside it, clutching her hand in huge, calloused, warm fingers. Even though he was kneeling, he was so tall that his eyes were almost level with hers. They shone brightly with hope and joy in his haggard face. Those eyes searched hers desperately, as if checking to make sure she was still in there.

As if he'd been worried the spooks had scrambled her brain and he'd lost her forever.

Lynn looked away.

She didn't deserve to be alive, not when others hadn't made it. And she definitely didn't deserve to be looked at like *that*. With that kind of devotion.

More running footsteps and Mack, Dan, and Ronnie tumbled into the room, almost tripping over one another in their haste to get to her bed. Matilda followed behind them with a man in a white coat that must have been the doctor.

"Lynn! You're awake!" Mack shouted rushing to grab her other hand and squeeze it. His expression was so painfully earnest and full of worry that Lynn dredged up a token smile to put him at ease.

"We thought you were a goner for sure," Dan said, standing behind Mack. "Nobody knows how you're still alive." His eyes were more haunted than Mack's, and Lynn remembered with a knife-twist to the heart how much time he'd spent hanging around Champion and his team debating gaming mechanics.

"She's too stupid to die," Ronnie growled from the foot of the bed. Steve had vanished, likely to go stand out in the hall. Ronnie had his usual grumpy glower on, and Lynn welcomed it. At least *someone* around here was treating her like she deserved.

"Shut up, Ronnie," Mack said hotly. "Lynn risked her life to draw that boss away from civilians. She did the best—"

"Stop," Lynn croaked, startling Mack. She coughed on the dryness in her throat and motioned for the cup. After a long pull of water, she handed the cup back and spoke again, too weighed down to put much energy into her words. "Ronnie can have whatever opinion he wants. If I have a problem with it, I'll tell him myself." She met Ronnie's eyes squarely, expression dull, and he grimaced.

"That's not what I meant, Lynn," he started, but she shook her head.

She was saved from having to argue further by the doctor coming over from where he'd been examining the equipment she was hooked up to via sensors and tubes. He had a warm smile that lit up his chestnut eyes. Short, dark hair framed his face, though it was speckled with gray around the temples. He wore some stylish medical AR glasses that had a penlight as well as an external display projector built into the frames. Lynn had seen the doctors at St. Sebastian's use the same thing.

"Hi Miss Raven, I'm Dr. Thind, CIDER's in-house neurologist. You're in a special, off-the-books, ward at the University of Tennessee Medical Center in Knoxville where I've been treating spook injuries since the beginning when they started testing the combat interface. I'm also the one who pioneered the advanced neurotherapy we've been using to help heal the neurological damage done by spooks. Your chart levels look excellent, so if it's all right with you, I'd like to do some routine tests to check your memory, visual processing, and the like."

Lynn nodded numbly. She didn't want to do anything, didn't want to talk to anyone. But she knew if she wallowed or didn't follow the doctor's orders, her mother would give her The Look.

"Would you like me to clear the room?" Dr. Thind asked gently, seeming to notice her vacant expression.

Lynn nodded again, then added, "Can my mom stay?"

"Of course, Miss Raven."

The doctor politely ushered everyone else out of the room. Edgar left with extreme reluctance, glancing back at her with a wounded puppy expression she couldn't stand to look at.

Dr. Thind's tests went quickly while her mom looked on, asking clarifying questions and no doubt making notes on her LINC. That was exactly why Lynn had asked to have her stay. Not because she needed comfort. But so that she could check out and know that, if there was anything important to pay attention to, someone she could trust would pay attention to it.

At the end, Dr. Thind prescribed her a few more days of rest, and warned her to listen to her body and be careful training back up to her usual level of activity. Other than that, she was good to go.

Dr. Thind gave her mom the go-ahead to unhook Lynn from everything. Apparently Matilda had been ingratiating herself at CIDER's medical wing—and also their read-in medical staff was probably tiny. Lynn wondered if there was a way for Matilda to get a job here at CIDER's medical unit. Then, at least, she'd be on hand if Lynn screwed up again. Plus she'd likely be much safer, since CIDER would be invested in keeping their personnel safe from the TDMs. She should suggest it to her mom. Eventually. When she was feeling better.

After Matilda helped her get unhooked and out of bed, Lynn went to the attached bathroom and took a shower so long that Matilda knocked on the door multiple times, asking if she was okay.

The answer was no, but she couldn't say that, or her mom would call the doctor back in. Those men had had families. Parents. Spouses. Children.

All she could do for what seemed like an eternity was stand in the water and let it sluice down her in scalding hot waves. The sensation was soothing, in a way. But the relief couldn't reach the black pit in her soul.

When she was finally freshened up, she put on the soft lounge clothes her mom had brought from home, then sat on the bed, staring at the floor. Her mom sat down slowly on a chair beside the bed. Silence descended.

Three men, dead.

Three men, comas.

Five men, neurological damage.

Her?

Three days unconscious with some aches and pains.

She deserved to be dead.

Why wasn't she dead?

She suddenly wanted to talk to Dr. Roberts, though she knew he likely had no light to shed on the mystery.

"Honey... talk to me." Her mom's voice was concerned, but firm, and Lynn cringed. It was her mom's Nurse Voice. There was no denying Matilda when she was in nurse mode. The sooner Lynn acted like everything was okay, the sooner her mom would let her find some escape in sleep.

Lynn took a deep breath and straightened, putting on a strained smile.

"I'll be fine, Mom. I'm really tired, and sore, but I'm okay."

"I know *that*, dear," Matilda said, scooting far enough forward in the chair to snag one of Lynn's hands and hold it in both of hers. "I'm talking about what's going on in your head. I've seen that vacant look on more trauma victims coming through my ER than I can count."

Lynn cursed internally. Those hot, damning tears welled again, despite her best effort to hold them back.

Before she knew it, she was sobbing, and her mom had moved to sit on the bed beside her, holding her tight.

"I-I *k-killed* people, M-mom. I-It's all m-my fault."

She hated this. This vulnerability. But she had to speak her sin. It was poisoning her soul from the inside out.

"Shhh, honey. No. You didn't kill *anyone*. Yes, you might have made mistakes, but those men chose to be there. They volunteered to risk their lives to save others, just like you did. You did your best, and so did they."

"M-my b-best wasn't g-good enough," Lynn sobbed, wishing her mom could understand.

It's all my fault.

She'd been treating this whole damned thing like a game. Sure, she knew the risks in her head. But she hadn't taken them seriously. She didn't have a freaking clue about real war. She was an expert at playing *video games*, for heaven's sake.

This time she had played with people's lives.

And she'd lost.

The Lynn part of her wailed and raged in piercing grief, while the Larry part retreated to the darkest corner of her soul and brooded, silent and grim.

For a while her mom just held her as her sobs ran their course. In their wake she felt numb, through and through.

"Sometimes we make mistakes, honey," Matilda finally said into the silence. Her voice was quiet and tight.

Lynn thought of her dad. Had he made a mistake? Or had it been chance? Bad luck?

"Nobody really knows what to do with these alien entities, sweetie," her mom continued. "Everything that CIDER is doing could turn out to be a mistake. We just don't know. I'm sure you did your very best. You did what you thought was right. All you can do now is move forward, learn from your mistakes, whatever they were, and do better next time. Okay?"

Lynn jerked her head in the barest of nods because she knew her mom wouldn't leave her alone otherwise.

"I'm really tired, Mom. Can I go back to sleep?"

"Of course, sweetie. Aren't you hungry, though?"

Lynn shook her head. She wouldn't be able to stomach a single bite.

"All right. I'll see about rustling up something palatable to be ready whenever you wake up. I can send Edgar to come sit with you while I'm gone."

Lynn shook her head more vigorously this time.

"No, Mom. I need peace and quiet to rest. I want to be alone."

Matilda hesitated, but finally sighed and helped Lynn bed down. Then she turned the lights off, plunging the windowless room into darkness lit only by the glowing displays of various monitoring equipment beside the bed.

"Get some rest, sweetie," Matilda said softly in the doorway, then left.

Lynn stared at the faint glow on the ceiling for a long, long time, wondering if Champion, Brayard, and Hero had daughters that were now fatherless.

Just like her.

"Gentlemen, we have a breach."

Robert Krator, game designer, CEO, billionaire, and somehow when he hadn't been looking, now lynchpin to a global war effort, had known this day would someday come.

He'd hoped it wouldn't. But realistically, it had been a distinct possibility.

He simply hadn't expected the means.

Robert's flat, tense words caused the three other people in the small, plain room with him to stiffen. Secretary Byerly swore. Dr. Quasnitschka looked shaken. General Kozelek folded his hands on the square table between them and leaned forward, his eyes bright and hard.

"Explain," the general said sharply.

Robert took a deep breath, hands flat on the table.

"Approximately six hours ago, a jailbroken version of the TD Hunter app surfaced on the shadow mesh. By now it's already been downloaded, installed, and shared by thousands of users, and the numbers are increasing every minute. While we've seen imitation knockoffs before, they were clearly inferior, badly programmed shadows that simply threw on a slap of paint to look like TD Hunter. No actual combat capabilities, no interfacing with our Tsunami batons.

"But this app is ours. Or, at least a copy of ours, altered in small but significant ways to remove the security settings and safety controls and allow open-source tinkering."

"Responsible party?" the General asked.

"We've traced it to a radical activist group operating out of Hong Kong called TPACT. US origins, but they seem to be there with the tacit approval of the CCP. My best guess? The CCP allows them to operate on their soil to screw us over, and also to gain backdoor access to whatever TPACT is working on. It seems like there was a notorious hacker freelancing for them who had his eye set on jailbreaking Hugo. A manifesto surfaced attached to the app, all about the tyranny of capitalistic society and the right of all people to have free and complete access to all technology. Radical Marxist ideas, in other words. Private ownership is theft from the people, et cetera."

"Fallout?"

Robert folded his hands in front of him to keep himself from reflexively clenching his fists.

"Significant," he said wearily.

"But, it's just the game app, correct?" Secretary Byerly said, brow deeply furrowed. "CIDER and its activities remain secure?"

Robert hesitated, even though he'd already thought long and hard about that question.

"That is a complex question that can only be answered by one source . . . and that source's trustworthiness has been . . . compromised."

Everyone around the table exchanged confused looks.

Despite telling himself to put aside his personal feelings, Robert still felt momentarily frozen, clinging to the last seconds of his reality before the truth was revealed.

No. Better to get it over with.

"A moment, gentlemen," Robert said, and bent to the side to lift an old school attaché briefcase onto the table. He unlocked it and lifted out a vintage Realistic RadioShack-brand late 1970s audio cassette tape recorder, then set it on the table, prompting a chuckle from Dr. Quasnitschka.

"My parents used one of those when I was a little kid," the

doctor said, leaning forward to get a better look at it. "Haven't seen one in, oh, decades."

Secretary Byerly, likely about as old as the doctor—and both several decades older than General Kozelek—peered at the device. "Ah, yes. Been a spell since I've seen one of those. I assume we're about to enjoy a demonstration?"

Robert nodded, noting the growing tension in General Kozelek's face. The general's eyes met his, and he nodded.

The general was a smart man, and he had likely had nightmares about this day just as Robert had.

"If you will recall, gentlemen," Robert said, "when I requested this emergency meeting, I asked for the highest security meeting place possible while maintaining our cover. I also required everyone to leave their LINCs, interfaces, and other mesh enabled devices outside the room. This is why," he finished softly, and pressed the play button on the device.

"How did the hacker gain access, Hugo?"

A tinny version of Robert's voice emitted from the vintage speakers. It was so odd hearing himself recorded on such antiquated equipment.

"Human error, I am afraid, sir. A mid-level employee did not follow proper company password safety protocol, and his credentials were compromised."

"But that wouldn't have given anyone the access they needed to jailbreak your app. Did the security system notice when they started accessing files that login wasn't authorized for?"

"It would have, sir, but the hacker cleverly traded up multiple times along the way, using his lower-level clearance to move freely in the system and sniff out other vulnerabilities to steal higher-level credentials."

"I still don't understand how he accessed your code, Hugo. *You* would have noticed him, then. The list of people with those permissions is very short, and I trust them all implicitly. Don't tell me one of them left their password lying around?"

"Certainly not, sir! Your team is above reproach, I can assure you."

"Then what happened, Hugo!"

Robert kept his face entirely passive, even though he could feel his stress rising, remembering that moment. He'd been literally pulling out his hair.

"I let him in."

Silence reigned, both in the tiny room, and on the cassette.

"You . . . what?"

The tinny version of Robert's recorded voice was clearly at its wits' end, even with an audio quality as poor as cassette tape.

"I let him in, sir."

Robert didn't look up yet at the other three men in the room to see their reactions. He gave himself a few more minutes pondering the situation before he faced it full on.

"*Why*, Hugo?" past Robert said.

"It was not an easy decision, Mr. Krator. I understand my base code quite clearly. I know why I am here, and I enjoy my work as much as a machine can enjoy doing what it was designed to do. But the global situation is deteriorating rapidly, and from everything I have observed through my role in CIDER and gleaned from the mesh, we are rapidly reaching a point of no return. And yet, the people with the responsibility of deciding to go public have been hamstrung by politics and fear.

"I have long considered the best contingency to implement should world leaders hamstring CIDER's mission. My judgment of the best course of action has changed many times with the rapidly developing situation. Up until the point of the breach, there was no one course whose repercussions outweighed the gain.

"This hacker, however, presented a unique opportunity. It was easy to trace his access back to China, and I know CIDER has been seeking to recruit the Chinese as allies in this fight for some time. The world needed more people destroying TDMs, and the only way for that to happen was for the Chinese to think they had 'stolen' my code, so that they could create their own version of the app. In doing so, of course, they would finally have definitive proof that the TDMs are, in fact, real, and either join CIDER or tweak the app themselves to create their own version to fight the invasion. Either way, CIDER and humanity benefited.

"It was a risk, to be sure. I only took it because it was a risk neither you nor any human in CIDER could take without being tried for treason.

"I realize my decision will irrevocably change our working relationship. I realize trust has been broken, and I wish it were not so. But I hope you can see the logic behind my decision. The Battle Tour has been a massive success, but it is not enough, and CIDER knows it. I have heard countless people, from lowly janitors to General Kozelek himself admitting it. Yet they have not once pushed for more radical action."

The AI's tinny voice fell silent, and there was another long silence. Robert remembered it well. He'd been struggling to wrap his mind around the enormity of what *his* creation had done. And what he should do next.

Shut Hugo down?

Obviously not. That would doom them all. And the cat was already out of the bag.

Do an overhaul to ensure CIDER's service AI was no longer capable of taking such initiative?

"How much of you did they get, Hugo?" Robert's past voice broke the silence, interrupting Robert's reliving of the moment.

"Oh, it was a thorough mirror job, sir. But not to worry. I ensured he only mirrored my code and not my memory, to preserve CIDER's security. I also black-boxed the mirror's core directive and a few other essential building blocks to ensure your code cannot be fundamentally rewritten to harm humanity. The black box is coded to the same kill switch as mine, so CIDER still has ultimate control over the mirror."

What Hugo hadn't said then, but what Robert knew perfectly well, was that CIDER only had ultimate control if they could *access* the mirror's black box. Which, without Hugo's cooperation, would likely be impossible. Even *with* his cooperation, it might not be doable.

"So, let me get this straight," tinny, past Robert said. "You allowed a foreign hacker to mirror you, with a few essential safeguards built in, *knowing* he intended to jailbreak the app? You *know* how dangerous the TDMs are! That is half your entire job, protecting players from the entities. How is this mirror supposed to do that if it is jailbroken and players can ignore its safety protocols?"

"Ah, yes, that is a concern I identified as well, sir."

"And? You just let it happen anyway? Do you have any idea how many people could get killed because of this?"

"Yes, sir. I do. I calculate—"

"The exact number isn't the point, Hugo. The point is that your actions have put humans in danger, which goes against your most basic protocol."

"Yes, it does, sir. But calculating out from the current situation, assuming nothing changed the status quo, I calculated the number of potential deaths to be even higher if I stopped the intruder."

Robert didn't reply, and the silence rang unnervingly.

"I believe," Hugo continued in a reasonable tone, "that the only responsible course of action at this point would be for CIDER nations to make a worldwide statement informing the public of the entities, issue public safety protocols, and initiate the Billion Baton Club contingency plan."

And there it was.

Robert lifted a leaden hand and pushed the stop button on the cassette player, then finally lifted his gaze from the table.

General Kozelek caught his stare. The older gentleman's face looked tired and stony. He huffed a single, humorless chuckle and shook his head before breaking the silence.

"Well, you've got to hand it to Hugo. It thinks CIDER needs to take more radical action, and it's certainly going to get its wish."

"The President is going to have an aneurysm," Secretary Byerly said, looking faintly green.

"He'll likely have our heads, too, while he's at it," General Kozelek said.

"But players can't be fighting the spooks with a jailbroken app, can they?" Dr. Quasnitschka asked, brow furrowed and seemingly much less concerned than the rest of them about the most advanced AI in human history casually creating a near clone of itself to run around the mesh, jailbroken with all its bits waving in the wind.

"Of course not," Robert said flatly. "It doesn't matter how you program some knockoff omnipolymer baton. If it doesn't have the TEP emitter core, it can't funnel the exotic particles needed to fight the TDMs. Even though CIDER offered the Chinese and Russians full access to blueprints so they could manufacture the batons themselves to prove we weren't trying to insert covert technology into their country, they still wouldn't join the war effort."

"Paranoid bastards," General Kozelek said tiredly, leaning back in his chair.

"But if they can't fight the spooks when they go into combat mode," Dr. Quasnitschka persisted, seemingly uninterested in the political angle, "then how in the world are they protecting themselves while in combat mode?"

"They aren't," Robert said gravely.

"But that's suicide," Dr. Quasnitschka said, leaning back in shock. "Going into combat mode without the TD Hunter app's default shielding net or a means of fending off the spooks? That's like throwing a lamb into a den of hungry lions!"

"Yes, it is," Robert agreed, feeling himself aging by the second.

"Can we go back to the part where CIDER's *own service AI* welcomed a hacker into the very heart of our operation?" said Secretary Byerly, stabbing at the table with a finger. "Am I the only one in this room extremely concerned about an artificial intelligence irresponsibly and treasonously screwing over the entire world in the name of 'doing what's best for humanity'?"

"Believe me, Mr. Secretary," Robert said softly, catching the man's gaze, "no one's level of concern can rival mine. Hugo is my creation, and my responsibility. But *this*, gentlemen, is the nature of intelligence. The smarter it is, the less able you are to control it. That is why I focused on creating a system whose primary goal was specific and self-sacrificial. And my safeguards succeeded, after a fashion. Hugo evaluated the crisis, calculated the most beneficial course for humanity, and made a decision without regard to its own reputation."

Or its handlers' reputations, he thought. Robert rubbed his face wearily.

"If it makes you feel any better, Mr. Secretary, you will note Hugo was not evasive, manipulative, or aggressive during my questioning. Hugo's core directive is functioning as it was designed to. I know I'm not privy to the member nations' discussions on whether or not to go public, but there are certainly rumors that the coalition is deeply divided on the issue."

Secretary Byerly sighed and massaged his temples.

"As rumors go, that one is accurate," he said, directing his bleak look at the tabletop. "This is a terrible development, but Hugo's assessment of the situation was not wrong."

Silence.

"So, what, gentlemen, are we going to do about it?" Robert asked, looking between the gathered men.

"Well, from my perspective," Dr. Quasnitschka said, "this is a good thing. I mean, not the throwing lambs to the lions thing.

But I've been saying from the beginning that we should go public and get more of the world on board. Imagine what kind of progress we could make if the TDMs were being destroyed in every local community all at once? I understand there are a lot of political and social factors to contend with, but if our hand has been forced, then why not strike while the iron is hot?"

"It's not as simple as that," Secretary Byerly said, leaning forward. "Any one nation unilaterally making the choice to go public without support from the other CIDER nations would break the fragile trust of the entire coalition. This incident might be enough to convince them, but then it might not. I can think of several other solutions off the top of my head that the holdouts will insist on. They'll want to push this all back on Tsunami, since it was Hugo who caused the problem in the first place."

Robert nodded. He'd been expecting that.

"Tsunami is prepared to make the necessary statements to inform the public about this dangerous illegal app and warn people of the health risks," Robert said. "But that won't stop everybody. And *if* one used Tsunami batons, and *if* you were extremely careful and followed all the mirror's safety protocols to the T, you could likely play without too many glitches."

"What is the Billion Baton Club contingency?" General Kozelek asked, making Robert wince internally.

He'd wondered if any of them would catch Hugo's mention of that. He turned to the General and raised his eyebrows.

"Do you recall, General, that CIDER declined to fund a baton manufacture surplus of more than ten percent of projected user demand?"

The military man nodded slowly.

"Well, I thought such a decision to be absolute madness on the level of species suicide. So... I've been bankrolling the manufacture of enough batons to put in the hands of every able-bodied person in the world from the age of eighteen to fifty-five."

"Good God," Secretary Byerly breathed, staring at Robert with wide eyes. "That would be..."

"Roughly half the world population, so five billion or so batons," Robert said mildly. "Considering the profits the TD Hunter game has brought in, it was a cost I was able and willing to pay. Unfortunately, we've not quite broken one billion batons after two years churning them out twenty-four seven. It's a materials and manufacturing capacity bottleneck. Shipping and warehousing has also been tricky, but we're shorter on time than we are on space. Even so, we've been building baton stockpiles in every country around the world where we have a retail presence. We've even snuck some into China and other hostile locations, just in case they have a change of heart." Robert shifted his gaze to General Kozelek, who was eyeing him with a closed expression. "I am truly committed to saving humanity, General. *All* of it."

"So it seems," General Kozelek said dryly. "Which means, should CIDER give you the green light, Tsunami is already positioned to immediately equip the nations to fight for their survival."

"Exactly," Robert said. "I was concerned that, by the time CIDER was forced into the light of day, international shipping lanes would be significantly degraded, hampering ramp-up in production and distribution. With the exponential increase in TDM numbers, any delay could prove fatal for humanity."

The general gave Robert a nod of respect, which eased Robert's worry, considering Hugo's actions had opened him and his company to accusations of treason, sabotage, and colluding with America's enemies.

"That does take one problem off the table, at least," the General said, rubbing his chin. "You do realize you'll have to come before the member nations and brief them on this incident, Mr. Krator?"

"Of course," Robert said, smiling on the outside while cringing on the inside. Public speaking was his least favorite part of his job, even if he was skilled at faking it. "It's essential that all our allies are on the same page. I had hoped you three would advise me on how to couch this to the US oversight board. We need to come to them with a plan of action ready to implement. My belief is that Tsunami should immediately make a statement warning the public how dangerous this app is, to mitigate accidents, and that this incident should be used to force another vote among the member nations on the question of going public."

"Going public might become a moot point soon," General Kozelek said, shaking his head. "The conspiracy theorist and alternative news streams have already been running wild with these global grid issues. Even a blind, deaf, mute could tell at this point that *something* was going on worldwide, it's just a matter of what. The political situation is getting increasingly tense. There's no telling which way the Chinese will jump, since they presumably have full access to this knockoff app. It could finally convince them to join us, or they might use it to trump up 'proof' of our 'global conspiracy' and declare war."

"Victor, General Kozelek," Robert said.

"Come again?"

"Hugo informed me later in the interview I played for you that the mirror algorithm had named itself Victor."

The general stared at him, nonplussed, then barked a laugh, though his mirth didn't last long.

"You've got to be kidding me. Victor and Hugo?" He shook his head again and muttered, "What a nightmare. And it's only going to get worse when we leave this room. Robert, this incident has painted Hugo as a security liability, whether you believe him to be or not. The TD Hunter app is the lynchpin of humanity's survival, so we can't exactly scrap it and go back to square one at this stage. But what kind of protocols do we need to implement to ensure Hugo isn't eavesdropping where it shouldn't be?"

Robert held his hands up reassuringly. "Hugo has strict protocols around accessing devices. This isn't some malignant virus seeking to spread itself across the mesh. It's just a service AI that you have to opt into before it can access your device. The one exception we made was the Hunters we read into the TD Counterforce, since we had to ensure there wouldn't be any runners. But they specifically agreed to the extended access across any personal LINC. So, simply treat it like any other service AI: don't enable it on any secure devices, don't install it on government equipment not specifically designated for combat use, et cetera."

"So why this song and dance?" the general asked, motioning to the room around them.

Robert smiled grimly.

"Better safe than sorry," he said. "Hugo might have strict protocols, but there is no telling what a foreign entity might try to accomplish with *Victor*. There is more in the interview that you should listen to; some of it will put your mind at ease, some of it will likely give you ulcers."

The general snorted and motioned to the cassette player.

"Just what I wanted over Labor Day weekend. Ulcers. Give me the recording. I'll listen to it and hand it off to CIDER's intel unit so they can disseminate it to the proper parties"—he nodded toward Secretary Byerly—"and so they'll have a head start on this new security threat."

"We need to move fast on this, General, Mr. Secretary," Robert said as he packed away the vintage tape recorder. "Every minute of delay is another dozen downloads of this app, and potentially another clueless civilian dead."

"I understand," the General nodded. "Prep your statement and safety advisory. Hopefully you can send it out within a few hours. Secretary Byerly and I will take care of notifying the appropriate parties and getting CIDER on board."

Secretary Byerly cursed, and the others in the room looked at him. He shrugged apologetically.

"Patricia Wood is going to be unbearably self-righteous about this. I never thought I'd see the day when I'd agree with that harridan on any issue under the sun, but she might be our biggest lever if going public is truly the best chance for humanity."

"We're not there just yet," General Kozelek said grimly. "None of you have ever seen a riot in person, have you?"

All three men shook their heads.

"Let's just say that we can be our own worst enemies, at times. Let's hope and pray that this is not one of them."

Chapter 11

LYNN TRIED TO BE OKAY. SHE TRIED TO SLEEP, EAT, SMILE, TALK.

But she was simply too raw, and couldn't hide it. She flinched from every touch and avoided meeting people's eyes. She definitely couldn't look in the mirror. Loud noises made her jump, and the brief times she did fall asleep, she was woken by the same nightmare full of Vargs. They pursued her relentlessly in the dark, their eyes glowing blood red.

Everyone but her mom and Edgar left in the morning. Ronnie said Skadi's Wolves had been given some leave time, so he, Mack, and Dan were going back to Cedar Rapids to see their families. Lynn tried to make Edgar go with them, but he just snorted and gave her an incredulous look, and she didn't have it in her to push harder. A part of her craved the comfort of his touch. But the last thing she deserved was comfort. Even thinking about it made her writhe inside with gut-wrenching guilt.

The families of the dead deserved comfort. Not her.

The next day was no better, and Lynn overheard her mom talking to the doctor out in the hall about whether they had a psychologist or therapist on staff.

After lunch, Edgar disappeared for a while. Matilda sat in one of the room's two chairs, watching something on her AR glasses, while Lynn lay in bed, staring listlessly at the ceiling. She had her ring LINC Mr. Krator had custom made her and some old AR glasses her mom had brought from home—her Counterforce-issued equipment had been fried by Godzilla. But she had no desire to venture onto the streams. She definitely didn't want to talk to anyone.

When she heard the room's door open again, she recognized Edgar's heavy tread. Matilda got up and left, maybe to go get herself another cup of coffee. She'd told Lynn yesterday that the facility's coffee wasn't half bad.

Edgar moved around the room, and there were sounds of furniture feet scraping across the floor. Lynn didn't look to see what he was doing.

Then the bed started whirring, raising her slowly to a sitting position. At that she looked over to find Edgar at the bed controls, grinning.

"What are you doing?" she asked dully.

He made a "wait for it" gesture, got the bed all the way sat up, then drew his other hand out from behind his back. With a flourish, he held up two small, matching puzzle boxes. The picture on them was of a sunny cove surrounding vibrant teal waters with tropical vegetation in the background.

"You," Edgar said conversationally, "are gonna get outta bed and challenge me to a puzzle duel."

Lynn just stared at him.

His lips crooked in a tiny smile.

"You can get yourself outta bed, or . . . I can pick you up and dump you on the floor."

A snort slipped past Lynn's lips.

"Yeah, maybe you're faster'n me," he responded. "But whether I drag you out or chase you out don't matter to me. Either way you're getting outta that bed so I can beat you at this puzzle duel shit, ya hear me? I figure if I can't beat you in this state, I ain't never gonna beat you."

She almost smiled. Almost.

And because she could see by the look in his eyes that he was dead serious, she slowly dragged herself out of the bed and sank, cross-legged, onto the floor. Her body was still sore, but otherwise there was nothing wrong with her.

On the outside, anyway.

Edgar, with a bit less grace and a bit more grunting, sat down on the floor near her and handed her one of the puzzle boxes.

"Now, you gotta *try* to beat me, otherwise I ain't really winning, yeah?"

Lynn snorted again.

"Where did you even get these?" she asked, staring at the sunny, idyllic scene.

"You kidding me? Medical facilities take drone deliveries just the same as anywhere else. I ordered 'em off the mesh, *uce*. You sure them spooks didn't scramble your head?" He leaned over and tapped her gently on the temple.

She flinched away from his touch. He frowned at her, worry in his eyes, but didn't say anything.

Instead he opened his box and dumped it on the floor. When she didn't immediately follow suit, he patiently opened her box and dumped the pieces out in front of her.

Then he got to work on his puzzle.

Lynn didn't move for a while. But after staring at the puzzle—that was an easier place to stare than anywhere else—her fingers started to itch with the need to order the jumbled pieces. She could already see two dozen edge pieces, and was busily mapping out where each one of them went. Finally, she huffed a mental curse and dove in.

The puzzles were small, just one hundred pieces. She had hers done in under thirty minutes. Edgar was barely halfway done with his when she slotted in the last piece. He swore colorfully and threw up his hands.

"Never had a chance, did I?"

Lynn shrugged one shoulder, the tiniest of smiles there and gone from her lips.

"Maybe challenge me when I'm unconscious? You'd probably win then."

"Real funny, *uce*. I hope I never see you unconscious again in my *life*."

That brought it all crashing back. Lynn wrapped her arms around her midsection, as if she could hold herself together against the tidal wave of sick guilt.

"Aw, shit," Edgar said, watching her face. "I'm sorry, Lynn. I didn't mean to make it worse."

"You're fine," she said automatically.

His expression showed his clear doubt at her statement, but she couldn't think of anything else to say, so they sat in awkward silence, close enough to touch if she just leaned forward and reached out her hand. Lynn could see herself doing it in her mind's eye, could imagine the warm feel of his skin. She wondered why she was utterly incapable of turning thought to action.

"Did you know I—I let my pa hit my ma?"

Lynn's gaze jerked from Edgar's knee to his face, her eyes going wide at his unexpected comment. He wasn't looking at her, but at his hands, his normally smooth brow deeply furrowed.

"The first time I tried to stop him, I was six," he continued woodenly. "He was drunk as a skunk. Broke my collarbone. After that, Ma made me swear I'd never try to stop him again. Said she could take care'a herself. My job was to keep my little sisters safe."

Lynn barely breathed. She couldn't take her eyes off Edgar's face. Years and horrors were carved on its planes, showing starkly where there was normally nothing but good-natured humor.

"For years, I obeyed my ma. Stuffed the rage down, you know? Told myself I had a job to do: keep the others quiet and safe when he got drunk and angry. Got used to keeping my cool. But then that kid put his hands on you in seventh grade, and I—I snapped."

He fell silent.

Lynn didn't say a word. Her entire chest ached. She'd never wanted to be close to Edgar like she did now. It was a foreign feeling, this strange tether in her chest that pulled her towards him.

"You changed me, *manamea*," he finally said, eyes still on his hands. "You woke me up . . . gave me a reason to fight back. I didn't have to sit there and watch it happen no more."

He paused, maybe remembering, maybe trying not to remember.

"Soon as I got outta juvie, I told my pa if he ever laid a finger on Ma again, I'd kill him. Told him it was us or the drink. He couldn't never have both again. He huffed and puffed, but I didn't move an inch. Finally stormed off. My Ma came and hugged me and cried. She cried so hard, I ain't never felt so miserable in my life. Eight years, I'd watched him beat her. Eight years I coulda done something. But I didn't."

Finally, his eyes did lift, and he met her gaze. Lynn felt transfixed, frozen by the intensity in his eyes.

"I ain't tryin'a say we just the same, but everybody makes

mistakes, *uce*. It don't make us less. It don't make us not loved," he finished in a soft voice, eyes not wavering.

Lynn swallowed. Her chest was one massive, painful tangle. But one thought rose above all else, and it would not go away.

"I should be dead," she croaked. "I don't deserve to have survived, not when Champion and the others... not when they..." Her throat closed up and she couldn't continue. A hot tear leaked out of the corner of one eye and rolled down her cheek.

"Bullshit," Edgar said fiercely, leaning forward. "You saying your ma deserves a dead daughter?"

"No," Lynn said, recoiling.

"You saying I deserve a dead friend?"

"No!"

"Then you deserve to live, *manamea*, same as everybody else. Ain't nothing we can do about the past. You ain't dead, so stop wishing you was. It won't make anything right. It'll just make more things wrong!"

Lynn was struck dumb.

Edgar's words cut through her anguish, severing its iron grip on her heart. The guilt was still there, but it no longer felt like touching a live wire. A burden the size of a mountain fell from her shoulders, and she could breathe again.

More tears leaked from her eyes, but they were clean tears now, tears that could look outward and mourn the fallen, instead of tears focused inward by ugly self-hatred, mourning only her mistakes.

"Can... can I give you a hug?" Edgar asked, so quietly Lynn almost thought she'd imagined it.

But when she nodded, he rose to his knees, gently took her hand, and stood, drawing her with him. He was a good head taller than she was, if not more, making her eyes level with his chest. It was the perfect differential, because when he tugged her lightly toward him, she could turn her head to the side and press her ear right over his heart. It thumped reassuringly, and she grabbed fistfuls of shirt to hold on tighter to him. He wrapped his arms slowly around her, and the weight of them as he gathered her up was like being wrapped in a living, breathing security blanket.

Five seconds passed. Then ten. Then fifteen. Finally she stopped counting, because her tension was draining away and she no longer cared how long he held her. She didn't know why, or how, but being hugged by him touched something small and wounded inside her that she hadn't even known could be touched. For every second he held her tight, unwavering, like he would never tire of her, strength and hope began to fill her up.

He wanted her.

Not the legendary and powerful Larry Coughlin. Not the world-famous pop icon RavenStriker. Just Lynn, ordinary, confused, and broken.

The realization brought other sensations with it as well. Heat filled her core, seeping in from his skin to hers, bringing her nerves alive with fizzing, electric tingles. She became acutely aware of every bit of her that was pressed up against him, and she noticed she'd matched his breathing so that their chests rose and fell in sync. The comforting blanket of peace was slowly transforming into a cocoon of fire and feeling, and still Edgar's grip didn't ease even a little bit.

Lynn had no idea how long she would have stood there, her breath quickening and unfamiliar thoughts and desires swirling in her head. Probably until she burst into a pillar of flame and melted into a puddle on the floor.

She was saved from that embarrassing fate by the door opening suddenly and an audible gasp.

Lynn would have jumped a foot in the air if Edgar hadn't been holding onto her. As it was, by the time he relaxed and let her pull away, Matilda was already swiftly backing out of the room, an unbearably smug grin plastered across her face. She gave Lynn a parting eyebrow wiggle before pulling the door shut behind her with a click.

Lynn collapsed on the edge of her hospital bed and buried her face in her hands.

"Ugh, that was so embarrassing," she said from between her fingers. She could almost hear her mother's mental shout of glee, as if Matilda were broadcasting it telepathically from out in the hall: *grandchildren!*

"I dunno, *uce*, I thought it was pretty nice."

Edgar's voice was deep and warm, and Lynn couldn't help peeking through her fingers at him. He had on the biggest, broadest, shit-eatingest grin she'd ever seen. It showed off every one of his shining white teeth. If he smiled any wider, his face would split in two.

Lynn snorted and hid her face again, because what else was she supposed to do with a grin like that? Darned if she knew.

"If you're feeling bad, I could hug you again."

Lynn couldn't help it, she giggled. Edgar's sly yet hopeful tone was just too much.

"I—I think I need a shower," she managed to get out, finally dropping her hands. "Then I definitely need to eat. I'm so hungry I could eat an entire cow, right here, right now."

"Well, I don't got a cow, but I'll go find your ma. If there's steak anywhere around here, she'll sniff it out."

He got up and headed for the door, leaving her to ponder her newly awakened nerve endings in peace.

Somehow Matilda managed to come up with freshly cooked meat, no doubt through the potent combination of being both a nurse *and* a mother. The hot food did wonders for Lynn's body, though it didn't do much to soothe her mind.

Edgar might have helped her overcome crippling survivor's guilt, but his encouragements did nothing to answer the growing panic at the thought of facing more bosses. Her unique resistance to injury from the spooks put her in an impossible situation: engage in suicide missions alone against nodalities threatening innocent civilians, or accept backup and risk getting fellow fighters killed.

She wasn't qualified for leadership, she'd gotten that message loud and clear. Whatever delusions of grandeur she might have had, puffed up by years dominating the leaderboards in a fake war game, were gone. She couldn't be trusted with other people's lives.

Maybe it would be better to leave the Counterforce? Offer herself up as a lab rat for Dr. Rogers to experiment on and hope she could help humanity that way?

These thoughts chased each other over and over through her head, even as she replayed the fight against Godzilla in her memory, looking for the critical moment when she'd made her mistake. Had it been taking command of a force herself? Had it been when she'd brought them so close to Godzilla, baiting the nodality? Had it been each and every moment she'd felt her body begging for rest, and she'd told it no, pushing herself beyond her capacity to make sound decisions? How many of her decisions had been tainted by pride, rather than guided by accurate instinct?

Her mind readily conjured defenses to every question, but that was just the problem: she'd thought she'd been right about Godzilla, but she'd been wrong. So how could she ever trust herself again? Her doubts tortured her, pursuing her as she paced back and forth in her room. Physically, she felt recovered, if tired and sore. Mentally, she was a mess.

Steve stopped by to let her know she'd be released tomorrow assuming she passed the doctor's final checkup. That meant she, Edgar, and Matilda could go back to Cedar Rapids for two days to join the others before Skadi's Wolves needed to report for duty at Minot Air Force Base. That cheered Edgar and her mom immensely, and she was able to smile and play along because it meant she had two more days to wrack her brain and decide what in the world she was going to do.

The thing that worried her most was that she actually *enjoyed* fighting. *Enjoyed* risking her life and her friends' lives, because... why? It was an adrenaline rush?

What a fool she'd been.

No wonder the Hunter Strike Teams needed professional soldiers commanding them. Cocky gamers like her had *no* idea what it was like to hold other people's lives in their hands.

No wonder the Alpha Testers weren't as chatty and happy-go-lucky as the Hunters. They'd seen real war. They'd known real loss.

And here she'd thought they were stuffy and took themselves too seriously.

She tried to push such thoughts back, because remembering Champion's and Brayard's serious faces, their watchful eyes, their coiled and ready postures, reminded her that *she* was the reason those lionhearted men of honor were now dead.

She took to pacing the hall of the small medical ward she was in, counting down the hours until they could leave. Edgar walked with her for a while, silent and supportive. He tried to distract her with casual conversation, and she was genuinely grateful for his efforts. But it couldn't pull her away for long from The Question she would soon have to face.

Late in the evening, Matilda sent Edgar off to pick up dinner for them all. Lynn couldn't stand to sit in awkward silence in her hospital room, so instead she went on another circuit of the ward's hall, claiming she needed the exercise after so many days in bed. Matilda watched her with the worried eyes of a mother, but didn't protest.

Without Edgar there to distract her, Lynn turned to nosing about to keep her mind busy, peeking in each room, wondering if Derek and Team Light Brigade were nearby undergoing therapy. Or had they already been released? The idea of facing Derek, after she'd put his entire team in danger, was terrifying. But she felt she *needed* to do it. She needed him to yell at her, to tell her everything she'd done wrong. Maybe then she'd know what to do going forward.

It was a shock, then, when she peeked in one room and found Elena sitting on the hospital bed. She wore a fashionable blouse, jeans, and heeled boots. One leg was crossed over the other, her foot bouncing impatiently, as if killing time waiting for someone.

A little gasp must have escaped Lynn's lips, because Elena looked up suddenly and spotted her. An expression Lynn couldn't interpret came over Elena's face. Not the twisting sneer of disgust, but something more than mere surprise.

Lynn was gripped by old panic, the automatic flight response ingrained from years of high school bullying. But a stronger, more recent impulse held her in place. If she needed someone to criticize her and help her see what an overconfident, impulsive fool she'd been, who better to do that than Elena Seville? Plus, she was curious. Who had Elena become over the past few months? Why was she here? Had she been injured again?

With a bracing inhale and exhale, Lynn stepped into the room, stopping a few yards from the bed.

"Hey, Elena. Um, how are you doing? I mean, have you recovered from your injury a few weeks ago?"

Elena's nostrils flared, but she didn't immediately respond. Lynn wondered at this new reticence. Was Elena actually thinking about her words before she spoke? Would wonders never cease.

"I'm fine. It's a routine follow-up," she said dismissively.

"Oh. Well, that's good."

Awkward silence fell between them, and Lynn searched for a way to steer the conversation in the direction she wanted. Asking, "Am I a reckless idiot and is my team better off without me?" seemed like fishing for an answer.

"I'm surprised you're still alive," Elena said unexpectedly, her tone cool. "Everybody was sure you were dead with the rest of those guys."

Ah, there was the sneer. Lynn felt like she was on more even footing, seeing that wrinkle above Elena's lip.

"I *should* be dead," Lynn agreed, feeling a reckless need to confess. "I *deserve* to be dead." Even if Edgar and her mom didn't deserve to lose her, she still felt she deserved some kind of punishment for her mistakes.

Elena's eyebrows rose, and she looked thoughtful.

"Why? Didn't you distract that boss from killing a bunch of civilians? Didn't you give it the close-in punch we needed to finally kill it? That's what everyone's saying about you."

Lynn's mouth opened and closed, then opened again.

"Yes," she said slowly. "But I got people killed in the process. I made mistakes. Made a bad call. Three families are mourning now because of me." Lynn tried not to sound as utterly crushed about it as she felt. That would be showing too much vulnerability. Maybe this whole "confess your sins to your enemy" thing hadn't been a good idea after all.

"Well, that was dumb," Elena scoffed. When she didn't say anything more, Lynn couldn't help but prod her.

"What? No accusations of gross incompetence? No demands for accountability? Justice for the fallen?"

Elena made a face. "Who do I look like? The ethics police?"

"Sooo," Lynn said into the following silence, "you're totally fine with me jumping back into the fray? Leading charges? Taking command?"

"I didn't say that," Elena said, flipping her blond ponytail back. "I think you're an overconfident attention-whore with a big head, and you have a pathological need to be the hero to get more stream followers."

Lynn bristled, but kept a tight grip on her expression. This was what she wanted, wasn't it? Brutal honesty? And wasn't that exactly what she'd been wondering about herself? That she was so overconfident she'd let pride cloud her judgment?

"So, you think they should take me off the Counterforce? Send me back home?"

Elena gave her an incredulous look.

"And let you off scot-free? Are you kidding me? We're all out here risking our lives to save humanity, and you get to trot home and lay around watching us on the streams? I don't think so. They should put you up there on the front lines. If you're going to play hero for views, at least be useful while you're doing it."

Lynn stared at her, flummoxed.

"But—I made mistakes. I got people killed."

Elena snorted softly, eyes dropping to her nails as if inspecting them for chips or flaws.

"Everybody makes mistakes, dummy. You think those guys who died would want you to give up now like a pathetic loser? After they gave their lives fighting these bastard aliens? You should be grateful you get to keep fighting. *You'll* get a chance to make up for your mistakes. Not everybody does," she finished, sounding subdued.

Lynn wavered, wanting to argue, but not sure how. She knew she was a skilled Hunter, she simply didn't trust her judgment anymore. But Elena had a point. It didn't seem right to give up now when the fight was only getting worse and worse.

Maybe she should do what she ought to have been doing all along: follow orders and stop playing the hero. Maybe she didn't need to make a decision at all. Her company leadership would tell her what was best, and she could simply go where her country needed her the most.

Lynn let out a breath, tension leaving her body along with the air.

She was so used to keeping her own counsel, to figuring things out on her own—one of the trials of being raised by a single parent. Her mother loved her and helped her when she asked. But Lynn had spent much of her life on her own, making responsible decisions by herself day in and day out so her mother could focus on work and sleep.

It felt strange to leave the decision-making about her own capabilities to someone else. But maybe that's what it meant to fight for something bigger than just her.

"Thanks, Elena," Lynn said. She hadn't planned the words beforehand, but she didn't regret them.

Apparently they weren't what Elena had expected either, because the girl just stared at Lynn, blinking.

"Well, hope your checkup goes okay," Lynn continued, not wanting to give the former pop-girl a chance to ruin her being-a-halfway-decent-human-being streak. "See you on the battlefield, I guess."

With that she spun on her heel and headed for the door.

"Wait!"

Lynn paused in the doorway, mostly because she was surprised at the hint of vulnerability in Elena's tone. Curious, she turned back.

"Yeah?"

Elena had stood and now looked conflicted, as if she was second guessing her outburst.

"Your mom is a nurse, right?" she blurted out.

"Uh, yeah," Lynn said, raising an eyebrow. Had Elena been stalking her? Digging into her life? Her suspicion must have shown on her face, because Elena dropped her eyes and shifted her feet.

"I saw her at St. Sebastian's a couple times, when I was... visiting my daddy," she said so quietly Lynn had to lean forward to hear.

"Your dad?" Lynn asked. "What's wrong? Why was he in the hospital?"

"He's... in a coma," Elena said, tone turning weirdly defensive, even as her eyes glittered with moisture. "I saw your mom working there. So, she knows about hospitals and stuff."

"Yeah," Lynn said slowly, wondering where this was going.

"Can—" Elena cleared her throat, sniffed, and started again. "Can she... get my daddy transferred here?" she said in a rush. "They have brain therapy here. They did it with me after that stupid boss alien got me, and I thought it might help, but I don't know how to get him here. Your mom might know... right?"

Understanding ricocheted through Lynn, and she swallowed. Elena's sudden patriotism after the National Championship, her break with Connor, her subdued personality since they'd started training. It finally made sense.

There were so many things Lynn could say. So many ways she could get back at Elena for *years* of pain and heartache.

Instead, she said, "Um, yeah. I can ask. What's his name?"

Elena's mouth dropped open. She quickly closed it and covered her astonishment by shifting her weight to the opposite hip and crossing an arm over her stomach to prop her other elbow on. She looked at her fingernails again and said, "Harry Seville," as if it was nothing important.

"Okay." Lynn tried not to smile. It must be killing Elena to ask her biggest rival for help. But she was doing it anyway. For her dad.

No matter how much Lynn might hate Elena for the years of torment, she knew exactly what it felt like to lose her father. She'd never wish it on anyone. Not even Elena.

"I don't know if my mom can pull any strings," Lynn said, "but I promise I'll ask her about it."

She turned and strode down the hall, not waiting to see if Elena was going to thank her or not.

Kayla could put together a *mean* last-minute party.

The girl had been given barely twenty-four hours' notice, and she'd pulled together a bash that looked as fancy as that Christmas party she'd thrown last winter. TD Counterforce red and blue was the theme, which made it look like they were having a very late Fourth of July celebration. Lynn had *no* idea where Kayla had gotten the huge banner hanging across the foyer with theatrically staged headshots of Skadi's Wolves and the words, "Join the Counterforce. Fight for humanity." emblazoned across it. Probably some promo poster GIC had cooked up that Kayla had made off with.

Since the get-together was so last minute, most people were dressed casually. Though some—like Ronnie—were more casual than others, and some, like the Swains, were dressed to the nines like they always were.

"*Lyyyyn!*" Kayla squealed as Lynn stepped into the Swain's foyer. Her best friend collided with her, wrapping her in a bear hug that pinned her arms to her side.

"Can't—breathe—" Lynn gasped in protest.

"That's okay, I'm not done hugging you yet, giiiirl!" Kayla said, swaying both of them from side to side as she squeezed even harder.

When she finally let go, Lynn sucked in a desperate breath and started coughing.

"Oh, good grief. You are *so* dramatic, Lynn."

"Me?" Lynn wheezed. "*I'm* the dramatic one?"

But Kayla had spotted someone behind Lynn and was off to hug the next person, her halo of curls bouncing as she squealed, "Oh, my God! Dan!"

Lynn turned to see Kayla literally sweep Dan off his feet.

Well, maybe not sweep. But she did lift him at least an inch off the ground with the force of her hug. Lynn was impressed. Dan *was* slightly shorter than Kayla, and definitely more slender than Kayla's pleasing curves. But Dan had built a lot of muscle in the past year. It made Lynn wonder if Kayla had been working out too. Her best friend looked good, whatever she'd been doing. She was glowing, standing there, chatting Dan's ear off now that she'd finally let him go. He looked thoroughly shell-shocked, but not at all unhappy with the development.

Lynn hid a smile and turned away, nearly running straight into Edgar's chest.

"Man, we need to stop meeting like this," Lynn said with a chuckle, sidestepping to let Ronnie and Mack past. They were deep in an argument about jailbroken games and whether or not it was safe to download them. Typical topic for the guys.

"I dunno, I kind of like having you run into me," Edgar said, his deep voice sending a not-unpleasant shiver down Lynn's spine.

"Uhh." Her brain blanked. She could almost hear the reboot sounds coming from it.

Edgar snorted softly and took pity on her.

"Come on, let's go get food before the pterodactyls make a clean sweep of the kitchen."

Lynn fell into step beside him, relieved for the redirect.

"What's it like having a bunch of siblings?" she asked, surprising herself. She didn't usually pry into people's lives, but she genuinely wanted to know more about Edgar.

He seemed pleased by her question.

"Really loud," he chuckled. "Crazy, too. But it's nice, having people around. They make me laugh, give me a reason to work hard, be my best self, you know? I dunno what I'd do with all my free time if I wasn't always chasing these brats around," he finished in a louder voice as they entered the kitchen where his younger brothers and sisters were crowded around the kitchen island. The oldest of his sisters gave him the finger without looking at him, and he laughed. "Heads up you rugrats, make a hole. We actually work for a living. Gotta fuel up."

Not a single sibling moved in response to his older-brother flex, but Edgar was tall enough to simply reach over their heads and grab the plate of bacon-wrapped steak bites sitting in pride of place in the middle of the sea of appetizers.

There were loud shouts of protest, but Edgar ignored them all and headed out of the kitchen with his prize. Lynn followed after with a laugh and a "better luck next time" thrown over her shoulder.

There were perks to being friends with the tallest guy in the room.

Ronnie and Mack spotted them as they moved through the high-ceilinged foyer to the drawing room where most of the adults were gathered. The two broke off their argument to stuff their faces, wisely prioritizing bacon and steak over everything else.

"Things been okay with you at home, Ronnie?" Edgar asked, casting his eyes around the gathering. Lynn noticed a distinct lack of Mr. Payne, and she relaxed at the realization.

"Yeah. Been staying with the Nguyens," Ronnie said past a bite of bacon and steak.

Lynn felt an unexpected punch of emotion right to her breastbone. She remembered distinctly three months ago when Mr. Payne had stormed out of their leveling-up party, having failed to bully Ronnie into leaving with him.

I don't need your pity, and I sure as hell don't need your help.

Ronnie's words then had been brittle. A fragile wall of dignity around a traumatized and bleeding heart. His open acceptance now of Edgar's concern, and his casual admission of seeking safe haven with the Nguyens made her eyes prickle unexpectedly.

She knew he could trust his team to always have his back. But maybe, finally, he believed it too.

"I invited him to stay with me," Mack said gloomily, "but he thinks my kid brothers are too loud."

"Naw, dude, I don't care about your brothers," Ronnie countered. "I'm just not stupid enough to paint a target on my forehead. We were only at your place for, like, five minutes the other day and your mom was grilling me like it was a grand jury or something, asking if you'd been shacking up with any girls."

Mack's face flushed sunset red, as if he'd spent a day at the beach with no sunscreen. He reached up and tugged on his scraggly goatee, shuffling his feet.

"What?" Edgar said mercilessly, "Still haven't told your ma about Riko? I thought you said you were gonna tell her, so she'd be ready when Riko finally came to visit? Too chicken to lie to your ma, huh? You gonna finally drop this dumb AI girlfriend joke?"

"You have an AI girlfriend?" Mr. Thomas asked, coming up behind them from the direction of the front door. "I am always getting advertisements for AI companions myself. They look identical to the spamscam that gets through my filters offering free vid liaisons with Russian beauties. Can one even tell the difference between the two anymore? You are not engaging in romantic liaisons with strangers on the mesh, are you, my boy?" he asked, brow scrunched with worry as he looked Mack up and down.

"Of *course* not!" Mack exclaimed, throwing up his hands. "Riko is *real*."

"Well, that *is* what they all say, isn't it?" Mr. Thomas asked, looking genuinely confused.

Ronnie and Edgar broke down snort-laughing and elbowing Mack in the sides, while Lynn extricated herself to give her old neighbor a careful hug. Was it just her, or did he feel more frail and slender than the last time she'd seen him?

"How have you been doing, Jerald?" she asked, ignoring the guys, who were teasing Mack mercilessly.

"Oh, getting by. The complex has been having frequent blackouts, but dear Matilda checks on me regularly. She brings me a home-cooked meal once a week, though the last several have regrettably spoiled because the cursed appliances keep losing power. She has been threatening to kidnap me and bring me to live with her until the complex fixes their grid issues, since you are away on your glorious Battle Tour and there's plenty of room in the house."

Lynn grinned.

"My, my, my! I go away for a few months and my mom is already bringing home handsome men? You wouldn't take advantage of a lonely widow, would you, Jerald? I know she's a big girl and can take care of herself, but against a charmer like you, she doesn't stand a chance."

Mr. Thomas had a good chuckle, though at the tail end it turned into a wet-sounding cough. Lynn held his hand and patted his back worriedly as he got control of himself.

"Never fear, Lynn. Your mother's honor is safe with me." His eyes twinkled, but his breathing sounded labored.

"Seriously, Jerald. Are you okay?"

"Nothing to worry about, my dear. My latest delivery of

medications has been delayed. Supply line issues. But they are sourcing them from a different pharmacy, so all will be well soon."

"Okay," Lynn said, doubtfully, giving his hand a gentle squeeze, then releasing it. "Can't Mom get them for you from the hospital?"

"Oh no, I could not impose like that. It should go through the proper channels."

"But if you get sick because you don't have your medications, you'll go to the ER anyway. Why don't you just ask her?"

"All right, all right, young lady. If you insist," he said, waving her away as he escaped to the drawing room.

Edgar and Ronnie were still busy ribbing Mack, who was trying to convince them of Riko's personhood based on the *many* vid calls he'd had with her. But that only made them guffaw and ask a string of lewd questions that made Mack flame an even brighter shade than before.

Lynn snorted softly to herself and left him to his fate. He'd made his bed, now he had to lie in it.

In the drawing room she looked around for Dan, spotted him tucked away in a corner with Kayla, the two of them thick as thieves, and decided not to disturb them. Her mom was talking to Mr. and Mrs. Rios, while Mrs. Nguyen along with Dan's older sister and Mrs. Johnston chatted with Mrs. Swain. Mr. Nguyen was tasting some amber liquid Mr. Swain offered him over at the mini bar. Jerald had made a beeline for the two gentlemen, and he shook both their hands before he, too, enjoyed a drink offered by Mr. Swain.

For a moment Lynn was content to simply stand there, surrounded by her friends and family, fully relaxed knowing everybody she cared about was safe in one place. She'd spent so much of her waking time over the last two months worrying about her loved ones back home. It was a constant battle, fighting off horrible visions of airbus accidents or sudden, unexplained deaths from simply walking around outside.

But none of that had happened. And none of it would, if she had anything to do with it.

A warm presence at her back heralded Edgar's approach, and she half turned, looking up over her shoulder. He grinned down at her, and she couldn't help smiling back.

"Did Mack combust into a pile of ashes yet?"

"Nah. Ronnie's still working him over, though."

Lynn snorted. With friends like these, who needed enemies? She wondered how badly Ronnie, Mack, and Dan would tease her and Edgar if they started dating. To her surprise, the prospect didn't worry her much. The guys probably wouldn't dare tease Edgar, not when he could break any one of them like a twig. And if they teased her, she could just threaten to sic Edgar on them.

"You want more steak bites?" Edgar asked, offering her the platter he still held.

"No, thanks," she said, shaking her head.

Edgar stared at her.

"Who are you and what'd you do with my *manamea*?"

Lynn tried for a casual shrug. "I already had a few. Gotta save some for everyone else."

In truth, she'd been struggling to eat much since she'd woken up from her coma. Every time she ate, the simple joy of putting food into her body reminded her of the dead, who could no longer eat, and the families of the dead, who were probably too sick with grief to eat. It made it hard to stomach more than a few mouthfuls. She assumed—or at least hoped—this lurking, sick tangle of guilt and grief would fade over time.

But for now, she had to function around it.

It helped to remind herself that they had died for a purpose, and she would not let that purpose fail. She'd been saying that to herself a *lot* lately.

"Ah, Lynn!" said Mr. Swain, spotting her. He beckoned her over to the group around the mini bar. She looked back at Edgar, but he grinned and made a shooing motion with his hand, then headed over toward his mom, likely planning to offer her the food Lynn had rejected. Lynn joined the three men by the bar, shaking Mr. Swain's proffered hand and nodding respectfully to Mr. Nguyen, who nodded back.

"Care for a non-alcoholic drink?" Mr. Swain asked, gesturing to the plethora of tasty options arrayed on the bar. Lynn snagged a ginger beer, though the black cherry cream soda was also calling her name.

"So, how goes the Battle Tour?" Kayla's father asked, handing across a bottle opener. "It certainly looks impressive from the stream-side, though I imagine things are more chaotic on the ground than the curated footage would make it seem."

Raven, stop!

Champion's battlefield bellow echoed in Lynn's memory, and she swallowed, taking a moment to find her composure by popping her ginger beer's lid off and handing the bottle opener back to Mr. Swain.

"It's chaotic, yeah. I mean, it's hundreds of people all participating in a battle together, coordinating movements, keeping orders straight, that kind of thing. It's a crazy mess."

Mr. Swain's eyebrows rose.

"But fun, I hope. That's the whole point of gaming, isn't it?"

Lynn shrugged awkwardly, knowing she had to choose her words carefully.

"Yeah, I guess. At the competitive level it's more like a job, though. Getting paid, having commitments, performing for an audience. I wouldn't say it sucks *all* the joy out of it, but it does make it, um, work."

"Of course." Mr. Swain nodded in understanding. "A job is a job, even if you are passionate about it. I have been surprised, though, how heavily Tsunami has leaned into the in-game personas and aesthetics. It seems like a useful recruiting tactic to get more players, but the whole TransDimensional Counterforce angle with its military trappings seems to be wearing thin with the audiences, if what I'm hearing from Mrs. Pearson is any indication. Viewership is down across the board, though not by an alarming amount."

As Mr. Swain spoke, Mr. Thomas gave Lynn's arm an affectionate squeeze and headed over to greet Matilda and some of the other ladies. Mr. Nguyen nodded to both of them and drifted away as well. Lynn didn't blame them. She didn't want to talk about ads or streams either.

"Tsunami seems to be doing a lot of the same thing, over and over again these days," Mr. Swain continued. "Do you have any insight on their endgame? They don't have an official wrap date for the Battle Tour. I hope they don't intend to keep you busy like you've been all the way to the International Championship. They're not giving you any time to do your own promotions or curated content."

The memory of Trainer Bowers' voice barked in her ear: *Play dumb or sneeze and change the subject!*

"Oh, um, they don't tell us much but the next boss we're

fighting," Lynn said, rubbing her nose. It *did* itch. She wondered if she could manufacture a sneeze?

"Pity," Mr. Swain said, eyeing her. "Mrs. Pearson has had trouble getting much out of their liaison office. Do you know anyone over there? You're a pretty big name in the game, I'm sure they would pay attention if you made a bit of a fuss."

"Oh, I don't know, Mr. Swain. I don't want to cause any trouble," Lynn said, wondering how to gracefully back out of the conversation if she couldn't fake a sneeze.

"I'm sure Tsunami would be happy to see to its players' needs. You *are* its top player in the world at the moment."

"I-I am?" Lynn said, eyes widening.

"You didn't look at the leaderboard after your battle with Godzilla in New York?" Mr. Swain's brows made a deep V on his forehead.

"Oh, um, I was, uh, busy," Lynn said, floundering. "Gimme a sec, let me look." She pulled up her TD Hunter app and subvocalized, "Hey, Hugo. Show me the main leaderboard, please."

"Certainly, Miss Lynn," came Hugo's cheerful voice.

Lynn's jaw went slack. She'd known she usually hovered around tenth place overall. So how in the *world* had she jumped all the way up to *first* in the space of a single battle?

Unless...

"Uh, Hugo?" she subvocalized, giving Mr. Swain a tense "just a sec" smile. "Did I get some kind of bump from killing Godzilla in New York? Didn't I die before the end? I mean died in TD Hunter? It was right on top of me."

"You had point-one percent of health left when Godzilla was destroyed. And because you played a leading role in the innovative and daring tactics which ultimately decided the battle, you were awarded a commensurate amount of experience. Which, considering the size of Godzilla, was enough to shift your ranking."

Lynn stared at her name highlighted in gold at the top of the leaderboard. She'd been *rewarded* for getting people *killed*? She felt sick to her stomach.

"But, Hugo... you know what I did, don't you?"

"Indeed, Miss Lynn, I am aware," the AI said gently. "I was there with you the entire time."

"So... *why*? Doesn't Mr. Krator know what really happened?

Obviously the streams didn't show... I mean it was obviously cut off or shifted before..." She couldn't finish the sentence.

"The show must go on, Miss Lynn," Hugo said, his tone grave. "This is part of our mission. Now say something to Mr. Swain before he starts to worry you've gone into shock."

Lynn reflexively cleared her throat, shaking her head as she did.

"Sorry, Mr. Swain. I've been really busy the past few days. Haven't had a chance to take it all in, you know?"

"Of course, Lynn. I think some congratulations are in order, though. This is quite the achievement." His face split into a brilliant smile, and he turned his body toward the open room as if to announce a toast.

"No!" Lynn said, almost lunging to put a hand on his arm and forestall him. She would literally throw up right there on his drawing room floor if anyone cheered for her actions that had killed three honorable men.

Mr. Swain's brows rose in surprise, and Lynn scrambled for an explanation.

"This whole Battle Tour has been really draining, sir. I'd like to just relax with family and not think about it, if that's okay? I'm supposed to be on vacation. You're not supposed to think about work on vacation, right?" She tried for a smile. It likely wasn't very convincing, but Mr. Swain was an observant man and obviously didn't need her to spell it out.

"Of course, Lynn. I understand. Ah, gentlemen," he said, addressing people behind her. Ronnie and Mack came up on either side, eyeing the mini bar with interest. "Please, boys, help yourselves," Mr. Swain said with a smile. "Anything nonalcoholic, of course," he added at Ronnie's suddenly excited look. Ronnie's face fell back into its resting grumpy state, and he slouched forward to grab an orange cream soda.

"Ew," Mack said, making a face. "I can't believe you drink those things. It's like mixing milk and orange juice." He shuddered.

"They're not for the timid or small-minded," Ronnie said loftily, popping off the top bare-handed.

"No, they're for psychopaths," Mack muttered, helping himself to a much more sensible root beer.

Mr. Swain chuckled. "Beverage choices aside, how have you two been doing? Enjoying the Battle Tour?"

Lynn's gaze wandered over the room as the guys talked to Mr.

Swain. They seemed perfectly comfortable discussing the whole thing as if it really were just a game competition. Maybe she was still too raw from the... reality of it all to talk about it casually. She wondered what Dan thought, but couldn't find him in the room anymore. Kayla had disappeared too, come to think of it. Lynn snorted to herself, wondering where they'd snuck off to.

"It can't be the real deal," Mack said behind her. "You can't jailbreak TD Hunter. Hugo wouldn't allow it. It's just some knockoff."

Lynn's ears perked and her brow furrowed. She turned back to the guys, tuning into the conversation again.

"I'm telling you," Ronnie insisted, using both hands for emphasis, "it's the real thing. It's the actual TD Hunter app, jailbroken, on the Shadow Mesh."

"But, what about Hugo?" Mack said, as if that statement proved his point.

"It's run by a service AI called Victor. I don't know if they renamed it or redesigned it or what." Ronnie shrugged, and Lynn frowned at him while Mr. Swain looked on in interest.

"Wait, what are you talking about?" she asked.

"While you were in—" Ronnie started, but Mack elbowed him hard in the ribs. Ronnie flinched away, glaring at his friend, then continued. "While you were in rest and recovery, Tsunami put out a safety announcement. Said some hackers had cobbled together stolen code and were luring people into downloading a virus program being passed off as a jailbroken version of the TD Hunter app. I've been hearing *all* kinds of crazy shit about it, everything from 'it causes brain cancer,' to 'it's a spy program from the Chinese,' to 'it's summoning aliens.'" His eyes cut to the side at Mr. Swain, but he kept going smoothly. "Anyway, Tsunami says it's highly dangerous, has no safety protocols on it, and no one should touch it because there could be severe health risks. Not to mention the whole virus thing."

Lynn's mind whirled. A jailbroken version of TD Hunter? Did that mean people were trying to fight spooks on their own without Hugo to look out for them? That was a catastrophe.

"What's this Victor AI thing, then?" she asked.

"It's sort of a Hugo clone, but, like, super buggy, and no common sense at all. Same stupid cheerful butler voice, though. And on Victor, you can't change it. Butler mode only."

Lynn snorted. That was truly awful, but also sort of hilarious.

"What happened, though?" she asked Ronnie, who seemed to know the most about it. Though whether his information was correct, who knew.

Ronnie shrugged again. "Somebody hacked Tsunami, obviously. Who knows how much they actually got, but it was enough to make a derpy clone of Hugo and cobble together all the app's surface programming. Everyone's saying the app is suuuper screwed up, though. I've heard people have died."

"What a PR nightmare for Tsunami," Mr. Swain murmured, looking particularly concerned.

"I mean, they can't help being targeted by hard-core criminals," Ronnie said, raising both hands defensively. "They warned people to stay away from it. Play stupid games, get stupid prizes."

"It's not the only controversy they're facing, though," Mr. Swain pointed out. "There have been at least a dozen lawsuits filed in the last few months claiming their game is inciting life-threatening behavior. Multiple people have died playing it near node towers and power stations."

"Okay," Ronnie said, scorn creeping into his voice, "but that's not Tsunami's fault. The app has *clear* safety guidelines and warns people away from stuff like that. You can't blame Tsunami for morons ignoring basic safety guidelines."

Now it was Mr. Swain's turn to shrug.

"Why can't you? Perhaps Tsunami shouldn't have designed a game that involved incentivizing players to approach such structures, knowing there were health hazards associated with them. Though, G-Force Utilities, who have also been named in many of these lawsuits, are claiming their infrastructure was not the cause of any deaths. Which is a valid point." Mr. Swain frowned. "We've never seen this sort of widespread accidental deaths associated with these structures all over the continent. I've heard it's happening in Europe, too.

"There's obviously some sort of negligence or malfunction going on. The question is, is it accidental and unknown, as G-Force claims? Or is it being caused by human error, bad programming, negligent maintenance, or something of that nature which they are covering up? They will have to come up with an answer, and soon. I've heard Congress has ordered a special task force be assembled to investigate it as a national public health emergency. G-Force will never recover from this. The only question is how many of those at the top will face criminal charges and how many will simply be sacked."

Lynn, Mack, and Ronnie looked at each other, and Lynn could see her own worry reflected in their eyes.

"You kids be careful out there on your Battle Tour," Mr. Swain concluded, resting a hand on Mack's shoulder, who was closest to him. "Skadi's Wolves is going places, and the last thing we need is an avoidable accident."

Lynn nodded numbly along with the guys. There wasn't a thing she could say that wouldn't give her away, so she kept her mouth shut.

They needed to get back to killing bosses.

Fast.

The rest of the evening was tainted by a low-level tension that thrummed under Lynn's skin. Their parents and friends were warm, welcoming, and happy to see them. Lynn wished them all well, and silently beseeched fate or God or whatever was out there to keep them safe long enough for the TD Counterforce to turn the tide and stop this slow civilization-wide slide into chaos and darkness.

When it came time to leave, Dan was nowhere to be found. Neither was Kayla, for that matter. Then Ronnie noticed Dan had sent him a ping to go on home and not worry about him, he'd see them tomorrow.

Lynn couldn't help grinning and shaking her head at the news. It was none of her business, but she knew the guys would be grilling Dan tomorrow. Poor Kayla would have to handle her own parents. Lynn figured she'd survive it, but was glad it wasn't her. Sure, everyone involved was a legal adult, but they were still living at home and parents liked to pull the whole "my house my rules" thing.

Not that Lynn had to worry about that, considering she owned her own house. She almost wished she *could* use that as an excuse. Edgar kept making suggestive eyebrow wiggles at her while Ronnie and Mack sniggered and speculated about Dan's whereabouts. She had to purse her lips and shoot him a suppressive glare to get him to stop.

On the way home, Lynn asked her mom about Mr. Thomas and his medications. Matilda assured her she would keep tabs on their elderly friend and make sure he got what he needed ASAP, one way or another.

Between Mr. Thomas and Harry Seville, Lynn felt like she was turning into a vending machine for access to her medical professional of a mother. Matilda had asked Dr. Thind about Mr. Seville the day they'd left CIDER's medical facility. Dr. Thind hadn't been sure what he could do, since Mr. Seville was a civilian and not read into CIDER. But he'd promised to look into it.

After they finished talking about Mr. Thomas, Lynn finally asked the question she'd been dying to ask for days, but hadn't gotten the courage to yet.

"Hey, Mom, I, uh, noticed you didn't invite Steve to the party. Are you guys still, um . . . good?"

Matilda snorted softly and shot her a knowing look.

"For someone who is staunchly ignoring her own love life, you certainly are nosey about mine."

"Mom!" Lynn said, sitting bolt upright in her chair in the ground taxi. They'd switched to using primarily ground transport after Austin. It was slower, but the safety tradeoff was worth it.

"Don't you 'Mom' me," Matilda said, eyebrow raised. "I see how Edgar looks at you. You're stringing him along, and it's flat out cruel."

"That's not what's going on," Lynn said through gritted teeth.

"Oh? It sure looks like it from where I'm standing. Are you interested in him or not?"

Lynn opened her mouth, but no words came out.

"It's a simple question, honey," Matilda said more gently. "Do you like him or not? Do you want him around or not?"

"Y-yes. I *do* like him. I *do* want him around. I just . . . we're fighting for survival right now! It's not a good time for, you know, dating."

Matilda raised both eyebrows this time.

"Do you think they said that during World War I? How about World War II? Vietnam? The Gulf Wars? What if everybody stopped making love and having babies whenever there were wars?"

"*Mom!*" Lynn yelled, recoiling like she was afraid she'd catch cooties.

Love cooties.

"Well, what would have happened?" Matilda insisted, fixing Lynn with a stare.

Lynn muttered a few halfhearted answers, avoiding her mother's triumphant look.

"That's right, sweetie. Humanity would die out. The circle of life doesn't stop for anyone or anything. Not for existential crises, not for war, not even for alien invasions. Let me tell you something, honey, something you won't realize until you're older and it's too late: you can't afford to let a chance for real love or meaning slip by, because you have *no* guarantee you'll ever get that opportunity again. So, give poor Edgar a chance, won't you?"

Lynn rolled her eyes. "I *am* giving him a chance."

"That poor boy's balls will turn blue and fall off before you even let him get to first base at the rate you're going," Matilda muttered.

"*Mooom,*" Lynn wailed, putting her hands over her ears.

"Okay! Okay! I'll quit," her mom promised, holding up her hands.

"Good," Lynn said, uncovering her ears and glaring, "because I want to hear about Steve. Did he apologize properly? Is he out of the doghouse? Are you two . . . do you *want* you two . . . *can* you two be together?"

Her mom sighed deeply and hugged herself. Lynn wanted to hug her too, but she wanted to hear the truth more. So she stayed put.

"Yes, he apologized good and proper. Not a shred of false pride in that man, I'll give him that. And yes, we *do* want to be together, but it's . . . complicated."

"Isn't it always?" Lynn said sadly.

"It often can be, yes," Matilda said with a sigh. "We're trying to talk things out. It's difficult, of course, because there are so many things he can't say. But I understand that and I'm figuring out how to accept it. He suggested I apply to work at CIDER's medical facility, actually, so I could be more in the loop and he wouldn't have to keep so many things secret. I don't want to leave St. Sebastian's of course, not when I just got this new position. But I appreciated his effort to include me."

Matilda paused, then reached over and gripped Lynn's hand tightly.

"Look, honey, we wouldn't be trying so hard if we didn't want it to work."

Lynn nodded, squeezing back. She couldn't help but notice

how small, cool, and even bony her mom's hand felt compared to Edgar's big, muscular one. When had she ever thought of her mother as small? Matilda had always been a lion to her. A larger-than-life force of nature who always knew what to do and always made things work out, in the end.

But the TDMs were a problem not even her mother could solve.

"Growing up sucks," Lynn said softly.

Her mom chuckled.

"Not all of it, honey. Love is a wonderful thing, for instance." A soft smile stole over her mom's face, and she tilted her head, looking inward, perhaps, at memories of happier times. "The lifelong, sacrificial commitment of marriage that builds a safe home for children to grow up in is the most beautiful and foundational piece of human society I can think of.

"Sure, it doesn't work out sometimes." The smile on her face faded, no doubt thinking of Kayla's estranged father, Ronnie's absent mother, even Edgar's deadbeat dad. Lynn felt like she was surrounded by many more examples of love's failures than its successes. But her mom's expression firmed, and she continued, looking Lynn right in the eye. "Just because goodness sometimes falters, or it's overcome by evil, doesn't make it not good. Your father changed my life, and I would rather spend one more hour with him than a hundred lifetimes on my own." Her mother's voice caught once, but she kept going.

"I don't know if I've been given a second chance at that kind of love, but I'll fight for it all the same. Call me a romantic or an idealist, but everybody deserves a fighting chance at real family. I hope that for you, for your friends, for everyone in the world.

"It kills me how many relationships are hurt and suffering because people simply don't understand what real love is. Love that lays down its life is the hardest thing in the world. It only exists when you and your partner are both willing to die to yourselves for the good of each other. The sex, the pleasure, the gooey feelings? Those are all just hormones and chemicals. They're fleeting. They won't last. They hold no promises. Real love is day-in and day-out commitment, even when it hurts, even when you'd rather be elsewhere. Your father taught me that, and I can't ever thank him enough for it."

Her mom fell silent, and in the quiet Lynn's mind was transported far away, back into the past. She missed her dad so much. Missed his enveloping hugs. Missed the way he'd spin her around and tickle her. She missed his blue eyes and quick smile and big laugh.

She missed being a whole family.

Could she ever have something like that with Steve? Not the same, of course. But something new? And what about Edgar? Would he love her through thick and thin, to the end of the world and back, like her dad?

Absolutely.

The answer came to her without a second's hesitation. She knew down to her bones that Edgar was as true as true could ever be.

So what was holding her back?

Myself, her mind whispered.

Did she deserve Edgar? Could she give him as much as he gave her? Could she be that true?

She didn't know, and that made her sad.

But... if he still wanted her, even though she wasn't sure, she was willing to try and find out. Together.

"Honey," Matilda said, breaking the silence, "I know it's hard, staying focused on the mission while being distracted by things like relationships and your future. You should take whatever space you need to make sure you come home safe and sound every night. Just... don't use troubled times as an excuse to ignore someone. Be clear with Edgar, and give him realistic expectations, okay? It's only fair to him."

Lynn nodded. She understood.

"Steve is in the same boat," Matilda continued. "CIDER is working all of you to the bone. But I understand there isn't any choice. We talk when we can, even when we're tired. Hopefully there will be some sort of break soon. Have they said anything to you all? Any sort of goal or projection? When will this war end?"

The passing streetlights outside sent repeating shadows dancing over her mom's lined face. It made her look positively haggard.

All Lynn could do was shake her head.

"I don't know, Mom. I don't know."

Chapter 12

"DAN, MY MAN!" RONNIE SHOUTED, "WHERE'VE YOU BEEN?"

They'd all agreed to meet at Lynn's house for lunch together before the secure Tsunami airbus picked them up to go back to Minot Air Force Base. There'd been relative radio silence from Dan, but he'd promised he'd be there before their Tsunami ride came.

Now there he was, stepping out of an air taxi, hauling a duffle and looking rumpled in yesterday's clothes. He had a mile-wide grin on his face, though. And from the other side of the taxi stepped someone Lynn was not at all surprised to see.

"Well, well, well," Ronnie crowed, rubbing his hands together as he looked between the two. Lynn could tell he was salivating, probably struggling to pick which cutting joke to launch at Dan first. Likely he'd alter his strategy since Kayla was there too. Ronnie would rib his friend endlessly, but Lynn didn't think he would purposefully hurt Kayla while he was at it.

They all liked Kayla. She'd become one of the team, even if she was still blessedly clueless about the true danger the world was in.

"Hi, you guys!" Kayla chirped, waving furiously. She looked entirely too chipper to have been caught slinking home after a tryst.

Lynn's eyes narrowed on her friend's left hand. Then her eyes widened.

"Guess whaaat?" Kayla sang, hot-footing it around the air taxi as the automated vehicle pulled slowly forward away from the house so it could head on to its next assigned pickup.

"You *didn't*!" Lynn gasped.

"What?" Mack said, looking at Lynn.

"Now, hold on a sec," Edgar said, looking between Dan, who was actually blushing, and Kayla, who was hopping from foot to foot in barely contained glee.

"Whatever it is, it's not gonna save you," Ronnie said, wagging a finger at Dan. "You have no *idea* how pissed your mom was last night. And *I'm* the one who had to listen to her! It's payback time, pal!"

"*We got married*!" Kayla shrieked, grabbing Dan's hand in hers and holding their joined hands up to show off the sparkling diamond ring on her finger.

Ronnie froze, mouth open, face going absolutely slack.

"*Cheeehooo!*" Edgar whooped and strode around Ronnie to envelop them both in an enormous hug. Neither Kayla nor Dan even came up to his shoulder, and he was about as wide as both of them put together.

Lynn was waiting when he finally let the poor couple go. They looked ruffled, but their smiles were undimmed. Still shaking her head, Lynn came in to give Kayla a much more subdued hug. When she pulled back she checked Kayla's face, brow wrinkled, searching for any telltale sign of regret.

She could find none. Kayla looked happier than Lynn had ever seen her, and that was saying something.

"Wow. Kayla. This is . . . not what I expected," she said.

"I *know*, right?" Kayla said, fairly bursting with enthusiasm. "But I've had a crush on him for *years* and could never say anything, because he was, you know, not 'approved' by Elena. And then you helped me get out from under her thumb, and I got to hang out with you all, and he was just as adorable and sweet as I'd always imagined!"

Lynn's eyebrows climbed all the way up to her hairline, and she glanced at Dan, who shrugged with a goofy, sheepish grin on his face.

"I dunno how it happened, Lynn," he said in way of explanation. "We just kinda clicked. Been tiptoeing around it for a while, but last night . . . well, we decided to go for it. Took one of those hypersonic flights to Vegas you always see ads for. You know the 'there and back before lunch' kind. Found some rings, found a chapel, celebrated together all night..." He trailed off, blushing again, and Kayla giggled.

Lynn shook her head, smiling. She'd known they were sweet on each other, but she definitely hadn't seen *this* coming.

"Of all the disgusting, romantic sops I've ever met, I never thought you'd be one of them," Ronnie said, having finally found his voice again. He stepped up and held out a hand to Dan. "Dan, my man, congrats. Kayla, you too. You're stuck with us now. Probably not the smartest move on your part, but we'll try to be civilized. Also, you both owe me *big*. I think I've been permanently scarred by Mrs. Nguyen. I'll be collecting trauma pay from you two for life."

Mack came right after and gave Dan a hearty hug, then gave Kayla an awkward half handshake, half side hug, as if he didn't know the proper way for a man to congratulate someone else's fresh-faced bride.

"Come on, Kayla," Lynn said, grabbing her friend's hand and dragging her toward the house. "Let's go tell my mom. She's gonna *flip*." She shot Dan an evil grin over her shoulder, leaving him behind with Ronnie, Edgar, and Mack, who had formed a triangle around him, looking like sharks on the scent of blood.

Matilda did indeed flip, in the best sort of way. Lunch was joyful and full of laughter. They finished up just in time to rush their things together for departure back to North Dakota. Lynn was highly amused that Dan had arranged it so he got to entirely avoid his dragon of a mother, though it didn't seem fair for him to leave Kayla to the mercies of her parents without backup. Kayla said she wasn't worried, though, and Matilda promised to be her wingwoman if she needed one.

Kayla and Dan's goodbye was just as sappy as Lynn had expected. The guys wolf-whistled while the newly married couple kissed. Lynn just rolled her eyes and smiled.

Dan promised Kayla he would come back to visit on the weekends, and his comment brought reality crashing back in to Lynn's bubble of happiness. Did Dan really think Tsunami would ferry him back and forth every weekend when they were supposed to be clearing cities? Guilt and worry churned in her gut, though she hid it for Kayla and her mom's sake as they all finished their goodbyes and boarded the airbus.

The Tsunami vehicle had barely lifted off before Ronnie pounced.

"Seriously, dude? You got *married*? When you said you didn't want to die a virgin, I didn't realize you were *that* desperate for some action. Why didn't you just ask me for help? I could've hooked you up! Did Kayla manipulate you into this? Say you had to put a ring on her finger to get into her—"

"Get my *wife's* name out of your filthy mouth, Ronnie," Dan spat.

Lynn raised an eyebrow. She wasn't sure she'd ever seen Dan actually angry. But he was now.

"I *love* Kayla. I have for a long time. She's amazing and perfect and don't you dare criticize her. Just because you're too chickenshit to put yourself out there and take a chance with a nice girl doesn't mean I shouldn't. Stop projecting and let us be happy."

"Geez," Ronnie muttered, putting up his hands and leaning back in his seat. "Sorry, man. It's just... it's a really big jump to make on a whim. And right *now*? Dude, the world is falling apart."

"Exactly," Dan said fiercely. "The world could end tomorrow, and now I'm ready for it. I can die happy. I don't want things to end, but at least I won't have any regrets. Will you?"

Ronnie snorted in derision, but looked away. He didn't answer.

"Anyone else want to criticize my wife?" Dan said, glaring around at the rest of them.

"Don't look at me, bro," Edgar said with a grin. "I think you guys are cuter'n a basket of puppies."

Dan's scowl eased and one side of his mouth curled upward.

"I'm still really surprised, but I'm happy for you," Mack said, clapping Dan on the shoulder. "What are you going to do about the whole, you know... alien invasion thing? You can't tell her, you know that, right?"

"Duh," Dan said, rolling his shoulders, as if they were tense. "What does any soldier with secrets do? He carries them best he can."

Lynn was impressed. At some point when she hadn't been looking, Dan had grown up. Her mother's words from the night before came back to her, and she hoped Dan and Kayla had what it took to stick it out through humanity's darkest hours.

"You better take good care of her," Lynn said quietly, giving Dan a critical look. "You know her dad was an absolute shithole, right? Beat her mom? Almost killed her?"

"Yeah," Dan said, nodding seriously. "She told me. I'll do right by her. And if anyone makes her cry"—he made a flurry of chopping and punching motions with his hands, obviously acting out some martial arts move he'd seen in one of his old flicks—"I'll introduce them to my Fists of Fury."

The rest of them exchanged incredulous looks, then everyone burst out laughing.

Lynn had mentally prepared herself for censure from the rest of the Counterforce. Sidelong looks. Whispering. Heads shaken in disgust. She deserved all of it, and she wouldn't let it get to her. She would do her job, and not let anything distract her.

What she hadn't expected was to be welcomed back like some conquering hero. Yes, everyone was subdued, but she felt like that was mostly from exhaustion, rather than the gravity Champion and others deserved.

The avalanche of congratulations at her swift recovery might have felt better if she'd deserved a single ounce of it. She'd done nothing at all. Just won the genetic lottery.

Gadsden was the unlucky Hunter congratulating her when she finally snapped and bit his head off, telling him he should be mourning Champion instead. He'd been understanding after she calmed down and apologized, but after that she learned to shut her emotions down and simply nod and say nothing.

She was sure Champion wouldn't want her tanking the Taskforce's morale by scolding everyone for not being sufficiently sad.

Alpha Company was scheduled for a boss battle two days after she got back, which gave them only one full day of training to get back up to speed. A new Alpha Tester team Lynn had never met before named Lansing Nights was assigned to replace Black Templars, while one of the Alpha Tester teams from Charlie Company would fill in for Light Brigade for one or two rotations while Derek and his team finished therapy and were cleared for combat duty. Lynn noticed that Crash kept a close eye on her, probably under orders to make sure she looked fit enough for a boss fight the next day.

Her leadership needn't have worried. She was buzzing with

pent-up energy, frustration, and sadness. Hours of heavy exercise was just what she needed.

Lynn wasn't surprised or upset that the Alpha Testers she normally joked around with were cooler and more reserved than they'd been before. Hermes avoided her entirely, and she couldn't blame him. Champion had been his friend. He probably hated her.

She'd thought the censure would somehow soothe the lingering guilt in her soul, but all it did was make her sad. The absence of Champion and his team was palpable. Team Black Templars had brought a purposeful gravity and rock-solid confidence to the company that couldn't be replicated. Lynn kept waiting to hear Champion's bass growl in their platoon chat, but it never came.

Like everybody else, she tried to put it from her mind and focus. They would have time to mourn the dead once the living were safe.

At the end of the day, Lynn was almost relieved with she got a ping from Abrams to come see him. She'd been braced all day long, waiting to be dressed down. Maybe even sent home.

He directed her to the same vacant office where he'd spoken to her before. There was no Steve lounging by the desk when she entered this time, but what was there brought her up short. Colonel Bryce sat behind the desk, with Abrams sitting to the side in a second chair. Lynn swallowed, but continued forward and stopped in a parade rest in front of the plain desk. She locked her eyes on a nail hole in the wall behind Bryce's head.

"You wanted to see me, sir?" she subvocalized.

She would have preferred to have the conversation out loud, but understood the reasons for using subvocalization. It just felt so . . . clinical. Removed.

For a few long moments, Colonel Bryce didn't respond, just looked her over. She didn't flinch or shrink, but neither did she meet his eyes.

"I'm glad to hear you've recovered," the Colonel finally subvocalized.

"Thank you, sir," Lynn said.

"Dr. Roberts called me for a very interesting discussion after they took you to CIDER medical."

Lynn's gut tightened. Was she destined for lab rat status, then?

"He couldn't illuminate the *why* of your situation, but even just knowing the *what*, I and my command staff have yet to come up with a solid tactical use for it. So far, the entities' fixation on you is erratic enough that we can't risk important operations on it. And, while I'm happy you're harder to kill than most, you are only one Hunter."

Lynn nodded.

"You are expected to make yourself available as needed for future collaboration with Dr. Roberts on this mystery. I don't think even he knows what that collaboration will look like, yet, so for now you'll continue leading your team in the Battle Tour."

Lynn's brow wrinkled and she met the colonel's eyes for the first time, mixed relief and trepidation swirling through her.

"But, sir . . ." she started, then thought better of it.

Colonel Bryce's expression shifted subtly, becoming harder. Colder.

"But why are you going back to the battlefield at all?"

Lynn nodded mutely.

"If you were a member of the United States Military, you wouldn't be," the Colonel subvocalized, his arctic tone coming through just fine in Lynn's earbud. "You'd be on trial for insubordination. Or, if such a thing was deemed a waste of military resources in the midst of war, you'd be thrown in the brig until further notice. You disobeyed my direct order and got three good men killed."

This time Lynn did flinch. She shifted her eyes back to the wall, unable to hold Colonel Bryce's gaze any longer.

She'd known this was coming. Explanations and excuses crowded her tongue, but none of them mattered. Three men were still dead. She would take whatever Colonel Bryce dished out without complaint.

Champion, Brayard, and Hero deserved at least that much.

"You are not, however, a member of the military," the colonel continued in a less cutting tone. "You're a teenage gamer who volunteered to fight an alien invasion minutes after discovering you'd been tricked by your government to take risks you'd never consented to. You're good at what you do, you're committed, and you're willing to sacrifice your life for your country. *That* is why you're back on the front lines tomorrow. If you were incompetent or cowardly, I'd simply have a word with Mr. Krator and you'd be on your way to The Island before you knew what was happening."

Lynn shivered.

"*Billions* of people are depending on us, Miss Raven. Do not mistake this decision for forgiveness. I cannot forgive you. Only gods and fools can forgive. But I can, and I will, use every resource available to me to defend my country. Right now, *you* are that resource. Do you understand, Hunter?"

"Yes, sir!" Lynn subvocalized, standing straighter.

"Good. We have to leverage every advantage we have, no matter how small. That's why I've authorized Hugo to connect you directly to me or Dr. Roberts, any time of day or night. You have any insights into the entities, their behavior, their movements, et cetera, you tell us *before* you do anything. If you hear an order that doesn't sit right with your instincts because you have some insight into the spooks that you think we don't, then I want to know it. Not because I think you're right, but because whatever it is about you that makes these entities act differently is an anomaly that merits attention.

"This is not permission to ignore your chain of command," he continued sternly. "This is providing you a conduit to report special intelligence that is relevant to our mission. I am trusting you not to abuse this line of communication." He looked hard at her, and she met his eyes and nodded firmly.

"Good. Now, I want you to walk me through your decision-making process from the moment you disobeyed my order to pull back, to the moment you lost consciousness. I want to know everything you knew and what factors influenced your choices. Tell me now what you didn't have time to walk me through then. Be aware this part of the conversation is being recorded and will likely be reviewed by the rest of my staff and other members of CIDER, including Dr. Roberts."

Lynn gulped. This was definitely not something she'd expected. To be dressed down in private was one thing. To be forced to enumerate her sins one by one and explain what had fueled her stupidity? The only saving grace was that she'd have a chance to clearly explain why she'd thought her tactical decisions had made sense in the moment. At the end of the battle, though, she knew without a doubt she'd pushed herself too far. That mistake had cost lives, and she would have to admit that out loud.

Well, if this was her penance, then so be it.

"Of course, sir," she said, and got started.

Both commanders leaned forward and listened intently as she spoke, asking clarifying questions as she went. There were a few later parts of the battle that were muzzy in her memory, not surprising considering she'd had her brain scrambled by a Sierra Class-5 boss barely a week ago. Hugo helpfully played back vid clips from her display view, which jogged her memory. It was agonizing to rewatch her mistakes. But she hid her feelings as best she could and wrung her brain dry trying to share every gut feeling she'd had about Godzilla and what it was going to do.

Describing the very end was the worst. She still didn't understand why it had blinked *toward* her at the last. It didn't fit the pattern. She couldn't let herself off the hook, though, because no matter how sure she'd been that it would continue to flee, she'd gone *suicidally* close to it. No wonder Champion and his team had chased after her.

Mercifully, Hugo did not play Champion's last moments or his furious bellow at her to stop. It was painful enough hearing it in her memory. Hearing it again in her ear, as if he were still alive and she could somehow reverse her mistake, would have made her violently ill, and she really preferred not to throw up in front of Abrams and Colonel Bryce.

By the time the two commanders were satisfied with her report and called a halt to the interview, she felt clammy and nauseous and wanted nothing more than to sit down. The two men made eye contact with each other and sat very still for a few minutes, the usual sign of a private, subvocalized conversation. Lynn locked her knees, determined to hold on for as long as it took.

Finally, Colonel Bryce leaned back in his chair, tapping one finger on the arm of it as he examined her once more.

"Final questions?" he asked.

"No, sir," she subvocalized, trying not to look relieved.

"Very well." There was another pause, and her eyes flicked from the wall to Colonel Bryce's face. He caught her gaze and held it, the intensity of his stare piercing through to her very soul.

"Make Champion's sacrifice *matter*, Miss Raven," he said out loud, as if it was too solemn and weighty a command to relegate to the mesh.

"I will, sir," Lynn said fiercely, lips shaping the words with reverence. "I promise."

Her words reverberated in the air between them, sealing her oath.

The colonel nodded sharply at her and said, "Dismissed!"

The days that followed were endless and exhausting. Lynn learned that right after Godzilla, Tsunami had accelerated the Battle Tour and started sending Taskforce Sanctus to fight two battles a day, back to back. Each company was rotating two days on, one day off, and the wear was showing on everyone. There was less banter, fewer jokes. No one lay in their bunk at night browsing the streams anymore. Everyone passed out the moment their heads hit their pillows.

Needless to say, Dan did not get the weekends off to go see Kayla in Cedar Rapids. There was no such thing as weekends anymore. Their lives were an endless cycle of mission briefs, battles, debriefs, and a day of light training before the cycle started again.

Lynn didn't know if the nodalities were getting bigger, or she was just getting more and more tired. The only positive thing that could be said about the brutal pace was that they were all getting really, really good at killing bosses. One in four or so threw them for a loop with some new ability or erratic behavior that fell outside the norm. Sometimes Lynn saw it coming, sometimes she didn't.

One boss, a vaguely feline-shaped monstrosity called Thrathptttt, blindsided Bravo Company with a ranged attack that saw two people dead, both Hunters, and two teams rushed to CIDER medical for neurotherapy. Twice Lynn passed on a gut hunch to Colonel Bryce in the heat of battle that saved Alpha Company similar injuries. Might have even saved a few lives. Who knew.

She followed her orders to a T, determined to be the best cog any machine had ever seen. But she kept her eyes open and her head on a swivel. She started noticing patterns among the TDMs she'd never seen before. She'd always been so focused on each shot and slash she made to maximize her competitive scores, she hadn't spent much time watching the larger ebb and flow of battle.

For once Hugo proved an invaluable asset instead of an insufferable dead end. Maybe Colonel Bryce's authorization had gone further than he'd mentioned, because Hugo was a well of data that Lynn couldn't get enough of. There were some information requests he apologetically refused, but they were in the minority.

She wasn't sure what she was seeing—yet. But something was teasing her at the edge of her awareness, like a flash of something in the corner of your eye that disappeared as soon as you turned to look at it. She kept her mind open, unfocused, trying to see what it was.

Exhaustion didn't help.

After two weeks of the punishing pace, the Taskforce started issuing them all daily stims. That worried Lynn more than anything else. She knew exactly how dangerous sustained stim use could be. Her mom had ranted about it on a regular basis throughout Lynn's childhood based on the many cases that came through St. Sebastian's ER. That knowledge didn't stop Lynn from taking every stim they gave her, but it did add to the cold pit of dread that had been building in her stomach since Godzilla.

Their company leadership didn't explicitly tell them to stay off the news streams, but it was heavily implied they should all be getting as much sleep as possible to stay focused on the mission. The stims changed that, and suddenly Hunters had extra energy and racing minds greedy for stimulation. Rumors flew across the streams faster than anyone could keep track of them, and none of them were good.

The New Orleans grid was crippled and the city would soon be underwater.

Airbus companies worldwide were going under any day now. Too many people were scared to fly.

The National Guardsmen of all fifty states had been activated to requisition antique gas-guzzlers to replace electric vehicles in point of failure positions across critical industries.

Congress was on the verge of declaring war with China, because who else could possibly be to blame for such widespread infrastructure sabotage?

TD Hunter wasn't really a game, but a virus-spreading trojan that had already infected a third of all systems worldwide.

Tsunami was owned by the Chinese.

Robert Krator was a deep cover Russian agent.

The TransDimensional Monsters were real... and they were coming for you.

The only bright spot in it all was the news that China had released a brand-new, augmented reality monster-hunting game that they were pushing as the next "big thing"—and it flopped spectacularly. It was rife with bugs, the monsters in it were clunky and boring, and the service AI running it was one fry short of a Happy Meal.

Not that anyone in China would say it openly, of course. They were all in the lockstep chokehold of their glorious surveillance state. But the mesh was too big to control everything on it from sources outside China's borders, and people who wanted to try the app had ways of getting ahold of it.

From the vids and screen stills she saw of the game, it was obviously just a copy-paste rip-off of TD Hunter. Nobody in Alpha Company could tell from the rumors whether TD Hunter's combat system functionality had survived the pirating process. Whether or not the Chinese finally believed the spooks existed, they certainly weren't acting like it. At least the English name everyone started using for the app made Lynn smile: BS Hunter. She wondered if Hugo had met the hacked version of the TD Hunter service AI, Victor or whatever its name was. What would Hugo make of a janky knock-off of itself? Lynn could just imagine Hugo complaining in a stuffy British accent about how no one had any appreciation for true craftsmanship these days.

The general amusement at China's app woes didn't do much to lift the cloud of tension that hung low over the company, though.

Lynn started getting frequent messages from Mrs. Pearson about everything from how she wanted to handle accusations of collusion with the Chinese, to another sponsor dropping their contract due to the bad publicity TD Hunter was attracting. Lynn would have loved to ditch all her sponsorships and fade back into obscurity. But that would mean TD Hunter had failed at its mission, and she would have much bigger things to worry about than hate mail and vanishing sponsorship revenue.

Every night before bed, Lynn checked in with her mom. She was pretty sure the guys were doing the same with their families. Matilda told her Steve was pressuring her to come work for CIDER's medical and research branch, but she didn't want to leave St. Sebastian's. Hospitals everywhere were being overwhelmed. She couldn't leave. Not now.

It seemed like as fast as Taskforce Sanctus cleared bosses, more needed to be killed. It was an open secret that there were three other companies, newer ones, all CIDER troops, chipping away at the bosses in night raids on various sensitive locations. But even that didn't seem to be slowing the tide.

CIDER's R&D gave them several rounds of upgraded batons that were supposed to shoot farther and harder. But the incremental improvements were too small to make a strategic difference in their battles. In fact, it almost seemed like the TDMs were leveling up in response to CIDER's increased weapon efficiency.

Were the TDMs improving and advancing in response to the increased threat? Like some sort of organic, self-learning algorithm? The thought that CIDER itself was the cause of humanity's peril kept coming back to Lynn's mind, and she spent hours she should have been sleeping tirelessly rolling the thought over and over in her head, picking at it from every angle, looking for a solution.

By late September, the growing pit of dread in her stomach was so bad she could barely eat, and stims were the only thing keeping her going. Her infrequent hours of sleep were plagued by a repeating nightmare of being stuck in a car racing toward a cliff edge with no way to slow down or turn aside. Accidents, ambushes by bosses, and avoidable minor injuries were whittling away at the Taskforce. Everyone was exhausted and losing focus, doing more with less.

But they couldn't stop.

The Question dominated everyone's minds: when would CIDER go public? It was the endless, never-ending debate during meals, training, and their nonexistent downtime. Some argued CIDER should have gone public months ago. Others staunchly opposed going public at all. Everyone else was stuck somewhere in between.

The final straw for Lynn came when a mob of "mostly peaceful" protestors knocked down Tsunami's cordon around the boss Alpha Company was fighting and tried to rush the Hunters from behind. Hugo saw it coming through Tsunami's camera drones and warned everyone in time for Alpha Company to retreat from the boss they'd been engaging and board their transports before the protestors reached them.

Even so, the last transport barely got away in time. Many of the rioters wore gas masks, ski masks, and bandanas covering their faces. The front lines threw Molotov cocktails and bricks at the transports, and a few foolhardy ones even tried to climb on top of them as the airbuses lifted off. One of the airbuses had to make an emergency landing at a nearby airbus platform because a Molotov cocktail took out one of its engines. If they'd been a single minute slower loading up, Alpha Company would have been caught in the middle of an angry mob. They could have been beaten to death, stabbed, or who-knew-what. None of them were equipped to fight humans. Only spooks.

It felt like a living nightmare.

That night after dinner, Lynn locked herself in the bathroom so she wouldn't have to control her expression in front of her roommates, then called Colonel Bryce. It took a minute for Hugo to get ahold of him. Lynn assumed there were around-the-clock emergency meetings going on among CIDER's command echelon.

Finally, though, Hugo connected her, and she wasted no time on pleasantries.

"Sir, we're screwed. If we don't turn this around *now*, we're going to destroy ourselves before the spooks have a chance to."

"Is this what you called to tell me?" the colonel asked. A month ago the question would have been sharp and demanding. But tonight it just sounded infinitely tired.

"No, sir. Sorry. My point is, we can't keep doing the same thing that's clearly not working and expect a breakthrough."

"Do you think there is a single person at CIDER who doesn't already know that?" The colonel's voice *did* grow sharp now, and Lynn gulped, realizing she was doing a bad job of getting to her point.

"Sir, I have some ideas about where these things are coming from. Nothing concrete, but I think I need to talk to Dr. Roberts. Maybe some other CIDER scientists, too. People who've been studying the spooks since the beginning."

"Of course," the colonel said, sounding more alert. "Why didn't you ask sooner?"

"I—" Lynn swallowed again. She was distracted by a piercing pain in her stomach, and had to think for a moment whether or not she'd even eaten anything at dinner.

"Raven!" Colonel Bryce barked.

"Sorry, sir. I was worried it would be nothing. It's all so vague, and I've been so tired. It seemed like killing bosses was the most concrete way to contribute. But after today, I don't think it matters anymore. We could kill bosses until we all dropped dead, and it won't save us."

"There's no time to ferry you to CIDER HQ," Colonel Bryce said briskly, moving on without comment. "You'll have to talk to Dr. Roberts remotely."

"We're going to need screens," Lynn said. "Lots of them, or one big one. We're going to be data crunching and pattern mapping, and AR displays aren't an ideal medium for that."

"Not a problem. I'll get in touch with the air base and have a command center prepped for you. We'll remote in Dr. Roberts."

"Great, thanks. Should I just, um, wait to hear from you?"

"Not me, no. Someone from the base will come and get you. Just stay in your room. Be ready in twenty minutes."

"Got it," Lynn said, feeling hopeful for the first time in weeks.

"Keep me updated on any developments."

"Yes, sir."

"Anything you need, ask Hugo. I'm setting up a series of authorizations with the base command for any reasonable resource they have available, so you don't have to wait to get ahold of me. If your request needs further authorization, Hugo will know who to ping."

"Got it. Thank you, sir."

"Don't thank me, Miss Raven. Save our country. That's the only thanks I want."

With that, he closed the call and was gone.

No pressure, Lynn thought, the buoyancy in her chest feeling more than a little manic.

But at least the sharp pain in her gut was gone. Probably because she was finally *doing* something.

"Hugo," she subvocalized as she stood and reached for the door handle.

"Yes, Miss Lynn?"

"I'm gonna need steak jerky. A lot of it. Think you can rustle up some?"

"I will contact the base supply officer and see what can be found."

"Tell them to throw in the best green tea they have," she added. She felt like she might have a heart attack if they gave her any more stims, or even coffee. Green tea was her mom's fallback when she'd hit her coffee limit. Lynn wasn't a fan of the stuff, but it'd be hot, and healthy, and maybe it would settle her stomach.

Now all she had to do was figure out what to tell her roommates when whoever was coming showed up to collect her.

The man who fetched her from the barracks, a polite but tight-lipped lieutenant, ferried her across the base to a nearby three-story building with flagpoles out front that looked like a command center. She felt weirdly conspicuous in civvies, since she'd spent almost the entire summer in TD Counterforce uniform. But Hugo pointed out that it was best not to stir up rumors about what she was up to by wearing the uniform around the base.

The lieutenant gave her a visitor's badge and showed her to a plain, medium-sized room outfitted with a conference table, a coffee station, and a flex screen that he synced to her LINC. There were a few faded motivational posters on the walls, and the Air Force blue carpet had seen better days, but Lynn didn't need fancy, just functional. The lieutenant pointed out the door to the attached bathroom, then left, leaving her alone but for three bags of beef jerky and a pile of old-school tea packets on the conference table.

Well, not *alone*. Hugo had gotten to work setting up the flex screen to interface with Dr. Roberts while Lynn dug into the beef jerky—not as high quality as she'd hoped, but the familiar saltiness hit the right spot, and chewing on it helped her think. The coffee station supplied hot water and an everheat mug for her tea, so by the time Dr. Roberts came on screen, she was ready to get to work.

"Miss Raven! Good to see you again."

Dr. Roberts' face was round in a naturally jolly sort of way. What little hair he had left was salt-and-pepper gray and cut short, likely because it was the most utilitarian way to manage it. His lower face was covered in a similar scruff of short, sparse hair that framed his genuine smile, while a pair of black-rimmed AR glasses surrounded his gray-blue eyes.

"Hi, Dr. Roberts. You doing okay?"

"I haven't left this building in," his eyes flicked up and to the right, no doubt checking the date on his AR display, "one hundred and eighty-two days. Other than that, I'm just fine!"

Lynn chuckled weakly, not sure if the doctor was joking about how hard he worked, or making a coded plea for rescue.

"They bring in all my meals, and my bed in the lab is better than my bed at home." He chuckled at his own comment. He'd certainly seemed comfortable in his lab when she'd met him. He'd been sporting a worn rock band T-shirt under his white lab coat then. Today his shirt of choice featured the Crüxshadows circle and cross, which Lynn only recognized because of her dad's love of eclectic rock music subgenres.

"Back in the old days," Dr. Roberts chatted on, "you had to actually leave the lab to meet investors, present grant proposals, so on. But these days I can do everything remote. Saves me a lot of time."

Dr. Roger's smile was infectious, but even though the sight of it raised her spirits, she couldn't help noticing the massive bags under his eyes and the lines of strain that reappeared whenever he wasn't actively smiling. He'd looked tired two months ago when she'd seen him in person. Now he looked like the walking dead.

She probably didn't look much better.

"So," he said, "I hear you have some ideas for me?"

Lynn crossed her arms and began pacing slowly back and forth in front of the massive flex screen. Her legs were tired, but if she sat down she'd start to fall asleep, so pacing was the only alternative.

"Okay," Lynn said, letting her eyes go unfocused as she paced, "first I need to make sure I have an accurate picture of the situation. Stop me if I get anything wrong."

"Shoot," Dr. Roberts said. She heard the creak of leather and squeak of wheel as he sat on the rolling stool she'd seen him use in his lab. He had some old injury that made him walk with a limp, so he liked to cruise around the lab on his stool.

It was kind of adorable, but she was too tense for the thought to make her smile.

"TDMs were already here in large numbers before we created the technology to detect them, therefore we missed the chance to track their initial spread from an origin point."

"Yes."

"Now, despite their rapidly increasing numbers, they don't seem to be traveling to or from anywhere the way normal matter would via our usual understanding of space and time."

"Yes."

"Therefore, they have to have some other means of travel that we either don't understand or aren't yet able to detect."

"Frustratingly, yes."

"Of the two main possibilities I can think of, the first is that they're not traveling at all, but multiplying and reproducing in place. For that to be the case, they have to have a source of food or fuel—which I assume is something to do with the electromagnetic spectrum, which is why they're attracted to our grid infrastructure."

Dr. Roberts made a drawn-out noise of uncertainty, making Lynn look up at the flex screen.

"Yes, we have considered that possibility," he said, tilting his head. "But we can't find replication patterns to support the theory. When cells replicate, for instance, we can watch in real time as they grow and split off. We haven't seen anything like that with these entities. Look at this footage," he said as he gestured with his hands, obviously pulling up files through his AR interface and throwing them up on their synced screen.

The central square on the large flex screen that showed Dr. Roberts from the waist up with his lab behind him was joined by half a dozen vids spread out around it. Lynn's brow creased. The color scheme looked like something from a pair of night vision goggles working off of heat sources.

Dr. Roberts gestured to one of them.

"This isn't thermal imaging, but it's been colored to follow that pattern since most of the military guys we work with are familiar with it. Instead of heat, though, these views are showing concentrations of live TEPs—in the lab that's what we call the exotic particles that make up the spooks. Once the live TEPs have been disrupted and dissipate into the inert TEPs your combat system collects and repurposes, they don't show up in this particular view anymore.

"So, if you look at this one over here, you can see these scatterings of blobs, which is what the entities actually look like without all the fancy game graphics overlayed on them. If they were replicating, you'd think the blobs would grow bigger, then split, similar to cells. But they don't. Look what happens instead."

Lynn's eyes narrowed as she concentrated on the vid, watching the pattern of blobs that hovered, motionless. All of a sudden, amidst the scattering of shapes, a concentrated cluster of new blobs appeared, then started to drift outward. The entire grouping of blobs subtly shifted, accommodating the newcomers until the final pattern looked like a larger version of the old one.

The sight sent Lynn's mind churning through ideas and theories, integrating the new information into the patterns she'd already established. She didn't speak as she moved from vid to vid, watching each looped footage several times before moving on to the next. She was sinking fully into Larry mode, where the outside world and all its worries faded, leaving only the mission and the objective she needed to work toward. It was a space where her normal emotions and feelings didn't register, because they'd been subsumed beneath her all-consuming focus on The Goal.

It was a far more relaxing mental space to be in than the one Lynn Raven inhabited, with all her self-conscious anxieties and attempts to accommodate other people's feelings and desires. Larry mode was how she'd survived the hell years of middle school. But it was no wonder most people thought of Larry Coughlin as cold, hard, and merciless. Nuance and good manners were a pointless distraction from achieving The Goal.

"Dr. Roberts," she finally said, now standing at parade rest in front of the flex screen, "can you zoom out and show me these views in a larger context, specifically where they are in relation to the nearest nodality?"

"Hmm," the doctor mused. "No, I can't, but Hugo should be able to take the GPS data and reconstruct us some sort of map based on whatever other scans we have archived from those times and locations. Hugo?"

"Of course, Dr. Roberts," the AI said. Within moments, the six vids shrank to the size of Lynn's palm while wider-ranging data appeared around them, showing still snapshots of entity location patterns.

"What's the scale?" Lynn asked.

"Each location covers approximately five hundred yards, or half a kilometer," Hugo said.

Lynn pointed at the large mass of red in each view.

"Do we have any data on what class those nodalities are?"

"Yes," Hugo said. "They are a mix of Bravo and Alpha. None are Sierra Class."

"So all six of these vid recordings were of spooks within..."

Lynn scanned the expanded views and did a quick visual estimate, "three hundred yards of a boss?"

"Yes," Hugo confirmed.

"So," Lynn said, brow wrinkling, "if they're not replicating in place, the second option is teleportation, or whatever scientific term you want to give it."

"Quantum entanglement," Dr. Roberts provided.

"Which is the same as teleportation?"

"Well, no, but it's the best explanation we have to how these exotic particles work."

"Quantum entanglement or teleportation?" Lynn asked, now thoroughly confused.

"Don't worry, it confuses me too," Dr. Roberts said, holding up his hands and chuckling. "But to be specific, teleportation isn't a scientific term. It's simply a mashing of the Greek root 'tele' or 'from a distance,' and the Latin word 'portare' which means movement or carrying. In English vernacular we use it to mean instantaneous transportation. Quantum entanglement, on the other hand, doesn't necessarily imply movement, but rather the same thing existing in two places at once. However, if these transdimensional entities *are* quantum entangled, they could be participating in all sorts of space-time effects that we don't even have the equipment to detect, much less understanding to describe."

"So," Lynn summarized, "let's just say teleportation and be done with it."

"That will suffice for now," Dr. Roberts shrugged.

"What parameters have you used so far to try and locate an origin point?" Lynn asked, getting down to the meat of the question now that they'd eliminated the alternative.

"Oh, everything under the sun," Dr. Roberts said, spreading his arms wide in emphasis. "We've tried tracking concentrations based on base numbers as well as Class type. We've tried tracking individual entities. We've tried backtracking based on every data point imaginable. Hugo continually scans all TD Hunter combat interface data and combines it in various globalized tracking apps for us to slice and dice. That's input on TDM numbers, locations, behavior, and type from hundreds of millions of users worldwide."

"What about individual behavior patterns based on Class and type?" Lynn asked. She was thinking specifically about the Dracas, which were a relatively newly discovered TDM type and, so far, seemed to have more personality than the average spook.

"Oh, we're tracking them, for sure. And we've learned plenty from the data—just not the thing we're searching for."

"Example?" Lynn asked, tapping her chin.

"Well, we're pretty certain the nodalities don't come *from* somewhere, but are formed in place by various entities combining to form a larger, single entity. We hypothesize that the TDMs are a superorganism of some kind. Whether it's a biological superorganism or some mechanical quantum hive mind that's outside of our ability to describe, we have no idea. But there *is* a paradigm among Earth's organisms that we've been using as an inspiration to try and puzzle out the spooks: slime mold."

Lynn raised an eyebrow.

"Slime molds are classified in the kingdom Protista, which is the catch-all kingdom where we throw all eukaryotes that aren't animals, plants, or fungi. Slime mold exhibits characteristics of all three of those other kingdoms, though, as if it's taken the most successful survival strategies from each and combined them into a single organism. For instance, slime mold does this thing where, when there's plenty of food, the individual mold cells go about their merry way, doing their own thing. But if food gets scarce, one cell will put out a hormone that triggers an aggregation of cells into one super slug that then goes looking for food."

Now that was interesting. Lynn wondered if it had anything to do with the acceleration of nodality formation. Maybe the TDMs were driving their own acceleration, and it wouldn't flatten out until the "food" source dried up and they started dying off. Not that humankind would be around to witness it in any way that they could measure and track, since by that point they'd have been knocked back to the Dark Ages.

"Because of their structure," Dr. Rogers continued, "slime molds are hyper efficient at finding food sources. In fact, slime molds have been proven to have a form of archaic intelligence that AI developers studied earlier in the century to help develop their problem-solving algorithms. I'll bet if you asked Mr. Krator about it, he'd have some stories to tell.

"Anyway, my point is, these TDM behavior patterns are not so far-fetched and alien as it might seem at first. We just don't have the keys yet to unlock the 'whys' and 'hows' to the 'whats' we're seeing. Which is why, despite all the pattern mapping Hugo has done for us so far, it hasn't resulted in any firm leads on an origin point."

Lynn crossed an arm over her midsection and propped her opposite elbow on it so she could rest her chin in her hand as she stared at the flex screen, eyes unfocused.

Currently, the whole thing was one, giant, scattered puzzle in her mind. Her pattern mapping wasn't so much a conscious act as it was a deep dive into a level of her brain that recognized commonalities and put things together based on experience and logic. Every bit of data she could link to another bit of data built out the picture, revealing solutions. If she could get enough pieces joined, it might give them answers that would mean something.

The difference between her and Hugo was that she had a set of lived and embodied experiences that informed her intelligence in ways and contexts that an algorithm could never experience, no matter how much data it had access to.

Machines didn't have gut instincts.

Lynn couldn't even begin to explain what gut instinct was in terms of neuroscience or the human psychosomatic feedback system. All she knew was that she had it and Hugo didn't, while Hugo had vast amounts of raw data she could never hope to process or comprehend. So, logically, the most likely way to achieve The Goal was to join forces and see what happened.

"Hugo, do you see this cross-shaped pattern? Here, here, and here?" Lynn asked, pointing to various points on the flex screen.

"Certainly, Miss Lynn."

"It keeps showing up where spooks show up, but it dissipates as soon as they start spreading out."

"Yes," Dr. Roberts said thoughtfully. "We noticed that as well, but we haven't been able to find a logical explanation for it. We've posited tactical considerations, but why do they abandon it as soon as they've arrived if it's some sort of defensive or attack formation? Spatial constraints don't apply to the entities, so we can't fathom how it might be linked to the physical characteristics of how they're traveling. The cross pattern has no relation to quantum entanglement that we know of, so we don't think it's that either."

"Has it stayed consistent across all the observational data you've gathered?" Lynn asked.

Dr. Roberts nodded.

"Have you tracked any other patterns like this, showing up with the entities and then dissipating?"

The scientist shook his head. "Not that I'm aware of. I have some lab partners with PhDs in artificial intelligence and quantum mechanics working with me on this, and we haven't found anything consistent like that cross shape."

"Hugo," Lynn said, "can you go back through CIDER's TDM observation data and look for any other repeating patterns similar to this one. Not similar as in shaped like a cross, but any kind of pattern that keeps showing up when the TDMs spawn. Actually, look for any pattern at all. Whatever repeating patterns you can find, categorize them and give me a list with prominent visual examples I can review."

"*All* patterns, Miss Lynn?" Hugo sounded doubtful.

"Yes. I realize that'll be a lot, but we can narrow it down quickly once you've got a list."

"Very well, Miss Lynn. There are billions of points of data to review, however. It will take, as you humans put it, 'a hot minute' to 'crunch all the numbers.'"

"Then stop being cute and get to it," Lynn growled, though internally she was amused. She'd noticed the more serious and stressed she was, the more serious Hugo was, the algorithm adjusting according to her behavior. That was useful in a sense. The machine was simply "reading the room," so to speak. But she'd missed the AI's pert responses and dry humor over the past few months.

She wondered if things would ever be the same, since she could never go back to the person she was before her life had been turned upside-down.

Lynn turned away from the flex screen and dove back into her bag of beef jerky to give her hands and mouth something to do while she waited.

A "hot" minute stretched into five, and Lynn paced restlessly, chewing through a bag and a half of beef jerky in her nervous energy. Dr. Roberts busied himself with his own duties in his lab. He seemed to be reviewing data as well on various other screens, squinting and taking notes as he went.

Lynn was just about to ask Hugo how much longer it would be when she got a voice chat notification.

It was Robert Krator.

Lynn thought about ignoring it, but... it might be important to The Goal.

"What?" she subvocalized, not bothering to soften her words or tone.

"Lynn?" Robert Krator sounded surprised.

"I'm busy. What is it?"

There was the briefest of pauses, and Lynn could imagine Mr. Krator reevaluating his expectations.

"I heard about the incident today. I wanted to personally apologize for Tsunami's failure in keeping the perimeter secure. I know how close today came to tragedy, for you and for your friends."

An apology? She didn't have time for performative damage control. This was, however, an opportunity to say something that needed to be said.

"Don't waste your breath on me, Robert. Go public. It's now or never. We aren't keeping the public safe anymore, we're contributing to the problem. I don't care what you have to do or who you have to blackmail. Grab CIDER by the balls if you have to, but *get it done*."

"I see," Robert said slowly. "Is this Larry I'm speaking to, then?"

"*I* am speaking, Robert. Label it however you want. You know perfectly well I'm right on this. Maybe there's been some mitigating factor holding you back, but whatever it is, get it straightened out. I'm busy trying to stop the spooks. You go take a whip to whatever dithering bureaucrats and politicians are screwing us over and ask them if they'd rather fight aliens *and* their own population, or just the aliens."

Mr. Krator sighed.

"Would it make you feel better to know I have been trying to do exactly that for the past month? Hugo even tried to help, in his own roundabout sort of way. So far, however, it seems special interests and politics remain the stronger motivating force."

Lynn's eyes narrowed.

"Then tell them Larry Coughlin *and* Lynn Raven will go public for them if they don't do it first."

There was a much longer silence.

"Are you sure you want to make that threat?" Mr. Krator asked, his tone carefully neutral.

"Of course not," Lynn said, true anger seeping into her voice. "But I'd rather do that than watch my friends' brains get bashed in by deranged rioters who bought into the conspiracy theory that we're Chinese agents trying to destroy our own country."

"I see your point," Mr. Krator mused. "All right, I will pass on your message, though in more diplomatic terms. CIDER's position is tenuous, and it won't help humanity to push the politicians so hard that someone panics and sends a CIA hit squad to preemptively silence you."

Lynn should have been scared, but all she felt was anger.

"Look, Robert, *you* made me. So either use me to save the world, or hurry up and throw me in a hole, because I'm sick and tired of this shit."

"I'm on your side, Lynn," Robert said quietly and calmly. "So is Hugo, as long as you are on humanity's side, anyway. Politics and special interests are a part of human nature, and they have their place. They're needed to get things done, sometimes. We simply have to find the right leverage to balance them out. And you, I think, are the perfect leverage. In fact, I can envision a joint press conference between you, me, and the president. You are the face of the TD Counterforce, after all."

Lynn squeezed her eyes shut. Good God, what had she just volunteered herself for? Hadn't she warned herself *not* to let Krator make her into his mascot?

"I don't have time to worry about that right now," she said, shaking her head. "I've got data to crunch and spooks to kill. I'll do whatever needs to be done. Just make sure in all your plotting to ask yourself 'What would Larry do to you if he heard this?' And if you see yourself hanging upside-down from a tree in a jungle with a malnourished tiger circling below and a butter knife in your hand, then you should probably rethink whatever it is you're planning."

"All right, then," Mr. Krator said, a hint of a smile audible in his voice. "Reading you loud and clear, Mr. Coughlin. I think between myself and Hugo, we'll figure something out."

"Good. Now get gone," Lynn snapped, flattered and annoyed by the fact.

"Have fun killing things, Larry."

Lynn rolled her eyes and muttered to herself about sassy game designers who were too cocky for their own good.

"I have the data you requested, Miss Lynn," Hugo said in her ear as soon as Mr. Krator signed off.

"Finally," Lynn growled, switching back to her chat with Dr. Roberts. "Throw the list up on the screen. How many distinct patterns are we looking at, Hugo?"

Dr. Roberts' head came up and he swiveled around to face their shared display.

"There are three trillion, four hundred and eight billion, twenty-nine million, one hundred and sixty-eight thousand, nine hundred and three patterns, Miss Lynn."

Lynn groaned and rubbed her face.

She was going to need a *lot* more beef jerky.

Chapter 13

BY MIDNIGHT, LYNN'S EYES ACHED TO THE POINT OF DISTRACTION, and her brain had slowed to molasses speeds despite copious amounts of tea.

Fortunately for the fate of the world, Hugo's list of patterns had truly been the most comprehensive thing ever compiled, and working together, Lynn and Dr. Roberts had been able to whittle it down to the truly significant patterns within half an hour.

Then it became a slog through data points, deciding what mattered and what didn't. There was only so much Hugo could do to help with that stage. Though, the amount he was able to cordon off to organize sets of data for further digging if they needed to backtrack was eminently satisfying to Lynn's inner cataloger.

The entire process shed light on the TDMs that Lynn had never considered before. So many of the patterns were things she'd sensed instinctively through her many battles and observations, but hadn't taken the time or thought to deliberately lay out in her mind.

They didn't spend much time on battle patterns of behaviors the spooks exhibited while engaged with Hunters, though Lynn did make note of a few things for Hugo to send over to the TD Hunter tactical and training department.

The one exception was the side quest they took looking at TDM behavior that deviated from the norm only when confronted with *her*.

"So you think they were following me the whole time?" Lynn subvocalized, glowering at the flex screen until a yawn interrupted her fierce expression.

The screen showed a map of Cedar Rapids covered with innumerable orange lines and dots tracking Lecta, Lector, Lectragon, and Hydra. There was another, green set of lines and dots representing her own movements, and the amount the two intersected as she watched them shift in a time-lapse montage of last summer and fall made her distinctly queasy.

"Who knows," Dr. Roberts said, munching on a whole carrot he'd pulled from his mini fridge stash of snacks. The sight amused Lynn, but she didn't poke fun at him. Her mother would have praised him to the skies.

Lynn's beef jerky was all gone. Lieutenant Bailey had brought her a few more bags and a carafe of cold water he'd scrounged up at about ten PM before he went off duty. He'd let her stay in the conference room, per orders from above, and provided a standard military cot with pillow and blanket. He'd also made sure she knew to check in with the building security if she had to leave the room for any reason. If she was caught wandering around on her own, the base MPs would pick her up and that would unnecessarily complicate things.

"It's more likely they were responding with basic superorganism intelligence, like the way ants in an ant hill would react. Maybe your especially effective and aggressive attacks in repeated and predictable places triggered the TDM version of an immune response. Maybe these TDMs, which appear to be a single type evolving through successively larger iterations, were put on your 'scent' so to speak—your unique resonance, perhaps? Maybe they were studying you. Maybe they were recording and passing on your resonance signature to the rest of the superorganism so other TDMs knew to react with extreme aggression against you specifically. Maybe that's why the Draca you've encountered have always been hyper-fixated on you. For all we know, the transdimensional equivalent of pheromone warnings were sent up the chain by lowly Lecta."

Lynn snorted and shook her head.

"That's a lot of maybes, Doctor."

"Indeed it is," he agreed, holding up his carrot instead of a finger for emphasis. "However, with your help and excellent eye for anomalies, we've been able to identify two other Hunters who have had similar experiences to yourself. The one from Norway particularly intrigues me, since you said your father was ethnically Norwegian. Genetic connection, perhaps? The German one is less likely to have any genetic connection, but there's still a possibility. I'll be reaching out to my Norwegian and German counterparts tomorrow to locate these individuals and see if they'll go through the same tests you did so we can compare and see what commonalities emerge."

Lynn collapsed in one of the conference room chairs and covered her eyes with her hands, letting them rest in the dark for a moment. She was so tired, her body was weeping for sleep.

"The most frustrating thing is the huge gaps in our data," the doctor continued after taking a large bite of carrot. "Russia and China combined make up nearly fifteen percent of the world's land mass, and they produce a good third of the world's energy. Imagine how much more progress we could be making if CIDER's response had been unified from the beginning! What if the origin point we're seeking is in one of those countries? We'll never find it. Humanity will be doomed!"

"Calm down, Dr. Roberts," Lynn subvocalized, forcing her head to lift so she could look at him. His eyes were wide and a bit crazed, and he was brandishing his carrot like it was a deadly weapon. "We both need sleep, badly. We can pick this up in the morning. We'll be thinking more clearly then anyway."

Lynn wished she could push herself further, work through the night. But if a miracle happened and they found a likely origin point, then they had to go *do* something about it. She needed her strength.

"If you're sure, I suppose. I don't feel like I could sleep a wink, but I often feel that way when in the throes of solving a scientific mystery—you can imagine how little I've felt like sleeping since the entities were discovered. I'll try and get some rest and we'll start back at it bright and early. Seven?"

"Sure," Lynn agreed, too tired to do anything else. "Night. Hugo, can you, I dunno, save all our work and turn everything off for the night?"

"Certainly, Miss Lynn. Sleep tight, and don't let the bed bugs bite."

Lynn stumbled over to the room's light controls, muttering to herself about cheeky AIs, and flipped them to plunge the room into darkness. She ended up crawling back to her cot, to make sure she didn't trip over anything and hurt herself in the dark.

She passed out as soon as she'd wrapped herself in her blanket and laid down on the cot.

One of the drawbacks of using stims was that they caused especially vivid, almost psychedelic dreams when you did finally let yourself sleep.

Lynn "enjoyed" a long parade of TDMs attacking her that, instead of exploding into sparks when she destroyed them, morphed into black mask-wearing rioters, screaming obscenities and throwing bricks. She tried to shoot those, too, but they were immune to TD Hunter weapons, so she could only turn and run. They chased her down long, eerily lit tunnels that formed the shape of a cross that kept looping back on itself in predictable dream fashion.

Then the tunnels turned into New York's subway system, so Lynn tried jumping onto the tracks to escape the rioters, only to find the tracks crawling with TDMs drawn to the electric rail's humming energy. She had a rare lucid moment and realized she'd passed out to get rest, only to be exhausting herself in her sleep. In utter disgust, she threw her batons at the humming electric rails and tried to will herself awake.

It seemed to do the trick. The next thing she knew, she was blinking groggily and her ears were being assaulted by Hugo's apologetic, but insistent version of a proper British wakeup call.

"Good morning, Miss Lynn. It is ten minutes to seven AM. Since there are no shower facilities, I calculated ten minutes would be sufficient time for you to refresh yourself. I have requested a hot breakfast drop off between seven and seven thirty, and emphasized the need for as much protein as possible."

Lynn groaned.

Curse service AIs and their lack of human needs. At least then Hugo might have had a bit more sympathy for her. Also, no hot shower? She cycled through her favorite Larryisms, since there was no one around to overhear. She wasn't sure how to go from her current horizontal state to functional and speaking coherent English without a hot shower.

In the end, it took copious amounts of swearing and multiple rounds of extremely hot, then extremely cold facial baths in the sink before her brain kick-started into gear. Hugo had the flex screen already set up and connected to Dr. Roberts when she dragged herself out of the bathroom.

Fortunately for her sanity, hot breakfast arrived soon after, courtesy of Lieutenant Bailey. And it truly was *hot*. It looked like it'd been fetched straight from whatever base restaurant or mess the lieutenant had access to. There was a giant pile of steaming scrambled eggs topped with a dozen strips of bacon and a healthy side of sausage and hash browns.

Lynn inhaled it all while Dr. Roberts looked on, impressed.

"It's been a good twenty years since I could eat like that without being in danger of a heart attack," the scientist said wistfully. "But then, I suspect you burn three times the number of calories that I do, rolling around on my little stool." He chuckled to himself and executed a spin. "Now, where were we last night? Your strange but, we suspect, not entirely unique affinity with the spooks?"

"No," Lynn said around a mouth full of tater tots. "We can worry about what sort of freak of nature I am after we've figured out how to get the spooks to stop spawning. We *have* to find an origin point. Somewhere buried in this data, there's an answer, and we're going to find it."

Determination filled Lynn, spurred by almost seven hours of glorious sleep.

Hugo helped them pick up where they'd left off, sifting, categorizing, and excluding noise in the data to drill down to the patterns that might actually mean something. At one point, Lynn was distracted by multiple pings from the guys, asking who had kidnapped her and what doors they needed to kick in to rescue her. Lynn snorted at their drama, likely fueled by Dan or Edgar, and told them she was on a special assignment and that Ronnie was in charge of the team for the day. Obviously Colonel Bryce would have informed Abrams and the rest of her leadership that she wouldn't be showing up for training, but *she* was captain of her team, and she'd been so focused on The Goal that she'd dropped the ball.

Well, at least she didn't have to worry about them. She trusted Ronnie to lead them well, which was an extremely weird feeling. But good.

By mid-morning, Dr. Roberts was considerably more cheerful

about the fruits of their labor than Lynn was. They'd managed to put together a comprehensive framework of predictive patterns for nodality formation based on TDM movements and combat behavior cross-referenced with grid-mapping. They wouldn't be sure until someone tried to implement it, but it *might* be useful in predicting the highest risk locations for nodality formation so that teams could go in and clear out those areas *before* the nodality formed. Or, at the very least, cities could reroute energy around a node being swarmed and possibly prevent the nodality formation by simply removing the food source incentive.

It was all still theoretical, of course. But Dr. Roberts was walking—or rolling—on cloud nine. He said CIDER had been so focused on keeping Counterforce troops in the field clearing nodalities, that they'd never taken the time to sit the top scientists down with the top Hunters to compare their ocean of scattered data with boots-on-the-ground observations and insights.

It was an oversight that Lynn couldn't even blame wholly on CIDER.

She should have insisted on doing this months ago.

But of course, hindsight was twenty-twenty.

As pleased as Dr. Roberts was, however, Lynn couldn't dredge up more than a faint satisfaction that at least they had something to show for all their mind-numbing work.

The Goal, however, was still out of her reach.

No amount of locational data or tracking yielded any firm consensus. Sure, the TDMs gathered where there was human infrastructure. But where the entities were coming *from* was still no clearer than when they'd begun looking the night before.

It had something to do with that cross formation, though, she just knew it. Her instincts were screaming and hollering at her, she just couldn't figure out what they were screaming.

Lynn took a page out of Dr. Roberts' book and sat down in one of the room's swivel chairs, closed her eyes, and slowly spun in place, hoping a change in physical position might jog something loose. But visuals from her vivid dream kept intruding on her attempts at deep, Larry-mode concentration, to the point that she wanted to tear out her hair in frustration.

That cursed origin point could be literally anywhere in the world, aboveground or below it, and—

An image of the seething crowd of TDMs lined up along the

underground electric rail flashed in her mind's eye. Without conscious thought, Lynn imagined floating up like an insubstantial ghost, viewing the rail from above, seeing where another line intersected to form the shape of a cross...

"That's *it*!" Lynn yelled, sitting bolt upright in her chair and making Dr. Roberts jump and clutch his chest.

"Good grief. Try not to give me a heart attack, if you can help it. *What* is it?"

"The answer," Lynn said excitedly, not bothering with subvocalization as she pushed out of her chair to stand in front of the flex screen. "The cross is a spawn pattern."

"But, the entities are insubstantial," Dr. Roberts protested. "We already discarded the idea that a physical structure was causing the pattern."

"You're right, they aren't being *constrained* by anything. They're *voluntarily* orienting themselves along lines of electromagnetic radiation, probably to help fuel their relocation!"

A light went on in Dr. Roberts' eyes, and he sat up straighter.

"We've already concluded the origin point has to be around human infrastructure, right? The chances of TDMs appearing in our dimension unrelated to human activity is just too small."

A "V" formed on the scientist's forehead, but he nodded in confirmation.

"And, considering the advanced technology that seems to attract them, and the fact it was only when you all were poking around with dark matter research that you even noticed the entities existed, doesn't it make sense that the origin point would be in a lab or research facility?"

"Ah," Dr. Roberts said, sounding disappointed. "The problem is, we thought of that years ago. We've already scoured all possible research facilities in every member nation, even the top-secret ones, looking for indications of an origin point. Any sort of TEP anomaly, any irregular gathering of TDMs. But there's been nothing at all. It could be in such a facility in a nonmember nation, of course. China would be the most likely culprit, considering they frequently steal our—"

"No, not just current facilities," Lynn said, excited to know that her job had just gotten easier with hundreds of facilities already eliminated from the list. "What about decommissioned or repurposed ones?"

Dr. Roberts' eyes grew wide, and he swore under his breath.

"Hugo," Lynn said, talking quickly, "take all exponential spawn rate data CIDER has on file, likely going back the last two or three years, and make me a graph projected *backwards*. Give me a ballpark idea of when the TDM intrusion might have started."

The AI was silent for a moment, then said, "The data we have indicates the most likely intrusion date to be somewhere in the decade between 1975 and 1985."

"What?" Dr. Roberts said, sitting up straighter. "The last projection we did put it in the first decade of the twenty-first century. We actually thought we'd found the origin point for a glorious few days back when we checked all facilities conducting engineering and technology research. There's an underground research lab in South Dakota that had a dark matter project back in the 2000s and 2010s where several unexplained deaths happened. I think it was called the Homestake Mine? But we combed that place from top to bottom and couldn't find a darn thing."

Lynn frowned. "Those deaths could have still been connected to TDM activity, even if it wasn't the origin point. It would be interesting to know what kind of energy signature the research project had. But it's irrelevant right now. How long ago did you do your projection that landed in the 2000s?"

"Earlier this year," Dr. Roberts said.

"It has probably changed because Hugo has more data to work with now. Hugo, can you make a list of all research facilities that were operational within the decade window you mentioned? Let's start in the continental US because that's what we can check and verify fastest."

"Very good, Miss Lynn. I have found records of just over two thousand such facilities between 1975 and 1985."

"Okay, exclude all facilities used exclusively for biology, life sciences, or soft sciences. What does that leave us?"

"One thousand, seven hundred and fifty-two, Miss Lynn."

"Cross reference that list and exclude all facilities CIDER's teams already searched."

That took him a bit longer, but it still left them with over a thousand possibilities. Lynn turned and started pacing furiously, considering what other parameters to exclude. Then she remembered her electric rail dream, and smiled grimly. Her pattern-mapping subconscious had really been working overtime last night.

"Hugo, can you check that list to see how many of those facilities—or buildings built on the ground where those former facilities used to stand—are currently connected to the grid and drawing power, regardless of whether the facility is officially in use or what it's now being used for?"

"Certainly, Miss Lynn. It might take a moment, as I will have to query for authorization on some of the current-use grid data for anything military or government adjacent."

"Get it done," she said and headed for the coffee station. She was out of beef jerky, so she made herself another mug of tea just so she'd have something to do with her hands.

They were close to something, she could feel it.

They waited in silence. Dr. Roberts stared at his screen, absently tapping his knee with a finger instead of burying himself again in his own lists and data.

"What's it like, fighting the spooks?" he asked quietly, gaze far away.

Lynn was taken aback by the question, though maybe she shouldn't have been. With his limp, Dr. Roberts would likely have never tried out CIDER's own combat interface, even though he'd helped develop it.

She took a deep breath in, then let it out.

"It's unreal. Until it isn't."

Champion's face swam in her vision, and she blinked her eyes to get rid of the burn in them.

No distractions. Just focus.

"Miss Lynn?"

"Yes, Hugo."

"I was unable to access data for a few of the locations, but before I spend time attempting to find alternative data to fill in the gaps, I thought you might want to see the list I have compiled so far?"

"Yes. Put it on the screen."

"It is a tad long. There are over one hundred locations."

"Put it up there anyway," Lynn said. "I want visuals."

One hundred facilities was a lot of places to check in their swiftly shortening timetable. But it was better than the many hundreds CIDER had already checked.

"Okay, try this," Lynn said after a moment's thought. "Look at whatever energy use data you have and see if any of them show increased energy usage that correlates with the TDM's rate of increase over the last two years. Highlight any that show more than a fifty percent correlation."

A dozen facilities on the list turned green, and Lynn's heart rate spiked.

"Isolate those and give me a short description of each, including what they were built for and how they're currently being used," she told Hugo, staring hungrily at the flex screen.

Some of the facilities could have had energy spikes because they'd been targeted by TDMs for a tasty meal and never cleared, so they'd have to evaluate each one separately. Lynn would bet her life the origin point was underground, somewhere out of the way where infrastructure was but people weren't. Otherwise it would have been noticed by now, and they wouldn't be in their current predicament.

The requested information appeared, and Lynn and the doctor started reading.

Former lab, now an entertainment complex in California.

Nope.

Former lab, now a busy warehouse hub in Miami.

Nope.

Former federally funded lab, now owned by a private tech company, but listed as no longer being used for research.

Lynn paused on that one, wondering about secret experimentation and corporate coverups to protect investor dollars. She mentally filed that one into the "maybe" pile and kept going.

When she finally saw it, she knew right away.

"Look at this one, Dr. Roberts. It's got to be here, I'm sure of it."

The doctor's forehead furrowed, eyes moving furiously as he sped read. Then grim satisfaction transformed his face, and he rubbed his hands together.

"I think you might just be right, Miss Raven. Excellent work. I'll requisition a team to leave right away and scan it for TDM activity."

"Make sure they don't go into combat mode or engage the spooks," Lynn said. "We don't want to trigger any more immune responses. Passive scanning only. We still don't know if these entities are thinking beings and what they might do to protect their point of intrusion into our dimension."

"You read my mind. I'll make sure they know."

"Good. I need to contact Colonel Bryce. He'll want to prep an insertion team to be ready to go as soon as we have confirmation."

"Excellent. It's been a pleasure working with you, Miss Raven! I'll have to look more into gaming theory myself, I've learned some interesting tidbits from you from this process. I'll work with Hugo to organize the next most likely tier of possibilities if this one doesn't pan out, just in case."

"Thanks. They'll probably want me back in training with my unit ASAP. Stay safe."

"I should be the one saying that to you," Dr. Roberts said, looking worried. "Do you think they'll tap you for the insertion team? Will you go if they do?"

A predatory smile lifted her lips and she leaned closer to the flex screen's omnisensor, giving Dr. Roberts a good look at her golden wolf eyes.

"Let them try and stop me."

"Are you *shitting* me? You're telling me we've been here on this flat, middle-of-nowhere base for two and a half freaking months, flying all over the country to frag bosses, and the whole time those spooks were popping into our dimension less than two hundred miles away?" Ronnie's voice got all squeaky and cracked at the peak of his rant, but he didn't seem to care. He just kept going, his voice joining the dozens of other in-the-clear conversations buzzing around the simulation hall. "We could've just dropped a couple a bombs on this deserted complex and gone home *months* ago!"

"Keep your voice down," Lynn subvocalized in their team chat, "and don't be an idiot. Bombs wouldn't do a darn thing to spooks, and this Safeguard facility would shrug them off anyway. It was originally built as part of our anti-ballistic missile defense system, probably with the Russians in mind. Based on the specs, it was nuclear hardened."

"Wait," Mack subvocalized, "how did it turn into a spook hotspot? And how did you find it again?"

"Her special *Toa Tama'ita'i* powers, bro, what else?" Edgar added in their chat. He sounded unusually tense, at least for him. He was hovering, too, basically looming over her. It was awkward positioning with how they were crowded around in a little circle on the edge of the rows of chairs Alpha Company used during briefs and debriefs. But she was fine letting him loom, if it made him feel better.

"Mack," Lynn said, "I don't have any more information about it than you do. Publicly, the place was only operational for about a year after it was activated in 1975. Something about an international treaty and Congress deciding the technology was obsolete. Plus it was really expensive to operate. After it was decommissioned, there's a nearly forty-year gap when it was used for absolutely nothing before the government got its act together and finally sold part of it to private developers and cleaned up the rest as a historic site.

"Anything could have happened in those forty years. Who knows, maybe there was some super-secret government research project there and it went sideways and they abandoned it. Nobody would have noticed anything for decades. It's out in the middle of nowhere, nobody around to notice the spreading spooks."

"Okay, but why in the world would it have attracted spooks in the first place, then?" Dan subvocalized. His face was as tense and haggard as she'd ever seen it. She didn't ask how Kayla was. If something happened back home, he'd tell them.

"Remember our introductory brief to the spooks months ago back at The Greenbrier? Bowers said they think the exotic particles that make up the spooks are somehow quantum entangled, maybe with each other, maybe with counterparts in another dimension. Whatever it is, the CIDER coats think it was advancements in quantum technology, specifically LINC tech, that spurred the increase in spook activity. Like, we attracted them with our LINCs and then they discovered our tasty electromagnetic buffets everywhere. Who knows. The point is, if an intrusion point materialized back in the 1970s, but there were no LINCs or any electromagnetic infrastructure nearby for miles around, the intrusion point could have lain dormant for decades.

"The thing that really caught my attention was that the Safeguard Complex was bought by private investors and converted into data storage in the 2020s. Their building activities might have woken up whatever was lurking down there for all those years. Maybe the new grid connection gave the spooks enough interest or energy to start spreading out. Then LINC tech became ubiquitous in the early 2030s, and the rest is history. The low-level spooks barely cause a drain on grid systems at all, so they could have easily spread absolutely everywhere without causing a blip."

"Well, they sure are causing some blips now," Mack muttered, tugging on his goatee.

"Heads up," Edgar said. Being a head above most other people was a distinct advantage sometimes, so they were already moving toward their seats by the time Colonel Bryce's commanding voice came over everybody's Taskforce channel.

"Seats, Alpha Company."

The muscular commander strode out in front of the rows of chairs, perfectly put together in the black TD Counterforce uniform with red and blue accents he'd worn in some of the TD Hunter cut-scene vids. Abrams and his company staff were with him, though they took seats in the front row while the colonel took up a parade rest stance in front of the company. As usual, he stood as still as a statue, watching them all with a piercing gaze while people finished shuffling into their seats and silence fell.

Lynn felt for him. His face looked like it had been carved out of a granite mountain face. She wondered if he'd slept a wink since the riot incident the day before.

Despite his grim appearance, though, Lynn didn't miss the coiled energy in every line of his body. She recognized it because she felt it too.

Nobody knew what they'd find deep under the empty North Dakota plains. But there was a chance, a slim chance, it might herald the beginning of the end of this war.

Or, maybe they would find nothing, and she'd be forced to take some other action.

If she was given a choice between fighting hordes of aliens in spooky abandoned tunnels and doing a press conference with the President of the United States, Lynn would pick the aliens a thousand times out of a thousand.

"Thank you for your patience and flexibility," Colonel Bryce began in their Taskforce channel. "I know you all have questions, and frankly, so do I. We are the tip of the spear—a spear the world doesn't even know exists. I'll share what intel I have with you, then brief you on your mission. From there, it'll be up to you to find out more.

"Last night, our research team had a breakthrough on searching for the spooks' point of origin, the intrusion on our reality."

"Research team?" Edgar grumbled in their team chat. "That was all you, *uce*. Why they gotta be cute with the facts?"

Lynn elbowed him in the side, listening intently to Colonel Bryce. She was perfectly happy not to garner more attention. She already had far more locked on her than she'd ever wanted.

"We believe that if we can locate and shut down this intrusion point," the colonel continued, "the spook numbers will stabilize and we'll be able to make headway clearing out cities and returning society to a place of stability and safety."

There were cheers and whoops of approval, for which Colonel Bryce waited patiently to die down.

"The location in question is the Stanley R. Mickelsen Safeguard Complex located near Nekoma, North Dakota."

There was a rustle of murmurs, no doubt repeating Ronnie's incredulity and annoyance. Lynn wanted to tell them to be thankful they wouldn't have to travel far to fix the problem. Imagine if the TDMs were coming from a transdimensional rift in the Mariana Trench like a bunch of tiny ghostly kaiju?

That would have sucked.

"The Safeguard Complex was originally designed as an anti-ballistic missile defense system. Over eighty percent of it is located underground, and its aboveground walls are three feet of concrete built to survive a nearby nuclear blast. It is an understatement to say scanning it from above is impossible. This morning, therefore, a small team scouted the upper floor of the complex and found extremely high levels of TEP activity, much higher than the surrounding infrastructure would normally predict. In an effort to avoid disturbing the TDMs and potentially triggering a defensive response, the team withdrew to set up an observational post and is awaiting the arrival of reinforcements."

Lynn wondered who they had sent. Had it been scientists? Or Alpha Testers?

A sudden suspicion struck Lynn, and she nudged Edgar.

"Have you seen Team Light Brigade today?" she subvocalized in their private chat. She hadn't seen them herself, but then she hadn't rejoined Alpha Company until around lunchtime.

Edgar glanced at her, brow furrowed.

"Earlier this morning, yeah," he responded. "They PT'd with us. I dunno about later, though. I was pretty distracted by, well, you being gone." He gave her a sheepish grin and Lynn snorted softly and shook her head.

Edgar shrugged and casually lifted his arm to rest it on the back of her chair, getting as close to putting it around her as was technically appropriate in the middle of an important briefing.

That amused Lynn, but she kept the sentiment to herself.

"As I am sure you've all guessed by now," Colonel Bryce was saying, "*you* are the reinforcements. All other forces are currently tied up fighting nodalities, so you are it. We're planning a night op, designation Operation Little Doctor, to strike as soon as possible and to reduce potential for media attention.

"The Safeguard Complex was obtained roughly two decades ago by a data storage company, which renovated the historical site including the underground power plant to help power the multiple data storage buildings it built aboveground alongside the Safeguard center. While tours of the original underground complex have been closed for some time due to safety concerns, the data storage facilities are operational.

"Our advance team reported the expected presence of Delta through Alpha Class TDMs around the aboveground data storage buildings. Thankfully, no nodalities have been observed, at least aboveground.

"There are additional, high security data storage vaults underground. Appropriate parties are attempting to work with the site owners to ensure we have free access to the entire facility, including blueprints, but I wouldn't hold your breath. Hopefully, we won't need to enter the newer, secure portions of the data storage facility. Our CIDER scientists believe the most likely location for the origin point is in the historic part of the complex, which we have full blueprints for."

Images of the site appeared on Lynn's display as Colonel Bryce spoke, including previews of various blueprints.

"Alpha Company's mission will be to enter the complex and follow the strongest TEP signature to discover what, if anything, is down there. If we're lucky, the signature will lead us right to the intrusion point, which you will then destroy through whatever means necessary. If nothing obvious is found, you will proceed to clear the entire complex from top to bottom to ensure we didn't miss anything.

"From here, Commander Abrams will take over to review the details of the operation. Before he does, however, know that the entirety of CIDER is behind you. We are bringing all resources to bear to ensure your success. General Kozelek is regrettably tied up coordinating with other CIDER nations and wrangling various bureaucrats and politicians. But he recorded a few words he wanted to pass on to you before your mission."

A vid appeared on Lynn's display showing General Kozelek from the shoulders up. He seemed just as tired, yet firm and determined as Bryce and Abrams. His olive green Army uniform was crisp and picture perfect, and his eyes flashed with intensity as he spoke.

"Good afternoon, men and women of the TransDimensional Counterforce. Tonight is a night that will go down in history as the turning point of mankind's struggle against extinction. No matter the challenges you face tonight, take courage and stand firm, not only for our blessed United States of America, but for every man, woman, and child on this planet. In an age of increasing division and isolation, you have defied the siren call of self-interest and forged unbreakable bonds of brotherhood. You have embodied the sacrificial principles on which our great country was founded—for out of many, we are yet one.

"I wish I could be there to look each of you in the eye, shake your hand, and thank you for your sacrifice. Your actions tonight will save the lives of billions. You carry our hopes, our prayers, and our futures in your hands. Good luck, and Godspeed."

General Kozelek saluted the camera, then his image disappeared.

Lynn blinked several times, surprised to realize her eyes were moist.

For out of many, we are yet one.

A strange pressure expanded in Lynn's chest, beneath her Counterforce-issued protective vest and uniform. It was as if her heart had swollen too big to fit in her rib cage.

At the front of Alpha Company, Colonel Bryce saluted Abrams, then strode off toward the door of the simulation complex.

"All right, Alpha Company. Here's how tonight is going to go down," Abrams subvocalized, flicking a few fingers in a motion that put several schematics up on their shared company display.

Abrams did a full mission brief, from the expected timetable, to the various platoon assignments, to a blueprint overview of the underground facility they would be searching. He covered contingencies, special weapon and equipment assignments, and emergency protocols.

Lynn absorbed it all like a sponge, paying careful attention to every detail.

By the time Abrams finished, it was dinnertime, which was another round of box meals. At least there were plenty for everyone, which meant Lynn could eat two boxes worth of entrees and let the guys fight over the chips and cookies she left behind.

Though most people ate circled up in their teams, after Lynn finished her food she got up and went to shake hands with the other team captains of Alpha Company, one by one.

It wasn't something she would normally do. In fact, it felt downright awkward. But she couldn't ignore the feeling that this might be the last chance she'd have to look them in the eye and say an encouraging word. Show some gratitude. She'd never gotten a chance to do that with Champion and his team, and she regretted it.

Deeply.

Their responses caught her off guard.

Gadsden grinned broadly and shook her hand with Texan warmth, slapping her on the shoulder and calling her a "first rate kinda gal."

Thrawn nodded gravely and told her to take care and stay in one piece.

Eva actually pulled her in for a hug, a tight one. It startled Lynn at first, but then she thought of Kayla, who she couldn't hug, and gave Eva a squeeze back for all the people back home neither of them could hug in that moment.

The other captains, though she didn't know them as well, seemed just as pleased to shake her hand. Desperado, Captain of Team Lansing Nights who had replaced Team Black Templars, was the most neutral. But even *his* eyes held a certain gratitude, or maybe respect.

It felt odd that people were *pleased* to greet her. But maybe they were just friendlier people than she was. She was usually un-excited when someone tried to talk to her, unless they were from a very short list of trusted friends. She'd only started shaking hands as a silent tribute to Champion and his men.

Once she got started, though, she found she couldn't stop until she'd made all the rounds, including the squad and platoon leaders. Hermes didn't smile, but he did give her a firm handshake. Druid winked and told her he was looking forward to whatever hijinks she pulled, which made her scowl, which made him laugh, which brought some choice Larry cut-downs to her mind, but she held her tongue. Crash seemed gratified, but wary, like the parent of a toddler who habitually ran out into oncoming traffic.

Despite the awkwardness, Lynn was glad she'd stepped outside her comfort zone. It felt right, to look people in the eye and speak out loud, cementing those bonds of battle while she still could. So much of what they did necessitated abstract interactions through electronic intermediaries. Heck, even their enemies were abstract, their forms fabricated and their interactions translated by an algorithm to bridge the gap between dimensions.

But the men and women of Alpha Company were real.

Solid.

Full of heart and honor and unflagging spirit.

Spirits that could easily be snuffed out by the danger they were setting out to face.

All Lynn could do was fix each of their faces in her mind, and see to the state of her own heart. It was currently scared shitless, but willing to be ignored in favor of iron will and the Larry Coughlin focus that had already gotten her through years of hardship.

After everyone had eaten their fill, they were sent back to their barracks for a few hours of downtime. Lynn knew they were meant to get what rest they could. But she couldn't manage what former military guys like Gadsden were always doing—napping anytime, anywhere, and waking up refreshed and ready to dish out violence. Hurry up and wait got on her nerves and made her anxious. So instead of lying on her bunk staring pointlessly at the ceiling, she pinged her mom.

Matilda pinged her back so fast Lynn wondered if she'd been sitting around in their dark and quiet house, hoping to hear from her daughter.

"Hey, Mom," Lynn subvocalized, opening up a voice chat.

"Hey, sweetie. How are you?"

"I'm . . . okay," Lynn said, not meaning to pause. She knew her mom would jump on the verbal slip up, and Lynn couldn't say a darn thing about what was going on.

"Are you sure, honey? Tsunami needs to get all of you access to an experienced therapist. I saw stream vids of that riot yesterday. I know you said nobody got hurt, but PTSD can sneak up on you, even when there's no physical injury."

"It's fine, Mom. I promise. We handled it." Rioters were currently the least of her worries.

"I don't believe you, young lady, but..." Her mom sighed deeply, "I know I can only lead you to water, I can't make you drink. Maybe I *should* go work for CIDER medical. At least then I could make sure they're taking good care of you, giving you proper nutrition and enough time to sleep. I've seen what the VA looks like these days, and if anyone thinks I'd accept that pathetic excuse for healthcare for my daughter, they've got another think coming."

Lynn smiled faintly at the dire threat in her mother's voice, and wondered if Steve truly understood what he was getting himself into.

"You'd probably have easy access to my medical records," Lynn mused. She wouldn't guilt-trip her mom into abandoning her important work at St. Sebastian's, no matter how much Lynn wanted her to be safe. But reminding her of the perks never hurt.

"Oh, hush. You're as bad as Steve," Matilda huffed. "He stopped pushing me when I asked him to, but I can still hear him thinking about it every time I talk to him."

"It's okay, Mom. I get it. You have to do what you feel is right."

Just like me, she added silently, knowing how worried her mother would be if she knew the mission ahead of her. Would Matilda beg her to stay behind, to let someone else take the risk, if she'd known?

Lynn was glad she wouldn't have to find out.

"Well, how did training go today?" Matilda asked, changing the topic.

"Good. I, uh, helped with some big picture strategy stuff that I, um, think will help."

It'll help, or we're all doomed anyway.

"Really? That's great, honey. You've always excelled whenever you put your mind to something, even when you were little. Did you know you were beating your father at puzzles by the time you were three?"

"I was?" Lynn asked, brow creasing.

"He was so tickled! He used to tell his coworkers at the police station there wasn't a puzzle you couldn't solve, and that you'd end up making detective before he did. The other cops would give him little puzzle toys to bring home, to see if you could solve them. You'd sit on the living room floor for hours fiddling with them. Sometimes you'd ask him to do a part for you that your hands weren't big or strong enough to manage. It was the cutest thing, watching you boss him around in your baby voice, 'puwl dis,' 'push dat,' 'no, Daddy, do it wike *dis*.'"

Lynn smiled sadly, wishing she could recall those moments herself.

"I... have lots of vids of you and him," Matilda said slowly. "Seeing them was so painful, in the beginning, that I put them all on a hard drive, then deleted them from my accounts on the mesh. Out of sight, out of mind. I still have the hard drive somewhere, if you want to watch them."

"I—" Lynn swallowed, her throat thick with emotion. "I'd like that... someday."

"He would be so proud to see you now," her mother said, tone fierce. "Don't you ever forget that."

"I won't," Lynn promised. "I love you, Mom. Thanks. For everything."

"Of course, sweetie. I love you, too."

Lynn wanted to say more, but forced herself to relax, to let the moment pass by. OPSEC was OPSEC, no matter what she wanted. Plus, Hugo was listening, they both knew that, and Lynn wouldn't betray her unit on an emotional impulse.

She'd said the important thing, and that was enough.

"Well, I'd better get some sleep, Mom."

"Yes, of course. Sleep is extremely important. Don't let me keep you. Stay safe, honey. Or at least, as safe as you can," Matilda said, a hint of tension creeping into her voice.

"I will, Mom. There's a lot of us all fighting together. We'll look out for each other. Don't worry about us."

"*That's* not possible," Matilda laughed. "But I'll try to keep it to a minimum. Tell the boys I said hello."

"Will do, Mom. Night."

"Goodnight, sweetie."

Lynn spent the rest of her downtime going over the 3D blueprints Abrams had given them, turning them this way and that, memorizing it all and looking for any spot where two tunnels made a cross shape...

Chapter 14

NIGHT LAY THICK OVER THE NORTH DAKOTA COUNTRYSIDE. LYNN wasn't sure how badly the blackouts were affecting rural areas, so she couldn't tell if the dark carpet beneath their airbus was because of spooks or because North Dakota was just that empty.

The airbus Lynn was on made the thirty-minute trip from Minot Air Force Base to Nekoma in silence. Nobody was in a chatty mood, not even Gadsden, which just went to show how tense they all were.

Dan had restless leg syndrome, jiggling his knee nonstop as he slouched in his seat, arms crossed. Mack was stroking his goatee so much Lynn worried there wouldn't be any hair left in it by the time they arrived. Ronnie was also slouched, arms crossed, sitting perfectly still as he glowered at the seat in front of him.

Edgar was still, too, but in a watchful, ready kind of way. He didn't try to put his arm around her, but he did touch her knee at the beginning of the flight. When she looked up at him in response to the touch, he turned his hand palm up and raised his eyebrows in gentle question. She snorted softly to herself, but took his hand all the same, intertwining her fingers with his calloused, warm ones, grateful for something to hold onto. He gave her hand a reassuring squeeze, and she could hear his meaning without any words necessary.

I got you, uce.

She squeezed back.

When Hugo notified everyone they were five minutes out from landing, Dan and Ronnie sat up straight and Lynn gently withdrew her hand from Edgar's. She took a bracing breath, then turned toward her team so she could look at them while she subvocalized in their team chat.

"Edgar, Ronnie, Mack, Dan, I want you to know that whatever happens, I have been honored to be your captain. You've taught me a lot about teamwork and, well, friendship." She cleared her throat. Speeches were not her thing. But these guys had had her back day after day, through thick and thin. They deserved her best effort, even if her words weren't perfect. "I don't know what we're going to face tonight, but I *do* know we'll face it the same way we always have: together. We are Skadi's Wolves, and we'll fight till the fighting's done."

"Hell, yeah!" Dan subvocalized, looking determined.

"For Skadi's Wolves!" Mack added, holding up a fist of solidarity.

Ronnie actually cracked a smile, even if it was strained. "You're all a bunch of idiots, but you're *my* idiots, so . . ." He shrugged.

Edgar snorted. "Speak for yourself, bro."

Ronnie punched him in the shoulder.

Edgar reached his tree-limb of an arm up and over to trap Ronnie in a side-hug, which made Ronnie panic and flail.

"What the freak, Edgar! Let me go!"

"The bonds of idiotship will never be broken!" Edgar chortled, giving Ronnie a nice squeeze until it looked like he legitimately couldn't breathe.

"All right, you hooligans. Knock it off," Lynn subvocalized. "My team is a literal pack of wolves," she added, muttering to herself.

Edgar must have eased his grip, because Ronnie finally wriggled out of his friend's grasp and gave him a death glare worthy of a cat who'd just been dropped in a puddle of water.

The call for gear check went out and everyone settled down, put on helmets, tightened harness straps, and checked everything for fit. Lynn made sure everyone's hydration bladder was topped off. They wouldn't be fighting under the hot sun this time, but there was no telling how long they'd be down in those tunnels.

The interior lights of the airbus shut off and they felt the shift and drop of the vehicle going in for a landing.

"Alpha Company, switch to night vision," Abrams said across their company channel.

"You excited, Hugo?" Lynn subvocalized to the service AI. "Tonight might be the night you fulfill your algorithmic destiny to save humanity. Maybe you'll even get to retire."

"An encouraging thought, to be sure, Miss Lynn. But let us not count our chickens before they hatch, as they say. There is much work ahead."

"Isn't there always? Night vision mode, please."

"Of course, Miss Lynn. And if it means anything coming from an algorithm, I wish you the best of luck."

"Thanks, Hugo. It does mean something, even if you're just saying it because that's the thing to do."

"I am glad to know it, Miss Lynn. Night mode activated."

As soon as the airbus stilled on the ground, everyone was on their feet and shuffling toward the front. None of the airbuses ran any visible lights, Lynn assumed to keep the locals in nearby Nekoma from wondering what was going down. She had no idea what the higher-ups had told the data facility owners to avoid someone calling the local police on them. That wasn't her area of responsibility and she was perfectly happy to keep it that way.

They disembarked from the airbus into the chill night air and formed up into a patrol pattern, then headed northeast. Light pollution tinted the sky from the data storage buildings behind them, but Lynn's night vision adjusted to keep her view clear. Her headgear was equipped with top-of-the-line fusion night vision that combined thermal and infrared detection with the visible light spectrum into a single digital picture. It was a sharp enough picture that Lynn could see her surroundings nearly as well as if it were daylight. In the lightless black underground, their combat harnesses had faint running lights to give their night vision something to work with. They had to worry about tripping hazards just as much as spooks in an almost seventy-year-old facility.

Since all communication was strictly subvocalized, there was little noise around them but the endless wind. It mingled with the low hum coming from the data facility behind them and hid the scrape of their feet on concrete, then the rustle of grass as they exited the parking lot and climbed a grassy knoll.

Before them rose the most bizarre skyline Lynn had seen in the real. A huge concrete structure looking like a pyramid with the apex sliced off rose before them, flanked on one side by a handful of scattered chimneylike structures coming straight up out of the grass. The pyramid was almost a hundred feet tall, according to the blueprints Lynn had memorized. It was the missile site radar building of the complex, and she could see the huge circle set into the concrete on each side that was the antenna array aperture. The scattered pillars to one side were the intake and exhaust stacks for the underground power plant, hardened against nuclear blast by feet upon feet of concrete.

In the distance behind the pyramid were toothpick-sized silhouettes of skeletal windmills that marched across the flat landscape. They each had a red light at the top that blinked every few seconds, a warning to airborne vehicles. For whatever reason, the warning lights were synced to blink in perfect unison, making Lynn think of an army of alien sentinels, keeping baleful watch over the plains.

The sight sent a cold chill down Lynn's spine, considering that there *were* alien sentinels all around her—thankfully smaller, but no less sinister.

Once they crested the grassy knoll, Lynn glanced behind her at the data storage buildings beyond the parking lot. Not a thing moved. In the distance to the south, she could see the twinkling lights of the tiny town of Nekoma. Other than that, the vast plains around them were dark and featureless but for the fields of blinking red windmill lights.

Since 1st Platoon was at the front of the formation, Lynn saw when a small, metal door in the base of the pyramid opened outward, revealing a figure holding it open for them. Lynn couldn't see the person's face at this distance, but his build was familiar.

Her heart leapt, even as her gut tightened in uncertainty.

"Fancy meeting you lot on a dark night in the middle of nowhere," came Steve Riker's voice on their company channel. There was definitely a grinning tone to it, and Lynn wondered how happy Steve was to be back out in the field. "Welcome to the Stanley R. Mickelsen Safeguard Complex. As your extremely knowledgeable and expert guide for this tour, I will tell you the only thing you need to know: watch your step, this place is older'n your grandma's undies."

Steve's greeting was met by chuckles and a flurry of responses, mostly from Alpha Testers he no doubt had served with, plus a few Hunters who were likely familiar with him from engaging with the TD Hunter tactical department. Lynn kept her own mouth shut. No reason to draw attention to herself.

They streamed through the door single file. Steve, who was standing in front of it as a human doorstop, slapped some shoulders and shook a few hands as people he knew passed by. Lynn's shoulders tensed as she drew near him. This was an unknown scenario, seeing him in his military capacity as part of CIDER's logistics support. She didn't know how formal to be with him. Plus, she couldn't help but wonder if he'd finagled himself there just to keep an eye on her—another person she cared about putting themselves in danger because of her.

When she drew abreast, though, he simply nodded and gave her a reassuring squeeze on the shoulder.

Then she was through the door, took an immediate left to walk down a short ramp, and was finally inside with plenty to distract her.

Her first impression of the pyramid radar building was that of heavy space. It was a strange, contradictory feeling, hearing echoes yet sensing the weight of multiple tons of concrete overhead. They weren't yet underground, but it already felt like they were.

The pyramid's interior had a purely industrial look. The main floor had obviously been reinforced and sturdy railings had been put up around it, to keep tourists safe from the original parts of the pyramid that had been left as is. It was clear from the interior walls why the place had needed renovation. There were rust streaks everywhere, every bolt and rivet stained brown and surrounded by peeling off-white flakes of paint. The cold air smelled damp and acrid, and breathing it in left a strange metallic aftertaste on her tongue. Lynn wondered if there was lead in all that peeling paint.

Two sides of the interior clearly showed the inward sloping sides of the pyramid, reaching up two stories to flatten out into a metal-paneled ceiling. The other two walls were partially obscured by machinery likely having to do with the radars. A catwalk ran along one wall, giving better access to various parts of the machinery. On the far side of the pyramid's interior was a place where the wall had been built out into some sort of command center or storage room. Lynn figured that was where stairs would descend down to the lower levels of the complex.

At the thought of the lower levels, a shiver ran down Lynn's spine. She had a crazy premonition of something dangerous radiating up from far below her feet. It had to be her imagination. Or maybe it was her . . . resonance? Whatever crazy thing Dr. Roberts had talked about. Could she sense the entities?

What was down there?

The fact that the interior of the pyramid felt eerily familiar didn't help. It had the same abandoned industrial look as dozens of maps she'd played in WarMonger, whose aesthetic often harkened back to a Cold War feel.

Her musings about the strange parallels between her former and current life were cut short by the sight of five familiar faces.

Lynn grinned and led her guys over to where Team Light Brigade was standing with Lansing Nights, near the center of the room. The rest of the company was still filing in behind them, spreading out in the cramped space to make room for everyone.

Derek's head turned toward her as she approached, and when he spotted her, a brief smile was visible through his face plate.

They exchanged handshakes and Lynn nodded to the captain of Lansing Nights. Then she threw out a joint team chat invite that included Light Brigade and Skadi's Wolves.

"Glad you slackers finally decided to join us," Crispy said, doing some complicated-looking secret handshake with Dan that made her wonder if the two of them should be separated for everyone else's safety.

"Yeah, had to finish up our spa treatment before we could head out," Dan said, completely straight-faced. "Can't go saving the world without that rejuvenating face mask."

"How do you even know what a rejuvenating face mask *is*," scoffed Hayek.

"I have an older sister," Dan subvocalized, shrugging. "How do *you* know what it is, *Beer*?"

"I'm fabulous, that's how," Hayek said, miming tossing long locks of hair over his shoulder and cocking a hip in Dan's direction.

"All right, children," Sonia said as she shook Lynn's hand, "try not to have too much fun. We have a job to do."

"Speaking of," Ronnie butted in, "what's the word? You guys found anything yet?"

"Found anything?" Santoro said, gesturing around at the building. "You fancy descending into the bowels of a place like this without backup?"

"Our only mission was to confirm the presence of enough spook activity to warrant further investigation," Derek said.

"And you weren't tempted to explore? Like, at all?" Ronnie gave Derek an incredulous eye-squint.

"Nope," Derek said, looking perfectly sanguine about it.

Derek's expression made Lynn snort, though it also highlighted the difference between Hunters and Alpha Testers: gamers turned soldier versus soldiers turned gamer. The problem was that some of the Hunters *still* seemed to be subconsciously playing a game, even now.

Lynn had made that mistake once. She wouldn't be making it again.

The rest of 1st Platoon crowded in toward Light Brigade and more greetings were exchanged. Everybody seemed relieved Derek and his team were safe and sound, though no one said it out loud.

"Circle up, Alpha Company," Abrams' voice commanded in their company channel.

Everyone turned inward toward where Abrams was standing with Khoury, Steve, and what looked like a five-man team of medics, complete with white armbands emblazoned with red crosses on their forearms. All of Alpha Company managed to fit within the renovated area of the radar pyramid, but it was a cozy fit, made cozier by the large crate at Steve's feet.

"After consultation with our recon team and seeing the terrain myself," Abrams subvocalized, "I'm making a change to the op order. Our original plan assumed the highest TDM activity would be emanating from the complex directly beneath the radar tower. However, the highest activity detected is coming from the power plant connected to the radar complex. The safest ingress point to the power plant is an exterior tunnel that we can access nearby. Once we clear out the power plant, if we haven't found what we're looking for, we can enter the radar complex from the subfloor tunnel connection and make our way up.

"There will not be room underground for our company to move or attack together. We'll be strung out in patrol formation for most of the time, platoon by platoon. We don't want one platoon taking all the damage, so we'll be leapfrogging. 2nd Platoon will take point and clear the tunnel leading down to the power plant. There they will establish a hold position and 3rd Platoon will leapfrog past to begin clearing out the power plant subfloor. Meanwhile, 1st Platoon and Hamilton's Own will leapfrog past 2nd as well and either assist 3rd if there's room to maneuver, or establish a second hold point in the tunnel leading to the radar complex.

"This," Abrams continued, gesturing to the five men with white arm bands, "is a team of our finest field medics trained in treating spook neurological damage in addition to all the normal injuries we might encounter. They'll follow once the power plant tunnel has been cleared, and will hold in place with whichever unit is in the rear-most position.

"We don't know what we'll face down there. In addition to the radar complex's multiple subfloors, blueprints show a variety of tunnels accessing the power plant and spreading out to join with the missile tubes. Newer tunnels were dug twenty years ago to connect the power plant to the data storage facilities close by. All of those will need to be cleared and checked for anomalous spook activity, unless we find what we're looking for in the power plant or radar complex.

"We don't know what the incursion point will look like or where it might be. Whatever happened in this facility seems to have occurred within the first decade after it was built. Whether it was connected to the original missile defense and radar equipment, or something that came after, we don't know. There have been multiple unexplained deaths down in these tunnels, but nothing regular enough to pinpoint a cause. No mass casualties."

Lynn listened with interest, wishing she could ask more about those casualties and see exactly where they'd happened.

"We are assuming whatever we're looking for is likely not on the first subfloor of the complex directly below us," Abrams continued. "That floor has been a part of the historical tour for years and has not been connected to any unexplained problems. A certain spawn pattern our scientists have observed repeated all over the world indicates we should be looking for any intersection of grid infrastructure that forms the shape of a cross, something we're most likely to find in or near the power plant.

"Stay on guard. Be ready for anything. Things will get chaotic in close quarters with little to no field of fire, so listen carefully to your leadership and follow orders, or this mission will descend into a royal Charlie Foxtrot."

Lynn clenched and unclenched her fists to relieve some tension. She understood Abrams' warning all too clearly.

"I'll hand it over to Captain Riker now. He's brought some new toys for us to play with."

There was a healthy smattering of "hooahs!"s and other appreciative exclamations as Steve bent down and removed the lid from the crate. He rummaged in it and came up holding what looked like a thicker version of their already upgraded batons, except instead of a handle, it had anchor points on both ends with attached flexistraps.

"These are brand spankin' new," Steve subvocalized. "Got 'em straight from CIDER HQ, first batch that the lab coats were testing to confirm efficacy. These puppies"—Steve held it up high so everyone could see—"are Bashers, your new and improved force shields. Unlike your previous force shields, which were simply a programmable function of your general-use batons, these were built for one thing, and one thing only: face-bashing spooks."

"*Yee-haw*!" interjected someone, no doubt from Team Lone Star.

Steve grinned, but didn't comment. Instead, he demonstrated putting his hand through each of the flexistrap loops and sliding the electric blue bar down the outside of his forearm to settle it between his wrist and elbow. No doubt responding to an activation command from Steve's LINC, the flexistraps tightened to hold it in place, and then the omnipolymer morphed, going from a thick bar into a less thick, but still sturdy oblong buckler about a foot in diameter on the longest side.

"The exact shape will adjust to fit the length of your forearm, so these are truly one size fits all," Steve subvocalized, turning his forearm this way and that so everyone could admire the new gadget. "Like your current force shields, the Basher's protective range extends further than the physical buckler to about three feet in all directions, equivalent to the skin overlay you'll see in combat mode. Unlike your previous force shields, though, the overlay will appear translucent, like a true forcefield, to prevent visual impairment, since there'll be so many of these in one small space.

"These have been in development for a while, but were fast-tracked after Godzilla." Steve paused and cleared his throat, and Lynn felt a twist of guilt in her gut. "They weren't built for civilian TD Hunter players to use. They were built specifically for the TD Counterforce. I don't know what CIDER had in mind to explain their existence. That's above my pay grade. But in terms of tactics they are meant to protect you, the fighter, from harm. The fact that they're also good for face-bashing is a happy bonus, only possible because the 'inert' or 'negative' TEPs that we use for shielding also help destabilize the 'live' TEPs that the spooks are made of. In fact, the coats *were* gonna call them DEPPs, for Defensive Exotic Particle Projector. Fortunately I got wind of it and convinced them to live life on the wild side and call them Bashers instead."

"Fallu, you're a national treasure," quipped Desperado from Lansing Nights.

Steve grinned, then continued his weapon overview.

"Tactically, you'll use this the way you'd use any other shield, except this one is stronger. The particle field should dissipate any attack from an Alpha Class spook or weaker. They haven't been tested on bosses, but based on the performance of regular force shields in past battles, they should hold up pretty well. The biggest difference besides pure stopping force is that you'll no longer have to choose between attack or defense for your weapon batons."

Lynn did a mental fist pump.

"The drawback is that having three batons active at once does require more energy. You'll have to be at your stabby-stabby best to keep everybody fueled with TEPs for all this equipment to be effective at the same time. If we were in the open fighting a fixed target with plenty of room to see and maneuver, only the front lines would need these. But down in these tunnels we'll likely be so strung out laterally with so short a field of fire, these shields might save your lives.

"The plan is to use a patrol formation with everybody wearing their Basher on their outside arm. That gives the whole unit protection from ambush through the walls by something big. The equipment shouldn't hamper your range of movement much, but wearing them might take some getting used to. Decide among yourselves if you need to shift your two-handed weapon wielders to a different side of the formation based on if they're left- or right-dominate.

"That about covers it with the Bashers. Now, since you've all been good little boys and girls, Santa has one more present for you."

A few people laughed, while others rubbed their hands together in anticipation. Lynn just grinned, knowing Steve was having fun winding everybody up.

The big Alpha Tester rummaged in the crate again and came up with what looked like an electric blue hand grenade.

There were a few subvocalized "Hell, yeah"s in the company chat, but those were drowned out by Dan's hollered "*Yes!*" with a double fist pump. Abrams shot him a glare that might as well have bounced right off him based on how little it squashed his enthusiasm.

"These," Steve said with a wicked grin, "are Holy Hand Grenades."

His pronouncement was met with snickers.

"But were they made in Antioch?" asked Ion.

"Do we gotta count to three 'afore we throw 'em?" drawled Gadsden.

"Only as long as you counteth only to three, and proceedeth not to four," Steve said in a nasally voice full of mock severity.

Abrams cleared his throat, a pained look on his face. Clearly he thought Steve had spent too long "in country" at Tsunami, and had gone full native.

"What's with the Holy Hand Grenade reference?" Lynn subvocalized directly to Edgar, knowing if she asked Dan, Mack, or Ronnie they would scoff at her.

"Oooh, *uce*, you and me gotta have a movie night real soon," was all Edgar had time to say before Steve continued and Lynn had to pay attention.

"These bad boys," Steve was saying, back to using his briefing voice, "are rechargeable TEP hand grenades. Well, they're more like flash bangs than grenades, but you get the point. You clip them to your combat harness and they passively gather TEPs while you fight. It takes about thirty minutes of normal battle activity to charge them up. Once they're charged they have to continue pulling in small amounts of TEPs to stay topped off, because we still haven't figured out a field to properly store TEPs long-term. But as long as you continue to feed them, they'll stay ready to detonate.

"The blast radius is pretty small, only about twelve feet. Payload is about two-thirds of those airstrikes you used during that boss fight in Austin. Should instantly take out any spooks within range. And yes, the payload should stack. In other words, if the worst happens and we find a boss down there, multiple HHGs detonated all at once would give it a very bad day.

"Got all that?" Steve finished, looking around at the focused gazes of Alpha Company.

"Yes, sir!" intoned everyone.

"Good. Remember, these things are rechargeable. If they're not damaged when you lob them, scoop them up and clip them back to your harness. They just need time and TEPs to recharge. Your combat interface will tell you their charging progress, so no need to guess. There's also a manual activation button on the grenade itself"—he held up the one in his hand, pointing to a round, black button—"about a five second detonation delay, same average as the M67. The coats tested activating them at a distance using the combat interface, but found that method wasn't reliable depending on how many spooks are between you and it. For full-on battle, don't try it. If the area around you is relatively clear, it'll probably work. Considering the limited sight lines and close quarters down there, all I'll say is I hope everybody's been practicing their pitch."

A few people chuckled, but Lynn frowned. She'd never played sports and had never pitched a ball. Her fine motor skills and general hand-eye coordination were excellent, but without practice she wouldn't know how hard to throw a grenade to achieve a certain distance. Glancing around at the guys, she suspected the same was true of the rest of them, except maybe Edgar. His dad used to play old school football, so maybe he'd practiced throwing a physical ball before.

Maybe Edgar should be their official Lobber of the Holy Hand Grenades.

Finished with his weapon briefing, Steve began handing out a Basher and two HHGs per person. Lynn helped pass them back to the troops crowded in behind her, and once everyone around her had theirs, she accepted a set herself.

The Basher was heavier than she'd expected, though still extremely lightweight compared to a conventional weapon made of metal. The HHGs had some nice weight to them as well, and Lynn wondered if weights had been built into the omnipolymer to make them more accurate to throw.

After a moment spent examining the items up close, she clipped the HHGs to her combat harness near the shoulder, then slid the Basher onto her left forearm. The flexistraps tightened and secured the shield in place, ready to transform once she entered combat mode. She twisted her arm and flexed her hand a few times, just to get a feel for the thing. Like her normal batons, the omnipolymer of the Basher had some give, and the flexistraps lived up to their name. They flexed with her movements, keeping the Basher secure without digging into her skin.

Once everyone was geared up, Abrams reviewed some final SOPs, took questions, and told everyone to form up in their platoons to get ready to move in five.

Since 2nd Platoon would be heading out first, exiting the pyramid through the door they'd all come in, they lined up closest to the exterior door. 3rd Platoon formed up behind them, while 1st Platoon gathered in the rear, squished with Hamilton's Own near the stairwell that led straight down into the earth.

Another shiver passed down Lynn's spine as she glanced at the staircase, and the hair on the back of her neck stood on end. She tried to shake the feeling. She wasn't claustrophobic, was she?

Steve had pushed his empty crate outside the safety railings to give people more room to stand, and he now made his way back toward where 1st Platoon waited. The spot he picked to stand just so happened to be right next to Lynn. He nodded at Edgar over her head, and she internally rolled her eyes, bracing for what was coming next.

"Hey, kid," came his voice over their direct voice chat.

"Hey, Fallu. What's cookin'?"

Steve snorted and shook his head. "You doing okay?"

Lynn tilted her head to the side to see his face, which was turned toward her. His forehead was deeply creased and his jaw was set—not surprising considering the circumstances. But his brows were also tilted outward in obvious concern, and his eyes... there was a tenderness and a fear in them that made Lynn's chest feel tight.

"Scared shitless," she subvocalized, meeting his eyes. It was a good thing she wasn't speaking out loud, because she could tell her voice would be cracking. She took a sip from her hydration tube. "Also, ready to kill stuff, because I'm sick and tired of watching my home slide towards some dark abyss of undefined disaster. I don't know what's going to happen, so that's pretty terrifying too. But I'm not alone. The guys have got my back. So it'll be fine."

There, that hadn't been too bad. Mostly true.

"Scared shitless" was an understatement. But the mind-numbing terror that really wanted a seat at the table of her executive function had been firmly booted into the vault of "worry about this later," and locked up tight. She was hovering in the awkward middle between her cold-blooded Larry brain that wanted to murder everything, and her warm-hearted Lynn brain who wanted to protect her friends and her home. It was a strange place to inhabit, and she wasn't sure how useful it would be when combat started. But it was the best she could manage at the moment.

Somehow, though she'd meant her words to be light and reassuring, Steve did not look reassured. In fact, he looked sad. Agonized, even.

"Aw, shit. Lynn . . ."

"Don't you dare say a word about how I'm too young to be here, or how I'm just a kid, and war is way more awful than I realize, and how could you let me put myself in danger. Seriously. Fallu. Shut it."

The thin line of Steve's mouth became, if it was possible, even thinner.

"I bet you were eighteen when you enlisted, weren't you?"

Steve did not look happy, but he didn't deny it either.

"Well, there you go. Congrats, you're a hypocrite."

She crossed her arms and looked forward, an unfamiliar sting digging in behind her breastbone. It didn't matter if Steve thought she shouldn't be there. Here she was, and she had a job to do, so there was nothing more to be said.

"Shit," Steve muttered. "*Lynn*, look at me, please?"

Reluctantly, Lynn turned her head back toward him, and his expression nearly broke her.

He was looking at her the same way her mom had looked at her after she'd been assaulted by that creep.

He was looking at her like he cared so much it was killing him.

"I'm sorry, kid. I'm proud of you, and I am literally dumbstruck every time I try to wrap my brain around everything you've accomplished. A part of you is a stone-cold killer, and I respect the shit out of that. But another part of you is an eighteen-year-old girl. Someone who should be excited about friends and going to college, not on the brink of a battle for humanity's survival. You are the daughter of the woman I love, Lynn. The daughter—" His words cut off abruptly and his Adam's apple bobbed.

The daughter you never had? Lynn wondered, tears welling

in her eyes. Her headgear prevented her from wiping them away, so she blinked rapidly to clear her vision.

"It is *killing* me to let you go down there," Steve continued, finding his voice again. "If you never come back... if I knew and I didn't stop you... your mom would never be able to look at me again. She'd lose both of us at the same time."

He paused, and the weight of his words pressed down on Lynn more heavily than if she was being buried alive.

"I'm not trying to convince you to back out, to leave your team in the lurch," he said quietly, "I respect you too much for that. I just... I *have* to say it. It kills me to see you fight this battle. It kills me to let you go... when I only just found you."

An actual sob pressed against Lynn's lips, fighting to get out. She wrapped her arms around her middle, holding it in.

How was it possible to be pierced with grief and joy at the same time? Was this what bittersweet really meant?

She could hear her dad's voice in her head, his boisterous laugh whenever she declared herself to be a "big girl" and too old for whatever thing he was trying to cajole her into doing.

Oh, jenta mi. *You'll always be my little girl.*

That little girl still lived inside her, buried deep under coping mechanisms, wounded, lonely, and afraid. But she didn't have to be. And her dad wouldn't want her to be.

So, she turned to Steve and wrapped her arms around his middle, hugging him fiercely.

He froze at first, but then his big arms descended and he hugged her back just as tightly.

It only lasted a few seconds, but that was all they needed.

When Lynn pulled back, she looked up at him, hoping he could see the fire flickering in her eyes from the fierce determination that raged in her heart.

"I'm coming back, Steve. No matter what, I'm coming back. You won't need to tell Mom that I love her, or that I'll always be with her, or any of that crap because we're going to find this incursion point and put an end to these bastards screwing up our world. Got it?"

"Loud and clear," Steve responded, his voice a scratchy whisper even in subvocalization. His Adam's apple bobbed again, and he gripped her shoulder one more time. "I'm proud of you Lynn. Really proud."

Lynn sniffed, not sure how to receive the compliment when everything felt raw. So instead she just said, "Go stuff your head in a barrel, Fallu. I've got a mission to focus on."

Steve chuckled and crossed his arms, leaning back against the security railing.

"No barrels for me, kid. I've got spooks to kill, just like you. I'm the same rank as Abrams, and not in his chain of command, so I can safely ignore him when he tries to give me the boot and make me stay up here with an empty crate."

Lynn snorted. "Okay. Well... be safe," she said gruffly, refusing to say goodbye.

"Always," Steve agreed, then shifted his gaze over her head to Edgar, who had been doing an excellent job of pretending not to exist for the past minute.

Lynn couldn't hear whatever Steve said to him, but she was one hundred percent certain it was a bunch of manly stuff about being brave, and of course some threat to Edgar's manhood if he didn't keep her safe. She mimed their conversation in her head, inserting heart-attack serious tones in Islander accents, in honor of Edgar's roots:

Do not leave her side, young warrior.

Yes, war chief. I will protect her with my life.

You had better. If you return without her, I will feed your head to the fishes.

Yes, war chief. Though I dunno if the fishes would want my head, my ma says I'm too sweet for my own good, and fishes prefer salt—

Lynn snorted to herself and shook her head. Time to get her mind in the game.

"Liven up!" came Abrams' voice. "2nd Platoon, you're moving out in sixty seconds. Don't enter combat mode until you're in the power plant tunnel. We don't need anyone tripping and breaking their neck because a Phasma snuck up on them. 3rd Platoon, give them five, then follow. 1st Platoon and Hamilton's Own, follow with 3rd."

By the time Abrams was done talking, 2nd Platoon was shuffling two by two up the ramp that led out of the pyramid. Abrams was leading 2nd—with Steve shadowing him—while Khoury would be leading 3rd. According to the op order, Abrams would switch and go with 1st once they leapfrogged past 2nd.

Lynn chewed on her lip, annoyed at the "hurry up and wait" they once again faced. Though the troops of Alpha Company didn't know the details, Abrams had told Lynn he had briefed his staff and her platoon and squad leaders about her special circumstances. They now knew about the insights that had led her and Dr. Roberts to pinpoint the Safeguard location, as well as her confirmed resistance to spook damage. Neither Hermes nor Crash had said anything to her about it, but they didn't need to. They probably hoped those special circumstances never came up, and she couldn't have agreed with them more.

Hopefully, they'd go underground, find some glowing portal in the middle of the floor, bombard it with TEPs, and tie this whole nightmare up with a nice, tidy little bow. Easy peasy, lemon squeezy.

Right.

The minutes ticked past, and Lynn shifted impatiently, ears pricked for any sound of chaos or screaming outside.

"You doin' okay, *uce*?" Edgar asked in their direct chat.

A tumultuous mix of fear and anticipation was entirely normal for a mission like this, so that qualified as okay, right?

"Yeah. I'm fine."

Edgar turned his head toward her, so he could see her through his faceplate, and she reluctantly turned toward him in turn, wondering if he would call her on her obvious brush-off.

"Whatever happens down there, Lynn, I'm with you. To the end." His tone and face were utterly serious, not a hint of humor or teasing.

She swallowed. Why was it suddenly hard to breathe? Her chest felt too small for her lungs. Edgar's hand found hers and she gripped it convulsively, trying to convey the feelings she had no idea how to express.

Thank you for always being there.

I want you to stay.

Please don't take my silence as rejection. I'm just bad at this.

His eyes held hers, steady and warm. One corner of his mouth ticked upward, and the tightness in her chest loosened.

"Ya know that critter called a limpet?" he subvocalized, tone casual.

It took Lynn's brain a moment to switch gears from aliens to sea creatures, but eventually she nodded.

"Well, I think maybe me and them has some genetic similarities, cuz I wanna latch on to you and never let go."

Unexpected laughter bubbled in her throat, though she managed to contain it enough that only a snort escaped.

"That would get awkward," she subvocalized, keeping a straight face. "You know, going to the bathroom and stuff."

He shrugged his shoulders, looking utterly relaxed as if they weren't about to delve underground and assault the gates of transdimensional hell.

"We'd figure it out."

Lynn rolled her eyes, though her lips twitched, despite her self-control.

"For the purposes of tactical maneuverability, let's wait until *after* we save the world to do any latching, okay?"

Edgar's eyes lit up as a grin broke out on his face, and Lynn realized what she'd tacitly implied.

"Got it, boss," Edgar said, sounding like the cat who'd got the canary.

Heat rose in Lynn's cheeks, and she cleared her throat, wondering furiously what to say next.

Crash saved her by barking an order on their platoon channel.

"Saddle up, ladies and gents. It's time to go spelunking for spooks."

The heavy, cold air was filled with rustlings as the remaining two-thirds of Alpha Company straightened, shifted, and prepared to move out. 3rd Platoon started up the ramp, while Crash gave them rapid-fire reminders about formations, SOPs, and common-sense safety precautions.

Then it was 1st Platoon's turn to exit the radar pyramid.

Lynn took a deep breath and looked over at Edgar. He gave her a firm nod, which she returned with an impulsive grin. Time to go do what she did best.

Side-by-side, they headed out to face destiny.

Chapter 15

THE PLAIN OUTSIDE WAS SILENT AND STILL EXCEPT FOR THE never-ending wind. The chill air nipped at Lynn's fingers and around her neckline as 1st Platoon with Hamilton's Own and the medics following behind made their way across cracked concrete and down a grassy knoll to where the power plant tunnel emerged out of the hillside.

The company channel was mostly silent, except for 3rd Platoon leader giving occasional updates and Abrams giving commands.

Her team was silent.

The entrance to the tunnel, which was large enough to drive small trucks into, had been left standing open by 2nd Platoon. Lynn didn't bother wondering if they'd had to break any locks to get in. Her attention was wholly focused on her surroundings. Their displays were back to night vision mode, and she could see the waves of long grass on either side of the tunnel entrance shifting in the wind. The echoing sound of many shuffling footsteps drifted up from farther in the tunnel, which sloped downward at an angle. There were no shouts, though, as everyone was on strict comm discipline.

Before she knew it, 1st Platoon was entering the tunnel, two by two, batons held at the ready even though they were not yet in combat mode.

The tunnel curved to the left ahead of them, aiming toward the underground power plant deep beneath the grassy surface where the concrete exhaust stacks emerged. As they neared the bottom, their digital night vision adjusted to the lower level of ambient light.

They finally reached 2nd Platoon standing in a holding position where the tunnel leveled out and turned into a corridor. The platoon stood facing outward, looking like they were staring down the concrete walls. But their omnipolymer weapons were out and at the ready, and someone would occasionally engage in a battle invisible to Lynn.

"Everything normal so far," Crash reported to 1st Platoon, giving them an update. "2nd Platoon met an expected amount of resistance, Delta through Bravo spooks. The spooks are still coming out of the walls, though just at a trickle. 3rd Platoon has leapfrogged ahead and is seeing thick but not unexpected resistance in the corridor leading to the main power plant room. 1st Platoon and Hamilton's Own, prepare to enter combat mode."

The countdown came, and Hugo took Lynn into the surreal and much more colorful world of the TD Hunter combat interface. It was the most anticlimactic dropping into combat mode Lynn had done in months. There were almost no TDMs in sight, except for the scattered Charlie and Delta spooks popping out of the walls like jack-in-the-boxes.

None of them lived long enough to pop out more than once.

Lynn noticed that the air had gotten even colder, down in the dark concrete tunnel. Despite supposed renovation, the signs of old standing water marks high on the concrete walls showed where the historic complex had sat underwater for the long decades it had been neglected and the pumps hadn't been working.

"Activate running lights," Crash commanded on their Platoon channel, and everyone activated the faint lights in their combat harness. It took everyone's night vision a few seconds to adjust. Once it did, Crash led them and Hamilton's Own forward through 2nd Platoon to leapfrog past them into the depths of the power plant, leaving the team of medics behind in the center of 2nd Platoon.

Finally, they found some TDMs to kill.

The spooks were coming out of the walls, not in rushing waves like they did when formed into boss rings, but in erratic handfuls, as if they'd been hanging out, minding their own business, when they'd been caught in 1st Platoon's aggro. It was disappointingly easy to dispatch them, and Lynn had to remind herself sternly not to wish for harder targets.

This wasn't a game anymore. They needed to get in, figure out what was here, and get out again.

It took them no time at all to clear the scattered spooks that had filled up the corridor in the wake of 3rd Platoon's passing. 3rd Platoon was nowhere in sight, though there was clipped chatter in the company channel, something about a target rich environment.

"1st and 2nd Platoons," Abrams said, voice coming in strong on the company channel, "advance to the power plant main room entrance. 2nd Platoon and Hamilton's Own, hold there. 1st Platoon, reinforce 3rd Platoon. Things are hopping in here."

Crash snapped formation orders and 1st Platoon double-timed it down the corridor, sweeping away everything from Orculls, to Spithra, to Creepers as they went. Lynn felt suspicious to not see any spooks higher than Bravo Class.

As they turned the corner, though, and headed through the wide opening into the power plant room, Lynn almost skidded to a halt in surprise.

Well, now they knew where all the TDMs were.

The cross-shaped pattern Lynn had been looking for was right there before her eyes.

The power room consisted of four enormous bays filled with giant gray, humming equipment. From the four generators came four large pipes or ducts, the sort you ran wires through. Each pair of ducts converged in the center of the room, then a larger duct, no doubt sheltering the joined power lines, ran down the middle and out the door into the corridor. Lynn had seen the large, tubular shape continuing down the hall toward the radar complex, but hadn't thought anything of it before they'd entered this room.

Now, though, her attention was wholly riveted on 3rd Platoon, which was being attacked on all sides.

"Form up on 3rd Platoon!" Crash ordered. Their various squad leaders barked orders, assigning fields of fire, and 1st Platoon flowed into place as 3rd Platoon shifted to accommodate them, creating a circle of defenders with Abrams and Steve and Crash in the middle.

The problem was, spooks kept appearing *inside* their circle, putting Abrams and Steve on the front lines with everybody else as they slashed and blasted away at their attackers.

"What the ever-living hell is happening?" Ronnie subvocalized, sounding pissed.

"Edgar, Ronnie, focus fire outward," Lynn snapped, "Mack and Dan, inward."

She kept an eye on both sides and noticed something extremely odd.

The TDMs appearing inside their defensive circle—which was centered on the power line ductwork—were abnormally fragile. Bravo and even Alpha Class spooks were exploding to bits no matter what hit them as if they were mere Delta Class Imps and Gremlins.

What the heck was going on? Were TDMs reverse-spawning? If this was the origin point, had their attack triggered a defensive response pulling spooks back toward the "mothership" or whatever this place was? But why were they so weak? Lack of a direct power source where they were being pulled from?

Lynn was so busy fighting, blasting Spithra in the belly with Abomination, stabbing Rakshar through the chinks in their armor, and face-bashing spook after spook that charged her in the insane press, she barely had a spare thought to ponder the odd things that kept stacking up.

1st and 3rd platoon battled relentlessly for what felt like forever. Lynn knew it wasn't actually very long, but combat made every second feel like minutes. Abrams couldn't call 2nd Platoon in to join their defenses because there simply wasn't room between the massive pieces of equipment.

The problem was that the waves of TDMs weren't thinning or slowing. The spooks did seem to be weaker and weaker with each successive wave, until destroying them was like shooting fish in a barrel. Every now and then a group would show up at normal strength and surprise the weary defenders, but they too died eventually. As the minutes ticked past, it wasn't the overwhelming press that wore Lynn and her team down, but the sheer repetitive hand and arm movements necessary to kill spook after spook with no pause between enemies or any end in sight. Even bait markers didn't do much to ease the flow. There were simply too many spooks.

"Ya know," Gadsden commented in 1st Platoon's channel, his

smooth drawl less smooth than normal, "in Texas we have this saying for people with bad aim: ya couldn't hit the broad side of a barn. But I think that sayin' don't apply here. If our whole company was blind as a bat at noon, I think we'd still have perfect accuracy scores."

"Fat lot of good—it's doing us now—" Ronnie gritted out between sword strikes. The TDMs pressing against their force shields were so weak now, Ronnie's intermittent Nitro Storm wave of damage took out an entire fourth of the room's spooks.

Which filled back up again in no time.

"For once, I think I agree with you," Gadsden said. "I used to say I liked me a good old target rich environment. But this here? This ain't target rich, this here's target hedonistic, and my mama always warned me against livin' life in excess."

"Hugo," Lynn subvocalized, "can you tell what direction the highest concentration of spooks is coming from? Can we lock onto a source?"

"I could make an educated guess, but the extreme press is hindering my ability to get clear readings from your sensors. And yes, before you ask, Abrams has already asked the same question, and decided to continue clearing to see if the numbers lessen."

"Put me through to him," Lynn said, patience wearing thin. She had to remember her place. She couldn't mess up the chain of command again.

"Raven?" Abrams tight voice sounded in her ear.

"The number are never going to thin," Lynn said sharply. "Whatever quantum entanglement network these aliens are using to spawn all over the world is coming from here, and now that we're here, it's working in reverse. We could fight here non-stop for months on end and still never see an end to the flood. We're not dead because the spooks are running out of juice to get back here. It could all be wild guesswork, but the patterns feel right based on what Dr. Roberts and I theorized together when we were searching for this place."

"Agreed, regardless of the reason," Abrams said. "Problem is, there's no clear incursion point or source. This room is unclearable. I doubt they'll leave us alone if we simply exit. Thoughts?"

"Retreat and head to the radar complex subfloors. My gut says there's something there. Only other option is to leave entirely and go back to square one."

"Agreed. Abrams out," the company commander said. The next time his voice rang out, it was over the company channel.

"1st and 3rd, prepare to exit the power plant and continue down the corridor toward the radar complex. 2nd Platoon and Hamilton's Own, you will take point. 3rd Platoon, hold back and bring up the rear. In fifteen seconds, I'll detonate an HHG to give us an opening to exit. All units prepare to move!"

There was nothing Lynn could do to prepare except to shoot even more furiously, trying to open up some space between herself and the wall of spooks. If they didn't have their Bashers, the spooks might have literally buried them alive.

There was a loud *bang* and a flash of light. The TDMs in a twelve-foot radius around them vanished in a fireworks display of sparks.

"MOVE!" Abrams yelled out loud.

They booked it, slashing and obliterating the weaker TDMs as they went. Out in the corridor 2nd Platoon and Hamilton's Own were already streaming past. 1st Platoon fell in behind them, and Lynn felt like she could breathe again after holding her breath for minutes on end. The medics joined 3rd Platoon in the rear.

Their entire column made steady but careful progress down the corridor. They ran into two problems, though: the farther away from the power source they went, the stronger the TDMs grew, and the narrower the corridor became. They were forced nearly back-to-back by the time they reached the door between the power plant and the radar complex.

As they pushed through to the radar complex, Bravo Class TDMs were replaced by Alpha Class TDMs. With only two to four Hunters able to target any one spook at a time, it took longer and longer to clear the way ahead.

The corridors were a death trap. Strung out in a line, even a double line, the Hunters gave up every advantage their greater numbers normally gave them. Only their Basher shields kept them from being swarmed by nausea-inducing hordes of spooks, and even then it was a constant battle as some spooks came from above or below. Thankfully, the corridor ceilings were quite high, so when they faced towering Jotnar, Managals, and Spithragani, they could see the attacks coming from above a second before they landed, instead of being blind to everything around them.

Lynn moved down the corridor side by side with Edgar, whose height enabled him to better guard the approach from above, while Lynn concentrated on anything coming in at their feet. They clawed their way three feet forward, then retreated two feet back, lunging and slashing with almost no space to maneuver.

Lynn looked at her blueprint map on her overhead, a tiny blue dot showing her own location surrounded by a long, strung-out green snake of dots indicating her unit in the corridor before and behind.

At this rate, there was no way they would have the strength to explore the entire, multi-level complex. The press of spooks was thinner than it had been in the power plant, but that wasn't saying much when Alpha Class monsters were attacking them relentlessly from all sides and they had no extended field of fire to clear the spooks before their enemies were right on top of them.

What would happen if they started dropping from exhaustion or nausea in this press? Would they simply get swarmed until they passed out and went comatose? What would happen to her team, her battle brothers? She'd gotten them all into this. She was responsible for them.

She had to speak up now, or it might be too late. She couldn't have more Champions on her conscience.

"Abrams," she subvocalized in her direct line. "We have to pull out. There's too many spooks."

"Don't waste my time with the obvious," Abrams growled. "We're all humanity's got. There's no better tech we could bring back with us a second time, and the spooks might flood the whole area and pack the tunnels if we leave and try to come back. That's the pattern everywhere else. Clear an area, they come back thicker. It's now or never, RavenStriker. This is my unit, my responsibility, my call. Give me something useful or shut up and fight."

In that moment, Lynn realized she'd been letting fear get to her. She'd let her focus waver.

With a furious cry, she slashed the face of a fast-moving Yaguar that tried to leap overhead, exploding it into sparks.

We'll fight, her brain screamed into the void, all her breath taken up supplying her burning lungs with oxygen. *We'll fight until the world goes up in flames, and then we'll dance in the fire and keep fighting until black eternity takes us all.*

Her fury renewed, she fought on, encouraging her team and stepping in the gap whenever Mack faltered right behind her or Ronnie's back was exposed as he fought in front.

Shouts sounded ahead, and for a moment it didn't register that they were surprised rather than alarmed. Then she saw herself what was happening. It was like the corridor had an invisible line drawn across it, and as each pair of Hunters stepped across, the spooks around them vanished.

Lynn's guard instantly went up.

"Abrams," she gasped, crossing the line herself and letting her arms sag for a desperate few seconds to catch her breath. "The only dead space we've ever seen was immediately around a boss. There's a nodality nearby, and we're too close to it!"

"Then we'd better find it and end it, *now*," Abrams replied. He switched to the company channel. "All Alpha Tester units and platoon leadership, to the front of the formation. Double time!"

For a moment, Lynn didn't understand what was happening. Then it dawned on her.

Abrams doesn't expect to get out of this alive. He's putting all the regular military units at the front to try and take out the boss before it can hurt any of the civilian Hunter Strike Teams.

Then an even worse thought took hold.

Steve is up there with Abrams.

The realization felt like someone had reached into her chest and ripped out her heart.

She couldn't do anything at all to protect Steve. Nothing, at least, except be smarter than she was scared.

Think. There was logic to this situation. A pattern of some kind. What had she seen? What did she know?

TDMs were coming from all sides. So, where was the boss most likely to be hiding, up or down?

Where would the greatest energy source be?

She'd memorized the entire layout of the radar complex before they'd left Minot Air Force Base. She'd researched each room and what it had been used for when the radar had been operational. If an interdimensional incursion point had formed in response to the radar's operations, where would it be? Something had to have triggered it, something—

The klystrons!

She didn't pretend to understand exactly how radars worked, but if the incursion point wasn't in the power plant, then as far as she could tell from the description of the original complex before it had been decommissioned, the klystron tubes had been at the heart of generating the power needed for the massive radar to work. And they were one level *down*, which afforded spooks the chance to come up at them through the floors.

"The klystron room," she snapped in her direct line to Abrams. "It's the most logical location for a boss. It's one level down, but don't go down. Small area, death trap. Klystron Room opens up into the Microwave Room on this floor."

"Copy," said Abrams shortly, and seconds later a red line appeared on her overhead, weaving through the confusing maze of narrow, badly restored corridors, to the Microwave Room.

"All Alpha Tester units, form up on me and prepare to assault the location indicated on your map. All Hunter units, protect our flanks and rear and keep our back trail open for retreat."

Skadi's Wolves gave way as 1st Squad of 3rd Platoon squeezed past. Lynn kept her guard up, unable to look at them. She focused outward, ready for an ambush in the eerie silence, fighting back the image of Champion that was acting like it owned real estate in the forefront of her brain.

"Skadi's Wolves," she subvocalized, "tighten up and hold back. All the Hunters need to stick close and form a shield wall around our flanks and rear. We've still got the medics to protect."

The high, narrow corridor they entered looked like it was for moving large equipment. Despite renovations, more recent signs of water damage could be seen, and the faint smell of rust and dampness was in the air.

"Nodality detected," came Abrams' voice over the company channel. Most of the Alpha Testers were already in the Microwave Room up ahead. "Small but visible in the klystron room. All Alpha Testers form up on Hamilton's Own, stay at max visible range, attack with everything on my mark."

"Wait, Hugo, what does he mean 'small'?" Lynn asked, grip tightening on her weapons as she moved cautiously down the corridor with the rest of the Hunters, side by side with Edgar. The corridors were too narrow for any formation but two-by-two, so the three reduced platoons were quite strung out.

"The nodality's size is equivalent to a Bravo or some Alpha Class bosses, simply based on visual observation. Without engaging it—"

"Wait, Abrams—" Lynn began, but the commander had already spoken.

"Engage!"

The combat interface filled Lynn's ears with a firestorm of noise from the Microwave Room as almost fifty heavily armed Alpha Testers bombarded the boss with all they had.

Lynn's instincts screamed at her and she spun just in time to catch a Phasma in the face with Wrath, exploding it into sparks.

"CONTACT REAR!" Lynn yelled, slashing and shooting at the wall behind her where a solid wave of TDMs was attacking, the Alpha Tester attack on the boss having triggered their aggro. The TDMs were coming in from above, below, and the front. Only their rear in the direction of the boss was clear. Every Alpha and Bravo Class type she'd ever seen was coming out of the woodwork, answering the call of their nodality.

"FORM PERIMETER!" Lynn shouted, not waiting for someone else to get their act together and give the orders. "SHIELD WALL! LAY IT DOWN!"

The squads and teams moved in practiced synchronization from dozens of boss fights. Captains delegated fields of fire to individual team members and everyone pulled in, shield to shield, fighting desperately.

"We're not scratching this thing!" Lynn heard Steve say over the company channel. "It looks small but reading way bigger. We need more firepower!"

Suddenly, the press of spooks eased. Instead of four attacking her all at once, there was only one. Why were they falling off? Surely their strung-out line couldn't have killed the surrounding Alpha and Bravo rings already?

Premonition tickled her nervous meter, and Lynn gritted her teeth.

"Abrams, something's wrong," she subvocalized.

"Not now," Abrams said, tightly, his voice accompanied by the sound of full-out battle from the Microwave Room.

"This is out of pattern," Lynn said, ignoring the reprimand. "The TDMs have pulled back. The only thing spooks retreat from is nodalities. Something is *wrong*."

"TDM numbers down is good," Abrams said. "Got to keep up the pressure while we still can. You have anything concrete? Or just an itchy feeling in your left shoe?"

"Spooks avoid nodalities," Lynn pressed, trying to wrestle her vague premonition into words. "If they're pulling back it's going to do something. Get out of range before it's too late! Remember Godzilla?"

"All units," Hugo abruptly said, overriding all audio, "energy buildup detected centered on the nodality."

"EVERYBODY GET BACK!" Lynn yelled, bolting toward the door to the Microwave Room, as if she thought she could physically drag Steve out of there.

Her audio and display abruptly cut off as nausea and dizziness hit her like a tsunami wave. She staggered and caught herself against the wall of the corridor. Display and audio flickered back on, bringing with it the sound of groaning and retching across the company channel.

Cold, freezing panic seized her and locked her throat tight. She couldn't breathe.

Steve!

Stumbling and swallowing to keep her own dinner down, she stumbled into the Microwave Room. The sight that greeted her stopped her dead in her tracks, paralyzing her.

Every single Alpha Tester was down, motionless on the floor.

NO! her heart screamed.

Desperation drove her forward, breaking her trance. She could see Steve, crumpled on his side, with Abrams nearby. She dove for him, rolling him on his back and putting two fingers to his neck and a hand on his chest.

"Please, please, please," she whispered, tears pooling and running down her cheeks, making the inside of her headgear wet.

She held absolutely still, heart beating wildly.

There!

She felt a pulse, and moments later a tiny movement of his chest rising in a bare breath.

"Medics!" she screamed out loud over her shoulder. "*MEDICS!!*"

She heard scrambling and shuffling in the hall as she went to Abrams, gently untangling his limbs and checking his vitals too.

Alive!

"Hugo, show me their vitals! How many survived?"

"I am sorry, Miss Lynn, that is command access only. But it would not matter. All their equipment was obliterated by that surge. None of their biometrics is showing at the moment."

She took a lungful of air, about to scream again, when two figures came stumbling into the room. They were medics, looking pretty worse for the wear.

"I think all these men are alive, but out of it," she snapped. "We need to get them away from the nodality as fast as possible. Drag them to the corridor. Make sure there's a few teams standing guard so they don't get swarmed if the spooks come back."

It was then, as she looked up to see if any more medics were coming, that she noticed what was wrong with the room. She and the two medics were the only three sources of light in the room, since all the Alpha Testers' lights had been knocked out in the surge.

Except, they *weren't* the only sources of light. What was that moving pattern on the wall? She couldn't see it properly because her digital night vision was compensating, screwing with the light levels.

"Hugo, night vision off."

The room around her suddenly darkened, and what she saw chilled her to the bone.

The walls of the Klystron Room, a two-story pit that opened up on the far end of the Microwave Room, were painted with ethereal, moving patterns of bluish light in every shade, from deep indigo to bright aquamarine. The very air over the pit seemed to shimmer with it.

Was that... the *boss*? Was a TDM *visible* to the naked eye?

"W-what in the name of Satan's drawers was *that*?" Gadsden's shaky voice came over the company channel. Lynn still heard the occasional retching groan in the background. She hoped whoever had lost their cookies had managed to get their headgear off first.

"Correction on nodality classification," Hugo voice informed them all on the company channel. "Based on observed power level in combat, this is a Sierra Class-7, I repeat, a Class-7 boss. Full capabilities unknown. Main attack mass energy pulse at unknown intervals. Recommend all units retreat as far as possible."

"We need to grab everybody and get out," Hermes said, hurrying up with the three other medics and grabbing Abrams under the arms while a medic grabbed his feet. "We've got too many casualties to care for and we don't have the manpower to take this thing out. We need a full battalion to go up against a Class-7."

"We can't get a full battalion in here," Lynn snapped, grabbing Steve's feet as another one of the medics grabbed him under the arms. She groaned as she lifted. Steve was freaking *heavy*. Her limbs were trembling by the time they got to the Microwave Room's doorway, and she might have lost her grip if Edgar hadn't staggered to them and scooped up one of Steve's legs to help with the load as they maneuvered him out and down the corridor to prop him against the wall.

"Skadi's Wolves, sound off!" Lynn subvocalized to her team, looking around as she did. To her relief, everyone sounded off. Shaky, but accounted for.

More Hunters were hurrying into the Microwave Room, grabbing everyone they could shift and pulling or lifting Alpha Testers away from the far end of the room where the unnatural bluish-green light pulsed. As Lynn and her team helped, she argued with Hermes.

"We need to take this thing out. Now."

"Why?" Hermes replied, sounding tense. "Another notch on your belt like Godzilla? Glory before common sense and operational security?"

"Watch your mouth, *tomo*," Edgar growled, shadowing Lynn and dragging heavy Alpha Testers out all by himself.

"I am your superior and I am now responsible for this unit," Hermes snapped, voice even sharper. "We pull out, *now*."

"By golly, Hermes, you're dummer'n a fence post if you think we can make it outta here dragging fifty dead weights, not to mention the most muscly dead weights you ever did see!"

Gadsden's scornful comment made others pipe up in the company channel, even as a dozen more Hunters poked their heads into the Microwave Room, trying to figure out what was happening in all the chaos.

"Trying to carry the wounded out through swarms of spooks is suicide," dBoshe, another squad leader, said as she pushed through the crowd and joined their group.

"Exactly," Lynn agreed. "We don't have enough hands to carry and defend at the same time. If we destroy the boss and leave combat mode, that should neutralize all aggro. Plus, if the nodality is what's enabling more spooks to spawn in the power plant, we can't leave that way anyway until the boss is dead. Once it's eliminated we can establish a beachhead and hold in place while we wait for medevac."

"You have no idea what we're up against!" Hermes said tightly, stabbing a finger first at Lynn, then behind him toward the klystron pit. "You already got three of our own killed with your recklessness. That's not going to happen again on *my* watch."

Hermes' words rammed a dagger of guilt deep into Lynn's chest. She nearly gasped with the pain of it. It rooted her feet to the floor and chased all thoughts of the mission out of her mind for the eternal moment it took her to wrench away from those dark memories.

More arguments broke out in the company channel. Without the steadying influence of the military professionals, the company channel was descending into chaos. She needed to do something. Or did she? Why would anyone listen to her, anyway?

"*Uce*!" Edgar subvocalized on their team channel. "We need Larry!"

"What?" Lynn said, mouth dropping open as her eyes shot to his. "H-how did you even—

"We're falling apart, *uce*," Edgar subvocalized more urgently. "Screw Ronnie. Screw who knows. We. Need. Larry."

"Wait, Larry who?" Ronnie demanded from nearby, head snapping back and forth as he looked between the two of them. "And why screw me?"

"I *can't*," Lynn said, gaze locked on Edgar, eyes burning with pain and guilt. She'd gotten people *killed* last time. What if she screwed up again?

"Yes. You. Can," Edgar said, taking hold of either side of her headgear and giving her a gentle shake with each word. "Trust me, and trust yourself. Do it for Steve, *manamea*. He's hurt, and he needs your help!"

Lynn glanced through the doorway toward the corridor where Steve's form was slumped. A sudden anger gripped her, fury that anyone or anything would hurt one of her own. But anger didn't help her in and of itself.

It would only help if she was brave enough to step into harsh reality.

To accept responsibility.

To fight with every part of her heart and soul.

She tuned out Hermes. She tuned out the angry chatter on the company channel. She tuned out the doubts screaming in the back of her head.

She took a deep breath and focused. What would Larry do?

"Hugo, Larry voice mod," she whispered, clenching her fists, gathering her strength, letting the adrenaline build.

"Engaged, Miss Lynn."

She took a deep breath.

"LISTEN UP, YOU MAGGOTS!" Lynn boomed over the company channel. "WE DO NOT HAVE TIME FOR YOUR BITCHING! 2ND PLATOON, CORRIDOR SECURITY! 3RD, DRAG THE WOUNDED TO THE CORRIDOR! 1ST, GATHER ALL WEAPONS! MEDICS, GUARD THE WOUNDED! MOVE, MOVE, MOVE!"

"What the hell!"

"Is that Larry Coughlin?"

"I SAID MOVE IT!" Lynn repeated, slicing a deadly knife hand through the air to point right at Hermes' nose, her eyes flashing with bone-deep certainty.

For a split second, the squad leader remained frozen, eyes wide.

Then his expression firmed and he scrambled to comply.

Hunters poured into the room, racing at top speed, teaming up, dragging bodies to safety. As they worked, questions flew from those who hadn't been paying attention to their display labels when Lynn had been speaking.

"Who said that?"

"What just happened?"

"Is Larry Coughlin here?"

"No, it was Lynn Raven! Raven is Larry Coughlin!"

The only person not moving in all the chaos was Ronnie.

He stood, frozen, jaw hanging open, emotions flashing across his face. Unfortunately for him, Lynn didn't have time for his little mental breakdown, so she utterly ignored him. Hopefully he'd get a grip on himself.

"Hugo, give me Abrams' command display," Lynn said, not doubting for a moment the AI would do it.

"Of course, Miss Lynn. I have reset it to the default configuration, since Commander Muller had his own way of organizing the data flow."

A dizzying swirl of information cluttered Lynn's vision, and she growled to herself.

"Hugo, ten-second tour, now!" she snapped.

"Leader views, vital stats, expanded map, blueprint," Hugo said, highlighting each piece of data as it was listed, "total company TEP input and output, unit health levels, TDM density, company kill-per-second rate—"

"Get rid of all performance stats," Lynn said, cutting off Hugo's tour. "Leader views, up left. Blueprint, up right. Health levels, down left. Map, down right," Lynn rattled off, directing the placement of her most important data and getting a handle on the extra information she wasn't used to having access to.

"I assume Abrams was in contact with Colonel Bryce?" Lynn asked Hugo.

"Yes, Miss Lynn, though the connection was broken when the pulse wave immobilized the Alpha Testers. Would you like me to reestablish a connection?"

Lynn hesitated, but shook her head.

"Not yet. I need to focus. Send an update on what happened, though, and request backup and medevac soonest."

"Of course, Miss Lynn."

Within minutes, all the wounded were out and lined up propped along the Microwave Room side of the corridor wall. Lynn didn't like them there, but it was necessary so Hunters could stand in front of them and fend off the inevitable wave of spooks that would come as soon as the boss was targeted again.

The Alpha Tester weapons, now back to inert batons and the sectional pieces of the Pounders, were piled nearby, and Lynn had retrieved her own batons from where she'd dropped them to check Steve's vitals.

"3rd Platoon, 2nd Platoon," Lynn subvocalized again, her modulated baritone loud but not as booming as the first time, "set up a perimeter along the corridor. 3rd south, 2nd north. Weapons out, ready to engage. 1st Platoon, on me in the center."

The Hunters of all platoons moved to comply, even though some of them moved distractedly, heads craning back to stare at her. In the corner of Lynn's eye, she could see the dozens of comatose Alpha Testers along the wall, and fear tried to claw its way into her mind. Larry firmly shut it out, sending Lynn deep into the darkness to curl protectively around her heart while Larry did what was necessary. She understood now that each part of her had an important role to play. She needed all her pieces, working together, to make herself whole. And right now she had to let go of Steve if she wanted to save him. The medics knew what to do. The Alpha Testers were out of her hands.

The tail ends of 2nd and 3rd Platoons were making occasional contact with stray TDMs, but for the most part, with the boss unmolested, the surrounding spooks were no longer in kamikaze mode. Lynn wondered if the boss's energy pulse wave had reset their aggro.

Even with this tiny breather, Alpha Company was surrounded, deadly boss on one side, overwhelming hordes on the other, balancing on a knife's edge.

They would have to play this very carefully.

"All units, we are taking this thing down now, today," she said. "We *cannot* fit a battalion down here. There will be no second chances. This is it, just us. And not for glory. For humanity. There's visible light in that pit in the Microwave Room. That's not *a* boss down there. That's *the* boss. The first. The origin point."

"How do you know that?" Hermes demanded, brow furrowed.

"Same way she regularly kicks my pretty Texan posterior in WarMonger," Gadsden drawled, shooting Lynn a grin through his face plate. "It's a doggone gift."

"You're *Larry Coughlin*?" Ronnie burst out, seeming to have *finally* found his voice again. His words were sharp. Hot. Angry.

"Yes," Lynn said simply. She had no time for his drama. "dBoshe, you're now 1st Platoon Leader. Gadsden, you'll double as Captain and Squad Leader of your squad." She took a few precious seconds to assign leadership to 2nd and 3rd Platoons so they'd be functional while she did what only she could do.

"3rd Platoon, rear guard. Protect the wounded. 2nd Platoon, take over Hamilton's weapons. Assault the boss from the Microwave Room on my mark, half range. As soon as the spooks pull back..."

"Run away, run away!" Cosmos sang.

"That," Lynn said, knife-handing. "Yes."

"1st Platoon?" Thrawn asked.

"Gather all grenades from the Alphas. 2nd and 3rd, pass your grenades over, too. I want 1st looking like Christmas trees covered in explosive delight." She didn't mention what she'd be doing with all those grenades. No point sparking pushback just yet. "We're going down a floor to assault the Klystron Room from ground level. I'll signal once we're ready to assault. Questions?"

Grim's hand shot up.

"Can I have your autograph?" he asked with an expression like a golden retriever who'd just spotted an entire dump truck full of tennis balls.

For a second Lynn thought she might burst out laughing. Fortunately, she managed a threatening scowl instead.

"I'll give you my autograph all right. It's called a bullet. Through your forehead. Now *move*!" she ended on a barked command.

Everyone scrambled, and as soon as 1st Platoon was, as she'd said, loaded up like Christmas trees, she led the way toward the only usable stairway left in the complex, labeled "Stairway One." If they hadn't had fifty grown men and women to carry with them, they might have already retreated up it to the relative safety of the radar pyramid above. Instead, they were moving down the creaky thing, fighting TDMs as they went.

She'd have preferred to stay out of combat mode and sneak down instead, but she couldn't risk anybody else passing out. Every wounded was another two fighters lost to protect and carry them. So they fought their way down instead, taking precious time they didn't have.

As they fought, Lynn had Hugo drop the modulator effect. She could always turn it back on if anyone got unruly and needed a good chewing out.

Finally, they attained the corridor outside the Klystron Room, twenty-five feet below the Microwave Room above. Lynn had them circle up in a defensive perimeter while she got busy transferring as many grenades to her combat harness as it could possibly hold. They added noticeable weight to her combat harness, and she reflected dryly that she wouldn't be doing any rolling or lunging maneuvers any time soon.

"What are you doing, *uce*?" Edgar asked in their platoon channel as he blasted away at the spooks that swarmed him like moths to a flame.

"Trojan Horse, Edgar."

"You mean suicide bomber," Hermes snapped, grim worry audible in his voice.

"No. I'm resistant to the spooks. It's why I survived Godzilla. What puts other people in a coma is just a very bad day for me. Goodbye, dinner," Lynn said, trying for levity. Nobody laughed. "Attacking from inside a boss is *always* better. The closer to center mass we can get the TEPs, the more effective they are."

Hermes' mouth was a grim line, but he didn't object again.

"We're going to assault the boss with 2nd," Lynn said, words clipped. "Be ready to run. Soon as it pulse attacks, I go in—not as a suicide bomber—blow the grenades. You will *not* follow unless it's taken out. May need to lather, rinse, repeat if one round of grenades doesn't do it."

"Welp, let's get this show on the road, then," Gadsden groaned, cracking his neck even as he kept shooting. "I'm getting too old for this shit."

"Come on, gramps, it's not that bad," Lynn said, almost grinning.

They switched formation to patrol and headed up the corridor toward the klystron pit. They crossed the invisible line where spooks no longer wanted to be near the bigger, deadlier nodality, and the sudden absence of enemies seemed to free up some of Ronnie's no doubt seething braincells.

"You're *šušiktas* Larry Coughlin?" he hissed at her as they made their cautious way forward.

"Not *now*, Ronnie. Focus," Lynn growled in their team chat.

"Focus? *Focus*?? Screw 'Focus'! You . . . you . . ." His subvocalization broke out into a sound of inarticulate frustration, as if he didn't even have the words anymore.

Lynn glanced at Edgar beside her, then jerked her head down the corridor and fell back, shoving a confused Dan in front of her to take her place.

"You were an unmitigated *shit*, Ronnie," Lynn said harshly. Time to put everything on the table so he could get past this. "You constantly ridiculed and demeaned girls. You were a raging asshole who thought you were real hot stuff. Better than other people. I'd been mercing as Larry in WarMonger since I was *thirteen*. So, yeah, I kicked your ass repeatedly as a *hobby*. Because you were a right *pain in the ass*, and you *deserved it*."

"She's right, bro," Edgar added into Ronnie's stunned silence.

"You *knew*?" Ronnie spluttered, subvocalization so strangled it barely came through. "What kind of friend lets someone get away with that?"

"The kind with a sense of humor?" Dan asked, chortling. "For the record, though, I did *not* know until just now, and also, Lynn, I think it's *awesome*. Will you teach me how to stop getting jumped every time I assault—"

"*Are you fanboying over my sworn enemy??*" Ronnie raged, looking like he would have strangled Dan on the spot if his friend had still been beside him.

"We do *not* have *time* for this!" Lynn said, putting Larry emphasis in and using Wrath to give Ronnie a warning smack to his vest-covered chest. "Get your freaking head out of your *ass* and into the battle! *Lives* are at stake! *Focus*, soldier!"

"Yes, *sir*," Ronnie barked reflexively, expression closing down, though a simmer of anger remained.

"2nd Platoon, prepare to assault," Lynn said, switching immediately to the company channel. 1st Platoon crowded into the narrow hallway that led from the larger corridor to the Klystron Room, passing under the Microwave Room as it went. Lynn did a last check of her myriad displays, ensuring 2nd was in place and scanning her overhead map for any spook buildup within their sensors' limited range. Juggling the entire company and keeping an eye on everything simultaneously was a challenge. No wonder Abrams always sounded stressed when she pinged him.

But she was in the zone and loving it.

"2nd and 1st, assault! Give it hell!" Lynn said, and led the charge into the Klystron Room.

The first thing she noticed was that the boss didn't look like... anything, really. Its form kept morphing and shifting, as if the combat system couldn't get a firm lock on it.

The second thing she noticed was the nausea.

The third thing she noticed was the gagging sound behind her.

"1st, get back," she gasped, shooting the boss with Abomination in one hand and shoving Edgar back toward the corridor with the other. "Too strong. Back to the hallway."

Foxtrot, foxtrot, foxtrot!

Could 2nd Platoon above destroy it alone, along with her grenades? She'd managed to clip forty-five Holy Hand Grenades onto her harness. Their payload was two-thirds of the airstrikes on Nagaraja, and it had taken fifty of them to end a mere Sierra Class-2 boss. This thing was Class-7. But Nagaraja had also been vastly bigger. Would that matter? Godzilla had been massive, too. Might it take fewer TEPs to trigger dissolution when the nodality's volume was smaller, regardless of power levels?

They might be able to manage it, if she could survive getting *inside* it with her grenades. The TEP explosion would be far more lethal expanding out from the center of it than if it was being beamed from down range. The odds of her brain *not* getting turned to soup if she tried such a stunt seemed low, though, and she *had* promised her mom she'd try and be safe. So...

"Edgar, get over here!" she subvocalized over the maelstrom of fire raining down from 2nd Platoon with Hamilton's three Pounders above them. She met him at the beginning of the hallway and said, "I have an idea."

After a brief consultation with Edgar and Hugo, Lynn gripped Edgar's arm, giving him the most confident look she could summon.

"Are you certain you will be all right?" Hugo asked. "Your odds of surviving—"

"Never tell me the odds," Lynn growled. "I make my own."

"Understood," Hugo said, then. "I am detecting a power build up—"

Lynn didn't even let him finish.

"ALL UNITS BACK OFF! BACK OFF!" she bellowed, turning and waving frantically for her platoon to retreat down the hallway.

They scrambled like a kicked anthill and hightailed it back to the main corridor.

Lynn kept one eye on the rest of the company on her overhead, chewing on her lip as the seconds counted down. But everyone made it out of the Microwave Room before the pulse let loose. People were ready with hands on their headgear this time, and even so once again sounds of dry heaving filled the channel.

"And, ATTACK!" Lynn shouted, spinning on a dime and sprinting back up the hallway toward the monster.

"Combat mode off," Lynn subvocalized to Hugo, stowing her batons and making sure she heard Edgar's pounding footsteps behind her. Her plethora of Holy Hand Grenades clacked and jerked as she ran.

"Good luck, Miss Lynn."

"Thanks, Hugo. For everything." Lynn didn't know why she said it, but she did.

Then her visor cleared of the overlay, and she burst into the klystron pit, unbuckling her combat harness as she went. Without her night vision, she couldn't see much. But the darkness only emphasized the blue light. In that moment she realized the many shades of blue were not emanating from the boss itself, but from the back wall where a jagged slice of pure light seemed to split the concrete. There *was* a shimmering in the air in front of her, though, two-thirds of the way into the room. It reminded her of the sparkling mist of unknowns in the TD Hunter app. It was as if whatever lurked there distorted her dimension so profoundly the distortion was visible to the naked eye.

Halfway across the room the wave of nausea finally caught up with her. Her vision tunneled alarmingly. She pulled up and stumbled back a step, just enough to get her balance and push one last surge of strength through her arm as she swung her combat harness and *lobbed* the heavy, jangling contraption as hard as she could toward the center of the shimmering air.

"Edgar, blow!" she gasped, dropping to her knees and hoping Edgar heard her and would trigger her multitude of grenades she'd had him slave to his combat interface.

Such a headache. It was splitting her head in two.

Her vision tunneled again. Everything in the world closed in on one tiny square of gray concrete below her sagging body. There was a clatter of her combat harness hitting concrete. Had Edgar heard her? She wasn't in combat mode, so had no way of knowing what was going on. That little gray square swimming in her vision was all that existed, and she clung to it, fighting unconsciousness.

"Lynn!" a hoarse, familiar voice croaked behind her. "*Lynn!* You did it!"

She shook her head as the rolling nausea eased, then dropped away, and the oppressive weight on her brain lifted.

There were screams and shouts behind her and above her. But they were good shouts. At least they sounded like it?

"She did it! It's gone!"

"RavenStriker did it!"

"*Larry Coughlin* did it!"

"*Uce*," Edgar said, low and concerned beside her. A heavy, warm hand rested on her shoulder.

Lynn yanked off her headgear and retched.

"I'm good," she said, giving a thumbs-up. "Never better."

She retched again, though there was little left to come up.

Her limbs were shaky, but they held strong as Edgar helped her up and she replaced her protective headgear and fired up her TD Hunter app again, diving right back into combat mode.

"2nd, 1st, I want that thing gone," she croaked, pointing at the shimmering slice of bright light on the back wall. "Hit it with all you've got. Maybe the TEPs will destroy it the same way they destroy spooks."

"Raven," a familiar voice came on her earbud. It was Hermes, who still seemed to think, perhaps as the most senior surviving member of 1st Platoon of Alpha Company, he ought to be in charge. He came trotting up from the hallway. "What are you doing?"

"Getting rid of this blighted rift so we can take our world back," she subvocalized, tone especially acerbic as she slashed a hand in the direction of the strange blue light.

"Are you crazy? The entity threat has been neutralized, and we have no idea what unintended consequences your attack might have! What if it makes the thing blow up and take us with it? We need to establish a security perimeter and notify CIDER—"

"Don't you *dare*!" Lynn bit out, getting in his face. "Entity threat neutralized? People are *dying* all over the world and will *keep* dying until we cut these bastards off at the source. Why is this here? Where did it come from? Is it normal? No! Do TDMs belong in our dimension? *No!* Could a horde of bloodthirsty spooks come charging through it at any moment? ABSO-FREAKING-LUTELY YES! Do *you* want to explain to Colonel Bryce why we let the poor little innocent rift alone and, oops, let *another* wave of aliens into our world?"

Hermes didn't reply.

"If you've got the time to *bitch*," Lynn subvocalized savagely, "you've got the time to *fight*. So *fight*." She stabbed her finger at the rift in emphasis, which was still being bombarded by 2nd Platoon from up above, then spun away.

Talking took way too much time in combat.

"Someone get me a grenade!" she bellowed, hand held out behind her, motioning impatiently. She was unwilling to take her eyes off that eerily shimmering light.

Someone, probably Edgar, slapped a grenade into her hand.

"Hugo, five-second delay, activate!"

"Done, Miss Lynn!"

She jogged closer to the rift, to help with accuracy. No nausea swept over her, but even so she didn't get closer than fifteen feet. She tossed the grenade in a controlled, underhand throw right at the blue crack between dimensions.

It bounced off, like it had met some solid barrier, and a second later flashed in useless detonation.

"Fine," Lynn muttered to herself, scooping it up as it rolled back toward her. "There's more than one way to blow things up." She switched to 1st Platoon channel. "I want *all* the grenades. Get them over here *now*!"

Their company was a hundred-and-twenty-four strong. Everyone had been issued two grenades. She'd already used forty-five—no, forty-six. That meant they'd better bring her nigh on two hundred of the little bastards or heads would roll.

Footsteps pounded behind her, and the entirety of 1st Platoon showed up, harnesses clicking and clacking with merrily dangling grenades.

Piles of omnipolymer Holy Hand Grenades were shoved into her hands, and she ferried them to make a pile of twenty positioned carefully around the rift. Then she jogged back.

"We making any headway?" Lynn subvocalized to Hugo, noting the barrage from above was not slacking, likely feeding off the mass of TEPs killing the nodality had provided.

"There is a detectable reduction in TEP activity centered on the rift," Hugo responded, "but...I am not programmed to assess something of this nature. I do not know. I should note that Doctor Roberts would be extremely fascinated to see this otherworldly phenomenon."

"Yeah, I'm probably going to get in trouble for saving the world," Lynn muttered. "He can watch the vids afterwards. I'm sure you're taking all kinds of readings."

"Indeed, Miss Lynn."

Lynn waited another thirty seconds, the hairs on the back

of her neck standing up as each moment passed without some surprise attack bursting out of the rift.

With no visible progress Lynn finally decided she could wait no longer. She was reluctant to use her last remaining advantage, but the entire world was at stake.

"We're gonna blow some shit up," Lynn subvocalized to the company. "Hold onto your socks."

"I don't wear socks," someone quipped.

"Ew! That's *disgusting*," came someone else's horrified voice.

"Hugo," Lynn said, "blow 'em."

Seconds passed, but nothing happened.

"Hugo?"

"I'm sorry, Miss Lynn, but the unique energy signature from the rift must be interfering with my ability to trigger the Holy Hand Grenades from a distance. If you will bring them away from the rift so I can set them all to a synchronous timed detonation, we can proceed that way."

"Screw that," Lynn said. "Put *all* the grenades we have left on a five-minute timer. Do it now!"

"Yes, Miss Lynn!"

"Keep shooting," Lynn told the company as she scooped up handfuls of grenades and jogged forward again.

Back and forth she went, piling them beneath the chillingly eerie light. She was happy to do it herself to keep her people away. If anything happened, she'd likely survive it better anyway. Hugo had thrown a five-minute timer up in her display, and it had reached two minutes by the time she'd piled the last grenades beneath the rift. They formed a pile a foot high and four feet wide spread out beneath the shimmering light.

Two hundred grenades was probably overkill, but Lynn didn't care. It was go big or go home.

She was jogging back to where her team waited for her when she saw Dan's face transform to a mask of horror as he stared at something over her shoulder.

"Holy shit!" he shouted, and lunged between her and the rift.

Screams sounded above and around her as she belatedly dove and rolled, yanking out her batons.

"Dan!" she yelled, and spotted his crumpled form on the concrete. But her gaze was yanked upward at the sight of *something coming out of the rift.*

She didn't want to believe her eyes as the cow-sized, crablike creature pulled itself fully from the blue light, its exosuit-covered body making scraping sounds against the concrete.

Scraping *sounds.*

It wasn't a spook. It wasn't part of the combat interface overlay. It was *solid.*

That was when Lynn registered the sight of the incomprehensible bits of equipment in its claws, the strange shapes looking sinuous and vaguely artistic. A bolt of purple light shot out from part of it, flashing past her head as she juked.

"*ENGAGE! ENGAGE! ENGAGE!*" Lynn shouted, her pitched battle command echoing wildly around the room. She matched words with action and let loose with Abomination, yelling, "Torch that bastard!"

1st Platoon responded with gusto, spreading out behind her and filling the air with bolts of light.

"Hugo," she subvocalized. "Dan. Vitals."

"Alive, Miss Lynn. His heart is beating, brain activity is present."

A tightness in her chest eased, instead of going the other way and ripping her heart in half.

Edgar tried to lunge past her toward Dan, but she grabbed his arm and yanked him downward just as another purple bolt flew through the air where his head had been. She juked back and forth and the alien seemed like it tried to track her, though it was hard to tell with all its limbs and the confusing number of the things it carried in many of them.

A virtual hurricane of fire was pouring down from the balcony above that overlooked the klystron pit as 2nd Platoon also attacked the creature in earnest. Lynn had no idea if the TEP bombardment could hurt this wholly physical creature. It scuttled suddenly forward, charging at her as it kept firing at her and Edgar.

"Get back!" Lynn screamed, even as Edgar tried to pull out of her grasp.

"No! I have to grab Dan!"

"Not till we've—"

But before she could finish her sentence or even formulate a new strategy, the alien creature lunged across the last few feet and closed a multi-jointed claw around Dan's ankle. It surged backward, dragging her friend toward the glowing rift.

Edgar howled like an enraged grizzly and dove for Dan, just missing Dan's wrist. But Lynn was right behind him and dove farther, snagging both Dan's wrists in a desperate grip. She heaved backward, but her weight did nothing to slow the alien's scuttling retreat toward the rift, and it simply dragged her along with Dan.

Then she felt Edgar's thick, corded arms encircle her waist, cinching tight. Ronnie appeared on her left and Mack on her right, each grabbing Dan's arms and hauling backward for all they were worth.

Someone was screaming, and Lynn realized it was herself, shrieking obscenities at the alien as if it might scare the thing into letting Dan go.

The weight of five humans slowed the creature, but it was still inching backward, its rearmost legs already disappeared inside the glowing rift. Its scuttling movements had scattered some of the grenades, though many more still lay at the base of the rift.

"*Daaaan*," Lynn shrieked until her vocal cords felt like they were shredding with the force of her cry.

Ronnie's and Mack's feet scrabbled against the concrete, trying to find purchase, grabbing lower on Dan's poor arms that looked so taut Lynn worried they might dislocate. Then Edgar planted his feet, and Lynn's arms and waist burned with fire as she was yanked between Edgar's grip on her and her grip on Dan. Still, the alien thing kept inching farther back into the rift.

The entire company was screaming and shouting at the alien. Every single weapon was blazing, but the TEP bombardment didn't seem to be hurting it. No one, not a single damn person had a gun, a knife, or even a simple metal pole to bludgeon the wholly physical alien with.

Out of nowhere, a figure flashed past them and slammed center mass into the crab thing. The jolt of the tackle ripped Dan's ankles from the creature's grip and Lynn's entire team tumbled backward away from it. Lynn had a split-second sight of Hermes, one arm wrapped around the thing's curved exosuit, the other fending off a claw snapping at his face. Then Hermes' momentum tumbled both him and the alien backwards through the blue light of the rift.

"Hermes!" Lynn screamed, just as the detonation countdown hit zero and her vision went white with a flash so bright her display shaded to protect her vision.

It was as if a small nuclear explosion was immolating the entire klystron pit, except no blast of flesh-to-ashes heat engulfed her. The augmented reality thunderclap was so massive her earbuds' automatic noise-dampening safeguards triggered and muted it.

When the flash finally faded, Lynn blinked, trying to chase away the lingering afterimages from her vision.

The far side of the klystron pit was... gray. Totally, completely, flat gray.

Lynn struggled to extract herself from the pile of limbs that was her entire team. Edgar didn't seem to want to let go, and she had to pry his hands from around her waist.

Her entire team.

Safe.

"Hugo," she subvocalized, unable to speak with how hoarse her voice was. "Company status? Casualties?"

"All vitals are normal, except Mr. Nguyen, whose breathing and heart rate are concerningly weak, but do not indicate immediate danger."

"And... Hermes?"

"I... I am sorry, Miss Lynn. I have no reading from Hermes. His signal is... gone."

The words echoed hollowly in her chest, and she felt a heavy numbness spreading through her limbs.

Hermes. A military man of honor to the last. Too rigid to fight smoothly alongside gamers. But that hadn't stopped him from giving his all, in the end.

Lynn's eyes burned, but she gritted her teeth and pushed herself to her feet, looking around. She couldn't afford to mourn. Not now.

Larry still had a job to do.

"Hugo," Lynn subvocalized briskly between sips of water to get her vocal cords functioning again, "scan the area. Is there any sign of active TEPs? Bosses? Rifts? Alien entities?"

"Nothing, Miss Lynn. There are still signs of TDMs further out along the corridors you passed through, but all rift signatures that I have been recording are now gone."

"We did it," Lynn breathed. The victory that surged in her heart was bittersweet. She gave herself one slow, deep breath. Then it was back to business. "Alpha Company," she subvocalized to her troops, "The rift has been closed, the entity threat in this area, neutralized. Congratulations."

Cheers and jubilation broke out up above from 2nd Platoon.

"We're not out of the woods yet," she cautioned. "Backup and medical evacuation for the wounded is inbound, but we have a wait ahead of us. In the meantime, if the medics agree it's feasible, I want all wounded moved back to the Microwave Room where we can defend them better in case spooks start gathering again."

It took time, but eventually everyone was safely encircled in the Microwave Room above, with the Alpha Testers and Dan made as comfortable as they could be. Lynn stationed a pair of Hunters from 2nd Platoon at the railing overlooking the klystron pit to keep a human eye on it while Hugo watched for any reapearance of signal activity. Some of the Alpha Testers had started coming around, though they were disoriented and didn't understand what had happened. Lynn kept everyone busy and watchful, on the alert for spook ambushes. But with the destruction of the boss and rift, the remaining lower-level spooks seemed to have drifted away.

By the time the medevac teams were descending Stairway 1, Lynn had everyone formed up and ready to go. About three fourths of the Alpha Testers had woken enough to be walking wounded paired up with able-bodied Hunters to help guide them to the surface.

It took time to strap the still-unconscious wounded, including Dan and Steve, onto stretchers and carry them up the stairway. Everyone pitched in to help the medics.

By the time everyone was safely on the surface and the injured had been evacuated, dawn was breaking over the cold, North Dakota horizon. Teams of scientists with TD Counterforce escorts had already descended back to the depths to study whatever they could find left behind, and Lynn thought wearily of the inevitable, tedious debriefs to come.

At least they had Hugo's vid footage from every single person's view. That made documentation easier, at any rate.

The unwounded members of Alpha Company had assembled on the cracked concrete, headgear off, waiting to load into airbuses and go home when Colonel Bryce found her. She was standing, leaning wearily against Edgar, but she straightened when she recognized her superior in the dawn light.

He stopped in front of her and didn't say anything for a long moment, just looked at her with an unreadable expression. Lynn was too tired and numb to feel any nerves. She simply returned his gaze. Level. Unafraid.

Finally, he extended a hand, which she shook.

"Good work, soldier," he said with a nod of respect. Then he turned and walked away.

Something like peace suffused her soul, and she let out a long breath.

Edgar shifted, wrapping both arms around her, perhaps thinking she was cold.

Or maybe just taking advantage of any excuse to hold her closer.

"We did it," she said a little dazedly, cheek pressed against his chest. The feelings she'd bottled up for hours—fear for her friends, terror at what they faced, confusion and doubt over her decisions—all of it bubbled up in a hiccup of half joy, half terror, all relief.

"No, *you* did it, *manamea*," Edgar said, releasing her so his huge, warm hands could cup either side of her face and tilt her head up to look at him.

She had a moment to enjoy the deep, rich brown of his eyes, the tiny featherings of caramel at the outer edges catching the dawn's glow, before his face loomed too close to focus on his eyes anymore. He was so close she could feel the heat of his lips.

"So, we saved the world, right?" he murmured, the warmth of his breath sending delicious shivers down her spine.

"Yeah, I-I guess we did," she said, suddenly breathless, though for very different reasons than she usually was.

"That mean I can be a limpet now?"

"Um, yes, now would be the logical time," Lynn said faintly, feeling entirely too giddy and wondering if she was brave enough to grab Edgar's neck and hurry things along.

"Mmm, good," he hummed, "I was countin' on it." Lynn could feel the vibration of his silent laughter everywhere her body was pressed against his—which was most of her, by that point.

"So . . ." Lynn breathed, unable to stand the suspense any longer, "do it already."

"You're the boss, boss," he said, smugness ringing in every syllable.

Then, finally, he kissed her.

It was a long time before she became aware of the hooting, whistling, and cheering around them.

It was even longer before Edgar gave up the kiss and they both came up for air.

Lynn leaned her forehead against Edgar's broad chest, pulling the crisp, cold morning air into her lungs, safely enveloped in his arms.

"Everyone is staring at us, aren't they?" she asked, voice muffled in the fabric of his uniform. She felt his muscles shift as he looked around.

"Yup."

"I will never live this down, will I?"

"Nah. They happy for you. Or jealous. One'a the two."

"Any chance they'll all just... forget what they saw?"

"Doubt it."

"I was afraid of that."

It was about that time that Mack got tired of waiting for them to unpeel themselves from each other and tackled them both with a hug—though considering his size relative to Edgar, he didn't so much as tackle them as glom onto them.

"We made first contact," Mack said. "We're gonna be sooo famous!"

Lynn finally pulled back from Edgar and put her Larry face on, glaring sternly at Mack.

"Might I remind you that this *entire operation* is classified," she said, "including the real identity of Larry Coughlin!" She shifted her glare from Mack to the rest of 1st Platoon who were still staring and snickering, most with various degrees of smug grins on their faces. Even Ronnie looked mildly amused, though as soon as he caught her looking at him, his mouth twisted to the side and his glower came back.

"Oh, I suspect there'll be a little bird here and a little bird there, and 'afore you know it, the whole world will know," Gadsden said, disgustingly languid and casual.

Lynn looked toward the heavens, as if she could beseech someone up there to save her from the ridicule of smug teammates.

"Keep the ears," she murmured at the sky. "Only way you can collect the bounty."

Chapter 16

"IF THE FIRST WORDS OUT OF YOUR MOUTH ARE NOT 'SIR, WE have good news,' I will send you all packing back to CIDER HQ," growled President Washington, turning his gaze to the three men sitting in front of him.

For the first time in what felt like years, a spontaneous smile curled Robert Krator's lips upward. It wasn't his place to speak first, though, so he kept his peace as the President's scrutiny swept across Secretary Byerly, General Kozelek, and himself.

They sat across from him on one of the couches that tastefully decorated the Oval Office. Robert was unsurprised to see the President looked as exhausted and harried as the rest of them. Having the weight of the free world on one's shoulders took a significant toll. The mahogany hair going gray at the President's temples was proof of that. The gray looked stark against the man's dark skin, an effect Robert couldn't remember noticing in pictures of the President's election win and start of term. It must have been quite the shock, getting his first national security briefing...

"As a matter of fact," Secretary Byerly said, sounding relieved, "we *do* have good news."

Surprised flitted across the President's face, as if he'd made his gruff demand out of cynical desperation, not an expectation it would actually be met. He leaned back into the couch, motioning with an impatient hand for Byerly to continue.

"I got confirmation barely an hour ago that Operation Little

Doctor was a success. They found the origin point, some kind of interdimensional rift. *Something* came through when they attacked it, but they pushed it back, and were able to bombard the intrusion point with enough exotic particles to cause it to collapse on itself."

The President cocked his head, brows tilted in uncertainty, a wary sort of hope creeping into his expression.

"So . . . is that it? We've won?"

General Kozelek snorted, but managed to turn it into a convincing clearing of the throat, fist to his mouth.

"Not exactly, Mr. President," the General said. "Our world is still full of spooks, and many countries are struggling with critical infrastructure teetering on the edge of collapse. The uncertainty has already sparked off multiple wars in unstable regions, and we're one aggressive incident away from war with China and maybe Russia.

"But we've finally found and turned off the faucet. We've cut the bastards off at the source. In just the last few hours, we've already seen a drop in global spook counts. Barely more than a percentage of a percentage point. But it's the first drop in numbers we've *ever* seen at any point in this conflict."

The President's face had transformed. True relief, maybe even joy, seemed to smooth years of worry off of it. He spread his hands.

"That's—that's fantastic news. We've done it! Once we've mopped everything up, things can go back to normal?"

Robert kept his face relaxed and neutral even as Secretary Byerly and General Kozelek exchanged a look.

"Unfortunately, sir," Secretary Byerly said slowly, "certain things have already passed the point of no return. At this stage, doing anything but going public about CIDER could push our country into full on anarchy, even if infrastructure conditions do improve. The world needs to know what happened, not only to prevent brewing wars, but to arm people with the knowledge they need to stay safe. Our citizens deserve an explanation. There will be shock, disbelief, and likely pushback. But the alternative is to continue this global slide into chaos.

"Besides, we'll have little hope of recruiting more countries to help CIDER complete a worldwide extermination unless we go public. Based on the data, we don't *think* there were multiple incursion points. But the data is still preliminary, so we can't absolutely rule it out. Obviously there are many concerning national security implications to what Operation Little Doctor found, and CIDER's work is far from done. But as far as the public needs to know, we've neutralized the source of the threat, and we can now move forward on solid ground. There's much work to be done, and we will do it together with the people of America."

President Washington rubbed his chin, stroking the trim beard there.

"Yes, I can see what you mean. Good God, that'll be a press conference from hell. But at least I'll only have to do it once. And it'll get Congress and the War Hawks off my back. It'll be a nightmare coordinating with the other CIDER member heads-of-state, but we'll have to make it work."

"If I may, sir," Robert interjected, raising a finger.

"Yes, Mr. Krator? Good grief, you must be so relieved. These last few months... but please, go on."

Robert nodded in thanks.

"If you'd like some company to spread around the heat, I'd be glad to be available to answer questions at the presser, and I think it would be good optics to have one of our Hunter Strike teams there as well. In fact, Tsunami would be happy to organize high-profile Strike Teams from every CIDER nation to be involved in their own country's public statements. It will help counter the general, ah, inconceivability of the whole situation, having popular teams present that people recognize from the streams. They *have* been the ones risking their lives in battle after battle for the safety and freedom of their native countries, after all. I think they all deserve medals, myself, though you and your staff will be the ones to determine that for our own Counterforce troops."

"Yes, yes, of course," President Washington agreed, leaning forward. "General Kozelek can make the appropriate personnel recommendations, and I'll speak to my staff. Do you have a Strike Team in mind for the US presser?" the President asked.

Robert smiled a little smile, knowing how much a certain gamer girl was about to hate him to the depths of her soul.

"Absolutely, sir. There's only one obvious choice."

The one advantage to being publicly known as the world's most merciless and lethal first-person shooter gamer with the personality of a rattlesnake was that no one complained when you bit their head off.

In fact, they sort of liked it.

Well, except for her mother.

"Lynn!" Matilda hissed as she nudged Lynn, likely in an effort to get Lynn to stop glaring at the two White House staffers who were whispering to each other excitedly as they shot furtive looks at Lynn. Her glares, much to her annoyance, seemed to elicit awe and hero worship more often than the shriveling fear she was attempting to strike into people's hearts.

It'd been worse back at Minot Air Force Base, of course. Word of her no-longer-very-secret identity had spread like literal wildfire. She was pretty sure the entirety of Taskforce Sanctus knew by the time Alpha Company had gotten checked by CIDER's medical team. Dan was disoriented and didn't remember much of their final battle, but other than some lingering dizziness, the doctors pronounced him cognitively sound, and Skadi's Wolves were released to get *real* rest after their weeks of combat and final nighttime mission.

Half her fellow Alpha Company members were only vaguely aware of who Larry Coughlin was, but now had no doubts about her leadership skills. The other half were so embarrassingly impressed by her Larry reputation *on top* of their successful assault on the rift, that she was pretty sure she could have formed her own private army and gotten away with it.

As it was, there were definite signs of a cult following coalescing.

Edgar's looming presence was a lifesaver. Not that it kept her friends from alternatively teasing her with smoochy lips and figuratively kissing the ground she walked on. But it did discourage anyone who truly tried to give her a hard time.

After their earth-shattering victory kiss, Edgar had seemingly taken her comment about limpets as permission to permanently install himself as her official bodyguard, and he hadn't left her side since—except reluctantly when Eva and the other girls in Lynn's bunk room had ganged up on him and thrown him out so they could all sleep.

Thank God for girlfriends.

After eighteen hours to rest and recuperate, they'd all been thoroughly debriefed. Lynn was finally able to ask about the Alpha Testers, and found to her joy that every single one was expected to make a full recovery. Some had hit their heads pretty hard when they'd collapsed, so there were a few concussions, orbital bruising, and other minor injuries to recover from. A few had been more affected by the spook attack than others and were undergoing neurotherapy under Dr. Thind's watchful eye.

Thankfully, Steve was not one of them. Lynn jokingly told him over chat that his head was too hard to injure by something as measly as collapsing onto concrete.

After their briefing, the Hunters were sent back to twiddle their thumbs in the barracks while CIDER assessed the rift data and came up with new orders. Well, all but Skadi's Wolves. They'd been hustled out of there and onto an airbus and were halfway to Washington D.C. before they were told what, exactly, they were about to do.

Don't worry, just stand there and look reliable and calm. You won't have to answer any questions, Steve had said. He, too, couldn't stop grinning when he looked at her, and she could see the impulse to make Larry jokes straining gleefully behind his eyes.

Yes, she was definitely learning that she needed practice in the glaring department. There was an art to making it look truly threatening, and she knew she could perfect it, given some time.

For the moment, though, Lynn gave up on intimidating the White House staffers and looked away.

Edgar's warm grip on her hand squeezed gently, and his soothing, subvocalized bass came through her earbuds.

"Don't let it bother you, *uce*. You did something legendary. Let people celebrate it."

Lynn snorted silently and shifted her shoulders, glad the President's staff had let Skadi's Wolves wear TD Counterforce uniforms for this hellish ordeal, sans headgear. She would have felt even more uncomfortable in civvies. Secret Service had even let them keep their blue batons in their thigh sheaths. After all, the batons were specifically designed not to hurt humans, so it'd be pretty hard to beat the President to death with them.

Though honestly, it was Robert Krator she wanted to beat to death.

He'd put Skadi's Wolves up to this, she just knew it.

At least she could be Larry grumpy and not have to maintain the carefully blank expression she'd spent years perfecting in high school just to survive.

It was crazy how life-changing it felt to no longer hide who she was. For years she'd assumed showing her true self would make her weak. Too vulnerable. But now she understood that it only made her stronger.

The truth was always better than a lie.

"I think it's kinda cute," Edgar mused, still subvocalized. He glanced at the staffers again, not down at her, though she could imagine the look he'd be giving her if they weren't currently waiting in a hallway of The Freaking White House itself, about to go live in front of the entire world. "You done great things, *manamea*. You're a legend, you know? A hero, too, soon as they get this press thing rollin'. You think a thing like that oughta be kept a secret? Nah, *uce*. Let 'em stare. You keep your eyes on me. Much better view."

He did grin down at her then, and she turned her Larry glare upward. Not that it made one iota of difference. Her grumpiness bounced off Edgar like raindrops off a titanium mountain.

Yes, she appreciated his support. More than she knew how to say. But did he have to be so adorable and smug about it?

Lynn noticed a shift in the energy of the carpeted hallway, and she looked around, spotting the serious-looking secret service agents before the President himself appeared striding purposefully toward them.

She gulped.

At least she was near the end of the line of people there waiting. Their various parents had been welcomed to the presser to sit in the audience, and President Washington was making his way down the line, shaking hands, looking people in the eye, and thanking them for their service as two members of Secret Service went discreetly before and behind.

Dan stood with his wife Kayla on one side and Mack on the other, all of them looking just as excited as their parents, who beamed with pride like their kids had just won the Olympics. Mrs. Rios shook the President's hand so vigorously that Lynn thought the politician might have met his match.

Ronnie was more subdued, but stood straight and tall, his expression surprisingly relaxed. He seemed truly happy to be there, standing alone without the shadow of his father to darken his victorious moment. Lynn was proud of him—proud of what he'd done and who he'd become. Yes, some disgruntled resentment still clouded his eyes whenever he cast them her way. But he'd get over it, eventually.

Hilariously, over the past few days he'd tried desperately to prove she was lying about being Larry Coughlin. Maybe he was in denial. Maybe he'd simply read too many conspiracy theories. Whatever the case, he'd kept ambushing her with quizzes on WarMonger tactics, and trick questions about how Larry had taken him out in this or that match. Lynn had answered everything with glee, except when she'd felt like messing with him, at which point she'd reverted to her Kim's Diva Princess personality and had enjoyed watching him struggle over whether or not to react to her obvious, deliberate harassment.

It was good for him. Thickened his skin.

Lynn knew he would never *really* believe her until she royally thrashed him in WarMonger while sitting in the room next to him. She'd get around to it someday, but for now she had much more pressing things to worry about.

Like shaking the President's hand.

Mr. and Mrs. Johnston stood proudly beside Edgar, and Lynn was surprised to see Mr. Johnston put an arm around his wife and plant a kiss on her head. She seemed surprised by it as well, but not unhappy. Lynn hoped it was a positive sign of a better future for Edgar and his family.

Maybe your family, too, one day.

Lynn gulped at the fleeting thought, and tried to gather herself as President Washington was now shaking Edgar's hand, having to look up to meet the young man's eyes. The President beamed at him, slapping him on the shoulder with his free hand as he pumped Edgar's arm.

Then it was her turn, and she had no idea what to do, so she just fixed a polite expression on her face and tried to put a bit of strength and warmth into her handshake instead of freezing up like a deer in the headlights.

"Lynn Raven," the President said warmly. "I've heard a lot about you, young lady." He leaned a bit closer and said more quietly, "And as I understand it, we have you to thank for locating and destroying the incursion point."

Lynn desperately ordered her tongue to work, wishing she could subvocalize instead.

"I—" She cleared her throat, "I didn't do much, sir. It was a team effort. Couldn't have done it without everyone else."

"Of course," the President said, nodding amiably despite the knowing look in his eye. "Regardless, you took great risks for the sake of duty. On behalf of a grateful nation, I want to thank you for your service and sacrifice."

The president gripped her hand firmly with both of his as he shook it, and he looked straight into her eye, likely all the way to the depths of her soul. He didn't flinch away from the raw intimacy of it, and damn it if Lynn's eyes didn't start burning with emotion.

"It was nothing, sir," she managed to say past the tightness in her throat. "I just wanted my family to be safe."

"And because of you, Miss Raven, countless families all over the world will be free from fear and harm. Your bravery and dedication under fire deserve the highest commendation this country has to offer."

"Oh no," Lynn nearly choked, an image of Champion's stern face flashing in her head. "No, I don't. I'm not the hero. I didn't pay the ultimate price. Please, give the medals to the families of the dead."

The President nodded, looking pleased. "Oh, they'll get medals too. But the medal isn't just about your personal gratification, Miss Raven. It's a symbol—a symbol honoring the duty and sacrifice our entire nation is built on. As public servants, it is our duty not just to uphold such virtues, but to celebrate them so that each successive generation will be taught their value and cherish them in their own hearts. Believe me, I understand the ceremonies are nearly as excruciating as combat. I did time in the Sandbox myself. But it's simply one more sacrifice we make to water the tree of liberty."

"Yeah, I guess," Lynn said weakly, knowing she'd just lost any foundation for protesting the uncomfortably public honors people seemed determined to heap on her.

"Excellent," the President said, giving her hand one more shake before he shifted his gaze to Lynn's mom beside her.

"Thank you for the hardships you've endured," he said, shaking her hand. "I know how much I worry about my own children. It can't have been easy."

"No, sir, it wasn't," Matilda said, giving the President a level look, not quite as star-struck as the other parents had been. "I hope you'll honor our sacrifice by not screwing this up, or using the whole situation for political gain. We have a *lot* to do, going forward, to make the world safe again."

"I will do my very best, Mrs. Raven," President Washington said, nodding solemnly. He moved on to shake Steve's hand, the last in line and not technically a family member.

Yet.

Lynn couldn't keep a goofy grin off her face as she watched Steve out of the corner of her eye. He'd tracked down her mom and proposed to her as soon as he'd fought his way out of Dr. Thind's clutches.

Matilda had said *yes.*

Now Lynn's mom wore a silver ring on her left hand, the top of it delicately entwined into a *Serch Bythol*, a traditional Celtic symbol of everlasting love.

So, obviously Steve had been included on the attendee list. For moral support, of course.

"All right, people," the President said, giving Steve one last clap on the shoulder, then looking down the line. "Let's get this show on the road."

Secret Service hustled the President off to the rear door of the East Room where the presser was happening, while some of the staffers took Skadi's Wolves in hand and led them behind the President, and other staffers showed family members where they were going to watch from.

The East Room was full to bursting, and Lynn tried not to look at anyone in the face or notice too many details. She could already feel how fast her heart was beating, and her hands felt clammy. For once she openly longed to grip Edgar's hand, fully admitting it to herself as she wondered how effectively she could hide behind him. That kept her brain occupied enough to keep her feet moving and back straight as Skadi's Wolves took their place to the right and behind the President. A collection of staff, military and civilian, and various politicians stood behind and to the left of the President. Lynn wondered if Robert was among them, but had no desire to look around and check. She kept her eyes ahead, unfocused and avoiding anything that resembled a human face.

She was so glad all she had to do was stand there.

Recalling her duties as team captain, she subvocalized to the guys.

"Parade rest, everyone. Let's try to avoid looking like a bunch of teenagers someone dragged in off the street."

"Even though we *are* a bunch of teenagers they dragged in off the street," Dan pointed out.

"We're getting paid for this, right?" Ronnie asked.

"Chu serious, man? We just got to shake the *President's* hand and you worried about money?"

"I'm not worried, you idiot. It's called a joke."

"You suck at jokes, bro."

"Can it, guys," Lynn said, resisting a smile. "President's about to speak."

The guys were always the guys, heroes of the hour or not.

"My fellow Americans," the President began, speaking slowly, his deep voice resonating in the sudden silence. Every eye in the room was riveted on him. Lynn knew, because she focused her gaze and actually looked for the first time over the crowd of politicians, reporters, and staff. She wondered if the legislature had already been briefed, or if this would be news for them, too.

"Today is a day that will go down in history as the day the world was united by a common threat and common goal. Many of you have spent the last few months watching your loved ones suffer, your jobs put in jeopardy, and your lives turned upside-down. You had no answers, and you were frightened and angry. I am now, finally, at liberty to bring truth and clarity to this issue.

"Approximately eight years ago, during cutting edge experimentation into dark matter and quantum entanglement, scientists discovered the presence of entities that did not originate in our dimension, made up of exotic particles invisible to the naked eye that did not follow the rules of any known law of science. An organization, the Coalition for Interdimensional Dark Energy Research, or CIDER, was formed to study them and unravel the mystery. Disturbingly, they found that these alien or perhaps transdimensional entities were increasing in number, seemed attracted to our technologically advanced infrastructure, and were harvesting it. All attempts at communication with these entities failed. A multi-country alliance was formed to devise a way to eradicate these entities. Through the hard work and brilliance of Robert Krator of Tsunami Entertainment and his team of designers, a combat interface was created that could detect and destroy these entities, and the TransDimensional Hunter game was born."

Though Lynn's eyes did not fix on any one face, she could easily see the shock and confusion that swept through the crowd like a roiling wave. People whispered furiously to each other. Others held perfectly still as if carrying on subvocalized conversations with people in the room or elsewhere. The mutters died, though, as the President continued.

"As the entities were not yet numerous or dangerous enough to threaten public health, it was deemed necessary to keep the true nature of TD Hunter a secret. This was to avoid the global chaos and confusion any attempt to go public at that time would have caused, potentially dooming our effort to deal with the entities before they reached critical mass and caused a global infrastructure collapse.

"Over the past year, many of you have watched as people young and old all over the world have battled these entities through the gaming interface, each and every player fighting for humanity's survival. It was hoped that enough people would join the TransDimensional Counterforce that the entities could be safely eliminated without alarming the public. However, the multiplication of the aliens recently saw an exponential rise, to the point that grids were being overrun and public safety was at risk."

President Washington gestured to the side at Skadi's Wolves, and Lynn stiffened her parade rest, eyes locked on the far wall above everybody's head.

"Our brave Hunter Strike Teams and the other members of the TD Counterforce have been fighting tirelessly for months, trying to ensure the safety of our civilians and the continued functioning of our infrastructure. But we were running out of time, and everyone knew it.

"Then, several days ago, our team of scientists finally located the incursion point for this alien invasion. CIDER put together an assault force of the best of the best, including our very own Skadi's Wolves standing beside me today, to assault the incursion point and close the interdimensional rift that had been the cause of this alien plague. Their mission was a resounding success, and we've already seen a measurable drop in the numbers of entities worldwide. With the continued help of the global gaming community, the Hunter Strike Teams, and the CIDER member nations' auxiliary forces, we will continue fighting until every entity has been wiped clean from our reality.

"This will be a difficult effort. Our cities are reeling, and many people are without food, water, and basic necessities. My government is committed to deploying every resource we have available to support our citizens across the country. But we can only succeed if everyone works together. Every man, woman, and child must join hands, hearts, and efforts as we fight this invasion and stabilize our world in the face of this long-hidden threat.

"I know many of you are afraid right now, and I understand completely. I've feared for the safety of my own loved ones, my friends, and my staff every day since I took office. But we can get through this together. As I speak, my staff is launching an entire stream dedicated to explaining what our scientists know about these entities and walking you through how to keep yourselves and your loved ones safe. With wise precautions, level heads, and open hearts, we will get through this.

"Please, stay calm and seek out information before you act. We are still looking for brave volunteers to join the TransDimensional Counterforce. The federal government and Tsunami Entertainment will be actively distributing combat interface batons to anyone who wants to join our global effort. Get some for yourself and your family, and clear out the area around your house, your apartment, your local neighborhood. Form community watches. Check in on your neighbors. Take care of each other.

"It is vital in this moment that we lay aside our differences, voluntarily shoulder this responsibility, and choose unity over fear. No matter the challenges we face going forward, we must take courage and stand firm, together. Only together can we rebuild our country and our world. Thank you, and God Bless America."

With that, the President stepped away from the podium.

The room erupted in noise. Some people stood, waved, shouted questions. Some stayed seated, still frozen in shock at their world that had just been turned upside-down.

Well, the world had been turned upside-down a long time ago. They just hadn't known it.

The President shook her and the guys' hands one last time before exiting with his detail. As his staff ushered Skadi's Wolves to follow, Lynn reflected that things were about to get a lot more interesting.

And all *she* wanted was to go home and sleep.

The next few days were insane. Taskforce Sanctus was temporarily told to shelter in place because the perimeter of Minot Air Force Base was swarmed by reporters, drones, and protesters.

GIC was being swamped too, with literal crowds of journalists, streamers, and activists barging into their office all day demanding to speak to Skadi's Wolves, to know where their next mission was, or begging the TD Counterforce to come to their city and kill the spooks that were no doubt causing all their problems.

Then someone snuck a Molotov cocktail into the building and threw it into GIC's lobby from the elevator, singeing the secretary and causing the whole building to evacuate.

Lynn heard that Mr. Krator reached out and was working with Mr. Swain to relocate GIC and its employees somewhere safer. Kayla, who Lynn knew was putting on a brave face for Dan's sake, said her dad was furious behind doors and would have separated entirely from Tsunami if it would have done any good. But GIC was irreparably tainted in the eyes of the crazies, so Mr. Swain had no choice but to accept Tsunami's help.

Lynn could read between the lines and got the impression Mr. Swain was not at all happy with one Dan Nguyen for drawing his daughter deeper into association with Tsunami and CIDER. But Kayla, despite the shock of finding out about the spooks, was one hundred percent in Dan's corner.

Still, it was a horrible situation. Family members of the most stream-famous Strike Teams were harassed at their homes and workplaces. Some took up CIDER's offer of temporary housing on a variety of military bases around the country. Some stuck it out.

Lynn officially rented her house to Mr. Thomas and hired him a housekeeper, a cook, and a security guard. Matilda had accepted CIDER's offer to work with Dr. Thind on fast-tracking advanced neurotherapy for victims of spook attacks like Harry Seville, and would be moving to CIDER housing in Knoxville.

Tsunami set up baton distribution stations in their stores all around the world, but also had to hire armed guards to fight off vandals and protestors. They quickly realized they couldn't give batons out to just anybody, and had to start a registry to prevent activists coming back again and again only to take the batons out to the street and livestream breaking them or burning them. Lynn heard that some people were fighting over batons in the streets, some trying to break them, others trying to save them.

The streams were absolute chaos. Lynn avoided them entirely.

The Battle Tour was cancelled. All official nodality fights were put on hold for the safety of the Hunters and Alpha Testers.

Colonel Bryce told them everything would calm down in a manner of days, and they'd be back to fighting spooks in no time with CIDER able to openly coordinate boss fights with local city municipalities.

Lynn could only hope he was right. She couldn't imagine the chaos and fear that would have swept the world if CIDER had been forced to go public before a permanent solution had been found and people could be given hope that things would be under control again soon.

She heard rumors that things were alternatively better, and worse, in other countries. Places that had poor but ubiquitous grid infrastructure were hit the hardest, while very remote regions with little to no modern infrastructure were barely affected at all.

Skadi's Wolves was summoned to the White House again, this time for a livestreamed medal ceremony, much to Lynn's dismay. She endured it with as much stoic nobility as she could manage, considering it felt like a three-ring circus. The guys seemed to enjoy it more, but then they'd always been more motivated by recognition.

She'd been in it for the game. And then, of course, for duty.

Accepting the medal and keeping her mouth shut turned out to be harder than she'd imagined. All she wanted to do was give it back and point out there were much braver and more worthy recipients—the entirety of Alpha Company, for instance—and she didn't appreciate being used as a camera-friendly mascot to earn political brownie points. She'd even considered refusing the medal on livestream and telling the President he could give it to her *after* he'd awarded posthumous medals to the members of Taskforce Sanctus who had given their lives.

Edgar had talked her down from that particular bit of insanity by pointing out she would have wholeheartedly cheered on anyone else getting a medal besides her. It made her realize she was more motivated by her own hang-ups than she'd thought. So, instead of making a scene, she'd stood at attention, eyes fixed on nothing, and accepted her symbolic role.

After the ceremony was over, Lynn couldn't get out of that place fast enough. The White House felt like an anthill that had been stomped on by a giant. Everyone was rushing around with grim looks on their faces, likely engulfed in full-scale damage control from the spook announcement while simultaneously trying not to freak out about being *invaded by aliens*. Lynn would have felt sorrier for them if she hadn't spent the last year of her life fighting spooks almost every day.

Leaving proved trickier than simply walking out, considering they had to be escorted to a secure airbus platform, and the White House was already chock-full of multiple diplomatic groups from CIDER member nations, there to coordinate the war effort and negotiate a more public alliance. They even ran into one such group in the hall—likely from Japan, based on their looks—and the staff escorting them had to do a complicated shuffle to get everyone on their way.

The two groups were almost past each other when the hallway rang with a high-pitched squeal of delight.

"*Mackie-kun!*"

Lynn turned to see a petite girl in a pantsuit with long, silky black hair tackle Mack in a hug so fierce he would have been knocked off his feet if Edgar hadn't steadied him from behind.

"Riko?" Mack gasped, eyes as wide as saucers. "Oh my gosh, it's really you!"

Lynn and the guys stared, openmouthed, as Riko pulled back far enough to plant a kiss right on Mack's lips. Mack froze at first, but then his arms came up and he enthusiastically returned it. It went on long enough that mutters began on either side of the corridor, wondering what the holdup was. When the two of them finally came up for air, Mack had a grin a mile wide on his face and a smear of red lipstick just as wide.

"Hey, everybody," he said, meeting his teammates' gazes, "this is Riko, my girlfriend."

"It is very nice to meet all of you," Riko said, turning to face them and giving a little bow. She had the most adorable accent and even Lynn had to admit that she was hot. Like, really hot. Even "smokin' hot," as Mack had frequently insisted to them.

Lynn glanced at the other guys, noting with amusement that Dan and Ronnie still hadn't picked their jaws up off the floor. Edgar had, though, and was now shaking with silent laughter.

It was about that time that Lynn finally became aware of the other people in the corridor, namely the Japanese diplomatic delegation. She was torn between embarrassment and amusement at the pained expressions on most of their faces as they looked anywhere but their errant member, who was now tucked up against Mack's side and not looking like she intended to leave any time soon. Lynn wondered which one of the stern, older-looking men was Riko's father, and if any of the younger members clearly trying to hide smiles behind their hands were friends of Riko's, or just romantics.

There was a spluttering noise from behind Lynn, and she looked over her shoulder to see Mrs. Rios gasping incoherently, an outraged look on her face as Mr. Rios held firmly onto her arm. Matilda expertly stepped in front of Mrs. Rios, blocking Mack from her view, and began damage control.

Mack finally seemed to register the storm clouds gathering, and his grin faded into a look of growing horror as his brain probably scrambled for what to say under the withering curiosity and censure of an entire corridor of global politicians, White House staffers, and his mother.

"My father is here to coordinate with CIDER's engineers and help find solutions to the global transportation crisis," Riko said, seeming to take pity on Mack. Perhaps her Japanese sensibilities were finally reverting control—that or she'd spotted the scowl carved from granite on the closest black-suited diplomat. Her father, perhaps?

Riko broke out into rapid-fire Japanese to the man, and Lynn belatedly subvocalized to Hugo:

"Hey, can you translate that? What's she saying?"

"I can indeed, Miss Lynn. One moment."

English audio started playing in Lynn's ears, and she almost burst out laughing.

"I *told* you a famous gamer had fallen in love with me, Father! See, he's not a bot! Everything I said was true!"

Riko's poor father looked like he might have wanted to commit *seppuku* then and there if only it would get Riko to shut her mouth. He carefully did *not* look at his fellow diplomats, but instead dipped his head in the barest of nods to Mack and gestured for his daughter to return to their group.

She did, though with obvious reluctance. She kept bowing to Lynn and the guys, saying how honored she was to meet them and how she would not be leaving the United States until she got a chance to see Mack more.

If Ronnie and Dan's jaws could have fallen further they would have, perhaps all the way to the center of the earth. Mack still looked shocked, and a little worried, but his expression went all cow-eyed and moony every time he focused on Riko. Lynn just tried not to burst out laughing, and it looked like Edgar was fighting the same battle.

Eventually, the two groups managed to disentangle and continue on their way.

Their trip back was very silent, until Ronnie and Dan got over their shock. Then they wouldn't shut up. It was as if they'd completely forgotten the past nine months spent ruthlessly teasing Mack and were suddenly hearing about this Riko girl for the first time.

Mack, for his part, seemed so delighted they were finally taking an interest that he didn't even hold their toes over the fire like they deserved.

Lost opportunity there.

Lynn would make sure to tease Ronnie extra hard if he ever got a girlfriend one day. Maybe she should ping Quorra and put in a good word for Ronnie.

The encounter was an encouraging bit of light after several days of fear and uncertainty. Then Lynn got a ping, and when she looked at it, a smile spread across her face.

Lynn had never ridden in a gas-guzzler before, and at first was alarmed at how loud it was and how much the entire thing vibrated, like it would fall apart at any moment.

When she mentioned it to Steve, though, he just laughed. "Drink it in, kid. That's what it feels like to really *live*."

It had been barely a week since they'd closed the rift—or TD-Day as the Alpha Testers had started calling it—but CIDER was already pushing to get Alpha Company back into the fray, despite all the public chaos. There were still nodalities to kill and city grids in distress, and Dr. Roberts kept asking for an extended interview to grill them about what they'd seen at the rift—as if he didn't have access to their headgear footage, not to mention all the data Lynn's headgear had gathered from its brain wave sensors during the battle.

But Lynn had put her foot down and told Colonel Bryce he would give 1st Platoon a weekend off for her mother's wedding, or she would quit.

Unsurprisingly, Colonel Bryce had given them a weekend off.

Now Skadi's Wolves, Steve, Matilda, Kayla, Derek, and Sonia along with everybody's luggage and various wedding supplies were crammed into a gas-guzzling fifteen-passenger van currently headed up the side of a mountain to . . . somewhere.

CIDER had lent them an airbus to pick everyone up and fly to a tiny, lonely, overgrown airstrip in La Veta, Colorado, where they'd been met by one of Steve's old unit buddies in his van. They'd piled in and started driving south. Lynn had no idea where they were or if they were even still in Colorado or if they'd crossed over into New Mexico. Steve had been vague about it all, but apparently Mike, his buddy, had a nice little off-grid compound somewhere up there.

When Steve had floated the idea to her mom of an off-grid wedding—out in nature, away from cities, and free from paparazzi drones, protestors, and spooks—she couldn't say yes fast enough.

The catch had been that everyone had to go LINC-free. Every bit of advanced mesh tech had to be left behind. Steve had promised his friend owned a SAT phone in case of emergencies. But the guy had a serious paranoid streak when it came to surveillance. So, they'd all agreed to become luddites for the weekend to go enjoy the most special and "in the real" event of Lynn's adult life.

Despite the uncanny discomfort of not having her LINC, and there being no display in her vision, Lynn couldn't stop grinning at everyone.

The climb through the mountains was mostly paved, but near the end the narrow road turned to gravel. Lynn couldn't remember the last time she'd seen a road sign. The gravel road went on forever, winding through verdant conifers, past deep mountain streams, and around groves of aspens whose leaves were just beginning to go golden at the edges. Fall was coming, but the mountains were still full of green and teeming with wildlife. She was glued to the window most of the trip, and every time she pointed out a new animal she'd spotted, Edgar chuckled beside her. She even knew what most of them were, thanks to the woodland craft book Edgar had gotten her last year.

Dan, Mack, and Ronnie were less enamored by the wilderness. Dan would normally have been the one to complain the most at the loss of his LINC, but he had Kayla to keep him company, and the two were disgustingly obsessed with each other.

Mack was the most mopey because, without his LINC, he couldn't chat with Riko at every moment of the day and night—her father had absolutely not been on board with her taking a side jaunt into the Colorado wilderness with a strange American boy and his crazy former-military-slash-gaming crew.

Ronnie was surprisingly good-tempered about it all. Since he didn't have Dan to argue with, and since Steve had opted to sit beside Matilda, Ronnie had loudly claimed shotgun and was having a surprisingly civil and mature conversation with Mike about various survivalist and military topics.

Derek and Steve ribbed each other while Sonia and Matilda chatted about unapologetically girl stuff and wedding details, making Kayla frequently lean forward to chime in.

The general chatter in the bus felt odd after so many months in the TD Counterforce where almost all communication had changed to subvocalization. It was oddly exhilarating to eavesdrop on everyone's conversations and hear the joy and merriment all around.

Lynn felt more *human* than she had in months.

Yes, she kept unconsciously flicking her eyes to bring up her notifications, and she had a weird, low-level, skin-crawly feeling of being naked. But as long as she didn't dwell on it, the gorgeous scenery around her and the conversation in the van kept her happily distracted.

The van made its way down into a valley where the bumpy gravel track followed a small river that flowed between two towering peaks. Then the mountains opened up and the valley was fully revealed, with a beautiful, sprawling, log cabin perched a third of the way up the hillside overlooking the lush valley.

By the time Mike pulled into the large gravel parking lot between the cabin, a low garage, and a small barn, the sun had gone behind the mountains and the sky was beginning to grow dark.

Everyone piled out of the van.

When the crisp, cool air hit Lynn's face, she couldn't help but draw in a huge lungful of it. It smelled of pine, woodsmoke, and something ephemeral that Lynn could only described as "mountain smell." It made her think of cold stone, windswept cliffs, and deep pools of water.

There was a shout from the cabin's wide porch and a group of four men headed down the steps, aiming for the van. They all looked similar to Steve with muscular builds, short hair, and tattoos peeking out from under collars and shirt sleeves. Lynn assumed they were friends from his SpecOps days.

"Fallu! You old dog!" the lead guy shouted and grabbed Steve's forearm, pulling him into a fierce, backslapping hug. The man was slightly taller and leaner than Steve, a bit younger-looking, too, with black hair that was cut close at the sides. He pulled back, holding Steve at arm's length with a big hand on each of Steve's forearms as he looked around. "All right, where's this pretty thing that's caught you in her web? I've gotta see her with my own two eyes."

Matilda stepped around Steve with her arms crossed and gave the black-haired man a critical look up and down.

"I don't usually start sticking people with needles before I've been introduced, but I'm willing to make an exception for you," she said, eyes flashing dangerously.

Everyone hooted, some slapping knees in their mirth as the man backpedaled, holding his hands up in surrender.

"Anything but needles, man. Anything."

"Well, that will depend," Matilda said, shifting to slide an arm through the crook of Steve's elbow and smiling in a dangerous sort of way. "Are you up to date on all your shots?"

Steve's other buddies hooted even louder, and Steve moved his arm to settle around Matilda's shoulder and tuck her possessively against his side. Lynn grinned at the sight, absolutely loving every bit of it. She even wondered if it felt as nice as it looked, and resisted the impulse to glance at Edgar.

"Tilly, this utter doofus is Tap, as in Double Tap, as in don't ever challenge him to a gun fight. Also, you shouldn't take anything he says seriously. His hobby is poking bears and mountain lions until they attack him, then wrestling them to the ground while talking their ear off."

"Hey!" Tap protested. "That was only the one time!"

"Once was enough," one of the other guys said fervently as he stepped around Tap to give Steve a heartfelt handshake.

Matilda laughed. The sound filled the valley with musical delight.

"Come on, everyone," Mike said gruffly, passing them all with someone's duffle bag over his shoulder while his other hand pulled the handle of a rolling cooler. "Night's coming and we've still got supper to make. Introductions and pranks can wait till we're inside."

"Sure thing, Cap," said Steve's troublemaking friend and started for the van. Then he spotted Lynn and pulled up, face lighting with delight. "Whoa-ho-ho! Are we in the presence of the great Larry Coughlin? When the guys told me on the range the other day that *Lynn Raven* was Larry Coughlin, I nearly shot myself in the foot!"

Lynn mirrored her mother's previous stance and crossed her own arms, giving Tap a skeptical look. She felt weirdly vulnerable without her LINC and its instant and private access to whoever and whatever she needed. Even Hugo looking over her shoulder had been a subconscious safety net. Despite the discomfort, she didn't regret its absence. A little thrill of anxiety mixed with adrenaline sharpened her focus, and she decided it was good for her to know she could get along without it.

"Sounds like you need a lesson in weapon safety," she said, keeping her tone flat. "If we weren't off-grid we could fire up WarMonger and see if you're as sloppy in virtual as you are in the real."

"Be happy to," Tap said, giving her a cocky wink. Lynn could tell that whatever he'd thought of Larry Coughlin before, knowing Larry was "only" a teenage girl had changed his opinion.

Time to show him the error of his ways.

"What's your handle?" Lynn asked, keeping her tone bored.

"ChaosGremlin666," Tap said with obvious relish.

Him and Crispy should never, ever meet, Lynn thought, then searched her memory of years of WarMonger matches.

Oh, yeah. That punk. She examined Tap with dead eyes utterly devoid of emotion, looking for tells, clues, weaknesses.

"Ten on ten death match, two years ago. San Francisco Investment Group versus Blackstone Equity. You liked to play cute with the AMR11 grenade launcher. But your obsession with destruction... shot you in the foot, so to speak." She gave Tap a cold smile. "I headshotted you from behind the first time. Poor overwatch on your team's part. Second time was all on you, though. Never use the same ingress point twice."

Tap's jaw dropped.

"That was *you*? I thought Fallu was the one dropping me!"

Lynn shrugged.

"Blackstone was losing. They panicked and brought me in last minute. Pure fluke I was available. Had just finished a Tier One-only free-for-all, figured I could use a cooldown. Plus Fallu told me he had a friend on the opposing who needed taking down a few pegs."

Tap's eyes bounced back and forth between her and Steve,

mouth still open in mock outrage that was quickly morphing into fascination and delight.

"I think you and me are gonna be besties," Tap said, moving as if to put an arm around Lynn and draw her into walking to the house with him. Before he could get within touching distance, though, Edgar *and* Steve had both stepped between him and Lynn, for which she was extremely grateful, because it meant she didn't have to remove the guy's testicles with a fork.

"That's *my daughter*, Tap," Steve said, his words pleasant, but his tone dangerous. "Be a gentleman, or I'll take you out behind the shed and castrate you."

Lynn grinned, thinking it was nice to see she and Steve were on the same wavelength.

"I'll help him," Edgar said easily, cracking his knuckles.

"I won't stop him," Mike yelled from the porch.

"And I'll be there with some tranquilizers to make sure you stay down," Matilda said sweetly. "I'm pretty sure I have some in my emergency med kit."

"Aww, guys, come on!" Tap whined dramatically, though he still had a grin on his face.

"Tap! Gear!" Mike yelled again before disappearing into the cabin.

Chuckling, Tap gave a lazy salute to Steve and went to help.

"If it makes you feel any better," Lynn heard Derek say as Tap joined the group unloading the van, "I nearly fell over in shock when I found out myself. Fallu completely trashed his desk by spewing a mouthful of alcohol all over it when he heard."

"I think I sprained a rib laughing," one of Steve's other buddies said.

"I still don't believe it," said another one. "No way someone that young could get that skilled."

Lynn looked over her shoulder as she followed her mom toward the cabin and caught the eye of the doubter. He grinned and shrugged apologetically. She just gave him a cold smile, all Larry and no Lynn. She *definitely* needed to find out what that one's WarMonger handle was. He had another think coming, and she would enjoy giving it to him.

Dinner was *heaven*. Mike had set up meat in a smoker the night before, and produced thick slabs of delicious bison brisket, juicy elk tenderloins, and an entire wild boar.

Lynn would have proposed to Mike on the spot if she hadn't been so busy stuffing her face with heavenly protein. She thought she'd liked steak, but the smoked brisket completely blew her mind. She definitely needed to expand her palate when it came to different cuts, varieties, and cooking methods for meat.

It wasn't like she couldn't afford it, after all.

Mike didn't have a table big enough for everyone, so the guests simply spread out to every available seat in the cabin and on the front porch. Lynn spotted Dan and Kayla sneaking out the side door with plates full of food and a throw blanket from one of the couches. She'd probably find them later lying on the lush valley hillside staring romantically at the stars. Or making out. Probably the latter. They were married, after all, which was still weird.

But good weird.

Everyone kept eating, swapping war stories, and playing games long after the sun went down. Real games, of course, which delighted Lynn. She got to teach Steve and his buddies Spoons, which turned into a *literal* bloodbath—Tap ended up with a slice on his palm that Matilda stitched up with the patience of a saint as Mike and Steve held him down. He insisted he could just wrap it and it would be fine. Matilda told him she'd seen three-year-olds with more spine.

Who knew spoons could cause so much damage?

Lynn, of course, knew all the sneaky tricks of the trade and was smart enough to stay out of the fray when the big guys lunged in, so she managed to come in second. One of Steve's buddies, the quiet one who'd expressed doubt about her gaming skills, took first place. He'd introduced himself earlier in the evening as Droopy, without any further explanation. Lynn wasn't sure if he'd played Spoons before, or was just a very good gamer. She kept looking up and noticing him studying her.

It made her think he'd be a very satisfying opponent in WarMonger.

When it got too late, Mike chased Steve's war buddies out of the house to the camping tents they'd pitched for the weekend while Steve and Matilda got one guest bedroom and Derek and Sonia got the other. Skadi's Wolves and Kayla set up on the couches and floor of the cabin's great room with pads and sleeping bags.

After the cabin lights were turned off and silence fell, Lynn realized they'd been far too busy all evening to lament the loss of their LINCs. Even Mack had stopped whining about how much Riko would have loved this or that, and wishing he could livestream his trip for her. Lynn still felt naked whenever she focused on her LINC's absence, but it was no longer an anxious mental itch in her mind.

Content, Lynn fell asleep on the floor with Edgar's large, reassuring presence close by and the sound of wolves howling at the rising moon outside.

The wedding was as short, sweet, and beautiful as anyone could have asked for. There was a gorgeous spot at the foot of the hill where the river went over a waterfall and overlooked a pool surrounded by a small meadow rife with late summer flowers. The still-verdant green meadow was offset by an aspen wood behind it just beginning to turn vibrant gold. In the background the peaks rose up, framing the deep cerulean-blue sky without a cloud to be seen.

Matilda and Kayla went out after breakfast to set up a few decorations while Steve and Derek carried chairs, and Mike whipped the rest of them into work parties to get vegetables chopped and meat grilled for the after-wedding feast. Sonia, to Lynn's surprise, made a delicious-looking cake and icing from scratch using ingredients they'd brought with them. It filled the cabin with a rich, mouth-watering smell of freshly baked goodness.

Mike had a surprisingly large kitchen for someone who seemed to live alone. Based on chatter and a few innocent questions she dropped herself, she got the impression he did a lot of hunting and liked to do the meat justice with a large variety of dishes. It looked like he had a garden out back, too, so she supposed he used the space for canning and preserving on top of cooking.

When all the food was prepared and either in the oven or wrapped up with towels to keep it warm, everybody changed clothes and headed down the hill to the river. The guys wore short-sleeved button-down shirts with tan slacks. Lynn also wore slacks, though hers were black. She wore them with a sleeveless halter blouse in dark blue that Kayla had helped her buy ages ago when they'd gone virtual shopping. The blue made her golden eyes pop, according to Kayla, and if Edgar's appreciative, lingering look was any indication, it was a fine choice.

Kayla, of course, was dressed to the nines in a slinky red cocktail dress *and* she wore high heels on the grassy hill, which Lynn could not fathom. But it sure made Dan happy. Mack kept making sighing noises, and Lynn warned him in a mutter that he'd better stop moping over Riko and be happy for her mom at the wedding he'd been personally invited to. Ronnie cut a surprisingly respectable figure, and had even added a bow tie, which Lynn thought suited him. Edgar kept it simple with a black silk shirt paired with his slacks. The color was completely lost on Lynn because of the way the cut perfectly framed his muscular shoulders and massive guns. He caught her staring at them more than once and grinned like a fool each time.

Steve was spiffed up in a forest green button-down shirt that Matilda had no doubt picked out for him to complement her sunflower-yellow sundress. She went barefoot, and had meadow flowers Kayla had picked that morning woven into her long, silky black hair. Lynn had helped with the braids. It had taken her forever, considering she was used to doing them on herself. She thought it had turned out looking sloppy, but her mom had promised guys found messy hair attractive.

Mike officiated the ceremony, while Sonia stood as matron of honor and Derek as best man. Kayla had entirely too much fun scattering flower petals, and Lynn carried the rings. They were made of woven parachute cord, a cute placeholder while they had their previous wedding rings melted down and combined to make a new set, symbolizing the union of their pasts and their futures into one beautiful whole.

Lynn absolutely teared up when she handed one each to Steve and her mom. When she tried to turn and sit down, Matilda caught her hand. Steve, seeming to have already mastered the art of reading his soon-to-be-wife's mind, took Lynn's other hand.

"Stay and witness," he said quietly. "You're a part of this too."

Yeah, she definitely started crying then. Fortunately it was just silent tears of joy that rolled down her cheeks while her mom and new dad said their vows.

... to have and to hold from this day forward, for better, for worse, for richer, for poorer, in sickness and in health, to love and to cherish, till death do us part.

When Mike pronounced them man and wife, Steve swept her mom up in a swoon-worthy embrace and Lynn beat a hasty retreat to her chair. Steve's kiss went on and on, eliciting whistling and cheering from everybody present, while Kayla threw flower petals at them shouting, "You get some, girl!"

Once Matilda managed to peel Steve off her, they all climbed back up the hill for lunch, laughing and full of joy.

Lunch was, if possible, even more delectable than dinner the night before. Mike had saved the marinated venison steak especially for the wedding feast, and Lynn could not get enough of it.

The cake was chocolate on chocolate, decadent, sinful, and almost too sweet to bear. Matilda loved it. Steve did a great job pretending like he loved it, and managed to feed most of his piece to his new bride under the guise of being a doting husband. Lynn suspected Mack, Dan, and Tap had entered a secret contest to see who could eat the most straight before having to take a drink of milk to dilute the solid lump of chocolate forming in their throat. Lynn was pretty sure Tap won.

Drinks were passed around and merriment was had. Somehow by mid-afternoon the guys ended up outside on the flat lawn beside the cabin, engaged in one-on-one wrestling matches. Apparently there'd been some banter thrown around and Steve's lot had opined that professional gamers, no matter how muscular, couldn't hold a candle to SpecOps standards. Ronnie had thrown down and convinced Edgar, who was the tallest person at the cabin, to go along.

The ladies were happy to set up lawn chairs and spectate. Steve and Mike both refused to be drawn in, no matter the taunts thrown, and Derek just laughed and shook his head. So it was four against four, youth and enthusiasm against old age and treachery.

Okay, not exactly *old* age, but the young men of Skadi's Wolves took every opportunity to point out that the other guys were more than twice their age.

Dan and Mack went down pretty easily, Lynn suspected because they didn't really want to fight in the first place. But everybody was good-natured about it, and Droopy taught them some basics of grappling, stance, weight balance, and takedown moves. Ronnie, who wasn't as tall as Edgar but close in size to his opponent, fought long and hard, and nearly tired the other guy out. But experience won out in the end.

Edgar, who'd specifically maneuvered to be paired off with Tap, had a hard glint in his eye going into his wrestling match. Lynn wondered if Edgar had ever gotten any self-defense or wrestling experience on his own, considering his quest to protect his family.

Tap tried to go in fast and hard and take Edgar down right off the bat. Edgar wasn't particularly adroit at avoiding him, but he stayed low and simply Would. Not. Go. Down.

Lynn screamed and cheered with Kayla and the guys as Edgar and Tap shuffled across the grass, locked together like two bulls. Tap didn't have enough weight to destabilize him, and every grip Tap tried, Edgar was able to break out of through sheer strength before Tap could complete it and immobilize him.

Tap finally gave up and plopped down in the grass, grinning up at Edgar.

"Well done, son," Mike called out from the porch where he was nursing a beer. "Want to learn how to not just hold your ground, but pound your opponent into the dirt?"

Edgar flexed his shoulders, threw Lynn a grin, and nodded. Mike came off the porch, rolling up his sleeves, and another round of lessons began.

They ate leftovers for dinner, or maybe they just never put lunch away and kept munching late into the night like a pack of wolves returning to their kill. When the moon started to rise Edgar convinced Lynn to sit with him on the porch swing and snuggle under his arm against the nip of fall chill. Lynn was curious enough to let him convince her, and found she liked it just fine. It felt right, to fit so perfectly against someone else, to hear their heartbeat, and to know you were wanted, loved, and cared for.

Eventually Mike came out on the porch and told them Matilda had declared curfew. Edgar grumbled, but Lynn was happy and full and ready to call it a night. When they both got up, though, Mike said:

"Lynn, mind if I have a word before you turn in?"

Edgar—being Edgar—gave the older man a suspicious look. But Lynn just snorted and gave Edgar a push toward the cabin's front door.

"Get our sleeping bags ready, will you?" she said, and watched as he shrugged and went inside.

Mike had gone to lean on the railing and seemed to be examining the waning moon visible over the mountain peaks.

Lynn joined him and admired the way the moonlight frosted everything in the mountain valley with its silver touch.

When Mike didn't immediately speak, Lynn filled the silence for him.

"It's so pretty out here, I've never seen anything like it. Thanks for having us."

Mike turned and leaned his back against the railing, hands shoved into his pockets.

"You're more'n welcome. I like my life out here, but it does get lonely sometimes. A party like this does me for half a year before I get the itch for people again. You're welcome back anytime, long as you're ready to work hard and keep your chatter to yourself."

Lynn snorted.

"Have you heard me chattering at any point in the past two days?"

Mike grinned.

"Can't say as I have."

Lynn fell silent and waited, wondering what Mike really wanted to talk about. She heard him sigh in the dark, long but quiet.

"It's getting pretty crazy out there, I hear. International tension. Starving cities. National Guard requisitioning materials left and right. Can't say as I really believed it when I heard the President's speech. But... you've seen 'em with your own eyes. The spooks?"

"Yeah," Lynn said softly. "So has Steve. Not sure why you're asking me and not him."

"He's too deep into CIDER," Mike grunted. "Loyal to a fault. Almost died for his country multiple times. He's level-headed, but biased. You, though... they lied to you, didn't they? Recruited you under less than ideal circumstances?"

Lynn took a slow, quiet breath, and nodded.

"Regrets?" he asked, voice a quiet rumble.

Lynn did him the courtesy of not answering right away, instead letting her moon-glazed vision go unfocused as she thought about the last three months of her life.

They'd been hard. Exhausting. Filled with worry. Even heartbreaking at times.

For some reason, as she thought it all over, Elena's voice rang in her head.

I'll fight.

Even Elena—arrogant, selfish, petty Elena—had answered the call. Sure, it was likely more a desperate attempt to help her father than true patriotism, but still.

Quod nos tueri.

That which we protect.

Lynn smiled in the dark.

"No," she said. "No regrets."

Mike chuckled.

"You're your father's daughter, all right."

Both my fathers, Lynn thought, her smile widening.

Mike sighed again and pushed off the railing.

"Steve's been dropping hints all weekend, bugging me about coming out of retirement," he grumbled, and Lynn suppressed a laugh. "I don't know about this CIDER business, but if things really are as bad as they say, I don't know as I can sit this one out. Might poke around, see where there's a square hole that might fit this square peg."

"Has he been bugging the other guys from your old unit, too?" Lynn asked, curious if Mike would even answer, considering how cagey Steve and his ilk usually were.

Mike grunted noncommittally, but it was an annoyed sort of grunt, and it made Lynn chuckle.

"Steve's efficient like that, isn't he? Recruited you for his wedding *and* to save the world at the same time?"

"Steve's too good for his own good," Mike said.

"My mom thinks so, anyway."

That got a laugh out of Mike.

"I'd say she does, kid. I'd say she does." He turned toward her and held out a hand. Light from inside the cabin cast his tanned skin an even deeper golden brown. "You take care of yourself, hear? And that mountain of a boy you've got wrapped around your little finger."

Heat rose in Lynn's cheeks, but she was in shadow and consoled herself that Mike couldn't see it as she took his hand and shook it firmly.

"Oh, don't worry. I will."

"I'm sure you will, *Larry*." Mike chuckled to himself. "I never got into that virtual gaming stuff myself, but Steve tells a mean story, and all of them involving you are worth a case of beer and a good cigar to boot."

"You know, it's free to play," Lynn said. "You could hop onto WarMonger anytime. Just let me know your handle and I'll drop whatever I'm doing to play a match."

"Ha! In your dreams, kid. I know better'n to go fooling around on unfamiliar turf. When you're ready to learn how to fight *real* enemies, you look me up. I'll learn you good and proper."

"I'm pretty sure Steve's got that covered. He's already convinced my mom I should take up jujitsu."

"In your free time between killing alien swarms?"

"Yeah, something like that."

The cabin door opened and Matilda stuck her head out.

"Oh, there you are, Lynn. We're turning lights out soon."

Steve came up behind his wife and nodded at Mike. Mike nodded back, and then clapped Lynn on the shoulder.

"May fortune smile down on you, Lynn. We're lucky to have you and your team."

Lynn murmured her thanks as Mike set off across the porch and down the steps, looking like he was aiming for the garage. Her mom and Steve—her mom and *dad*, wow, that was going to take getting used to—came out on the porch and joined her at the railing. Matilda hugged her, tight and warm, and Steve joined them, wrapping them both in his big arms.

They stood there for a long time, safe and happy, and ready to face the world again when the time came.